HEIR *to* FROST & STORM

BOOKS BY BEN ALDERSON

Heir *to* FROST & STORM

BEN ALDERSON

SECOND SKY

Published by Second Sky in 2023

An imprint of Storyfire Ltd.
Carmelite House
50 Victoria Embankment
London EC4Y 0DZ

www.secondskybooks.com

ISBN: 978-1-83790-925-4
eBook ISBN: 978-1-83790-924-7

Kellen, our bond is as unbreakable as one forged between dragon and their rider. I have found not only a friend for life, but one that stretches far beyond such human concepts.

Voltar

The Unknown Isle

The Thassa
Ocean

ALDIAN

PART ONE

FRAGMENTED BONDS

PROLOGUE

The nightmare was always the same. I stood in a field of ruin. Above me, the sky hissed with fire; below my feet, the ground withered. I was alone, until I wasn't. Before me, stretching out for a league, an army of shadows waited. Faceless and shapeless, everything they touched was left in decay.

Then there was the woman. Her back was always to me, the details of her body distorted. The more I studied her, the more her outline wavered. Although I knew I was scared, deep in the body which was not mine at all, fear uncoiled and sparked.

Even though I knew I was dreaming, terror ruled me.

I was rooted to the ground—the last tree left to watch as the pending doom came. But whose doom? It was an answer I could never reach. The thing about dreams is they never felt as real as this. I could smell the blood in the air and hear the crunch of bones beneath feet as the army moved forward.

Still, I couldn't look away. I was forced to watch, kept in place by a hand I could feel but not see.

The woman turned, as though finally sensing my presence, my *plan* and before her eyes found me, I—

Someone slammed past my shoulder, drawing me from the lingering vision. They barely turned around to apologise as they raced towards the growing crowd ahead. I followed suit, focusing on getting myself to the best vantage point for what was to come.

Despite the winter sun beating down in the cloudless sky, there was a chill that settled deep in my bones. A wind tore over the city of Wycombe, bringing with it the bite of ice. It brewed in the snowy landscape of the Avarian Crest, the three-peaked mountains like a crown set into the far reaches of Aldian. And it was in that direction I looked, waiting, with bated breath, for the father of dragons to make his blessed appearance.

Ruin had carved itself into the very bones of the city. It had been close to three weeks since the phoenix's attack on Wycombe, and, with every inhale, I could still taste the acrid bite of smoke in the back of my throat. Buildings were either piles of rubble or demolished skeletons of charred stone and glass. Although most of the wytchfire's devastation had been focused within the centre of the great city, especially around the Heart Oak and castle in Wycombe's core, the outskirts had been affected too.

Civilians had become refugees, simply seeking somewhere to live.

It had rained for two days after the wytchfire was extinguished, alongside Camron Calzmir's life. Muddied puddles of ash-covered cobbled streets squelched beneath my feet. Rumours abounded that it was the nymphs, using their magic to help clear Wycombe of the pain and suffering. But it would take more to wash away the memories of what happened.

No magic-conjured storm could wage war against the one inside of me. One look around, and I wouldn't have known any of it had happened. All I saw was smiling faces, eyes alight with the anticipation of the pending conscription. The Claim. When battlemages of age signed up to partake in trials, in the hope to find themselves with their own dragon. Something I had been forbidden to do. Which only made me want it more.

Elder Leia Hawthorn hadn't explicitly banned me from signing my name up for the Claim. But her words had been as clear as her meaning. Perhaps if she hadn't told me what to do, I wouldn't have been here. Then again, I had other motivations as to why I could possibly want a dragon of my own, and the power that gave a mage.

It was my nightmares, lingering in the far corners of my mind, which kept me focused.

I had been aware of the shadow following me since I arrived in Wycombe's central square. What I hadn't noticed was who the shadow was. Not until I stopped, faced them directly and prepared to call their bluff.

'Simion Hawthorn.'

The crowd parted around him like water to stone. He was garbed from head to toe in his gleamer regalia—the cream tunic overlaid with perfectly formed silver armour and a cloak that billowed from clasps at his shoulder. He was both a warrior and a beauty. His stance was straight-backed, chin lifted so the glare of the sun highlighted the lines of his sculpted face and full lips. Simion's left hand never strayed far from the pommel of his sword, the other carefully folded to his side, what looked to be a lump wrapped in brown paper nestled beneath it.

I drank him in, because it was impossible not to.

'Maximus,' Simion said my name in reply. He lifted my hand, bringing the knuckles to his lips and pressing a slight kiss. Dryads, his fingers were smooth to the touch. Gentle, even if it had the capability of causing me desperate agony. Gooseflesh erupted over freckled skin, but it was the glowing silver lines of my handfasting mark that had me snatching my fingers back. If Simion noticed, he didn't show it.

'*She* sent you, didn't she?' My gaze shifted to the Council members. They towered over the gathering crowd, stood upon an erected podium. Elder Leia, Simion's aunt and the acting Head of Wycombe, seemed to sense my gaze, raising her eyes over the crowd to meet mine.

'Is it that obvious?' Simion said, his voice light as though there wasn't literal thorns between us. I dared look down to the silver marks on my arm, for fear acknowledging it would cause me pain.

'The look of guilt gives it away. So, are you going to stop me?' I asked, looking back to the gathering crowds at the base of the podium. Ink and parchment waited for those brave enough to sign their name.

'No.' Simion joined into step with me, his arm brushing mine ever so slightly. It was enough contact to make me hold my breath, as though I expected pain to follow. It didn't. 'Although I think an escort would help you navigate the danger zone which is my aunt.'

I wanted to tell him I was fine, that I didn't need his company. But I would be lying to him, and myself.

'What do you think my punishment will be?' I asked, as the silence between us grew uncomfortable. 'She's made it clear she doesn't want me to do this.'

Exile? Imprisonment like Beatrice who still awaited trial for her involvement in Camron's attack, the Queen's death... my father's murder.

No. I refused myself to think about it.

'Your guess is as good as mine,' Simion replied, navigating us through the thickening crowd. At one point, his hand grasped my elbow, steering me in the right direction. Towards the podium, not away. 'Then again, disappointing my aunt has been rather enjoyable recently.'

'When she is the only thing standing between Beatrice's freedom, I don't think toying with her would be wise,' I said, sparing him a sideways glance. Dryads, his smile was enough to spark a fire in my chest. *Literally.*

'Yet here you stand, prepared to go against her command.'

He caught me.

'Do you truly want this?' Simion asked, bringing us both to a stop. I could see the table ahead with the old man with wide owl eyes and a feather-tipped quill, waiting for others to sign their names down. He was so close—as was Leia. Her breath was practically itching down the back of my neck.

'If I didn't want it, I wouldn't be here.' I wanted this because it was my choice. Something I hadn't been privileged to exercise in a long time. 'If you've followed me all this way just to tell me it is a mistake, you're wasting your time.'

'That is not why I am here,' Simion answered quickly, almost too quickly. 'Surprised?'

'Don't you have some duties to attend to?' I asked, as we continued forward. What I meant was: *Don't you have a sister to visit in prison?*

I had hardly seen Simion because he had been occupied preparing for Beatrice's pending trial. There was a part of me who longed to help, but another who couldn't forget.

Simion's touch softened, whereas his voice hardened. '*They* can wait. Anyway, this is for you. It's custom for those who partake in the Claim to receive a gift as good luck.'

'But I haven't signed my name yet.'

Simion rearranged the wrapped item from beneath his arm and handed it to me. 'Yet.'

Yes, he really had caught me.

'Take it, please. It would be awfully rude if you didn't.'

Curiosity had me reaching out, our fingers brushing ever so slightly. 'You didn't need to do this.'

'It's just a little something.'

The object was lightweight, soft to the touch. Clothing of sorts, it had to be. 'You took a risk. What if Leia jumps down and snatches the pen from my hand before I even sign my name? Then the gift would go to waste.'

'I know you enough to know that you wouldn't let that happen.' *I know you.* 'Plus, I enjoy rubbing salt in the wounds of the person who is, once again, keeping my family from me.'

A shadow passed behind his eyes, darkening the vibrant gold of his iris. The storm lasted all but a second before I interrupted it from overspilling.

'Well, thank you.' I couldn't hide the smile. It was natural around Simion, even if I wished it wasn't.

'Which brings me to my next question. That gift... it doesn't need to go to waste, it has a purpose.'

I rolled my eyes. 'Here we go.'

'As I am sure you are aware, all initiates partaking in the Claim are expected to attend a Ball.' Simion fiddled with his hands, picking at the skin around his thumb. It wasn't like him to act without confidence, but there was something about this moment that reduced him to a nervous mess. It was endearing. 'It's just a pompous excuse to drink, dance and parade the initiates around the nobility.'

'Yes,' I replied. 'I'm *very* aware.'

He looked everywhere but me, rubbing his hand down the back of his head. 'Well, then you know... I mean I was just thinking...'

'Spit it out, Simion Hawthorn.' I raised my finger to his chin, lifting his face up so his eyes settled back on mine. Forgotten was the silver handfasting mark, the reason why I couldn't get close to him. 'Ask me the question.'

'Go with me, to the Ball I mean. I know dancing isn't really your thing, but there is more we can do than dance. There is food and wine, and I mean who doesn't like wine? And I had that made for you...' Simion gestured to the package I held. 'Because I took another risk that you would say yes and...'

'Simion,' I stopped him with a single word. There was a part of me that wanted to say yes, to accept his invitation and pretend that everything was normal; that Beatrice wasn't locked away awaiting trial for her crimes; that my father wasn't dead; or I hadn't killed my husband—even though he filled my dreams and still marked my skin by the fast-mark. But a larger part of me, a louder more demanding part, had me grasping for an excuse.

'I—' But I couldn't finish, Simion added one final and hopeful statement.

'It *would* be my honour.' Simion's golden eyes widened, hopeful. Perhaps he could see the impending doom that was my answer, almost preparing himself for the disappointment.

'I'll think about it,' I said, not noticing just how quiet the crowd had become.

'That's better than a no, I suppose.'

I had been so lost to him, his touch and his gaze, that I hadn't noticed we'd reached the front of the crowd. If the man behind the book hadn't cleared his throat, we may never have turned from one another.

'Mage Oaken,' he said, his voice rough as stone. I didn't need to ask how he knew my name, not from the fearful glance he shot towards the Council members. He too scrutinised me with a wary glance. 'And you are here for?'

'I would like to put my name forward for the Claim.' I spoke with the most confidence I could muster.

He hesitated, chewing the inside of his lip as he searched for a valid excuse to stop me.

'I believe it is my choice, and I have been blessed by Oribon, so that confirms it is also my birthright. Unless you have a reason as to why I cannot?'

Simion's deep laugh sounded behind me, warming me from the inside out. 'He is not wrong.'

The older man looked between us, then back to the Council. Any moment now, Leia would leap down and stop this. When the quill was lifted from the inkpot and handed to me, I almost stopped breathing.

'This is binding, Maximus Oaken,' the old man said, deep voice like grinding stones. 'There is no going back.'

I opened my mouth to reply, but the words were ripped away by a sky-shattering roar. My head snapped back in the direction where the Avarian Crest lingered. It was as though a shape had broken away from the shadows, large and monstrous, and it flew towards the city.

Oribon. Father of dragons.

He was coming.

Lost in my awe, I didn't notice Simion slip behind me, nestling his hard stomach into my back, his hands carefully anchoring me on either side. Where his thumb traced circles over my jacket, it was as though he touched bare skin. Even his cool breath disturbed the chestnut curls of my hair.

I should have pulled away, but I didn't. I didn't because I was selfish, and Simion was all I craved, even if I was too scared to admit it to myself.

'Oribon is an incredible creature,' Simion whispered, his voice buried beneath the powerful beat of wings as Oribon flew closer. 'As are you.'

My mouth dried. There was nothing I could say. Instead, I locked my eyes on Oribon and focused on the details.

He was a large dragon, far greater in size than Glamora. His wingspan stretched out, casting the shadow of a storm beneath him. Legends told that Oribon was the one who tore the mountain in two, freeing himself and his children from their earthly imprisonment. Without seeing him now, it would have been easier to pretend that was impossible. But if anything had the power to tear mountains apart, it was Oribon.

Crafted from silvered scales, its armoured body glowed beneath the sun. Curled horns protruded from its skull, twisting like a crown of granite. The closer it came, the more scars I could see across his body. Old wounds from battles, only proving the myths for truth.

Dark clouds billowed in his wake, coating the sky and blanketing the sun. Winds sang, snow fell and winter had finally arrived as though brought on by the god of the sky. The crowd erupted in cheers and screams, arms reaching up to the sky as though Oribon would bless them, give them access to his ancient and *great* magic.

Which was exactly why I was prepared to sign my name up for the Claim. Not only was it my right, but it was my way of preparing. Simion had not asked me why I had finally decided to compete, and I was glad for it. Because how could I tell him every morning I woke from the grasp of a nightmare, a vision given to me when I touched the Heart Oak and drew on its power. I couldn't explain it, but deep in my chest, there was a seed of impending doom. It had sunk its roots into my chest and refused to let go.

Something was coming. This peace was short-lived. And, this time, I wasn't prepared to sit back and allow others to protect me —protect what I love. I would be ready, whether it was to face the wrath of the Council, the memory of Camron Calzmir, or, worse, the monster who filled my dreams.

As Oribon's shadow passed over me, I lowered the quill to the page and scrawled my name. My hand was steady, as was my heart. By the time I finished writing it, I held the quill so long that the ink began to smudge beneath its tip.

'Congratulations,' the man said, looking over the frame of his glasses. 'And good luck. May you survive the trials, may you prove Oribon of your worth.'

It was done. I had signed my name in ink. But if I did not prepare for the Claim, it would be my death signed in blood. Because what I did know was not everyone made it out alive.

But I would. I *would* survive.

CHAPTER 1

The fist connected with my face, followed by the sound of shattered bone. Blood seeped from my broken nose into my mouth. The copper taste exploded across my tongue and stained my teeth a tacky pink. I swallowed it down hard, keeping my focus pinned to the battlemage before me. I dared not drop my defensive position, fists clenched and raised in front of my face, to clear the blood away. If I did, a broken nose would've been the least of my worries.

'There goes that pretty face of yours,' Leska sneered with a knowing smile.

'You think I'm pretty?' I replied, unable to stifle the sarcasm. It was as much a shield as my raised fists.

She rolled her eyes. 'Focus. Hold your guard.'

I shifted from one foot to the other, mirroring the thunderous beat of my heart. It was one of Leska's first lessons when our training began almost three weeks ago.

Never stop moving, don't give your enemy the chance to snare you.

I found the warning rather apt, considering Leska made it clear that she disliked me. I'm sure she took great pleasure in breaking my nose over and over. I didn't know what had become more a part of my routine: the broken bones or the continuous visits to Saylam Academy's in-house infirmary.

Both, perhaps.

'Can't you pick another bone to take your hate out on?' I asked, gathering a ball of spit laced with blood, hacking it on the smooth stone floor of the training hall.

Leska narrowed her bright azure eyes, judgement and enjoyment blending as one. 'I go for your face because it is the most pleasurable part of you to hit. Say the word, and I'll shift my focus elsewhere.'

A pang of discomfort jolted in my groin. It was an echo from a week prior, when Leska had driven her knee so hard into it that there was nothing the gleamers could do to calm the swelling. My pride also kept them from coming anywhere near enough to truly work their *magic*. If there was anything that would make me fight harder, it was the warning glittering in Leska's cobalt eyes.

I threw my left fist forward, only to miss as she sidestepped out of my way. Leska was ready, as she always was. The momentum, and my exhaustion from the hours of combative training, made me slow. I lost my footing, my body weight following through my initial jab. All it took was a fast smack of Leska's knuckles into the side of my stomach, followed by the smooth sweep of her leg beneath my uneven stance, to send me careening to the ground.

I met the stone with a *thump*; it sang through every bone in my body.

'You're sloppy,' Leska said from above me, casting a shadow where I lay, panting on the floor. 'You don't think before you act, you just throw that useless body around without care.'

Her words should've hurt, but I was in too much physical pain to care. 'I'll get better.'

She laughed at that. 'Who are you kidding?'

What I meant was I *had* to get better. The Claim was fast approaching, and I was still weak and powerless. Literally powerless.

A deep cramp of agony reverberated through my lower stomach, reminding me of the thrashing magic left untapped within me. Even if I wanted to reach for it, I couldn't without an amplifier—something Leska was working hard to keep away from me until my physical training improved. I convinced myself she wished to keep me away from my magic because she knew I could best her with it, but one look into her eyes and I knew that wasn't the case. If Leska enjoyed thrashing me with her fists, I could only imagine how she would enjoy doing so with her magic.

'In the South we have a saying,' I said, breathless. 'Don't blame the tools but the person who wields them. Perhaps it is your teachings that should be—'

Stars burst behind my eyes a second after the boot connected with my jaw. Blood sprayed out of my torn lip. Before I could take a breath through the agony, or open my eyes, a weight was atop me.

Leska straddled my waist, wrapped her fingers around my blood-slicked chin and held me firm. 'Careful, Maximus.'

'Get—off.' I struggled, but it was useless.

'Take that as a reminder you are *not* in the South anymore,' Leska sneered, spittle crashing across my face. 'And before you offend me again, remember it is my training that will keep you alive during the Claim. I am not here to make you a warrior, I haven't the years for that.'

I smiled through the blood and agony. 'Then what do you want to make me?'

'Good. Good *enough*. Now, get up,' Leska snapped. 'We run again.'

I inched my face towards Leska, feeling the swell of fury rise in my chest like a viper from a wicker basket. Anger was as much a companion as the shattered bones in my nose. Since my father was murdered by my husband, the feeling had never left me.

'You're punishing me, you're trying to break me. How can I improve if I spend most of the time on my back?'

'A position you enjoy, no doubt.' Leska's sneer broke into a grin.

'Fuck. You.'

'You're not wrong. I *am* trying to punish you, but not break you. Regardless of what I desire, my job is to make you unbreakable. I cannot teach you how to fight, or hold a blade, or wield the years of knowledge you've missed out on. I am to make you as resistive as the roots of the oldest tree. You have to work harder, faster, *be* stronger than those around you.'

'Does kicking me when I'm down help towards that goal of yours?' I asked, body trembling with unspent rage.

'If you think your enemies will care if you're lying on your front, back or side, they will do far worse than anything I might do to you.' Leska removed herself from me in a flash, the lack of her weight helping me take in a proper breath.

I stood quickly, feeling the solid ground beneath me sway. 'I won't be a sack for you to take your feelings out on.'

'Then don't be the *fucking* sack, Max. Get up and *be* something else. Prove to me I am not wasting my time. Otherwise, consider your name revoked from the...'

I didn't let her finish. The pain from my nose, my bruised body and aching bones, I took it all and buried it deep, *deep* down, where my grief lay. It fuelled me. My fist connected with the side of her stomach. Her surprise encouraged me to push forward as a vicious snarl broke out of me. Leska jumped over my next attack, a sweep of a foot meant to knock her over. What she didn't expect was me to throw all my body weight into her middle, knocking her to the ground.

It was only a handful of seconds worth of duelling, and I felt as though I had climbed a mountain.

'Don't—threaten—me—*again.*'

I held my breath, trying to count to ten before I continued. I had found my temper to be frayed and short, my tongue sharp and quicker than my mind since Camron.

In the most dramatic flair, which made me all the more jealous of Leska's control over her body, she sprang from the floor with a kick of her legs.

'Then do that more often,' she scoffed, leaning her weight onto her left hip, dark hair shifting across her damp forehead. At least that was new; Leska didn't usually break a sweat during our training. She may not have been bruised and broken-boned, but the glistening across her forehead told me I was improving.

The Claim was what kept me going. It was a focus during a time when drowning in grief was the easiest option. I wouldn't admit it aloud, especially not to Leska, but I was more desperate to partake in the Claim than anything else. Since being here, watching the dragons—the glorious gods of air as they danced around the Nests—it had become an obsession to claim one for myself.

It was my right, a deep-rooted need that I could not explain.

'I'm calling an end to today's training. Visit the infirmary and see that they fix you up.' Leska snapped me out of my thoughts, drawing me back to the moment at hand. 'I would prefer to train when I have a nose to break, and since yours is already... well, I think it best if I give my fists a rest.'

The broken flesh of my lower lip stung as I brushed my tongue over it, inspecting. I knew, without the need for a mirror, that my eyes were ringed with bruises, and the skin around my cheekbones swollen. It was nothing Dayn, the novice gleamer, hadn't already dealt with.

'You speak as though I care to prove anything to you,' I said. 'Your opinion means little to me, Leska.'

'As does the opinion of the Traitor Mage. It means fuck all to me.' Leska held her fist to her chest as she glared at me. One glance down, I noticed the torn skin across her knuckles. I may not have meant to hurt her, but knowing she would walk away today with her own wound made me fight the urge to smile.

There were times I was beginning to grow used to Leska's company, and then it all crashed back to reality when I remembered why she despised me.

I had killed someone close to her. And she would make me pay every moment she could.

* * *

'Would you just keep *still!*' Dayn said, face pinched in concentration.

Keeping still was easier said than done when his shaking fingers clutched my nose, grasping shattered bone and bruised skin.

'I'm trying.' I winced as a short finger prodded the mess Leska had left across my face.

'Well, try harder. I need to focus, and I can't do that if you keep wriggling like some unfortunate worm on a hook.'

I fought the urge to laugh at Dayn's ridiculous analogy, but I dared not move unless I wanted my nose fixed in a wonky position permanently. 'You do realise, if a worm is on the end of a hook, it is likely dead, thus not moving anymore.'

Dayn tutted, as though he was the adult when he was, actually, many years younger than me. 'Then *be* a worm on the end of a hook and keep still!'

Dayn had seen no more than thirteen winters. Although there was something ancient that lingered in his violet eyes. It was as though he had seen the world in ways no one else could understand. Framed by short brown hair, spot-covered skin, full red cheeks and short, stumpy fingers, which continued to prod and poke at my bruised face. He was one of the youngest gleamer novices enrolled in Saylam Academy, and one who had the least experience in healing. Which was exactly the reason he was always asked to see to my injuries. It had little to do with his need to practise—which he did in fact require—but everything to do with the fact no other gleamer cared to lay their hands on me. To them, regardless of what I had done to help save this city, I was still the Traitor Mage.

It was a title I was growing rather used to—in truth, I

preferred it more than the others I had before.

Julian Gathrax. The False Son. The Lost Mage. Now, The Traitor Mage.

At least it led with my name, Maximus Oaken, not anyone else's.

'All right, I think I got it,' Dayn said, his light voice raising in pitch before it lowered into a whisper. 'I think.'

I pinched my eyes closed, feeling the hopeful swell of his calming power as it eased into my face. First came the numbing of pain, then the pop and crack as bone reformed and moved into the position they belonged in, not the position Leska left them in.

For a gleamer to heal, they had to understand the human body inside out. They studied anatomy, every layer that made up a person from their skin to their veins, bones and muscles. Their ability to fix was limited to knowledge of the area they worked in. Dayn had explained it all during the many hours we'd spent together. He couldn't simply heal a bone without understanding its form, its density and structure. Luckily for me, he'd become all too familiar with the formation of my nose.

Unlike me, Dayn was an academic. I admired how his eyes brightened when he discussed his studies. And his favoured subject, the one that practically made the young boy salivate from the mouth, was history.

'At least the bruises will fade before the Ball,' Dayn said, although I wished he didn't. I would've preferred if he focused on the task at hand.

'Honestly, I haven't decided if I'm going or not,' I replied, mind lingering on Simion's invitation from days prior.

'Has no one asked you?'

Ouch.

'Yes, in fact, someone has.'

His eyes widened like a child being offered something excessively sugary to eat. 'Who? Who?'

I dismissed his question with the sweep of a hand. 'No one of importance. Anyway, I'd prefer to sit at home and read a book than embarrass myself dancing in front of a crowd who hate me.'

It was only half a lie. The thought of parading around Saylam Academy before Elder Leia and her Council displeased me. Anything relating to Simion and Beatrice's aunt displeased me. But the truth was far deeper. It was because going with Simion, allowing myself to get close enough to him, would risk the hand-fasting mark still inked across my skin. I wasn't ready to test its boundaries, to find out if it caused me pain, and what that would mean...

The young novice smiled at that, flashing the gap between his two front teeth. 'I suppose it is good you are not coming. I haven't mastered the art of fading bruises yet. All those broken vessels, there are so many I cannot focus on them one at a time.'

'Don't worry about it, I don't mind a bruise or two. Makes me look scary.'

Dayn laughed, his voice breaking from deep to high-pitched, which he proceeded to cover up with a cough. He leaned in, suddenly cautious of those who moved around us. 'They make bets, you know. They put wagers on how many bones need healing, or how many bruises that battlemage leaves on you. I don't join in, but I... I thought you should know.'

My eyes left Dayn and scanned the room behind him. A heavy smell of disinfectant, lavender and citrus filled the air. Ivory-cloaked gleamers moved on soundless feet, the swell of power in the air so palpable I could taste it. Dayn's amplifier was designed to be practical in his work; around his wrist was a band of polished wood. It was slightly too big for him, allowing for the growth expected as he became a man.

'Then I better make them lose their wagers,' I whispered, returning my focus on Dayn. 'Their opinions do not upset me.'

'*Who* upsets you?' A voice called out from my side. It was deep and powerful enough to cast the entire room into a tense silence.

Dayn pulled back, eyes wide and posture stiffened. There was admiration as well as fear in his gaze as he regarded the visitor. It lasted a moment before he bowed his head, as did every other gleamer occupying the room.

Only the scholar overseeing the gleamers' training stayed standing, face void of any expression. 'Mage Hawthorn, by what do we have the pleasure of your visit?' The scholar said, clearly displeased by the interruption.

In the back of my mind, just beyond the fortress I always kept up, I felt the brush of cold fingers. It was the gentle kiss of winter winds against bare skin, the touch of ice across water.

It was Simion's magic, attempting to mind-speak.

'I am here for Maximus,' Simion Hawthorn answered the elder, his golden eyes drinking me in entirely. No matter how I longed to bury the swell in my chest, I couldn't.

Dayn looked between us, reading the unspent tension. His brows raised, eyes widened, as though he found the answer to the question he had not long asked. 'It was him, wasn't it? Mage Hawthorn was the one who asked you to the Ball.'

I shot him a look. Dayn's hissed whisper was still loud enough to make Simion smirk. I couldn't move, not even to nod in agreement, as a scarlet blush crept up my face.

'Anything I can help you with?' I asked, hating how distant I sounded. I fortified the steel barrier around my mind, feeding strength into it. I couldn't read his mind, but I could read the change in his posture, his demeanour.

Something was wrong.

'In fact, there is.' Simion approached the side of my chair, extended a hand and waited for me to take it. The whites of his eyes were stained with red veins, the lines across his forehead confirming the tension he harboured. As much as I longed to reach out for him, I didn't. I couldn't. Not with the handfasting lines still inked around my skin. Marks I had hoped would fade. Marks that still glowed as bright as they had the day they etched across my skin when I was married off to Camron Calzmir.

Simion kept his hand extended, even after I didn't take it and stood from the chair myself. His eyes traced across my face. Beneath his gaze, I longed to lift my fingers to my newly healed nose and the bruises that lingered around it.

'You are hurt,' he said, grimacing as though it pained him to look at me.

'It's nothing.' I refused to look away, fighting the urge to touch my wounded face.

'To you, it may not be.' Simion broke our connection, unable to look at me. 'To me, it matters.'

I looked down to my hands, feeling shame for causing his reaction. That was when I noticed, out the corner of my eye, just how violently his own hands shook as he balled them into fists.

'Have you come to escort me home?' I asked, although, somehow, I knew that was not the case.

'I am afraid not.' He spoke like a man infected with rigid tension. Gone was the person I had spoken with days ago, the one who still waited for my answer to his invitation to the Ball. This was Simion Hawthorn, the Elder's nephew. 'Leia and the Council have requested an audience with you.'

He was unable to hide the desperation in his voice. Everyone heard it. Holding his gaze, I couldn't help but recognise how exhausted he looked.

'What have I done this time?' I asked, attempting to keep the atmosphere light.

It didn't work. Simion didn't crack a smile to show me everything was okay. In fact, he could still hardly look at me without the lines of fury across his face deepening.

He only broke when I reached out and laid a hand on his arm. 'Is it bad, Simion?'

Simion leaned in close until his lips were so close to my ear. To anyone else, he was whispering sweet nothings in my ear. When I heard his response, I wish he had.

'I cannot say it here. Just… trust me, please. I won't let them do anything to you.'

It didn't matter if there was anything else to say. All I could focus on was his final words and the raw, undiluted terror behind them.

I won't let them do anything to you.

CHAPTER 2

A bead of sweat trickled down my temple. It raced along the side of my face, falling beneath the collar of my training leathers. I dared not move to clear it. Beneath the scrutiny of the Council, I was immobile. If it wasn't for Simion, who stood in front of me, attempting to shield me from his aunt's fiery gaze, I would've faltered the second he had escorted me here. But it wasn't only the Council who had me rooted to the spot.

It was the room around me.

I hadn't been in the throne room since the fateful day when everything had changed. And yet it was as though I had never left. I fought the urge to look towards the step that had cracked Simion's skull. Or the place my father's body had burned to a crisp. It all captured my attention, but nothing more so than the charred body of the Heart Oak.

It pulsed with a faint green light. As it had when I first saw it, except this time it was dull. Weaker. As though the life of the tree was fading.

No—it was dying.

If Wycombe was the scar left in Camron Calzmir's wake, this room was where the rot lingered.

I'd not visited the castle in the weeks since the attack, but in the depths of my dreams, it was as though I'd not left. Every night had been different versions of the same event. But there was one detail that never wavered. Fire as black as night, as I was held in the uncaring hands of Camron Calzmir. Ash, screaming and death.

Then the woman and her army of shadows. A monstrous force, something I feared I could never put into words. I told no one. Not even Mother, when she asked me why every morning I looked more exhausted than the night before.

Even as I stood in the centre of the room, I tried everything in my power not to look to the spot where my father was reduced to ash.

'Finally, you arrive.' Elder Leia's voice rang through my skull, as did the disappointment lingering in it. 'I do hope my summons hasn't interrupted your training, Maximus Oaken.'

She was dressed in an emerald gown that spilled around her feet like the algae-coated water of a lake in summer. Silver hair fell over her shoulders, complimenting the rich gleam of her brown skin. Her pointed nails tapped on the armrest of her chair, one finger at a time, the rhythm drumming into my bones.

I bowed, as was custom, although my own nails bit into my palm just at being in her presence. 'I get the impression I have done something wrong.'

'Well, have you, Maximus?' Leia's beautiful smile faltered. 'Done something wrong, that is?'

'You're the one who requested my presence, Elder Leia,' I replied.

'I see Leska has done little to knock that attitude out of you,' Leia snapped, back straightening. She shot her nephew a look, one that silently asked if he would stand by and allow me to speak to her in such a way.

His silence was answer enough.

'You know this is ridiculous,' Simion finally said, 'clutching at straws. Max has been accounted for, every hour of every day. He is innocent in this.'

In what? My mind screamed the question.

An ominous smile lifted across Elder Leia's face, bright and all knowing. It set me at unease and twisted my stomach into knots. 'I wish that was true, nephew. But evidence suggests that Maximus Oaken here has not been entirely honest with us.'

My body stiffened, blood cooling to rivers of ice. 'What evidence is this?'

Simion's expression hardened when he looked at me. 'Maximus hasn't had the time to conspire against you.'

Conspire? My breathing faltered.

Leia leaned forward, nails pinching into the armrest of her chair. 'Perhaps, but that does not take away from the *fact* that Maximus's husband has provided him an army. No matter how many times Maximus has refuted this claim, we now know the truth behind it.'

Blood thundered in my ears. For a moment, there was relief— relief that Leia didn't bring up my mother or my ties to the Heart Oak. Since the Queen died, I had kept that secret to myself.

Whatever they spoke of now seemed like another secret, one I didn't even know I was supposed to hide.

'I've told you everything,' I said, reiterating the very statement I had been forced to repeat in the weeks following Camron's attack. 'I have answered every question, over and over. There is no army. There never was, and there will never be. I'm sure we don't need the reminder that Camron is dead. Unless you brought me here to tell me a pile of ashes can have that much influence?'

'Unfortunately, as much as I wish I did, I do *not* believe you.' Leia leaned forward, a predatory glint in her eyes. 'So, I shall give you a chance to tell us what it is you are hiding.'

'Leia,' Simion scorned, hands raised, holding them up between me and his aunt. 'Stop.'

Elder Leia tutted, tongue smacking against her lips. The sound grated my skin, prickling as though I'd been thrown into a hedge of poisoned ivy. 'Stop what, Simion? Protecting this city? Preventing any further innocents being murdered? No, I will not stop. I will ask you, Maximus, what were Camron's plans for the South?'

My jaw ached as I gritted my teeth, refusing to take my eyes off her. If I did, it was an admission of guilt. 'Whatever you think you are trying to get out of me, I'm afraid to let you down. *Again.*'

'I can see you do not wish to be honest with us, even after everything we have given you. Shame, a real shame.' Elder Leia waved her hand, eyes rolling with dismissal. 'Guards, please can you see that our *guests* are brought in. Perhaps they will provide the necessary insight that Maximus Oaken refuses to provide.'

Footsteps sounded at our backs. I was the last to turn to see who the battlemages escorted into the room. When I did, my heart almost stopped.

There were eleven of them, men, women and three children, the youngest couldn't have seen more than eleven winters. They each wore the white shawls of Wycombe's infirmary, barefoot and wide-eyed as though they'd survived a battle, physically and mentally.

Behind them, masked healers from the infirmary fanned out, casting careful eyes across their patients. I could see they were all gleamer mages, as most of the infirmary staff were. They wore ivory cloaks, trimmed in grey, with a dryad's face stitched into the cloak's breast.

It took my mind a moment to register where I had seen the face of the leading woman before. It was not that she had changed, just that this was never a place I expected to see her. Not ever.

Striking beauty on display, uncovered by hair. Hazel eyes, which, even exhausted, held the spirit of a warrior.

'Queen Stephine Romar,' I spoke aloud, as though that would make this impossible vision real.

'Mage Oaken,' she replied, tipping her head in a bow.

I had last seen Stephine Romar during my handfasting ceremony to Camron Calzmir. Not only was her presence here shocking, but I also couldn't believe how it was possible. The

Romar Kingdom was the furthest South of Galloway Forest. Not only that, I understood the dangers that lurked in the shadows of the forest all too personally.

Yet here they stood, alive and well.

'*Queen* Romar was found with a small band of her followers, traipsing along our borders.' Elder Leia paced before her chair, eyes never leaving me. 'Stephine, would you care to explain what it is you told us earlier today? I think it may jog some of Maximus's memories of... home.'

Home. She said it as though it meant something.

Simion raised a finger and pointed at his aunt. He shook violently, eyes wide and lips flashing in a snarl. 'Do you ever give up? This endless interrogation of Maximus *must* stop.'

'And it will.' Her reply was so cold it chilled me to the bone. 'As soon as he is honest with us. Stephine Romar, I apologise for my nephew's outburst. Please, share with the audience what drove you out of the South?'

'We fled,' Stephine said so plainly it snatched my breath away.

My body hardened to stone. All around me, people reacted the same, except the Council members, who looked on as though none of this was news to them.

'Fled from what exactly?' Elder Leia was enjoying this. She knew she had me in a corner.

'There is a plague passing through the Calzmir Estate,' Stephine continued, looking at me as she spoke. It was as if we were the only ones in the room. Her brown eyes glanced down at the silver mark just shy of my shirt's cuff. 'People are dying, burning from the inside out. If they survive, they do so *changed*.'

My knees almost gave out, the room swaying. Even if I longed to speak, I couldn't.

'Does that sound familiar, Maximus?' Leia encouraged with a flick of her wrist.

The room spun violently. 'No.'

'And still he lies,' Leia said, the talons of her magic scratching the outskirts of my mind's wall. 'This would be the moment to tell the truth—'

'He answered your question,' Simion spat.

'—or let me into that mind and I will glean the answers out.'

The shields keeping my thoughts hidden strengthened. Then I reached out and touched Simion. Not because I wanted to calm him, but because I needed to calm myself. 'I've got this. I haven't got anything to hide.'

Now that was another lie. But what I had to hide had nothing to do with what Queen Romar had just said.

Elder Leia paused, looked at me and grinned. 'Words. Believable or not, that is all they are.'

I straightened, trying to grasp some calm in my mind. 'I know you wish to use me as a shovel to dig yourself out of the hole you find yourself in, but not once have I lied about any of this. Believe it, or don't. I know nothing of this.'

Leia ignored me this time, focusing back on the Southern Queen. 'Stephine, who let you into Wycombe?'

I paused, wondering the same. The city was guarded by dryads, the gods of earth whose essence ran through my blood.

'I… I don't know.' Confusion rippled over the Southern Queen's face before she broke into a fit of coughs. 'My memory is foggy in places.'

'Altered,' Leia corrected. 'We believe a skilled gleamer has shrouded their memories. Although I can't possibly begin to wonder who did that.'

I held my ground as Elder Leia stepped towards me. She stopped only when her boots tapped into mine. 'Do *you* know who let them in?'

My jaw set firm, eyes widening as I knew she was attempting to blame me. 'Your guess is as good as mine.'

Leia recoiled with such furious speed I thought she would strike me. 'What would you have me do to an army of wytchfire-wielding monsters? Talk to them? Find out what it is they want before they burn this Aldian to the ground?'

'Forgive me, but you are now asking my opinion on matters? I thought you made it clear that you don't care to hear my suggestions.'

Heat rose in her cheeks, the whites of her eyes stained red. Unseen claws scratched across my mind again, trying to gouge their way in. I strained against the discomfort, fuelling steel into my shield whilst trying to keep her out.

'I *will* see into that mind,' Elder Leia hissed, panic in her wide eyes.

She didn't do this because she wanted to, but because she needed to.

'What of the aid I have requested?' Stephine called out, pulling forward from the line of guards who stood behind her. It became suddenly clear that she was no welcome guest in the North. Although her wrists were not bound by manacles, the guards reached to grab her.

As suddenly as it began, Leia sheathed her mental claws, withdrawing them from the shield around my thoughts. She looked at Stephine as she replied. 'Unfortunately, we are in no position to help you.'

'The South—'

'The South must deal with its own, just as I will deal with mine,' Elder Leia snapped. 'That has been the way for a long time, and it will stay as such. We do not involve ourselves with the South, and we ask that you do not involve yourselves with us.'

Stephine Romar caught my gaze. Her eyes overspilled with her silent plea. It sang in every crease and wrinkle that formed around her eyes. 'Mage Oaken, we swore ourselves to you. No matter what you think, you are still our King. If *they* won't help us, you must.'

Help us. King. It was a request I felt tug at my soul. Everyone stilled as they waited for my response. Before I opened my mouth, I knew this was a test. Leia would be waiting for me to prove where my loyalties lay.

Regardless of my wants, Wycombe was my home now. The

cottage nestled on the outskirts of Wycombe city was home. A place we called our own.

I wouldn't jeopardise it.

'I'm sorry,' I said, unable to hold her eyes. 'I can't.'

I longed to tell her why, but I couldn't.

There was a part of me that expected Stephine to spit at my feet. To tell me how I had failed them, even though I never asked to lead or rule. Instead, she surprised me with her reply. 'There will come a time when you will.'

One look at Elder Leia and I knew any attempt to beg for her to help would have been wasted.

'The phoenix's attempt to destroy the Heart Oak was perhaps not its only task.' Leia kept as still as stone, emotion void from her expression as she surveyed the crowd. At our backs, the rest of her Council positioned themselves as a shield. 'I wanted you to see this so you can understand what we must face.'

'Understand what?' I asked, sensing the strange unspoken tension that hung between Leia and the Council.

'You are a smart man, Maximus. Look at them, truly look at them and tell me what you see.'

I did as she asked, settling my eyes on Queen Romar and the refugees who escaped the South with her. It was as though I truly saw them for the first time, or maybe I just didn't know what I searched for before.

There was a mutilation of burns covering their exposed skin. Arms had been blistered and healed in folded, scarred skin, as had necks and faces. The youngest of the children—a small girl with wide and wet blue eyes, and a face framed by poppy red hair, had half her neck twisted by healed burn marks.

'They are infected,' one of the Council members answered for me, stepping forward with a quick bow of his head. I had not seen him before, but there was something familiar about him. He was a man between forty and fifty winters. His thick beard was peppered with silver, which made up for the lack of hair across his head. He surveyed me with eyes that were a dark, ocean blue. Eyes that were perpetually tired. It clicked why he looked so familiar. He looked like Leska. They looked almost identical; I didn't need the confirmation to know they were related in some capacity.

'Infected?' Simion repeated the word as though it made little sense. To him maybe not, to me it meant everything.

'Like Camron,' I answered.

'Exactly, Maximus,' Leia added. 'Just like your husband had been.'

Her use of titles should have hurt me, but it didn't. My focus was on Stephine and her people. Queen Romar lowered her eyes to her boots. It was enough confirmation that Elder Leia was right.

'Can we heal them?' I snapped.

Leia gestured to the man to take the floor. 'Elder Cyder, would you care to explain to Maximus Oaken just how impossible that is?'

'We believe, whoever has let Queen Romar and her people into Wycombe, did so with the hopes that they would destroy it.' Cyder lifted a white mask to his mouth, lacing the loops around his ears to keep it in place. When he spoke again, his words were muffled but clear enough. 'One look into their minds, you will see the war that rages inside.'

My gaze veered between Leia and Cyder, searching for a sign that this was all some misunderstanding, or misdiagnosis.

'So, you see now why I wanted to speak with you.' Leia gestured to the crowd. 'These are your people, after all, and it would seem they have also been touched by the same power that poisoned your husband's blood.'

'He is not my husband,' I spat.

Leia's gaze fell to the hint of silver marks on my arm. She didn't need to say anything, but I read the words from her eyes. *Oh, is he not?*

'We have access to magic,' Simion stammered, 'the least we can do is heal them if you are not prepared to spare numbers to help them.'

'Our gleamers are unable to heal them, Simion,' Elder Cyder continued, pacing the line of unflinching people. It was as if they didn't know where they were, not a single one of them looked at anything of importance. 'They hold onto a temperature that surpasses anything our bodies are built to withstand. Their burns continue to spread as though a fire kindles, unseen, beneath their skin. But it is their minds that reveal all—frantic, hazed and...'

'Loud,' Leia finished for Cyder. 'See for yourself, Simion, but do not get close. We are unsure on how the plague is spread.'

I watched Simion focus on the crowd. His brow furrowed, setting deep lines of concentration across his forehead. He scanned the line, searching for the one he would gleam. Then his eyes settled on one of the children. The silence lasted all but a moment before Simion rocked back, eyes glassy and distant.

'Indulge me, Simion. What did you find?' Elder Leia encouraged.

Simion gazed at me, before steeling his expression. 'When I connect with Maximus, his mind is as bright as a summer's sky and clear as newly blown glass. But Stephine's mind is a haze of fog—no, smoke. Thick plumes of lung-shattering smog. I saw... flashes of fire and heard the... the screeching of a creature in anguish or agony, I couldn't tell.'

'And where have you seen this before?'

Simion looked at me, even though it was Leia who asked the question. 'Camron.'

A hand rested on my back, followed by the seeping ease of a healing presence. I looked to find Elder Cyder, offering me his power and taking my anxiety away. It helped clear my mind, enough for me not to break down.

'Proof,' Elder Leia barked, 'that they too are possessed by the firebird, Camron Calzmir. He too was once an ordinary man whose soul burned with the wytchfire of the phoenix.'

Dread cut through every muscle in my body. I looked back to the line of people and saw them in a new light.

They were all like Camron. They each had the potential to destroy, ruin, burn and raze. Suddenly, the suffocating scent of the Heart Oak overwhelmed me, stung my eyes and scorched my throat.

But I couldn't take my eyes off the children. There was a glint of fear in their gazes, at least that is what I first thought. Then I saw it, the flecks of red and yellow, twisting unnaturally around their pupils.

'Queen Romar, is it true?' I asked.

'Camron has spread his infection to the South with the disease he brought from his travels,' Queen Romar replied, her voice resonating in the silent room. 'Those remaining attempt to keep the infected bound in Calzmir lands, but it has become impossible. They have magic... we can't resist them. So, we came not only to ask for aid, but to ask for healing. The North has access to magic, to powers that can help us. Please—'

'No. This is an act of war, sneaking into our city.' Sudden fury radiated off Leia, so potent I felt it in waves. 'What did you wish to do, finish the destruction your creator began?'

'No,' Stephine snapped, eyes wide with pleading. 'I swear, we came to ask for aid. That was all.'

As though sensing the change, the line of infected Southerners shifted their gazes, in tandem, to where Leia stood. They were so entirely focused on her, the beacon of power she was, that they didn't notice the shards of stone that broke from the slabs beneath their feet, rising slowly in the air beside them.

'Stop it,' I whispered, unsure who the command was for. 'They're children, you can't.'

'Elder Leia, perhaps if I could have more time with them,' Elder Cyder added, hands raised between Leia and the infected. 'There *are* avenues I have yet to investigate, potential cures—'

Leia silenced him with a stare. 'You know as well as I, we don't have the time for investigations.'

There was no looking away at the sharpened bullets of stone which hovered beside the temples of each of the infected.

'Sometimes, the hardest path is the only path,' Leia said, as her eyes emitted light from the power of her amplifier. The Heart Oak seemed to groan, begging Leia to stop, or encouraging her to continue, I couldn't be sure.

I looked to Elder Cyder, to Simion, silently pleading for them to do something.

'I hope you find your peace,' Leia called out, an unignorable sadness lingering in her voice.

I should've looked away, but I refused myself. In a blink, the stones moved. They passed through bone, brain matter and flesh, only to pierce out the other side of their heads, completely encased in blood.

One by one, they fell, life swept from their eyes. The crash of bodies thundered through me, choking on a sob in my throat. Queen Romar was the last to fall, the last for death to claim.

A violent grasp broke out of me. In moments, I was encased in Simion's arms, face nestled into the crook of his shoulder, and I pinched my eyes closed. All I saw was darkness and the flashing of life as it left the eyes of Queen Romar and her people.

Your people, the inner voice reminded me.

Leia turned her back on the lifeless bodies. 'The Heart Oak is damaged and is showing signs of weakening with every passing day. Without the Queen, it will perish, leaving us without a supply for the amplifiers. We will not be able to fund an army from the war that is to come. Beatrice's thirst for revenge has weakened us. It allowed the enemy into our home in hopes to burn what is left from the inside out.' Leia pushed her cloak aside, replacing the short staff back into its holder.

'You see now, nephew,' she continued, 'this burden has been placed upon my shoulders. It may not seem it now, but, for the sake of Wycombe, it had to be done.'

'Death seems to be a price you are most confident paying,

Leia,' I said, tears rolling down my face, Simion refused to release me. His presence was the only thing keeping me standing.

She winced, pity flashing in her golden eyes. 'It was not the easy decision, but it was the only decision. You may think me a monster, you may hate me, but this is only the beginning. They must die to keep us safe. To purge this sickness, we must send our numbers to the South and eradicate any further threat. Do you think it would be any different if it was the other way around?'

My body trembled; lightning fizzed over my arms as though I could connect with it even without an amplifier. I couldn't speak, my tongue swollen, mind fixated on both my relief and the line of dead bodies spread out across the floor.

'We cannot simply watch as the wytchfire burns through the rest of those we love,' Leia spoke to Simion, her voice as cold as ice. 'If you wish to protect *him*, this is how.'

Him. Me. She looked at me, grimacing at the concept.

The words fell out of me before I could stop them. 'Do not speak of love as though it is a concept you understand.'

'Oh, but I do.' Her hand fell upon my shoulder. 'I will root out every phoenix-possessed soul in Aldian and see them destroyed. Love matters little in the face of doom. I hope you come to understand that before it is too late.'

CHAPTER 3

I couldn't banish the execution of Queen Romar and the other refugees from my mind. There was no scrubbing the puddles of blood, the lifeless eyes or the paling of flesh, as it was etched into my memory, a fresh scar, another one added to my collection.

Could I have done more to save them? I played the events over in my mind, searching for something I could have done to stop Leia, something I could have said. But it always led to their eventual murder.

Because they were sick, with the same plague that changed Camron.

Phoenix-possessed.

I sat in the carriage, the journey passing in a blur. No one spoke. There were no words to share. Simion sat opposite me, his knee brushing mine as he stared outside the misty window. I should have asked where he was taking me. But it didn't matter, none of it did. All I could do was stare down at my hands. They were not covered in blood, but they might as well have been. After helping Elder Cyder clear the corpses, he had ushed Simion and me from the room and back out onto the streets. There had been words shared between both men, but nothing I cared to listen to.

The only sound that occupied me was the slick smattering of stone through flesh and the *thud* of bodies hitting the floor.

Camron had spread the same plague he and his father had suffered with. Queen Romar was proof that Leia was right—there *had* been an army he built in my name. Not one with pitchforks as I first believed, but an army of phoenix-possessed humans. The thought alone was horrifying; the reality was worse.

Leia would destroy them all.

History told of when the Queen rode on her dragon, with an army of masked army, to eradicate the four Southern mages. But this, this would end in far more turmoil. If it meant protecting the North, would she level the South entirely?

The carriage stopped, followed by a knocking on the wooden shutter between us and our horseman. Simion leaned forward, opening the door and gesturing for me to exit. Truthfully, I expected to exit onto the grasslands outside my new home—the cottage overlooking the Nests miles outside from Wycombe city. Instead, I was faced with Saylam Academy.

A rush of cool winds wrapped around us, tugging hair from my face.

'If you brought me here for more training, then forget it.' I heard my voice as though I was a witness. It was detached, cold and as blunt as an old blade.

'That is not what we are here for.'

Simion paced to the front of the carriage and asked them to wait for us, proving we wouldn't be long. He then moved for the sweeping steps that led up to the entrance. I reached out and snatched his wrist.

'Talk to me,' I demanded. 'Why are we here, Simion?'

He looked at me. Where the gold of his eyes touched my skin, it shivered in response. 'What we saw... what Leia did... it only proves that you need to be able to protect yourself. As much as I want to be the one, I can't. I mean, look what happened with Bea...'

He couldn't finish, but he didn't have to. I knew what he spoke of. Simion gazed from me, back to the spire behind us. 'You like libraries, from what I remember.'

'I do.'

He nodded, forcing a smile that was the least convincing thing I had ever seen. 'Then you will appreciate this one.'

'And how is a book going to help me protect myself?'

'Not books, Maximus. Amplifiers.'

It turned out that Saylam Academy did have a library, but it wasn't as I expected. I didn't expect the library to be located in the levels beneath the ground floor. Like the roots of a tree, it stretched four floors deep into the earth, accessible by stairs, unlike the floating podiums of stone that were required to move upwards through the tower.

The further we descended into the Academy's underbelly, the colder the air became and the more the scent of moist earth hung in the atmosphere. Down there, the silence was grating, maddening. Only the echoing of footsteps and the scuff of leather over stone shattered the quiet.

Simion led the way, silent and stoic as a sentinel of stone. He didn't even attempt to reach out and glean my mind. His anger was palpable, and I felt as though I was to blame.

Whether I liked it or not, I was named the South's ruler. And I had left them, selfishly enjoying the bliss of my new life whilst leaving them to squander in a plague left by the man who swore to love me, protect me—the man I killed.

A faint oozing of light shone from the veins of white stone throughout the walls at our side. Avarian stone, I had learned, captured the light of day and released it in a low buzz when required. Without it, I may not have seen the muscles in Simion's jaw flutter with resistance. The material came from the northern mountain range, which was aptly named as the Avarian Crest, the birthplace to the Aldian dragons. I supposed Dayn's history lessons were sticking.

It was one of his first, telling of how the Queen worked alongside the dragons, who carried the stone from the mountains and helped craft Saylam Academy alongside the other grand buildings in the city of Wycombe.

But now I did not crave stories to keep me occupied. I *required* Simion.

'I can't bear the quiet. Please, say something,' I begged.

Distract me.

'And what would you have me say?' Simion said, his voice a murmur through tightly pulled lips.

'Anything,' I pleaded, eyes stinging with the promise of more tears. 'Tell me this isn't my fault. Tell me it isn't my burden.'

His sudden attention had me stopping dead in my tracks. I stood on the step above him yet still he towered over me, having to look down his nose at me. The wash of silver light cast across his face, brightening the cold of his eyes and accentuating the exhaustion around them. The fury he harboured seemed to fade as he finally looked at me. Sorrow passed over Simion's face before he dropped his chin to his chest, looking down at the floor beneath him. 'Max, I'm sorry.'

'You are going to have to be more specific,' I said, unable to ignore the trembling in my body.

I reached out without thought, tracing my fingers down his forearm until they rested over his balled fist. Simion took his eyes from the floor and shifted them to the connection of our hands. He didn't need to vocalise it, but I knew he looked to the silver marks that wrapped around my wrist like iron manacles.

'Everything is falling apart,' Simion finally admitted, relaxing his fist enough for me to slip my fingers inside. 'Beatrice is up for a trial she has no hope of winning, every time I see you it is with a face painted in darker blues and purples. Wycombe is shattered and barely on the cusp of healing. And now there is the threat of a plague, one with the power to turn innocent people into the same monster who ruined your...' He stopped himself, taking in a giant breath.

'Life?' I answered for him.

'I'm trying, Maximus. I'm trying to find the light in this situation, but I fear it is hiding behind clouds that never seem to pass.'

I exhaled, unable to look away from Simion's velveteen-brown lashes. 'It is not your sole responsibility to fix the world, Simion.'

'Nor is it solely your burden to carry.'

There was more to say, but I couldn't seem to find the right words.

'Then whose is it?' I asked, my voice broken and soft.

'Who is going to worry about my sister? And you? If everyone else seems intent on punishing you, blaming you... I promised to be the one, Max. And I *will*.'

The shuffling of feet was quiet, but, in the taut silence that followed Simion's words, it was the loudest sound in the world. I wasn't aware just how close we had become. Too close. I had let my guard down; forgotten the very reason we couldn't get close like this. Bowing my head, I stepped past Simion and moved ahead. The conversation may have been interrupted, but I knew it was far from over.

Shelves upon shelves lined the modest room. There was barely enough space to walk between them, let alone move without smearing a thick layer of dust across myself. Cloaked figures shifted on silent feet, moving boxes and containers from one dust-ridden spot on the shelves to another. The air was thick and stale, lit by globes of Avarian stone set in flameless sconces. Where the silver light didn't reach, impenetrable shadow hung in the corners. Every now and then another cloaked figure would step from the darkness as though born from it, carrying large branches of wood or small boxes full of smaller wooden cuts.

I drank in the room, every pile of dust and glow of Avarian stone. 'So, this is where the power is kept.'

'Amazing, isn't it?' I was vaguely aware of Simion sulking in the shadows of the doorway, watching, eyes pinned on me. 'This library is where the Keepers of the Chamber store the offerings from the Heart Oak. You are looking at years of collection. A collection that will come in handy due to the Heart Oak's current state.'

More guilt spiked in me. I had heard the rumours, but seeing the Heart Oak today was confirmation enough to know there was truth behind them. It was dying. Without the Queen to fuel it, to provide her essence to sustain it, the Heart Oak would follow soon in death.

'I know you already *had* an amplifier, but after this afternoon's events I think it sensible you have another. Having access to an amplifier will be pivotal to your training, but, more importantly, the Claim.'

The Claim. When Leia requested my audience, I thought it was finally to punish me for going against her command not to put myself forward. In a way, I wish it was. Dealing with that would've been easier than the prospect of more monsters like Camron.

'I can... feel it,' I said as my ears tickled against the siren call of magic. It was hard to explain, and from Simion's response, I gathered it was not something that was said often.

'Strange. Maybe your separation from your magic makes you more susceptible to its presence.'

Or maybe it is because dryad blood runs in my veins. I kept that thought to myself, locked behind the shield around my mind.

The mage-mark across my palm tingled as I looked around the room with a new sense of vision. It was a tomb. A place the Heart Oak had been dissected, limbs chopped and cut, only to be stored in this dank place like bodies would be stowed in a catacomb.

I stepped forward. Drawn by the thrum of power, I almost didn't notice it at first. It was like the faint chime of bells caught in the wind from miles away. It tickled across my conscience, urging me to find its source. Unlike when Jonathan Gathrax had kept my wand from me, since Camron destroyed it, the agony of separation was not as intense.

'Has Elder Leia agreed to this?' I asked, unsure why I cared what Simion's aunt thought.

'No,' Simion replied.

'I'm all for pissing her off, but I don't think—'

'Leave the wrath of Leia to Elder Cyder,' Simion said. 'It is nothing he hasn't faced before.'

'Why Cyder?' I asked, thinking back to the balding man with kind, familiar eyes.

'We did him a favour, so instead of harbouring one in return, I called on it. He deals with these stores. Yes, my aunt is the one to have the final say, but Elder Cyder is still part of the Council. He can make decisions that he sees fit. The Heart Oak is not recovering,' Simion said without moving from his position against the shelf. 'Elder Cyder and his colleagues are preserving as much of the tree as possible, in case it fails to heal, and we lose access to it. He can spare a piece for you.'

Remorse coursed through me. It wasn't a new feeling, nor was it particularly jarring—I'd grown used to its company in the past weeks.

Through the shadows in my mind, I heard the Queen's voice repeat the same revelation she had shared with me in the catacombs beneath her castle.

The Heart Oak needs us to survive... This tree is a product of my essence, just as it is yours.

'Maximus, peruse the shelves. They say that a novice finds the piece of Heart Oak that resonates personally with them. Let it call to you.'

What if the Heart Oak entirely resonates with me? The question hummed in my mind, reminding me exactly why I kept Simion from gleaming my thoughts. *What if I can restore the Heart Oak by letting it drain my essence just as the Queen had me created for? The reason my mother stole me away.*

'Go on,' he whispered, concern lowering his thick brows. 'I will wait for you.'

In truth, I could've claimed myself a new amplifier whenever I wanted. As the Queen had said, I can create one from any piece of wood. But, in doing so, it would only generate more questions—questions about my birth, *questions* I had avoided since the attack.

I was beginning to grow comfortable here, in my new home. Mother was happy, providing assistance and carving a new life for herself. If I wanted to ensure it was never jeopardised again, I needed access to my magic. Especially with the threat of fire-wielding monsters an ever-present reality.

And if I was to help the South, I *would* need my magic.

As I walked the length of shelves, fingers tracing over dusty containers and boxes, each holding a different-sized piece of Heart Oak, I contemplated what my amplifier could have been. It had been something I'd spent a long time thinking about. Would I have chosen to present my amplifier as a wand again, or perhaps a staff, a wooden mace, a bracelet? A mage's amplifier in the North was as much a fashion statement as the clothes they wore. Since training with Leska, I'd learned the importance of having my hands free to use.

It didn't take long for me to pick one of the many boxes. My choice was not because the wood within called out to me, because, in truth, the entire room seemed to scream for my attention. I chose it because it was small, lightweight. I lifted the lid to expose a chunk of brown wood no bigger than the palm of my hand. For what I wanted, I didn't need much.

'I'm done,' I said, stepping back around to where I'd left Simion.

'That was in record time,' he replied.

A blush crept over my cheeks. 'Efficient is my middle name.'

I held the box in my hand, feeling the pulse of my heartbeat beneath my fingertips. We stood there, looking at each other, awkward tension hanging heavy between us. I felt it before it happened, the opening of a conversation I had been avoiding.

'I should get home, Simion.'

He snapped out of his daze, nodding frantically. 'Yes, of course. Forgive me for bringing it up, but...' *Here it comes.* 'I was wondering, as the Ball is tomorrow, have you decided if you are to come?'

'The Ball,' I repeated, feeling sick at the mere mention. 'No, I haven't decided yet.'

Simion expelled a breath, one loud enough for us both to hear. 'I gathered as much.'

'I *will* think about it,' I said with almost too much urgency.

Not a beat after, Simion mumbled something beneath his breath. *'I hope so.'*

I wanted to go. I did. But I couldn't think about celebrating, not after what I had seen. Nor did I want to put myself under the glare of Leia's eye. Yet the expectant glow in Simion's rich eyes was almost harrowing. I could see he, too, longed to know my answer; he had been waiting for it since he asked me to join him.

* * *

I had decided to keep what had happened from my mother long before I returned home. There was no point worrying her with the idea that Leia believed I was working with the South in some way. It was easier to lie, to plaster on a smile and pretend everything was okay. When, in reality, everything I vowed to protect was crumbling inside of me.

Dusk painted the sky in shades of navy and violet, the sun slipping over the horizon of the Thassalic, setting the ocean ablaze. To my luck, when the carriage arrived at the cottage, I found it empty.

It was not uncommon for my mother to be late home. She helped in Wycombe town—aiding those who had been affected by Camron's attack. She was a gleamer mage, her abilities sought after in the past weeks. Caring was in her blood. And it kept her busy, filling her time with others instead of facing her own grief.

Silence surrounded me as I entered my room. The more time that passed, the deeper the seed of panic settled. I couldn't sit around, contemplating her safety. We were safe here, I reminded myself. The plague was in the South, not here.

Instead of sitting and dwelling in my anxieties, I gave into the Heart Oak's draw. It was a test of my own will. A way to prove to myself that I never needed this magic, magic I had hated—magic that had taken so much from me.

I sat upon my bed, legs crossed before me and the wedge of Heart Oak resting on the sheets between. A shiver raced across my bare skin, sending every hair to stand. As I lost myself to the cutting of Heart Oak, I listened to the crashing of waves against chalk cliffs and the distant roars of dragons as they cut through the night sky beyond the Nests.

I'd yet to touch the wood, although my entire being longed for it. I couldn't explain it, but power thrummed around me. Perhaps it was my proximity to the Heart Oak's cutting, or the anticipation of familiar magic, but my entire body trembled with the desire to reach out and touch it.

More than ever, I hated magic. But, more than ever, I needed it. Magic was more than the access to power; it was strength and knowledge. It was a chance. A chance to hold this life together, to carve a future for me and my mother, one where she no longer needed to suffer. And one where I didn't need to look over my shoulder at every given moment.

The fast-marks caught my eye as I reached for the cutting of Heart Oak. It was a sour reminder of Camron, and only begged for more questions, questions I didn't have the energy to contemplate.

Only in death shall you part. It was the caveat in the union I'd found myself forced in. I'd killed Camron with a bolt of power that broke apart his body in an explosion of flesh, ash and feather. Yet the mark was still as clear as the day it spread across my skin.

I feared what it could mean.

Pushing thoughts of Camron to the back of my mind where

he usually lingered, I picked up the piece of Heart Oak I had chosen. The moment my fingers brushed the coarse surface, a rush of renewed energy flooded through my lungs. Just as it had when I grasped the roots of the Heart Oak, I felt magic thrash and crash around in my stomach, like a beast trying to break free of chains. Connected to my power, I sensed the threads of earth far beneath the cottage. Stone, dirt, wood and soil. It all sang to me.

Thunder crashed across the skies, answering my freeing cry. It echoed in my bones. A flash of stark-blue light cast across the world, bathing my room in a sudden harsh glow. Time slipped away, marked only by the booming claps of thunder and the slithering song of vines as they crept up the walls of the cottage like snakes. The world was alive, colourful and loud.

When I opened my eyes, uncurled my fingers and extended my open palm, the cutting was no longer the lump of misshaped wood it had been when I first held it. Dust and shavings coated my hand, falling between my fingers like ash. And there, nestled amongst it, was the smooth circular band my power had carved. My amplifier. A ring.

As I sensed the power, it, too, sensed what I desired.

I picked the ring up carefully, pinched between my forefinger and thumb. Slowly, I lowered it over the middle finger on my left hand. There was enough room to turn the wooden ring around with little resistance.

Drunk on power, I laid back on the bed, head spinning from the constant connection that tethered me to the earth and skies. It wasn't until I felt the familiar coiling of ice at the back of my mind that I realised my distraction had torn down the fortress in my mind.

Maximus Oaken, are you to blame for the storm?

Yes.

Panic clawed its way up my throat, threatening to choke me. I scrambled for the protective layer, preparing it to be put back in place. But, before I did, I needed Simion to know something. *I accept your invitation to the Ball.*

His relief flooded into me, a powerful wave of emotion that I could not ignore. *Are you certain?*

Don't be late.

I forced him from my mind before he had the chance to uncover the secrets I wished to keep buried. Even if I wanted the opposite. The rational side of my mind reminded me that this reaction, this burning and sudden need for Simion was my power. The rush, it was intoxicating. But that didn't take away from my desires. I longed to hear his voice, to feel his calming presence. The closer I got to Simion, the more I played with the boundary of the fasting mark. When I had kissed Simion, betraying the bond between Camron and me, it had afflicted me with world-shattering pain.

'Only in death shall you part,' I said aloud as I lifted my arm before my face, inspecting the silver-inked marks. 'Camron is dead. He can't hurt me anymore.'

What if I gave into my desires with Simion, what if I tested the bond that should be broken, only to discover pain?

I didn't need anyone to tell me the answer. It was clear as day. Pain meant the bond was still forged. Pain meant Camron Calzmir would forever haunt me.

CHAPTER 4

I fiddled with my amplifier, turning the ring over and over with the flick of my nail. It was an unconscious act, one I had quickly picked up. The wood was still damp from my soak in the bath, my skin scented with camomile soap and sandalwood oil.

Who are you? The question filled my mind as I stared at my reflection. The jacket I wore was crafted from a thin but durable material. Two shades of black, one a light drinking obsidian, whereas another was lighter and formed a formation of large golden roses across my torso all the way to the sharp-edged hem. The sleeves fit the slender shape of my arms, whilst another layer of material billowed at my elbows that fell freely to my sides like black water. A thick belt wrapped around my waist, narrowing it and making my shoulders look wider than they were. Velvet trousers clung to my legs, giving way to knee high boots with silver clasps falling on the outer side.

I couldn't stop looking at my reflection. Not because I was self-absorbed. It had nothing to do with me, and *everything* to do with the outfit. As I ran my hands down the soft material, delighting in the craftmanship and beauty, I couldn't fathom how Simion had managed this. It had been waiting inside the brown-paper package he had given me the day I signed up for the Claim.

Since then, I hadn't been brave enough to open it until this morning.

What I found had snatched my breath away.

My hair no longer held the light orange tinge from when the Gathrax maids cut and dyed it, turning me into the illusion of Julian Gathrax. It was comforting to see the dye fade, replaced by the familiar chestnut brown hue. I had curls that required managing. My hair had naturally dried, been swept back from my face and tucked behind my ears to keep from falling before my eyes.

Even if my appearance changed, it was the way I stood, the way I moved, which took longer to return to normal. I had spent a short time pretending to be the Heir to the Gathrax Kingdom, but long enough for the essence of Julian to blend with my own.

Lines blurred, making it hard to see where he ended and I began.

Simion had arrived at my cottage not long ago, his deep voice resonating beyond the closed door to my room. He spoke freely with my mother, laughing about something. The sound of her joining in warmed me.

By the time I left the room to face them both, I felt sick with nerves.

Simion sat in a chair with his broad back to me. I didn't need to announce myself to have him turning his head to the side, gold eyes catching me.

'Incredible.' The word slipped out of him as he drank in every inch of me. I almost felt his eyes move over my dressed body like unseen hands, leaving a trail of shivers in their wake.

I caught my mother raise a hand to her mouth, covering the smile that blossomed behind it. 'Oh, Maximus.'

Tears started in her eyes, which surprised me when I, too, reacted in the same way. She wrapped me in her arms, pulling me close as though she refused to let go. Nor did I want her to.

'Don't you dare cry,' I warned her, and myself.

'Simion,' Mother said, patting her hand on his shoulder. 'This was all you?'

I fought the urge to look down at myself, to watch my fingers leave marks in the velvet of my trousers.

'It was.'

Pride glowed across her face.

'Are you sure you don't want to join us, Deborah?' Simion asked, drawing my attention back to him.

She drew back, sniffling with a red-tipped nose. 'No, no. You both go and have fun.'

I nodded, smiling naturally for the first time in days. 'Thanks, Mum.'

'Don't thank me, Max. Thank Mage Hawthorn, or I should for getting you out of my hair! Now, should I be waiting up, Simion? Or do I need to give you some firm warning about looking after my son?'

Simion laughed, a deep resounding chuckle that warmed my blood. 'He is in safe hands with me, I promise.'

Safe hands. Hands I kept imagining leaving their own marks in the velvet material I wore.

My mother gave me a fluttering kiss, patted my shoulder and shot Simion a look of satisfaction. Then she was off, shuffling towards her rooms with a skip in her step.

Simion didn't react, he didn't do anything but look at me as my mother left. In truth, I couldn't focus on anything but him either.

I was self-conscious beneath his stare, my hands brushing the smooth material of the black jacket I wore, as though there were creases to smooth even though there weren't any.

The outfit was the most handsome thing I had ever had on my body. It was form-fitting, clinging to my limbs as though someone had measured it to the nearest inch and stitched it for me. The thought alone had my cheeks warming, knowing Simion had this made for me—all without the need for measurements. I longed to ask him how he did it, but the way his eyes drank me in was enough of an answer.

'Do you like it?' he asked, the question tempered.

'Yes,' I exhaled, not in control of myself. 'Do you?'

Dryads, why did I ask that?

Simion's eyes widened, ceased their shifting and levelled with mine. 'It was everything I could have hoped for.'

He stepped in close, eliminating the space between us. I found myself holding my breath, bubbles popping in my chest one by one.

'May I?' Simion said finally, gesturing downwards.

'May you what?' I barked, suddenly panicked I had left my zipper down.

Simion enjoyed my fussing from the grin that brightened his face. 'Your boots.'

The clasps. I had yet to do them up, which Simion noticed. I must have said yes, because he dropped to his knees before me.

I looked down at him, warmth spreading across my shoulders as his gloved hands reached for the clasps and clicked them together one by one. He did it all without taking his eyes off me.

'Much better.' Simion stayed on his knee before me, even after he finished clasping my boots. Through the thick polished leather, I felt his fingers, the press of them making the skin beneath tingle. How was it possible to feel his touch through leather?

'Are you going to stay down there forever, or…'

Simion shook his head, smiling awkwardly as he stood back up. I was used to his height, but suddenly he seemed to tower over me like a giant. 'Apologies, I was distracted.'

I wanted to clap my hand over his mouth and stop him for saying another word. But then the thought of his mouth brushing my palm, his breath caressing the skin, almost undid me.

Dread chose that moment to rise up in my chest. To remind me of why this was wrong. Any given moment and the pain would come—and I wasn't ready to face it.

'You look nice too,' I said, surveying him. He wore a cream collared shirt that clung to his thick neck, flashing most of his sculpted chest. Gold trim slipped across the pockets and seams, almost covering his build in thorned vines. From head to toe, he looked regal. Princely.

'I live to please.' His eyes fell to my hand, landing on the band of Heart Oak around my finger. 'Simple yet effective.'

I almost placed my hand behind my back, but Simion grasped my fingers before I could retreat.

'I half expected Elder Leia to turn up today and confiscate it,' I said, overly aware of every brush of his skin against mine.

Simion huffed a laugh, the left side of his lip turning up into a shy smile. 'I would be lying to you if I said I didn't share the same concern. If she did not sense it last night, Leia will see it in person tonight.'

Good, because that is the only reason I am going. Of course, I didn't tell that to Simion when I accepted his invite last night.

'Simion, we both know I'm in no position to play with her tolerance.'

He paused, taking in my words. I watched him turn them over in his mind, narrowing his eyes in concentration as he searched for the right reply. 'I will not deny you, knowing my aunt will feel a swell of discomfort pleases me.'

'Is that what this is?' I asked, 'A chance for you to get back at her?'

His eyes widened. 'No.'

Shame, I thought.

'Then why do it?' I asked, tilting my head slightly to the side, as he continued brushing his thumb across my hand. 'We don't need to go, we could... I don't know stay here and talk.'

'As much as that entices me, we are going. I promised to keep you safe. I am grown enough to know the only way of doing so is making sure you have control over your life, your power. If you are to partake in the Claim, you will need it. If you are to truly integrate yourself into Wycombe's society, to really accept it as your home, we must first stop treating you as an outsider. My aunt, no matter her position of influence, cannot prevent you from having something that is as much a part of you as the very hand I am holding. To me, this is the only option.'

I felt as though there was something else he was not telling me —I knew him enough to recognise that the small moments when his eyes left mine, only proved he concealed something.

He looked almost... frightened.

'Well, if you think I'm going to dance with you, I am afraid you are sorely wrong.'

'Maximus,' Simion said my name as though it was the most beautiful word in the world. 'If you have not realised it yet, I am a man who enjoys a challenge.'

'Is that what I am to you, a challenge?' I asked, although I didn't want to hear the answer. Not because of what he would say, but I feared if I gave into this tension between us, the agonising pain would spread beneath my handfasting mark, proving my worst fears true.

'You are far more than a challenge,' Simion said, turning his body whilst threading my arm into his.

'Indulge me, Simion Hawthorn. What am I to you if more than a challenge?'

'Well, you are a friend, Max.'

My silence spoke volumes, it betrayed me as much as my facial expression, which slipped beyond my control.

'Something wrong with my answer?' Simion's voice peaked. One side-eyed glance and I saw the pleased look pinched across his face. For the first time, it seemed utterly honest. I hadn't seen that glint in his eye since... Beatrice.

He needed this night; he needed the distraction.

'Not at all. Well, what're we waiting for?' I asked, ignoring his question. 'Let's go and make an entire room of people highly uncomfortable.'

'Sounds excellent.'

* * *

Uncertainty squeezed my chest, worsening with every passing second. Simion didn't need to acknowledge my reaction, even with the steel barrier around my mind, he could sense it. He didn't offer me words of comfort, because there was nothing he could say to take away how I felt.

Instead, Simion did the only thing that helped clear my mind. He laid a careful hand on my wrist and drew my anxiety away—not completely, but enough for me to take a large enough breath.

'You don't need to do that, you know,' I said, as crowds of people swelled around us.

He looked at me seriously, the side of his face bathed in the iridescent glow from the piles of Avarian stone recently erected on the streets beyond. 'I want you to have a good night. Dryads know you deserve it.'

Deserve it. Did I? It felt wrong, misplaced, to be enjoying myself when Beatrice was locked away. Wrong to smile and dance, as though my father had not long been swept from the floor, ashes collected into a pot that sat on the mantlepiece back at the cottage.

'This year there are more initiates to Saylam Academy than any year before. What you are seeing is families, immediate and distant, coming to witness their children be sworn into the Academy. It happens every year—just a lot of drinking, eating and small talk.'

'Sounds hideous,' I groaned, delighting in the fact no one spared us much mind. There were a few untoward glances, but nothing to suggest we were the centre of attention.

'That all depends,' Simion said, as our carriage began to move on, leaving us alone on the street bathed in silvered light.

'On what?'

He threaded my arm into the crook of his, pulling me close to his side with a pat of his gloved hand on the back of mine. 'The company.'

'I preferred it when you weren't nice to me,' I lied, as we slipped into the sea of bodies.

'Is that so, because I can stop any time.' Simion couldn't hide the jest from his tone.

'These drinks better be strong.'

Simion laughed beneath his breath. 'Am I insufferable?'

It was my turn to laugh, something that felt so natural when I was with him. 'Ask me again at the end of the night.'

'Oh, I shall.'

The throne room was filled with a sea of bodies. All around us people mingled, talked over glasses of bubbling liquid, ate bite-sized creations of food and danced. Beneath the Heart Oak, a long banquet table had been erected, with a delicious-looking feast piled upon plates with gold trim.

My fingers tightened on the stem of my glass as I surveyed those who danced within the cleared-out centre of the room. Where they smiled and laughed, I couldn't think past the ominous thoughts in my mind.

All these people had no idea of the true horror that occurred in this very room. Although the floor may have been swept and the walls washed from the ash and char—nothing could remove the knowledge of what had happened.

My father died in that very spot. As the dryads burned in wytchfire and my husband—bound by more than just law—broke my heart in more ways than one. Queen Romar and her followers had been murdered. There was so much death lingering, all the while music played and people danced.

As if that was not all consuming—the Heart Oak practically called for me. Over and over, its presence lingered at my back, glowing as bright as the pillars of Avarian stone whilst exhaling a low-toned hum that never seemed to cease.

A hand squeezed my shoulder, distracting me. 'If it gets too much, we can leave,' Simion said.

I forced a smile, a skill I had become rather adept to in the past months. 'No, it is fine. *I'm* fine.' Simion didn't believe me, and why would he. I could tell from his pinched expression that being here was difficult too. But we had to face this place eventually, why not when we were together? Moral support or something.

I hadn't come this far not to speak with Leia. I longed for conversation that had to be had.

Whenever there was a pause or moment of silence, I asked Simion a ridiculous question, just to keep him talking. Roast or boiled potatoes? Winter or spring? Green or blue? I didn't care how stupid I sounded, how strange the question was, I couldn't afford a moment without hearing him say something. Because when he stopped, even if it was to survey me with a confused look, I felt the Heart Oak drawing me towards it, a moth to flame.

Even with its charred bark, dead limbs and lifeless branches, it still held the faint glow I had seen around it the first time.

I focused on Simion's face, trying to memorise the lines in his skin, the scars, every curl of dark hair across his head. If I could take the time to count each silver strand at his temples, I would have. Anything to distract me from the Heart Oak and its pulsing call.

An unwanted gaze scratched across the back of my neck. I turned my head enough to catch Elder Leia in my peripheral. As expected, she was looking at me. More importantly, the amplifier wrapped around my finger. She hardly blinked, the whites of her eyes an almost red stain, as she spoke to—*fuck*, Leska.

'Your aunt has seen me,' I said, feeling her gaze scratch over my skin.

'I know,' Simion said, a faint wrinkle formed between his brows. 'Let her get a good, hard look.'

'I should go and speak with her, before...'

'There is not much she will be able to do now. She is not the only one who sees you with your amplifier, Max. The crowd sees you. All of them.'

My blood drained from my face. 'So *this* was your plan all along, wasn't it?'

I noticed the wall of people watching us, surrounding the centre of the ballroom in a barrier of sorts.

'Yes,' Simion said, squeezing my hand. 'Leia has not been able to stifle the rumours that have been circulating. These people—Wycombe—they all know what you did. What was sacrificed for you to save the city from complete destruction. Even if Leia and her Council long to stifle the whispers, the gossip, that is one thing her reach does not have the power to do.'

'And what has this got to do with them seeing my amplifier, Simion?' I wanted to feel anger, I wanted to feel used. But I didn't.

'They must see you for the saviour you are,' Simion said. 'The person I see.'

I read between the lines, shifting through his words until I found the core of his reasoning. 'Leia cannot take my amplifier away because now everyone else has seen me with it. Clever, I'll give you that.'

Lights blurred behind Simion, haloing his face in a glow of incandescent glow. He was breathtaking, equal measures beautiful and handsome. I didn't long to think such things, but I couldn't stop myself.

'Exactly,' Simion said. 'Leia cannot do anything. She can simmer in her displeasure and get over it. Now is not the time for the city to be thinking badly of her. If she acts against you, it will not do her any favours.'

Elder Leia disappeared behind the blurring wall of bodies, but I felt her presence like lightning over skin. I didn't blame her for disliking me—not completely. She shouldn't trust me, no one should.

Regardless of the secrets I harboured, I wasn't involved in the phoenix-possessed. That still didn't mean I would allow her to send an army to the South to destroy them. There had to be another way. The need to speak with her was boiling, but I also couldn't bring myself to leave Simion.

'I hardly imagine she will let this go, Simion. Even if she can't openly act against me, Leska will ensure I face punishment during my training. Especially since I have access to my magic again. Leska's been dying to unleash her own upon me. That or they will force me to withdraw from the Claim.'

'That is not going to happen.' His grip tightened on my hand. 'I do not doubt your power, Maximus Oaken. Neither should you. Show them who you are, show them what you are.'

What if I can't? The thought was scolding and sharp. Once again, the call of the Heart Oak grew louder, the glow brighter.

Simion glanced down at me, exhaling a tempered breath out his nose as he surveyed my face with a caress of his eyes. Where they moved, I felt it. It was such a still, peaceful moment, I found my body moving closer to his. The press of his hard chest held against mine, the brush of his thumb across the back of my hand.

There were no thoughts of anything but him—his touch, his expression, his mouth.

'How about another drink?' I spat, knowing I had to break away from him. I feared if we didn't move, I would have come to do something I regretted.

Would he regret it?

'Or two—'

'Well, wasn't that just delightful.' A voice called out, inter-rupting Simion before he could finish. It seemed the entire room shifted in a heartbeat, turning towards the person who made the sound. They parted, creating a pathway, allowing Elder Leia to stride through, a smile cut across her face, hands clapping together in a slow, prolonged rhythm.

'Aunt—'

Elder Leia raised a hand and silenced Simion. She gave him a scolding look that spoke a thousand unsaid things. 'Not another word, Simion.'

I had the urge to put my body between them, but I also couldn't bring myself to move.

Her gaze set upon me, veering from my amplifier to my face, a sickly sweet smile breaking her face. 'Maximus, please follow me.'

CHAPTER 5

I held Simion's gaze as he watched on from the crowd opposite me. He stood out like a rose amongst thorns, refusing to look away. Even at a distance, I saw the muscles in his jaw flutter. It didn't help the unease that rippled in my stomach.

Two people stood in a line on either of my sides. They were all young, no older than thirteen winters at most. Novices, the other four students of Saylam Academy who would be partaking in the Claim.

Dayn was one of them.

I couldn't believe what I witnessed as he parted from the crowd, only to come and stand beside me. As he did so, I couldn't spare a thought as to what else was happening around me.

'Dayn,' I said from the corner of my mouth. 'And here I was thinking you were just a gleamer.'

Rosy cheeks swelled as Dayn's face broke into a youthful smile. 'My mother says it is better to be underestimated and over deliver, then to be overestimated only to disappoint.'

'That's one way of putting it,' I said. 'You're an elder?'

It was rare for a mage to have both the power of a battlemage and a gleamer. Not once did I imagine Dayn had that capability, which I supposed was his mother's entire point.

'Surprise,' Dayn replied through thin, taut lips, as someone from the Council line cleared their throat, demanding our attention—and silence.

Elder Leia and her Council sat before us in a line of chairs that had been erected only moments before. At her back, the Heart Oak towered broken and burned.

The stone throne had not been removed from the wreckage—shattered and cleaved in two by the fissure I had created. A bunch of bright red flowers had been laid upon the seat, next to the breast plate of armour I had last seen on the Queen's body. It was a memorial, and a reminder. A way of mourning someone I had not known, whilst being reminded of the burden she had left upon me.

What stole my attention was a portrait, set in a gilded frame, resting against the tree. It was of a woman with bright forest eyes, lengths of brown hair. At first glance, I thought it was my mother. Then again, it was in a way.

It was the Queen, in her youth. It was no wonder why my mother was chosen to carry the Queen's egg. Their looks were so similar it was striking.

I stiffened, feeling every eye set upon me in the crowd. Did they see it? The same features, the details. Did they know the Heart Oak drove me mad with its incessant begging for my essence?

'This year we will be lucky enough to see four—five of our new students of Saylam Academy complete the Claim and return to us each with their own dragon eggs.' Elder Leia's voice raised over the silent crowd, although she never looked away from me. 'The Council has found it important that, in the shadow of recent events, we do not allow our traditions to be ruined. The Children of the Forest are a formidable force, and now more than ever we will look to our new battlemages, gleamers and elders, to train with the knowledge they much protect one another from forces that wish to put harm against us.'

Everyone hung on Leia's every word, clinging to it with clawed fingers. Her eyes stayed on me, long enough to make her comment clear.

I was the threat—still she believed it.

'In a handful of weeks, the novices who stand before us will find themselves in the middle of their greatest task yet. Oribon chooses only the strongest willed of the Children of the Forest—he sees in them what the dryads saw in our dearly departed Queen—'

Limbs shifted, hands lifting from the novices' sides and placed above their hearts. I was the last to follow suit, not knowing the custom of respect when the deceased was spoken of. I knew Elder Leia noticed, because her smile grew brighter.

'—but being blessed by Oribon is nothing more than an invitation for our brave soldiers to face unknown terrain and challenges we could never begin to expect. Not even the Council know what occurs during the Claim—those who partake are asked not to speak of the trials faced, to ensure those who face them next succeed from the same will Oribon first saw in them. Except this year, we see something unfamiliar occur. Mage Oaken, please step forward.'

I knew it was coming—I felt the uncertainty stir in the air around me. This was her chance to humiliate me. Punish me for the band around my finger. Remind me who was in control.

Compliance is the key. The voice of a ghost filtered through my mind, loud and clear as the whispers erupting around me.

I fought the urge to look down at my boots, fixing my eyes on Elder Leia and refusing her the satisfaction of seeing me weak.

'I believe I can speak for everyone in this room when I say, I never expected you to return… home, to us.'

Home. Us. Two words that didn't correspond in my mind.

I kept myself still, face void of any emotion. It was strange, to focus on keeping a smile lifted and forehead smoothed of unforgiving lines. It was more effort than not.

'Are you happy?'

'The welcome has been so warm, how could I not be?' I answered, mouth dry as stone.

When Elder Leia smiled, I noticed it was from the left corner of her mouth. Just like Simion. My sarcasm didn't go unmissed.

'You must miss the South.' It wasn't a question, but a statement. 'That has been all you have known.'

Shivers coursed across my arms. 'No, I don't miss it.'

'Good.' The word was sharp, silver-tongued. 'As the mouthpiece of the Council, I would like to grasp this moment and show our appreciation for you. Considering we may not have all had the pleasure of sharing this event tonight if you had not saved Wycombe from Camron Calzmir.' Elder Leia clapped, encouraging the entire crowd to follow suit. All but Simion, who kept his rigid gaze boiling. The clapping ceased, giving way to a silence. It seemed controlling tension was yet another one of Elder Leia's gifts.

'It must have been a great sacrifice, choosing us over your husband.'

'He was not...' I stopped myself, biting hard on my tongue until I tasted iron.

'No.' Elder Leia laughed. 'Perhaps husband is the wrong term to use. Because, he was more than that, was he not? Do *your people* not view a handfasting as a sacred bond, one coveted by great power?'

It was as though every word she chose was meant to harm me. Each was a stab of a blade, a knock of a fist.

I steeled myself, taking a moment to think before I spoke. It was hard to grasp exactly what I would say, the strings of comments filling my mind, just like the faint shimmering cords of power I saw around me.

Simion took a step from the crowd, but I stopped him with a single look. My smile was honest, telling him that I did not need him to come and save me from this.

It was someone else who offered me a reprieve from my emotions. Knuckles brushed over mine, the touch fleeting. Magic peppered the air. Dayn only needed to touch me for a moment to draw out the embarrassment, the hesitation. I grasped the clarity his magic offered and used it to my advantage.

It was time for me to strike back. 'Camron Calzmir killed my father. Just there, where you are sitting comfortably, his body reduced to nothing but ash and scorched bone. I don't want you or those watching now to think for a moment I killed Camron to save the city. I did it for my father.'

An audible shared gasp burst across the crowd. Slowly but surely, Elder Leia's smile faded. She had attempted to embarrass me, to push me in the corner and ruin the vision those around us had built of me from the rumours and gossip.

No one would do that to me. I would control my reputation, not her. Not her Council.

'I fight for my family. I am loyal to them,' I spat, knowing Elder Leia had no understanding of such a concept. She had locked her niece in a tower, knowing an unbalanced trial would lead to her punishment. She had placed the deciding vote on her own sister's and niece's respective exiles.

'Then what are we to you, Maximus Oaken, family or strangers?' Elder Leia said, tension so thick between us my limbs weighed heavy with it.

Every person in the room waited for my answer. This was her attempt to get me to admit my loyalty to the South. I wouldn't do it, not because I did not feel a sense of responsibility, but because it would only prevent me from helping them.

Doors slammed open behind us, saving me from the need to answer. I turned and watched a regiment of battlemages rushing through, Leska at the head. I had not noticed her departure until now, but, dryads, from the look on her face, something was wrong.

The crowd shifted, a wave of bodies moving, to allow for the battlemages to pass. I couldn't hear what Leska said to Leia, but whatever was said didn't bode well for the tension. Leia lost her gaze to a place on the floor as Leska muttered into her ear, trapped in a maze of thoughts. She handed something over, a sprig of leaf and berry. It was a strange gift to give, but, from the horror on Leia's face, it proved the sprig was not something to be taken lightly.

Simion brushed his presence against the back of my mind, willing me to let him in.

I didn't.

By the time Elder Leia straightened, Leska pulling away, the smile worn was the most fake I had seen yet.

'I am afraid I must take a short leave. Please, enjoy yourselves. Share this moment with your loved ones before they embark on a journey unlike any other. I look forward to welcoming these five *fine* mages home. I have no doubt they will reach the bounty they set out to find.'

It seemed she had spoken something else into the minds of the Council, as they all stood abruptly, chairs skidding over the floor. Leska led them away, her eyes catching mine as she passed. I had never seen her so troubled; shadows clung beneath her eyes, her skin an ashen pale tint.

Simion was suddenly before me, blocking my view. If he was worried, he didn't show it.

'You did well,' he said, hand resting on the small of my back. 'All considering.'

Did I? I could hardly remember the words I used as I spoke to Leia, my mind a race with adrenaline and blood.

'I had some help,' I said, glancing to Dayn who stood beside a young girl with long sun-gold hair, eyes of raw opal and cheeks littered with freckles. She was one of the other novices who had been in our line. I understood now that she was something more to Dayn, from the way his hand grasped hers at his side.

'I *will* speak to her. Leia cannot continue doing this to you.'

I grabbed Simion's hand and squeezed. 'Don't... poke the hornets' nest again. What's done is done.'

'What she did was wrong—'

'Please,' I said, fluttering my eyelashes. 'Do it, or better yet don't, for me.'

Simion paused, his lips pouting as my words settled in. 'Fuck, Max.'

I smiled, releasing his hand, knowing I had just won. 'This is between me and her. We will sort it. What I need is to speak with her myself, alone.'

But all hopes of that tonight had just traipsed out the door.

'In the meantime, I need another drink,' I said, replaying the haunting reaction Leia had to the sprig Leska gave her.

'I think you have earned more than one.'

Simion wrapped me in a protective arm, pulling me close to his side. I didn't notice it at first, but it soon became apparent that he was not only offering me comfort—he was keeping the crowd from speaking to me.

Without the Council around, people swarmed me with questions on the tips of tongues.

I pulled back, resisting the urge to give into Simion's drawing pull.

'Forget the drink, Simion. Take me home.' The words broke out of me, straight from the vulnerable part deep inside.

He paused, drawing my face in his hands until I could look nowhere but him.

'As much as I want to do whatever you ask of me, I will not do this one thing. Do not hide from them, just as I would not want you to hide from yourself. This is your home; you deserve to be here. *I* need you here.'

I felt the fasting mark stirring then, as I gave into the twisting cyclone that was Simion's allure. It began around my wrist, twisting and coiling, pinching and scratching.

The silver ink reminded me of the very reason I could not get close to him. Reminding me what I was too scared to find if I gave into my wants, leaned up on my tiptoes and…

Simion leaned into me, his mouth inches from mine, his scent overwhelming me, his touch distracting and all consuming. I blinked, worried that if I moved an inch, it would shatter this moment. He was so close; *we* were so close. A hair's breadth apart, his hand in mine, his thumb circling my skin. 'Let them see you, as I do.'

CHAPTER 6

Let them see you, as I do.

On one hand I longed to punch Simion in the jaw, knocking such sweet words out of his mouth. On the other hand, I wanted him to say it over and over. Only he had the power to warm me from the inside out.

It didn't take long before I was glad Simion refused my request to take me home. By my sixth drink, I was rather enjoying myself. Music swelled and crashed, bodies swaying to the beat. I found my foot tapping, fingers clutching the stem of a glass whilst pale wine bubbled and fizzed within.

The stares had lessened. It had started as obvious glares but now was no more than a few side-eyed glances. I could live with that. Truthfully, I didn't care much for their attention. I was here, so I might as well have made the most of it.

Simion stood at my side, his arm brushing against mine. I wondered if he wanted to say something, because dryads know I did. But I couldn't find the right words.

Instead, I busied myself with watching the crowd.

Dayn was dancing with the young blonde-haired girl. Their movements were awkward, but they were smiling, and that made me smile. Or was it the alcohol I had consumed?

What I could be certain of was a slight swell of jealously. I wanted to feel arms around me, touching me.

Now that *was* the drink talking.

But still, it simply grasped my desires. Right now, I wanted touch. Even if people still watched me. Even if the silver marks lingering on my skin would send pain lancing through my body.

I downed my glass, glad for the liquid courage that warmed my throat. One of the servers walked past holding a silver tray afloat with more offerings. I didn't take another, instead I put my glass down.

'Drink up,' I said to Simion, gesturing to his glass. 'We have plans.'

He straightened, the left side of his mouth quirking up.

'You've got the look of scheming in your eyes, Maximus.'

'Oh?' I asked, snatching the drink from him, because it had suddenly become an afterthought. I knew why. Because he looked at me as though there was nothing else in this room. It made my skin prickle, in a good way.

'Dance with me.' It was a command, and I knew without a doubt that Simion wouldn't refuse me. 'Or shall we just stand here in silence?'

Simion seemed to grow taller before me, unfurling like a vine beneath the sun. Stepping in close, he looked down his nose, both sides of his mouth now lifted into a grin.

He took one of my hands, and then the other. 'No need to hold a knife to my throat.'

Heat flooded my cheeks and spread over my chest. 'Careful, Simion Hawthorn. Someone might overhear you and think something nefarious about that comment.'

'Maybe there is.'

The ice kiss of his magic caressed the wall around my thoughts. I had lost the ability to hold my tongue by the fourth drink I had downed, so my words came flying out. 'Is there something you're searching for?'

Simion raised a brow, his gaze holding strong to mine. 'I

suppose I've relied heavily on my power when it comes to knowing what you want from me.'

My fingers tightened around him. I tugged him forward, towards the middle of the room.

Voices around us hushed to whispers as we entered the crowd. The Traitor Mage and the Hawthorn heir, I could hear them all. I could also imagine exactly what Elder Leia would've thought if she saw me dancing with her nephew.

Not that I did it for a reaction, but that certainly made it more enjoyable.

Yes, it was certainly the alcohol that was in control now. I gave into it willingly. It pulled at my limbs as though I was a puppet on string. It dampened my worries, my anxieties. Perhaps I shouldn't have relied on it in such a way, but dryads, it was a relief.

Even the Heart Oak's call had quietened to a faint whisper, dulled with each glass I had downed.

It wasn't until we stood, facing one another in the midst of the crowd, that I suddenly felt a rush of panic. Simion noticed, reading my expressions instead of my mind. 'You haven't done this before, have you?'

He began moving my arms into position. He took one and placed it upon the hard bone of his hip and then held the other to his side.

'No, never,' I breathed, feeling the patter of his heart beneath every fingertip—or perhaps it was my own.

'Then I feel honoured to be your first.'

A blush crept over my face, betraying me. There was something about the way he said it, emphasised by the glint in his amber eyes, which revealed a hidden meaning.

Simion was gentle with me as he rearranged my body. His fingers traced my arms, carefully guiding them until they both rested over his shoulders. There was hardly an inch between us. His breathing laboured, as was mine. I knew there was something I should be worried about, but it seemed buried. Lost somewhere deep within me, just out of reach.

'I'll lead,' Simion whispered, as he placed his hands on my hips, his fingers drumming on the fleshy part of my sides. 'You follow.'

My eyes dropped to his feet, using them as my cue for when to move.

I barely noticed the lack of pressure on my side until fingers pressed beneath my chin. He lifted my head up, forcing me to look at him. As our eyes locked, the room faded. The music stilled to silence; the crowd disappeared until it was as though we were the only ones in the room.

'Don't overthink it,' Simion said, lips glistening with the reflected glow of the Avarian stone lights.

'What if I step on your toes?' It was such a childish, stupid question. I regretted it the second it fumbled out of my mouth.

'It isn't my toes you should be worrying about,' Simion replied, returning his hand to my hip. His touch still lingered across my chin.

'Dare I ask what I should be worried about?'

Simion narrowed his eyes. 'If you think of anything else but me in this moment, I will take it as a personal failure.'

My heart stuttered in my chest. And, just like that, the music flourished, and the crowd spun around us. We were not the only people in the world, even if he made me feel that way.

Simion led with the confidence of a man who had done this many times before. I focused on him, worrying less about the beat of the music. Soon enough, it was as though we floated. I had no clue how long we danced for. There was no conversation, no need to talk. But I didn't take my eyes off him, not once.

Neither did he look away from me.

Every time my mind tried to warn me off losing myself to him, the light seemed to shift, and I forgot my train of thought.

I felt like a sculptor, studying my subject before I crafted them from stone. Except Simion was already carved from stone, wasn't he? His body was hard and firm. Muscles hidden beneath clothes, material keeping me from reaching out and discovering him.

'You're smiling,' Simion muttered beneath the symphony of instruments.

I hadn't noticed. Perhaps because I was far too lost to him to even worry about what I was doing. He controlled me, just as he said he would. I didn't need to think of anything in his arms, but I did.

I thought of him.

'Am I?' I replied, refusing to drop my gaze.

'Can I inquire as to what you are thinking about?'

His question hung between us as he spun me around, catching another rising wave of music.

The answer was simple. *You.* But I couldn't bring myself to say it. The alcohol might have been in control, but at least I had some sense of clarity to know better.

'How did you get that scar?' I asked, altering the attention.

His brow raised, the very one that was marked by the V-shaped line of an old wound. 'If I tell you, it will shatter the illusion of this strong warrior you see.'

It was my turn to chuckle. 'And who in this world told you that I saw you as a strong warrior?'

Simion forced a pout, winking his amber eye at me. Then his face turned suddenly serious. 'When I was younger, before…'

He didn't need to say what before meant. I knew. Before his family was torn apart.

'Before everything happened, I was teaching Beatrice what I had learned at the Academy. Mother had brought us these wooden swords for practice, I thought I could practise with my younger sister, but in truth I was confident I would best her.'

Hearing her name was sobering, but the way Simion smiled as he spoke of her made me feel somewhat lighter. As though there had been a time of peace for him and his family—before my existence ruined it.

'That doesn't sound like a fair set-up,' I said, wishing to reach out and touch the scar in question.

There was so much I didn't know about Beatrice. I had

thought I knew everything about her, but I had been so wrong. There had been six years of her life before she was exiled to the South. Six years of stories, tales. Six years of a life I hadn't the chance to ask her about.

'You'd think that. But Beatrice bested me,' Simion added, wiggling the brow in question. 'She always was the more natural one with a weapon.'

I opened my mouth to reply, but Simion stopped suddenly, pulling us to a halt.

'I'm sorry,' I said, reading his sudden change in demeanour as my fault. 'I shouldn't have asked.'

Simion offered me a smile. 'No. I like talking about her. It isn't that… I just…'

His eyes flickered over my shoulder. I followed his attention to what had distracted him. It was the Council, they had returned, flooding back into the room. An atmosphere seemed to follow in their wake, settling over everything in a haze.

'Well, it was enjoyable whilst it lasted,' I mumbled.

Simion grasped me before I could pull away. 'I'm not stopping because I don't want them to see us. Trust me.'

I believed him. How could I not? Honesty radiated from him.

Still, it didn't take away from the fact that something had changed in Simion. His focus was… distracted. As was I, because Elder Leia had just swept into the room.

This was my chance.

'Another drink?' I asked, as he guided me out of the crowd.

'One more,' he replied, 'then I think I should get you home before your mother sends out a search party.'

Elder Cyder stood by the main doors, his attention pinned on us. He offered me a smile, his eyes glowing with the mist of magic. Just like Simion's eyes were. It lasted but a moment, something only I could see.

'I'll be back in a moment,' Simion said in a daze, as though he was physically in the room but mentally elsewhere. 'Will you be okay?'

I nodded. 'Go. I'm fine.'

Simion left promptly, sweeping out of the double doors after Elder Cyder. His offer to get me a drink was clearly forgotten, but so was my need for one. I took my chance and pushed through the crowd. I didn't stop until Elder Leia was before me.

'I am glad I caught you.' My blood pressure spiked, as did the crowd's attention. There was something distracted about Leia's eyes, as though her mind was occupied and, for once, it didn't involve me.

'Is there something I can help you with?' she asked, almost hesitant.

I extended a hand, ready to put what Simion had just taught me into practice. 'Care to dance?'

Elder Leia didn't refuse. She grasped my offered arm, nails gripping just a little bit too hard. 'I think that would be a good idea.'

We quickly swept into the music, feet finding the rhythm as we moved as one. Leia maintained her smile, though it never quite reached her eyes. Something was on her mind, I could tell.

'Well, this is a surprise, Maximus.'

'I've been wanting to talk with you,' I said, attempting to level the playing field between us.

'You have got me now. Share what is burning in that *closed off* mind of yours.'

'Is there a problem?' I asked, gazing out to the doors Simion and Elder Cyder had just walked through.

'I don't know,' she replied, sharp-tongued. 'Is there?'

Her expression changed. Perhaps if there weren't so many people watching us, she would've replied with something equally as silver-tongued. But she didn't.

Her magic scratched at the walls of my thoughts. I pressed back. And, as quickly as her magic entered my mind, it left.

'Don't repeat history,' I whispered, 'Please.'

There wasn't the need to elaborate. Leia had made her plans clear, her need to eradicate any possible threat to the North. The threat being the army of phoenix-possessed growing in the South.

'Maximus, you know I will do anything to protect my people. Anything.'

I straightened, pulling free from her hands. 'The South is not the enemy. I swear it. They are families, just like those you want to protect here.'

She moved and I smelled it, the faint char of smoke. How did I not notice it before? Elder Leia leaned in, rested her hand on my shoulder and brought her lips to my ear. 'You are lucky that your movements can be accounted for tonight.'

'Pardon?' I couldn't ignore the scent of smoke that oozed from her. It was strong, invading my senses, clogging my throat and nose. It was a smell that reminded me of another time, another person.

It reminded me of Camron.

Leia lifted my arm, the silver ink flashing as she patted the back of my hand. 'Maximus, what would you have me do if you learned of an army of monsters, who could turn this entire city to ash with little effort?'

'Find a way to save them. Don't massacre innocent people.'

My people. The persistent voice echoed in the back of my mind.

'You think I am the monster. I see the answer in your eyes.'

I shook my head. 'I think you are simply in a position no one else wants to be in.'

'That we can agree on. But I *will* root out every phoenix-possessed in the South and cleanse the land. You see it as a massacre, I see it as an act of mercy. Now, if you do not mind, I have matters to attend to.'

I bowed my head as she swept away from me. Even if I longed to say something to her, I couldn't. The chance for conversation was over.

My heart was in my throat, the scent of smoke following me as I fought across the crowd, making my way to the doors where

Simion and Elder Cyder had left. The remnants of wine quickly seeped from my mind and body. The short interaction with Leia had sobered me. On quickened footsteps, I reached the shadows for a sign of Simion. I needed him, more than I cared to admit. In the corridor beyond, lit by pillars of Avarian stone, people stared at me as I passed them.

I stared right back.

'—it is important they are found.'

I stopped, hearing Simion's voice, filled with concern. Off the corridor were double doors, barely closed. They led to a small balcony outside, the sky speckled with stars like jewels sewn into a blanket of obsidian.

'And they will be, in time,' Elder Cyder replied, his voice equally worried. 'Saylam Academy will be closed from usual activity for the foreseeable future. Until the missing novices are located and returned. Safely.'

Missing mages?

Simion's fists clenched, singing of his tension. 'Why would *they* do it?'

Elder Cyder gazed out across the night. 'Everyone has their reasons. Until we get our hands on one of the rebels, we will never—'

Amber eyes lifted, gazing at me through the glass. Simion saw me. 'Maximus.'

'Everything all right?' I asked, sweeping my gaze between them.

'All fine. Nothing to concern yourself with.' Elder Cyder practically sprinted from the balcony, a rush of cool winds racing in from behind him. Like Elder Leia, he also smelled of smoke. It was a scent that haunted me, one I would recognise anywhere.

It was fire, scorch and ash. It was ruin.

It was the scent of Camron Calzmir.

CHAPTER 7

I woke to the pounding of drums in my head. Of course, it wasn't really drumming, just the hateful rhythm of punishment—a punishment well-earned after devouring countless glasses of wine.

A dull light streamed through my window, making me wince. My fists grasped the bedsheets, anchoring myself to this world. I was breathless, my heart thundering. It took a while for the nightmare to spill away from me, claws slowly lessening their hold.

Since touching the Heart Oak, I had the same dream every night. Fire. Destruction. The woman. A chant. I tried to reach in my mind and draw out the words, but I could never grasp them.

But it was just a dream. A figment of my imagination. Wasn't it?

Tonight, Camron had been there too. His glowing smile, warm hands and skin inked by the silver fast-mark.

I pushed myself up, refusing to dwell on him. My mouth was dry as the bottom of a birdcage, and likely smelled like one too. I gave myself a moment to gather my breathing, mind racing through the events of last night. Thinking of Simion was likely the only thing with the power to make me forget about the dream, so I held onto it.

My memory was muddied by the hangover. I could not recall the words we had shared during the carriage journey back to the cottage, but the feeling lasted. It was weightless. Even though my legs ached from dancing and my arms felt stiff, I couldn't deny the feeling that lingered beneath it all.

Enjoyment. No matter if my conversation with Elder Leia didn't go to plan, no matter if the Heart Oak sang louder than any music the string band could create. Simion had made it his mission—one he didn't need to say with words—for me to have a good night.

Until the end, he had succeeded.

I rolled out of bed, moaning aloud, wishing the universe felt sorry for me. My brain felt as though it was loose within the confines of my skull, banging around with even the slightest of movements.

Two steps from the door and Leska sprang to mind. *Fuck*. She would be here any moment, ready to wreak whatever hell she was going to put me through during training. The Claim was still weeks away, but I didn't feel nearly as prepared. It didn't help I wasn't privy to what happened during it. How could I prepare myself for the unknown?

I changed quickly into my training leathers, tears of discomfort and regret filling my eyes. As always, the sound of Leska's carriage reached me first. I only hoped she had been drinking too and suffered from a headache as bad as mine. Perhaps then she wouldn't be as heavy-handed.

I paced towards the door when something caught in the corner of my eye.

Mother's bedroom door was closed. Strange. She had normally left for Wycombe city before I woke, even before dawn. I knocked on it, calling out her name. There was no answer. I knocked again and caught the faint sound of ruffled sheets and a breathy groan.

The warmth of the air hit me first. Before I even opened the door fully, I felt as though a furnace had been lit in the bedroom and left burning all night.

'Mother?' Thick, warm air assaulted me the moment I took a breath. It almost choked me as I entered. Panic had me looking to the hearth, but it was cold and without flame. In fact, it clearly hadn't been lit in weeks.

My mother was in the bed, sheets draped over her body. Her eyes were closed, but a deep crease had etched itself across her forehead. Curls of chestnut hair clung to her face in sticky strands and splayed over the pillow.

I quickly moved for the window, throwing it open to allow some fresh air to enter the room. Still, she didn't open her eyes.

My footsteps creaked over the floorboards, loud and demanding. I stood beside the bed and reached a hand to her forehead. I didn't even need to touch it to know the heat was coming from her.

Dread seized my throat and squeezed.

Tired eyes fluttered open, the whites as crimson as blood. It was as though she couldn't focus at first, not until she blinked a few times. 'What time is it?'

'You're sick.' It was the only answer I could muster as my skin itched with the warmth radiating off her.

She attempted to sit up, groaning as though it pained her. 'I'll be fine, Maximus.'

My eyes saw the mottled flesh before she had a chance to lay herself back down. It crept beneath the collar of her night shirt— a twisted pink that looked more like old burns than a fresh rash.

I stumbled back, gagging on the air, on my thoughts. 'No.'

'It is just... it is just a...' Mother couldn't finish before the hacking coughs began. She barely had a moment to lift a hand to her mouth to catch the spray of blood that spat out across her chest.

My world was crumbling before my eyes. I didn't dare blink for fear of what I would miss. All I could do was watch the stains of blood that spread across the damp, white sheets.

The burns were just like the scars that had marred Queen Romar and the other Southern refugees. The very same ones that had covered Camron's back, like wings hidden beneath flesh.

'Tell me it isn't what I think it is.'

Mother buried her face in her shaking hands. 'Maximus...'

'How?' I muttered, tears blurring my vision. 'How?'

She winced, her grassland eyes hardly able to stay open. 'I will get better, I promise I will survive this, for you. I've failed you, time and time again. I kept you from your truth, stole you away from your duty and put us all on this path. This is my doing, and I am so, so sorry.'

I longed for her to deny me. I longed for her to say something that would prove my fears wrong.

'Camron has done this,' I said, nails biting into my palm. 'He made you sick.'

A single tear slipped down her cheek, steaming as it rolled across her warm skin. All I could hear for a few moments was the rush of blood in my ears. Mother coughed again into a closed fist, the sound harsh and painful. More blood spread across her knuckles, smudging across her lips and chin.

'Simion can help you,' I stuttered, unable to form a single coherent thought. 'He will know what to do. I can't lose you too.'

Mother shook her head. 'I hear it calling, Maximus. It wants me to give in.'

It. The phoenix. The plague.

'And... do you?' Fear kept me in one place.

I knew what would happen to her, there were three clear endings. Mother would either die like Camron's father, or she would survive... but she would no longer be the person I knew. The final and most scorching option was Leia would kill her. Just like Queen Romar.

How could I keep her safe in a place where she would soon become their greatest threat?

Her emerald eyes found mine, the whites almost entirely red

with veins. We held each other's stare as she nodded once in confirmation. 'I do.'

Fury boiled through me. For the first time, I hoped Camron was still alive, just so I could punish him all over again. I longed to take this pain I harboured, and burden someone else with it.

My body trembled with the need for vengeance.

Mother was the last thread tethering me to sanity; without her I feared it would snap. She was all I had, and I'd do anything, *anything* to keep it that way.

A heavy pounding sounded at the bedroom door behind me. Leska. Dryads, I couldn't let her see my mother like this.

'Go,' Mother gasped, eyes fluttering closed. 'Let me rest. All I need is to…'

I warred with myself. Part of me longed to leave for help, to defy my mother and get someone to heal her.

I had seen what became of the phoenix-possessed.

Death.

Another slam of fist against door jolted through me. My entire body tensed, each muscle hardened to stone. I stared at my mother, unable to grasp the reality of what laid before me. All I could think about was *how, how, how.* That one word rang out across my mind, demanding an answer I could not give.

'Maximus Oaken.' My name rang out. Leska was inside. A sudden spike of wrath erupted within me. Magic swirled, the cords of power brightening around me as though demanding my attention. Outside, thunder rumbled, echoing the storm within me.

I left my mother quickly, closing the door behind me. Leska stood in the middle of our living room, head turning to face me as I walked down the corridor to greet her. Each footstep was forced, each breath laboured and harsh.

Leska's mouth turned up, lips curling over teeth. 'I knocked—'

'Get—out.'

Another rolling of thunder sounded outside. Looking beyond the open door, I could see the sky was no longer blue but speckled with clouds of dark grey. Lightning flashed as rain fell in thick sheets.

Leska's hand rested upon her amplifier—the spiked mace hanging at her waist.

'So, you are ready for some *real* training,' Leska said, turning on her heel and walking calmly back to the door. 'Good.'

Gone was the joy from last night. Gone was the hope I had that I had found the peace I had so long sought. I knew, without a doubt, I had to leave Wycombe. Withdrawing from the Claim and getting my mother as far away from Leia as possible was my only option. But first, I had to survive Leska.

CHAPTER 8

The carriage didn't take us to Saylam Academy. Instead, it navigated us to training fields far outside the city. Something I heard Elder Cyder say last night filtered into my raging mind. *Saylam Academy will be closed from usual requirement for the foreseeable future.* It should've mattered to me, but it didn't.

Magic had built inside of me, pressing out of my skin, oozing from my pores. The second I left the carriage, I let it out.

The ground rumbled beneath our feet, shaking as I buried more power into it. It split apart into a fissure so large a dragon could've been swallowed whole by the earth, never to be seen again. It followed where my hand moved, guided by the unseen force that my amplifier connected me to—the split raced towards were Leska waited, doubled over and panting.

Wide-eyed, she saw it and acted. A pillar of earth and stone shot up beneath her feet, thrusting her skywards. Her evasion worked, until my power shattered the pillar she conjured. Without it, she was sent soaring.

Power spoiled the air. Leska's eyes burned with a blue mist as she gathered her magic. It melted the ground she fell forward, turning it to mud, enough to soften her fall but not enough to stop the impact from stealing the air from her lungs.

Silver cords of magic danced around me, each one begging for me to choose it. *Cords. Visualise. Intention.* Three simple rules to use magic. Simion had taught me that. Even being separated from my power, it was as though no time had passed. The only difference was it controlled me, fuelled by my emotions, my anxieties, instead of me controlling it.

'Using your magic isn't always about grand impressive displays,' Leska shouted, mace slick with mud. Her black hair was smattered with it, as was her face. It made her look all the more ominous. 'The best manoeuvres are small yet effective.'

My legs caught on something as I attempted to step forward. I looked down to see my feet stuck beneath a layer of earth. It was as though the ground was devouring me.

I thrust out a wave of power, attempting to knock Leska over, but failed.

'Cheap shots, you're better than that!' Leska snapped as power thrummed around her, echoed in the growl she emitted.

I fell awkwardly, the bones in my legs crying out in agony. Leska pointed her mace towards me, keeping me in place. But her hate for me didn't scare me, nor did the unspoken desire for pain that she harboured in her eyes when she looked at me. Nothing mattered. Nothing but my mother who I had been forced to leave, dwindling in a sickness I had no knowledge on how to solve.

In a move of pure desperation, I reached into the skies and called down a bolt of boiling light. It didn't hit Leska, for that was not my hope. It crashed into the ground at her side, distracting her. With her focus and her connection to her magic broken, I took my moment and called for the roots that lingered far beneath us. With towering trees all around the training field, there were many to draw on. Slithering serpents of earth exploded from the ground. I grasped one, urging it up and up and up.

It pulled me from the puddle of earth, my bones aching in their sockets at the effort.

Even after I was free, the roots continued to shoot upwards. I forced them towards Leska, ready to tangle her in a web of my own design. She leaped over them, lithe and well-timed, evading each potential strike. One clipped her ankle at the last moment. A swell of pride filled me, but to my detriment. The root exploded in shards of wood, littering me with debris. I shielded my face, blocking the view, just as the full weight of her shoulder slammed into my middle.

I hit the ground, again. The air knocked from my lungs.

When I opened my eyes, it was to see the mud-slick spikes across the circular head of Leska's mace, inches from my face.

'Yield,' she snarled.

Lightning cut across the dark sky. 'No.'

I lifted my hand, ready to grasp at all the cords of power that filled the world. I may not have been the master of subtlety, but I could draw on everything and hope something hit.

Leska slammed her body down on mine, legs straddling my waist. Power glowed from her eyes, as she drew on her magic once more. This time, we sank together, Leska's mace pressed to my chest. Mud covered my hands, my arms, my shoulders, drawing us both into its embrace.

'Bring one of those bolts down on me, and you will feel it too.' Leska leaned in close. 'Go on, I dare you.'

She didn't need to dare me. The last man who had straddled me and threatened me had ended up with a bolt to the chest.

Julian Gathrax had died. Would she survive?

Hot light fizzed around us. It crackled in the air, stinging my face and setting the hairs of my neck on end. Leska's eyes widened a fraction before a bolt cast down upon her, the sharp whipped tail aimed for her back.

Leska hoisted her mace skywards, like a hammer to an anvil. She caught the bolt of blue-white light, collecting it around her amplifier. Strands of light hissed like serpents made of blue flame, before she continued her arch and sent it careering away. The lightning crashed into a tree, shattering it apart in shards of bark and ruin.

Splinters rained over my face, over Leska. Fire crackled to life, burning hot and red. The sight of the flames and the smell of smoke reignited the fear for my mother.

It immobilised me.

'You are sloppy and rushed,' Leska snarled, returning her mace back to my chest. 'You'll soon burn yourself out with such large displays of power. Carry on and you'll be dead before you pass the first of Oribon's trials.'

I thrust myself up as much as the muddy bindings allowed. My nose cracked, bone breaking, beneath the force of it smashing into Leska's face. She reeled back, blood spraying down her face —a mix of mine and hers. Her power receded enough for me to pull myself free, shift our positions, until I was the one above her.

'Yield,' I repeated her command, iron pooling in my mouth from my broken nose. At least this time I had broken it on the attack. And Leska was no better off.

'It seems you have found something to fight for.' Leska barely moved beneath me. Her mace was out of her hand, fallen to the ground at her side. A gash had split between her eyebrows, dripping blood that mixed with the mud.

'Did you give *Aaron* the option to yield, before you killed him?'

Her question slammed into me, knocking the little air my lungs had left. I released her and stood. The ground swayed, but not from my connection to it. A rush of exhaustion and weakness crashed over me.

Leska pushed herself from the ground. She didn't bother to retrieve her amplifier. Her fists were balled into dirt-caked boulders, practically trembling with unspent tension. For the first time, it wasn't only anger in her azure eyes. It was an emotion more familiar.

It was grief.

'No,' I replied, unable to fathom a lie. 'Nor did he give me the opportunity to yield. He was hell-bent on killing me.'

I waited for Leska to deny my accusation. She didn't.

'Did you even know his name before you took him from me?'

This conversation had been brewing for weeks. I had felt it stir in the air between us, felt it in every smack of her fist, every snap of my bones. There were times I almost brought it up myself but feared the repercussions. I supposed those fears were justified in the way Leska treated me, in the way she looked at me as though I was the most offensive, disgusting thing in the world.

'There wasn't exactly the chance to find out. Like I said, he tried to kill me and I—'

'Say it,' Leska sneered, tears slicing down her dirtied face. 'I want to hear you say his name. Aaron. Say—it.'

I held my breath, biting down on my tongue to stop myself from saying the wrong thing. This grief displayed before me was so familiar it hurt.

'What good would it do?' I asked.

'Pathetic,' Leska said, calm but ferocious. 'You do not deserve that amplifier.'

'Your father disagreed.'

Leska's eyes flared wide, she reeled her fist back and slammed it towards me. I closed my eyes, expecting to feel it connect with my face, but it was the ground beside me which suffered. 'No more than you are the judge of who lives and dies, Maximus.'

Like Queen Romar? Like my mother?

'And yet you keep brushing over the fact that *Aaron* was the one who wished me dead first.'

Leska's mouth gaped, her eyes widening as though I'd physically hit her.

Saying his name, even knowing it, was agonising. Leska grimaced as I said it, as though she wanted to hear it but couldn't stand the way it slipped easily from my mouth. She turned her back on me and retrieved her amplifier from the ground. I expected her to unleash another attack. I even prepared myself, although the draw to my magic was faint from exhaustion.

Instead, she slumped forward, shoulders sagging inwards. All I could hear, beside the thundering of my heart, was her shallow breathing.

'I'm sorry, Leska.' The apology came out without contemplation. If I expected a weight to lift from my shoulders, it didn't. 'Everything that has happened, I would have never wished for it to go this way.'

'But it has.' She turned around, eyes red and mouth drawn into a firm line. 'Do you truly think you will succeed during the Claim? Being chosen by Oribon does not mean you have the potential to survive. That is earned by more than sheer will. You signed your name down, you signed your fate. Whether you pass or fail is your own issue, not mine.'

I hadn't realised it, not at first, but Leska was dragon-blessed too. Like Aaron, she was able to deflect my lightning, which not every battlemage had the ability to do.

'Where's your dragon?' I asked.

Leska held my gaze, refusing to look away. 'Do you ever listen? I told you, not everyone walks out of the Claim a victor. Not everyone walks out alive. There are tests. Trials. I—Aaron was the best of us. He was...' She paused, swallowing hard to allow herself a moment. 'He was better than you, than me. I can work you into the ground, I can punish you for what you took from me. But it will be Oribon who places the final judgement on you. Only he will determine your fate.'

I read between the lines, deciding for myself what Leska refused to say aloud. She had failed the Claim. No one was able to discuss what occurred during it, but from Leska's comments, it was clear she had not returned with a dragon egg.

'Then you'll be satisfised because that's exactly what you want... you want me to fail,' I said.

There was more to say. It lingered on the tip of my tongue, to tell Leska that I had to withdraw. But there was something in her eyes, a hopefulness that silenced me. Until now I believed Leska hated me to my core, but the emotion in her eyes suggested otherwise.

'If that was the case, I wouldn't push you so hard.' Leska extended a hand for me. I stared at it as though it was a viper, caked in dirt and blood. But I took it, watching how she winced with the shifting of my weight. She hoisted me from the ground, grip as firm as her settled gaze.

'Then what *do* you want?'

With a great tug, she pulled me in close until we were inches apart. Her sorrow lingered deep within her, concealed by an exterior she had forged. It had lasted all but a moment before the Leska I had come to know had returned. 'To understand.'

I snatched my hand from her. 'I told you. He was going to—'

'Not why you killed him, Max. But why he found it so important to try and murder you. That was not the man I knew; he was a protector. I want to understand what changed. Sadly, those answers died with him.'

CHAPTER 9

Saylam Academy was quiet. Too quiet. The usual bustle of novices had been replaced with the silence of stern battlemages who stood watching. Guarding. My eyes were almost swollen shut, the skin tender and my nose blocked with dried blood. I only hoped the infirmary was not as deserted.

It wasn't Dayn who greeted me upon arrival. The only person occupying the room was Elder Cyder. He must not have heard me arrive. For a moment, I almost felt as though I was interrupting something. I cleared my throat, signalling my presence. Elder Cyder jumped from whatever he was doing. His surprise quickly faded as soon as he laid his eyes upon me. 'Maximus, I wasn't expecting you.'

Nor was I.

I lifted a muddied finger and pointed to my face. 'I had an accident in training.'

'Accident?' Cyder asked, wincing. Where his blue eyes looked, my skin prickled, as though he physically touched me.

All I could do was nod. He exhaled and gestured towards one of the beds at his side. 'Take a seat.'

I did as he asked.

'Is my daughter teaching you how to hone your powers, or

how to best break a bone?' His question was as tense as the expression he gave me.

'Oh, this—this was my doing,' I replied, almost proud that it wasn't a lie.

Elder Cyder tutted, shaking his head. 'Never mind, let me see you put back together. Please, keep as still as you can for me.'

Elder Cyder was gentle and sure-handed. I caught a glimpse of his amplifier, in the form of a band around his thin wrist. His bright eyes gave off a faint mist as he opened himself up to his magic, allowing it to flow freely from his hands.

It ebbed into my skin, easing my pain whilst snapping, reforming, moving and mending my bones. Unlike when Dayn worked, Elder Cyder had confidence and experience in the art of healing. He moved with the sureness of someone who could map out the human body with their eyes closed.

'Where's Dayn?' I asked, as he withdrew his hands from my newly mended face.

What I really wanted to ask was 'where are all the novices?' I remembered Elder Cyder and Simion whispering about missing mages. How the Academy would be vacated until they were found. Seeing it for myself further confirmed that what I heard wasn't induced by the amount of drink I'd had.

However, I didn't only go there to heal my face and sate my curiosity. If there was any place I could find something to help my mother, it would've been there. Amongst the shelves of vials, glass containers and boxes of dried herbs, there must be something I could take for her.

'His talents, as well as the other novices and trained gleamers, have been requested within Wycombe. Last night, as you saw, there was an issue in the city. We've requested all healers to assist.'

A cold chill raced down my spine. 'Were people hurt?'

'Nothing that you need to concern yourself with.' Elder Cyder patted me on the shoulder. 'It is lucky you came when you did. I was just heading into the city myself, once I picked up a few of our supplies.'

I hadn't noticed until he pointed towards it, but a leather satchel rested beside one of the desks. Vials and small bottles filled it, stuffed next to wrapped bandages and packets of gauze. This was what he had been hunched over when I arrived.

Was there something in that bag that could help my mother? Elder Cyder had pleaded with Leia to let him continue his investigation into the phoenix-possessed. He believed he had a way of helping them.

'It looks like you have your work cut out for you,' I said, returning my attention back to Leska's father. A crease of worry formed between his brows as he noticed where my attention had been.

'Indeed. And so do you. So, tell me Maximus, do I need to speak with my daughter regarding her training tactics?'

'I think it is best I sort this one out,' I said.

He didn't look convinced. 'My daughter has been through a lot in her twenty-six years. It is a big ask of me, but please take the time to see through her illusions. She means well.'

'Leska told me about Aaron.' The words fell out of me. I regretted them the moment I said it. In truth, I hadn't stopped thinking about him since Leska had revealed his name. It was as though knowing it made the reality of what I did that much greater. Before, he was simply a nameless person who wished me dead. Now he was a person with a name, which meant he had a past, a story.

Elder Cyder paused, looking between the satchel and me. I thought he was about to come up with some excuse to leave—he did the opposite. 'Leska was a quiet child. For as long as I remembered she was focused on her education and physical training—never paying mind to friends. In her eyes, having people to care for simply placed a barrier between her and her goal. It was her determination that nearly killed her...'

'During the Claim?' I asked, although I already knew the answer.

He gripped his chest as though it pained him to speak of her.

'The Claim is dangerous. It is not as simple as visiting the Avarian Crest to obtain your dragon egg. But you will also be aware that those who partake are not allowed to discuss what takes place there. The details of what happened during that time are not for me to know, and, perhaps even if I did, I would not be able to tell you out of respect for my daughter. But Leska returned from the Claim cradled in Aaron's arms, hanging onto life by a thread. He saved my daughter, from what I am unsure.'

Leska didn't have a dragon, which meant she was not successful in claiming an egg during the trial. Whereas Aaron had attacked me from the back of a dragon, which told me he passed his. Beatrice had killed it before the red beast devoured me. And Camron had worn the dragon's scales as armour when he killed my father.

'I didn't know the Claim could be passed or failed.'

'Being dragon-blessed only means Oribon saw potential in you. It is up to you to prove him right.'

'How do I do that when I don't understand what being dragon-blessed even entails?'

Elder Cyder laid a hand on my shoulder. A wave of cooling essence spread over my skin like ice. It was comforting... a fatherly touch. 'When a child is born, they are taken to the Avarian Crest by a Council representative. It is there that they are presented before the gates to Oribon's home. From the shadows of his dwelling, he is said to breathe the kiss of his power over the child, seeing into their soul, searching for kinship. If it is found, they are blessed. If not, well, nothing changes. So you see, Oribon sees potential in you.'

'And yet I can fail?' Would I have signed up if I knew death was a possibility? Not that it mattered. Unless I could find a cure for Mother, I had no intention of proceeding. Doing so meant leaving her, leaving here meant...

It wasn't worth thinking about.

'Between us,' Elder Cyder said, leaning in, 'I do not imagine an Oaken even recognises failure. I... knew your mother. Failure was not a word she understood. And whereas others may not, I believe in you.'

'I need to withdraw.' The words came out of me without control.

His large hand eased on my shoulder, his blue gaze softening. I hadn't noticed it before, but a faint layer of freckles spread over his nose.

'Do not be frightened, Maximus. If you are anything like your mother, you will survive whatever the world can throw at you.'

My mother. Pain jolted through my chest, piercing me from one side to the other. Elder Cyder could not know how wrong he was. If he noticed my reaction, he didn't say anything. He carried on speaking about Leska and Aaron as though the memory was both fond and agonising.

'For those who partake in the Claim, coming away without a mount is seen as failure. To the rest of us, coming away with your life is success. Of course, Leska didn't see it like that. She fell into a dark place after her time during the Claim. A place I couldn't bring her out of, no matter my power and abilities. I couldn't reach her. Only Aaron could. He saved her in ways I will never understand—he saved her long after that too. He was her lifeline.'

Blood thrummed in my ears like a violent crash of waves caught in a storm. 'And I took him away from her...' I mumbled, to myself more than to him.

'Aaron was many things, but he, too, had his troubles. He... struggled to follow commands and respect our traditions.'

'I heard you speak with Simion last night about rebels.'

Cyder offered me a knowing smile. 'Ah, I was wondering how much you heard.'

'Was Aaron one of... them?' I asked. There was no pointing denying it. The Academy was empty and guarded. I had seen Leia's reaction after Leska interrupted the Ball. Something was going on, and I wanted to know.

Elder Cyder withdrew his hand and returned it back to his lap. 'There are people in Wycombe who do not agree with the way we are ruled. The Queen, the Council—as I am sure you understand, their decisions have not always been popular.'

'Decisions like preparing a force to wipe out the South, just because of a threat of more phoenix-possessed?'

'Yes,' he replied, face drained of emotion. 'Decisions such as that.'

'Then stop her,' I said, grasping Cyder's arm before he moved away. He looked at my hand, then at me, brows pinched until his forehead was littered with lines. 'You're part of the Council. Vote, resist. Do something or Leia will kill innocent people unless she is stopped. War is not the answer.'

A vein bulged in his neck. I didn't think he would say anything, but when he finally replied, his words kindled like fire. 'I will do what I can.'

I felt some relief, but mainly the expression he held when he said them. It was determined, honest.

'My focus currently is assisting Simion on saving his sister from exile... or worse.'

Or worse. 'You're helping him?'

Guilt reared its ugly head. I had barely asked Simion about his task. It wasn't that I didn't care. I did. But I was pathetic and weak. When I thought about Beatrice, it was shrouded by the clouds of what she had done... what her actions led too.

'I owe it to Simion and Beatrice. You see, I knew Celia Hawthorn well, as I knew your mother.' Elder Cyder said Simion's mother's name as though it was the hardest thing to voice in the world. There was a story there, one I thirsted for. 'She was the most brilliant battlemage of us all. Her exile hurt many people—deeply. So much so that they decided to create new rules for themselves. Rules outside of those governed by our Council.'

My mind went back to a time weeks before this, to something the Queen said before she died. She had not requested the battlemage to kill me. Now, I saw that statement in a new light.

Not all people believe I act with their best interest in mind. Many would wish to see me fail.

Aaron came to kill me at the orders of those he followed. People who saw my value to the Queen and wanted to keep me from her. It wasn't because of what I had done, or what I stood for as the Lost Mage in the South. It was because I was important —a tool that would be used in ways they did not understand.

The truth tumbled out of me, raw and honest. 'It still does not diminish Leska's loss. I took her lifeline from her. I took the one person away from her who gave her something to live for during her darkest times. It is no wonder she despises me, and truthfully, I don't blame her. I hate myself for killing Aaron. I hate myself for killing others, even if they wished to harm me or use me.'

Elder Cyder took a deep breath in and exhaled slowly through his nose. 'It takes a brave person to admit that death is not the answer. Believe it or not, that was the very sentiment that inspired the rebellion. But it seems they lost their way too—in their attempts to harm you.'

Regret hung in his bright eyes.

'If they wanted me dead, what's stopping them from trying again?'

I had grown complacent in recent weeks. No other attempts had been made on my life. Truthfully, I had more to worry about than unseen enemies when corporeal ones stood before me.

'It would seem the rebellion have shifted their focus to other things they deem as more important than you,' Elder Cyder said. I didn't miss the way his gaze moved back to the satchel of supplies.

The phoenix-possessed.

'Do you think they are working with the South?' I asked, sitting up straight, as a flush of heat crest over me.

Cyder stiffened before quickly standing from the bedside. 'I think I have said far more than enough. Just know that *you* are safe.'

I allowed his words to settle over me, attempting to convince myself to believe them. 'You said you think you can help them... the phoenix-possessed.'

Cyder didn't agree or disagree. He kept silent, studying me as though he could find the right answer. But his silence was enough of one.

Hope swelled in my chest so violently I almost choked on it.

'The Claim will begin within a handful of weeks,' Elder Cyder said, 'your focus should remain on that. You must train, although I suggest you try and stop anymore bones from breaking. Leave the talk of rebels to us.'

I almost laughed. How could I focus on anything with so many horrors before me? I was the King of the South and the rightful heir to the North, and I couldn't decide where my loyalties lay. I was being pulled from both sides, when my focus should have been on saving my mother.

'I am glad we bumped into each other, Max. If you need a friend, you have one in me. Anything, and I mean anything you need, please do not hesitate to ask.'

He was dismissing me in his polite manner.

'There is something,' I said, stopping him from gathering his bag and leaving. 'Leska said there are trials to pass.'

'We are not allowed to speak on—'

'I need to know what I'm facing.' It wasn't a request, but a command. Even if I longed to bite my tongue, I couldn't.

Elder Cyder eyed the room as though people lurked in the shadows. 'I trust you, Max. I also feel some sense of responsibility since you are more familiar with my daughter's knuckles than anyone else. But I trust you will keep this to yourself.'

I nodded, urgency racing through my veins. Knowledge was power, I had always known this. It was the very reason the Gathrax family didn't allow their servants to read. 'I swear, Cyder.'

'Very well.' Cyder looked carefully around the room, checking for others who could be listening. Satisfied we were alone, he leaned in and spoke. 'The trials you are to face are not linear nor obvious. As Oribon watches you, there are three traits you must prove to him. Traits he would've sensed in your infant soul. Although it is hard to explain, they can be boiled down to three important qualities. Selflessness, sanity and sacrifice. I wish I could tell you more, but these tests are personal to the dragon-blessed. There is no knowing how Oribon will present them to you—I have said enough.'

'Thank you,' I said, trying to grasp the knowledge he had given. 'And what if someone wishes to withdraw from the Claim?'

His eyes widened to moons, brows furrowing until his entire forehead was littered with deep grooves. 'Why do you ask?'

I scrambled for a lie. 'If I don't believe I can pass the trials, what is the point of proceeding?'

'You are an Oaken, dear boy. Your mother's child. I have no doubt in your ability to prove yourself, nor should you.'

'But what if I have to withdraw?'

His power trickled over my mind, attempting to reach inside and read me. He sensed my shields and pulled back, not before I recognised the brushing of scales that his essence presented itself as.

'There is no withdrawing, Maximus. Not without a justified reason that can be presented before the Council. Elder Leia must hear your reasonings but, most importantly, see them. You are welcome to show them your mind, allow them access and then perhaps they will vote to allow your withdrawal—'

'No,' I snapped, interrupting him as a surge of panic burst within me. 'I can't allow that to happen.'

It didn't matter the tests I had to face, or the deep desire of obtaining myself a dragon egg. Not when my mother burned from the inside out back at the cottage.

'What is it, Maximus?'

I practically melted beneath his calming touch.

'My mother—' I quickly stopped myself, biting down on my tongue. This man and his fatherly aura overwhelmed me.

He read it on my face. Then I felt the tendrils of his power ease around the wall protecting my mind, before quickly retreating.

'Is Deborah *well?*'

'She is… fine,' I said quickly, back-pedalling, 'I think she has caught some type of winter flu.'

'What are her symptoms?' There was no emotion in the way he asked his question.

I waved his hand off, throat swelling as though my body wanted to stop me from speaking. 'It's nothing.'

But what if he can help? The thought was invasive and loud. What if it is just a flu, delirious mumblings brought on by a high temperature. Though the scars across her skin proved otherwise.

'You can talk to me,' he said, eyes wide and riddled with concern. 'What you say between these walls stays between us.'

I swallowed hard, unable to take my eyes from him. Perhaps it was my weakness, or the way Cyder stepped perfectly into the fatherly role, that had me spill my guts. 'This morning I found her in bed. I think she is—'

He pressed a finger to my mouth, silencing me.

'Leia,' Cyder mumbled beneath his breath, almost too quiet for me to hear, but there was no confusing the name. I would recognise it anywhere. 'There is no need to say anything more. I understand.'

My heart hammered in my chest, threatening to crack ribs. Did he?

Before I could question him, Elder Cyder dove a hand into his satchel and produced a vial of aqua-blue liquid. It was mostly clear, all beside the thin strip of what looked like a weed languishing within it. He turned back and offered it to me.

'Give this to her in two doses a day,' Elder Cyder said, dropping the vial into my palm. His fingers shook as he did so. 'See that she has access to plenty of liquids. Cold baths. Fresh air. All the normal remedies for a *normal* flu.'

The way his voice lingered on the word 'normal' told me everything I needed to know. It was far from mundane.

'And Maximus,' he said, 'tell no one. My offer stands, if you need me for anything, then you come and find me. But do not tell another soul that your mother is… unwell. Not Simion. Not Leska. Not anyone.'

'But—'

Gone was his soft demeanour. The man who stood before me was striking and sharp. He was his daughter's father. 'Two doses a day. Fluids. Rest. I will visit you in the coming days, if you need me before then, I will come. But no one must know. Promise me.'

The glass strained beneath my grasp, as my entire body seized beneath the urgency of Elder Cyder's stare. 'Okay.'

He physically relaxed, shoulders lowered and forehead smoothed of lines. Even the smile he displayed was of relief. 'I do hope the next time I see you, it is without bruises and broken bones.'

'Elder Cyder,' I called, as he moved for the door. He stopped in his tracks. 'You said something. Something about Elder Leia, just then. What was it?'

He turned around and stared at me; there was no denying the glittering tears that clung to his wide, bright eyes.

'Elder Leia personally visited your mother, the morning of the Ball.'

It was as though the world fell away from me. 'What are you suggesting?'

He shook his head. 'Nothing, I am sure it is nothing.' Cyder forced a smile, one that didn't reach his gaze. 'See that Deborah takes the vial. She needs rest, and fluids. And remember, tell no one.'

His warning rang loud throughout my mind—slamming like brass bells between my skull, over and over.

Do not tell another soul.

Those five words were the key that had snapped the lock shut, keeping my secrets from ever spilling again. Whatever Elder Cyder believed, it scared him. I knew fear well. But who did he fear for? Himself? My mother… Or me?

* * *

Mother could barely keep her eyes open as I lifted the metal spoon to her lips and poured the medicine past her pale, cracked lips. She expelled a groan of exhaustion, discomfort and pain.

The air in the room was thick with unnatural heat. Even with the windows open and the door left ajar to encourage a draft, nothing could lower the fever that boiled below her skin.

'You're going to be okay,' I said, brushing the strands of sweat-coated hair from her damp brow. 'I'm going to find a solution and fix this.'

If she heard me, she showed no signs of it.

My mother lost herself to another bout of grumbling nonsense. There was no making sense of the string of words that slipped past her mouth. Every now and then I would lift her head up and encourage her to drink, but most of the water spilled down her chin and soaked across her chest. In seconds, it had evaporated due to the sheer warmth of her body.

I blinked, transporting myself to another time.

Camron had been warm to the touch, comfortable and welcoming—not scalding as my mother was. His scars had been so beautiful to me but seeing them across my mother's skin was horrific. If I could have taken them off her myself and carried the burden of her sickness, I would have.

The only noise she made was when she called out for my father every now and then. Each time his name broke out of her, I shattered into another broken fragment. No matter how it pained me to see her like this, to hear her childish calls—I didn't leave her side.

Broken sleep followed. I would wake and try to get her to drink, run a damp cloth across her skin and sob until my tears hissed as they crashed against her. Then I slept, a light dream-poisoned sleep that was the same as every night.

The dream welcomed me. Ruin. Fire-filled skies. The army of shadow. A burning star falling from Aldian's skies.

I woke to my mother's voice. At first it was as though the dream had bled into reality, because the same chant that the army of shadows repeated suddenly sounded as though it was being whispered into my ear.

And it was. With her eyes still closed, her pale lips quivering and hands clutching the sheets, my mother muttered something beneath her breath. Aching and exhausted, I leaned in, the warm breath tickling the side of my face. But there was no denying what she said.

'Mother is coming... Mother is coming.'

CHAPTER 10

It had been hours since Mother had woken me with her strange words, and they haunted me still.

Mother is coming.

What did it mean, and how did she reach inside my dreams and pluck them out? As soon as I heard it fall from her pale lips, I recognised it as the chant which I heard every night. It didn't bear contemplating, not when I had to focus on getting her better.

And there were only two things with the power to distract me. One was Simion and the other was books. Since the first option came with complications, I chose reading. Saved putting on a face and lying to Simion—avoiding him was the easier option.

Wycombe's *actual* library was one of the world's many wonders. The building was constructed from Avarian stone, large stained-glass windows allowing brilliant light to wash the large room. It made the Gathrax library look like a storage cupboard.

The air was thick with the scent of stories. I was practically shrouded in them from the towering shelves on either side of me. The top shelves were so tall there was no ladder that could reach them. To request a book was simple. It required speaking to the shuffling librarians who used magic to call down the novels.

It was so quiet I could hear ancient pages being turned over from leagues away. The crinkling of pages and the cracking of spines sounded strangely loud.

I had sat myself alone, away from the tables of students and civilians utilising the library and its quiet. As I flicked through the dusty book, careful not to rip the frail pages, I searched for my answers. I didn't know what I was looking for, only that I needed to know more about the phoenixes and possession.

I fiddled with my amplifier, twisting it around my finger with a nudge of my thumb, studying the drawing of a dragon on the page with a keener interest than I would've before. The illustrator had drawn it with green scales, slick with rain that caught the sun cutting through an abundance of clouds. Like sea-glass across a bed of sand, the dragon's body winked against the dull light. And it wasn't alone. A bird made of flame warred against it, breathing plumes of fire from its beak as the dragon spewed a pillar of ice. It was a depiction of an old tale called *The Ashes*. It spoke of one of Oribon's first children who ventured to an island called Voltar—the name was both strange and familiar.

A dragon named Dacraire had killed the first Phoenix King, for reasons the author didn't know. She speculated it was for power. What started as an assault on the phoenix ended with Dacraire's demise. After destroying the god of fire, reducing it to torn flesh and feather, the story told of the phoenix resurrecting more of its kind from its ashes. Dragons were hatched from eggs, whereas phoenixes multiplied from the ruined mounds of their fallen.

My finger traced the script as I read the words aloud. 'From the ashes, we rise.'

A cold sweat broke over the back of my neck as the words repeated in my mind. I looked up, breaking away from the story, stretching my eyes down the endless row of shelves before me.

There was no hiding from the stares my way, nor the way they scratched over my skin. But it was the grace of ice across my mind that told me my first option of a distraction had found me.

'Maximus Oaken, the bookworm. Out of all the titles you've obtained, that might be the most accurate.'

I looked up to find Simion. He was leaning against one of the shelves, arms crossed over his broad chest. Dust puffed up before me as I closed the book with a slam, pushing it over the table as though it was some incriminating evidence.

'Leska told you where to find me then?'

I had known her willingness to forgo training this morning was suspicious. Leska seemed occupied so much so that she didn't put up resistance when I asked for the day off. It was too good to be true that I had found myself with spare time.

Simion pushed from the shelf, lifted a chair from the desk opposite me and brought it to my side. 'She did. I almost visited your home to check on you, but—'

I slapped my palm on the table, panicked. 'Why?'

Simion raised his arms in defeat. 'I was worried, especially after the last time I saw you after training. Leska told me she dropped you off here and… Well, I thought, you might need an escort home, so I came.'

'You should know that I don't need your help.'

'Need or want?' His question stumped me. 'If it makes you feel better, I came to do some research for myself. Elder Cyder has been… helping me prepare. He suggested there were some books here that may help.'

I didn't want to reveal that I already knew this information, because doing so would lead to why I had seen Cyder and what that interaction entailed.

'That is helpful of him.' Dryads, I sounded short even to my ears. And from the way Simion studied me, he noticed it too.

Although Elder Cyder made certain there was not a single mark for Simion to find—no bruises or swelling—I still raised a finger to press it against my newly healed nose. All I had to hide from him was the internal turmoil I suffered and what waited for me back in the cottage.

It didn't stop Simion from tracing his eyes over every inch of my face. 'Very.'

I forced a smile, rolling my eyes as though I was embarrassed at my own reaction to hearing Simion went to my house. 'Would you stop looking at me like that?' I said, tugging the cloak tighter around my shoulders. 'You'll only find something you don't like.'

'That wouldn't be possible,' he said softly. 'I admit, every day I wonder what state I am going to find you in. Yesterday's training went well then?'

'Not exactly,' I said, unable to stop myself from being short. Conversation meant I had to talk, talking meant I had to think over what I was to say.

'What are you researching?' Simion asked quietly. 'Anything I can help with?'

'The Claim,' I half lied. 'Sounds like it will be more challenging than I first expected. I thought I might find something here that will help me prepare.'

He walked closer, bringing with him the fresh scent of pine. Against the backdrop of the library, Simion looked as much at home as I felt. 'I like to pride myself on my knowledge, but sadly that is one thing I am useless to help with.'

'The great Simion Hawthorn, finally without answers,' I said, unable to hold the sarcasm from my voice. 'And here I was thinking you were a smart man.'

Simion's eyes narrowed; the corner of his lip turned up. 'So, you think I'm smart?'

I rolled my eyes, eliciting a laugh from Simion. 'You're insufferable.'

'Smart and insufferable,' Simion said. 'Well, I am really multifaceted.'

'Care for me to continue?' I retorted. 'Because I have a few more descriptions I could add to that list.'

Simion shook his head, eyes glinting. 'As much as my ego enjoys you speaking about me, I would rather the conversation shifted.'

A warm shiver passed over me. It felt wrong to smile so naturally when I was hiding something from Simion. I was too frightened to hold his stare for too long, in case he slipped through the shield of my mind and found out about my mother.

Elder Cyder was right; I couldn't tell Simion. Not because I didn't trust him, but because it was not his burden to bear.

'Ah, I know this book. We are forced to read through the stories during the earlier years at the Academy. The author of this one is rather descriptive.'

'I didn't put you down as a reader,' I replied.

Simion nudged my arm with his, flashing me a half smile. 'I'm not, but this one has pictures.'

My skin tingled as he picked the book up, opened it and began flicking through the pages. Although he didn't touch me, dryads it felt like it. Where his thumb traced the brittle pages, it was as though he touched my skin.

'I'm finished with that one, your welcome to it... for your research.'

'This isn't going to help me free Beatrice.' Simion shot me a look, one that made me hold my tongue. 'As much as I think this read is entertaining, I do not exactly have a dragon I could fly on and break her out.'

Simion then picked up another book, riffling through the small pile I had requested, reading each of the spines. My heart sank as he quietly uncovered my lie. The books each had one thing in common, and it had nothing to do with the Claim.

'Phoenixes,' Simion hissed the word as though he spat fire. When he drew his eyes back to me, they settled not on my face but the silver ink marks lingering outside the cuff of my shirt. 'And what would phoenixes have to do with the Claim, Max?'

'Caught me,' I muttered beneath my breath, metaphorically raising my hands in surrender.

The thud of the book made me jump as he dropped it back to the table. 'You won't find *him* in the pages of these books, Max.'

I should've felt relief knowing that Simion believed I was

reading about the fire gods because of Camron. 'Believe it or not, I cannot sit back and wait for your aunt to deploy battlemages to destroy the South. I thought I could find answers here... something to help stave off a potential disaster.'

Save the phoenix-possessed. Save my mother.

Simion chewed on his lower lip, finger fiddling with the corner of a page. 'The Council could recite these books over and over. There is nothing you'll find to stop a war, Max.'

'War suggests it is two-sided. Leia will destroy the South before it can react.'

His stare fell back to the book, to another sketch of a phoenix, burning wings outspread, feathers a multitude of gold, red and yellow. 'The phoenix-possessed are a threat. I do not agree with Leia's plans, but something must be done.'

'I know, but what if there is a way to heal them?'

He shook his head, pulling a seat up next to me. His proximity sent a shockwave of shivers over my skin. 'There isn't—'

'Elder Cyder believes there is.' My thoughts went to the vial he had given, and how it had calmed Mother's temperature and suffering. It might not be a cure, but it would help.

Simion didn't question me again. He gestured to the pile of books. 'Then I should let you get back to your personal research. We have a good afternoon of reading ahead by the looks of it.'

'We?'

He took up a seat beside me. 'You didn't think I would let you suffer through all these old tomes alone, did you?'

There was something about the way he said it, with such clear confidence, I felt as though he truly was on my side. He wanted to help me. His willingness was as encouraging as a hand pressed to my back, urging me forward.

It made me feel less like I faced my challenges alone.

The Claim was still weeks away, I had time to find a way to withdraw from it. Of course, there was another option, one I didn't wish to contemplate yet. But if it came to it... desperate times called for equally desperate measures.

We read for hours. The more time slipped away, the busier the library became.

A sudden touch tore my gaze from the passage I read about Voltar, describing the island with mountains that spewed destruction from chambers of liquid fire. Simion was so enthralled in the book before him, he must not have noticed his fingers brushed mine.

Glad from a break from the words, I drank him in. From the thick velveteen lashes framing the glow of his amber eyes, to the way the light from the windows glowed across his brown skin, I devoured every detail.

As though sensing my gaze, Simion turned and looked at me. His lips pulled closed as his eyes met mine and the world seemed to fade into silence. It no longer mattered what I wanted to find here, not as we focused on one another as though the world beyond meant nothing.

'Distracted?' he whispered.

I blinked, feeling heat rise to my cheeks. Without needing to look down at our hands, I knew his thumb traced those familiar circles. 'A little,' I replied.

I couldn't help but retract the wall around my mind, enough to call out and welcome him in, but not enough for him to access all my memories.

Thank you. I forced the words into the void of my mind, feeling them echo across the boundaries of my skull as Simion slid his cool presence within. *For looking out for me.*

He should be using this time to prepare for Beatrice's trial, and here he was sitting with me, routing through books in search for dryads knew what.

For you, Maximus Oaken, anything.

I closed my eyes, allowing myself a deep breath to flood my lungs. There was something about the way Simion made me feel that encouraged me to reveal every secret to him. His touch was encouragement, his smooth voice a guiding force.

By the time I opened my eyes, Simion was closer than he had

been before. I memorised him, from the scar across his eyebrow, the gold flecks that glittered in his eyes, the way his lips bowed at their tip and to his left-sided smile.

It seemed there was a draw between us. During the Ball, we escaped the inevitable by the skin of our teeth, drunk on wine and enjoyment. Now, in this moment, there was nothing clouding my judgement.

I didn't dare look away. Not as we closed in, the world forgotten, our lips brushing one another.

Fire flashed in my peripheral. A burst of boiling air raced down the row of shelves, slamming into us both, drawing us away.

Black flame, so dark the outline glowed with an almost white light. The warmth stung at the side of my face, drawing me away from Simion in an instant.

The library was no longer still and silent. It bustled with chaos, students running, knocking chairs and desks over, piles of books spilling over the ground. We barely stood before the wave of screaming people crashed into us. As we turned to face it, trying to make sense of what happened, Simion was yanked out of my hand.

'Max!' Simion called, his voice muffled by the panicked crowd he drowned within.

In a blink, he was gone. Swallowed by the chaos and panic, leaving me alone to face the black flame and what it meant.

I couldn't form his name, nor draw a deep enough breath to say anything, as the crowd shifted around me, pulling and pushing. I tried to find the fire, to prove to my mind that I had made it up, when another explosion of obsidian fire shot skywards from the crowd.

The air tainted with the scent of charred flesh and screams of fear and pain. Panic clawed up my throat, as the realisation overcame me, just as a single word cried out above the rest.

'*Wytchfire!*'

CHAPTER 11

The crowd pushed around me, snatching my limbs, crashing into me with a frantic force that almost sent me falling to the ground. I couldn't move by my own will even if I longed to. Between the bedlam of bodies and the immobilising view of black flames, I was lost to fear.

Elbows drove into my sides, fingers clawed at my shoulders and neck, as the panicked crowd swelled away from the fire. Black flames crawled up shelves, devouring books and wood as though they were doused in oil.

It was spreading, and fast.

Maximus, Maximus! Simion's presence in my mind drew me out of my shock, enough for me to steel my core and push against the wave of flesh and screams. *Say something.*

From the leaf caught in a storm, I became a rock, using my arms to fight against the crowd of bodies. *I'm fine. Get as many away from the fire as possible, I will find you.*

No, Maximus, don't you dare—

Simion must've sensed what I was to do. Before he could truly glean the reasons behind my sparked fury. Before the steel wall erected, fortified and powerful, I sent out a final sentiment, hoping Simion heeded it. *Trust me.*

I couldn't allow him such free access when I was not in control of my own thoughts.

Satisfied at my mental protection, I pushed towards the flashing of black fire until I found the source. It wasn't that I expected to find Camron, but I couldn't help but search for him. His presence still affected Aldian in the form of his plague. He might have been dead, but he was still very much alive in my mind.

The all too familiar scent of scorched flesh and charred bone filtered into my nose, lathering my tongue with its acrid taste. After my father's death, it had taken days for the scent to truly fade. Smelling it now, so pungent and strong, it was as if I was transported back into the throne room all those weeks ago.

Power throbbed beneath my skin, strengthened by my continuous connection to my new amplifier.

Ire filled my muscles; fury was the symphony that kept me pushing forward. Wytchfire licked up the wooden shelves to my left, leaving its boiling kiss across the side of my face. There were still too many people before me, fighting their way to safety, for me to see the source. However, far across the library, I saw more flashes of black fire. The attack was not limited—it had spread.

There must be a phoenix-possessed, someone with the power to conjure wytchfire.

But who?

I knew, first-hand, how to extinguish wytchfire. In the back of my mind, I saw Camron's body exploding beneath the force of my power, flesh and feathers left behind. I had to find the phoenix and destroy it. Dryads help me, I wouldn't let another perish to the power of the gods of fire.

Focused on pushing forward, I didn't see the puddle of melted flesh beneath my foot until I stood upon it. I looked down, distracted, a violent wave of sickness overwhelming me. My focus was on the flesh, the blood, the gore, that I didn't notice the blast of fire until it singed my skin. I ducked, just in time. A pillar of black flame shot over me, slamming directly into the back of an innocent trying to run for their life. As soon as the fire connected, the body exploded, entirely engulfed. Their pained wails and screams melded seamlessly with the roaring, unnatural flames.

I rolled out of the way, body encased in agony, hands coated in blood and crisp bits of flesh. Determination smothered my pain, enough to push myself to stand and rub the gore down my jacket.

A stab of ice slammed through my skull. A warning. I looked behind me just as a woman stepped into view.

'You will all burn,' the woman said, her voice broken and rasped.

It took me a moment to see that the woman before me was not my mother. She had the same wild curls of chestnut hair, the heart-shaped face and freckled bridge of her nose. But her eyes were not green. No, they twisted with a multitude of gold, red and yellow, twisting like a storm around the obsidian pupil that jewelled in the centre. The right side of her face was a mess of scarring that stretched down her neck and across her ear, which looked more like a stump of melted flesh.

Obscure fire dripped from the woman's hands, hissing across the wooden floor at her feet where it spread and rippled, akin to water in a lake. Like Camron, she had the scars from recent burns, her eyes glowed with the power of the phoenix.

Sorrow mixed with the storm of fury that filled me.

'Don't do this,' I pleaded, skin smarting with proximity to the fire. 'I can help you.'

'You, help me?' She cocked her head. 'You left us to suffer, Mage Oaken.'

I was frozen, entrapped beneath her fiery gaze. 'I can—'

'The South sends its love,' she interrupted, flames burning hotter, taller, brighter.

All around the woman were puddles of melted flesh, charred bones sticking out like reeds from a lake. Already, she had killed so many. If she wasn't stopped, she would destroy more. To me, each one of those melted piles was my father. From the deep pits of my soul, where I'd buried my grief and placed a lid of iron atop it, a resounding crack announced itself.

'I'm so sorry,' I breathed, lifting my hands as my power seeped out of my flesh and connected me to the earth around me. Dark clouds billowed across the skies beyond the library, the ground far beneath me trembled, sending the possessed woman off kilter.

My presence lingered everywhere.

Threads of power linked me from the wood beneath my feet, to the promise of hot light that hovered in the newly conjured storm clouds. I was spoiled for choice, unsure how to save the phoenix-possessed, whilst also protecting any more innocent people from dying.

A tear cut down my cheek as I grasped the earth and called it. Splinters of burning wood raised at her back. Her focus was on me; she didn't realise her demise waited behind her, until it was too late.

She gathered a ball of wytchfire, cocked her arm back and prepared to engulf me with it. But before she could unleash her wytchfire, she was dead. Blood misted the air as my wooden spears sliced through her from the back. Holes covered her unexpecting face, torso and limbs.

A great whoosh of air sucked in around me as the black fires extinguished in a single breath.

Releasing my power, a deep horror grasped my body. I closed the space to the nameless woman before her body hit the ground. I caught her, ceasing her fall and aiding her down to the ground.

I held the woman in my lap, hands shaking violently as I finally took in the natural colour of her eyes. Honey brown. Eyes I would never forget as her death etched itself onto the amplifier on my finger. Without the host, the phoenix couldn't survive. By killing this woman—a victim in her own right—I had freed her of the sickness she was not strong enough to stave off herself.

It was then I noticed something horrifying. Her clothes. She wore a torn, burned jacket of rich azure. Her trousers too. She stood out compared to the darker tones of Wycombe fashion.

Calzmir blue. The colour of Camron's kingdom.

Hands grasped my shoulders. I didn't have the strength to lift my eyes from the woman. I kept looking at her face, expecting to blink and see my mother. This would be her fate. She either died from the sickness or was killed for surviving and becoming the monster the phoenix wished to create.

'Are you hurt?' Simion said, fingers holding firm onto my shoulders. I hadn't realised I was crying until he touched me, the steady hold of his hands contrasted to the shaking of my torso.

'I killed her,' I said, rocking the body against my chest.

'You did what you had to,' Simion said, refusing to let go. 'Maximus, you've saved many lives doing what you did.'

'But it wasn't her fault,' I shouted, as guilt sank its blade through my chest. 'She didn't ask to be sick, she didn't ask to survive the plague.'

Simion pulled me from the lifeless body. She slipped out of my blood-stained hands, falling to the burned floor where she stayed, shards of black-slick stones scattered around her.

'I know,' Simion said, drawing me into him. His hand cupped the back of my head, his arm wrapped around my shoulders. I didn't fight back as I pressed my face into his hard chest. Blood and tears dampened his tunic. With each deep, shaking inhale, all I could smell was smoke. It filled my nose, scorched my lungs. Since the wytchfire had been extinguished, it left pillars of dark smoke to slither into the skies.

I had smelled it before, during the Ball. This same smell had oozed from Elder Leia's clothes, like an unwanted perfume.

This had not been the first attack, and nor would it be the last.

Simion allowed me a moment of weakness. In truth, I don't think he would've ever pulled away. But the chaos was far from over. The street beyond the library was alight with screams and shouts, the ground thundering with hundreds of running feet. Smoke billowed outside of shattered glass windows, filling the sky in a haze. Ash fell like snow, littering everything.

'I need to get you away from here,' Simion said, pulling me

from his chest until he held my face with both of his hands. His thumb brushed a stubborn tear from my cheek, leaving a cool shiver in its wake.

'Wycombe isn't safe—I can't just leave them,' I said, drinking in the horror of burned, screaming people and bodies sprawled down the steps of the library.

There was some part of me that felt solely responsible for the destruction. I might not have allowed Camron to enter Wycombe, but he'd used me to get here. He'd used Beatrice. Weeks after his death, his presence still lingered.

'Maximus.' Simion used my name as a way of drawing me back to him, and only him. 'Right now, your safety is all that matters to me. I cannot let anything happen to you. You are all I have left, I cannot fail you as I have failed my sister.' The urgency in his amber eyes, the deep resonating thunder in his voice, proved there was no arguing with him.

'Why?' I asked.

'Selfishly, I need you.'

His words were so raw, they barrelled into me, distracting me from the chaos of the street. I grasped his face, soot-covered hands pressing into his skin. 'I'm not going anywhere.'

Simion leaned his forehead down and pressed it to mine. He closed his eyes and exhaled a long breath, overspilling with tension. 'Dryads, Max. I thought I lost you.'

I had to focus on not faltering beneath his words. They had the power to undo me; the cracks within me spread wider, breaking apart. 'I'm—here.'

In that moment, I longed to tell him everything. It was on the tip of my tongue, spoiled and sour. I shifted my eyes from him, back to the lifeless body of the woman I had freed from her possession. Again, I saw my mother, and was reminded why I couldn't tell him.

This is my mother's fate.

CHAPTER 12

The street bustled with battlemages, dressed in silver and ivory, doing everything they could to calm the crowd. Bodies were stretched out across the street, being tended to by gleamers. Legs were entirely melted to the bone, flesh and material seamlessly blended into one. I could smell the blood on the air, hear the screams of the wounded like a song, feel the kiss of wytchfire across my dirtied, bloodied skin.

Simion didn't release me. His arm was wrapped around my waist, guiding me through the gathering crowds. I wanted to ask him where he was taking me, but I couldn't form a single word. All I could think about was the woman I had just killed. Yes, I might have saved others, but I couldn't save her.

Like a river around a rock, the crowd parted as Leska cut directly towards us. Her scowl softened, for a moment, before being replaced with the usual sharpened glare she always gave me.

'I should have refused your request,' Leska snapped, fury bubbling in her eyes. 'This is my fault.'

I quickly realised her fury was actually masked worry. Her eyes trailed over me, relaxing only when she couldn't find a wound on me.

'What's going on, Leska?' Simion asked, gaze sweeping the street. 'What has taken you so long to get here?'

It was true. Time had stretched after the attack. It seemed no one was coming to help, until the rush of battlemages arrived.

'My apologies, Mage Hawthorn.' Her tone was bitter with sarcasm. 'But this has not been the only attack. There have been more, all throughout the city. Small pockets of solitary phoenix-possessed. All have been dealt with.'

More attacks? My blood thrummed as though fire filled my veins. 'We need to speak to Leia. She will use this as the perfect excuse to attack—'

My hand was snatched, lifted by Leska as she studied the ring on my finger. 'Already a death notch, not even a week after you get your amplifier.' Her fingers tightened. 'Do you enjoy decorating it?'

'Let him go, Leska.' Simion's deep voice resonated at my back, his cool presence casting across the shield over my mind. 'Maximus killed the *possessed*; he saved lives in your absence.'

A look of disbelief crossed her eyes as she looked between Simion and then back to me. I cringed as her thumbnail pressed into my amplifier's surface. My breath hitched as the small carved notch suddenly came into view. It hadn't been there before, but I knew all too well what it meant.

My last amplifier had been scarred with many death notches. Disgust ran through me as I studied the mark, wide-eyed.

'I did what I had to,' I said. It was hard to swallow past the lump in my throat.

Beneath Leska's gaze, I felt exposed. I could only imagine what I looked like, coated in blood and burns. 'Yes, you did.'

'The other attacks, where were they?' Simion asked.

I dreaded the answer.

'Mainly areas around the city centre. Spread out enough to occupy us, distract us. Shift our attentions elsewhere, whilst their main goal was completed.'

'Main goal?' I sensed there was more to it.

People passed us, making Leska drop her voice. 'Not here. It will cause more panic.'

'My apartment is close,' Simion said, his hold tightening around me.

Leska grimaced, glanced to one of the carriages nearby. It was a silent suggestion, one Simion agreed to. Within moments, we were inside one with the scent of burning and blood lingering on us both. Simion gave the directions to the coachman. The carriage jolted forward, leaving behind the library and the chaos until all I could see was smoke drifting skywards. Leska was right, the library was not the only place attacked. Out the window I saw countless strands of smoke.

I blinked and was transported back to another time, when Camron had attacked Wycombe. Then I looked back to the fast-marks on my arm.

'It is Camron,' I said, 'it has to be.'

Leska and Simion shared a look, clearly agreeing.

'But you killed him, enough witnesses saw that,' Leska said. I appreciated her attempt to dispel my fears, but it didn't make me feel better. 'My father said his ashes are stored with Elder Leia.'

'Leska is right,' Simion said. 'I've seen them. Camron died, that is the end of it.'

My mouth dried. 'Why didn't you tell me?'

He held my combative stare, refusing to look away. 'I thought I was protecting you.'

Moisture clung to the window, blurring the view beyond. I raised a hand and wiped the glass; my palm came away dewy. At least I could distract myself with the view beyond.

Wycombe city was wounded after Camron Calzmir's attack. Seeing the remnants of destruction up close was a sour reminder of what had been lost that day. My father was not the only one to die, many had burned in the fires, been crushed beneath the weight of fallen buildings. Some buildings were untouched, whilst those beside them were no more than a cavernous hole. Battlemages had helped shift the rubble, allowing space for newly crafted buildings to replace those that had been destroyed, but to completely repair the city would require months, if not years. Camron's attack had almost razed Wycombe completely. And now he was not the only one attacking the city. His creations were.

'What matters now is locating those responsible for all of this,' Simion said, breaking the silence. 'Not chasing ghosts.'

'It's the South,' I admitted, hating saying it aloud. 'There is no denying that anymore.'

The South sends its love. That was what the woman said to me before I killed her. She wore the telltale clothes of the Calzmir kingdom. Just like Queen Romar, someone had let them in. And I had an inkling as to who that was.

'No, not entirely,' Leska replied. 'Intel points to another. The Council think it's the Hawthorns.'

In the reflection of the window, I could just make out the outlines of their faces. This bothered Simion, evident from the creases across his forehead.

He leaned forward. 'Are you confident?'

'Who?' I asked before Leska could reply.

'The rebellion, and, yes, I am sure. More novices are missing. I don't know what they're planning, but I'm sure it's all connected. Despite the attacks in the city, it was to draw the attention away from something greater.' Leska leaned in, eyeing the closed shutter keeping the coachman from hearing. Her voice dipped to a whisper. 'The rebels have attacked the armoury.'

'Why?' Simion muttered, gaze lost to the view beyond the window.

'To stall Leia from sending her numbers to attack the South,' I answered for him, knowing it without the need to be told.

Leska eyed me as though my knowledge was incriminating. 'If I was you, keep that to yourself, otherwise the Council will start pointing fingers, and, trust me—they need someone to blame to stifle the panic this city will be grasped in.'

My thoughts drifted back to the Ball and what I had heard Simion and Cyder speak about.

'Fuck,' Simion spat, burying his face in his hands. 'We know who they will blame.'

There wasn't time to contemplate who he meant when Leska answered my thoughts after a beat. 'Beatrice is innocent.'

'I know that,' Simion shouted, cheeks flushing crimson. 'But she is the perfect scapegoat.'

'So is…'

They both turned their gaze to me.

My fingers dug into my thighs, pinching skin. There was no stopping my mind from whirling. 'They are sick, it still doesn't explain how the South are sending sick people over the borders.'

They shared that look again. It anything displeased me more, it was being kept in the dark.

'I care little for you, Max. But I don't wish you to be blamed for something you haven't done. I don't like you, but I dislike injustice more.'

Leska's comment should have taken some of the burden from my shoulders, whereas it did the opposite.

'Nothing will happen to him. Nothing. I will see to that,' Simion said, lost in his emotion. 'Even if it is the South trying to ruin us, it is the *Hawthorns* who keep claiming responsibility.'

'Well,' Leska added, leaning back, seemingly unbothered by the revelation, or Simion's raw reaction, 'they are back, perhaps they never went away. The rebels always left something behind, a token to taunt the Queen and Council. The Hawthorn tree is known for producing berries of the ripest reds, those berries are always left. If a token is found at the library, it will only cement their involvement in the abductions.'

'And has it?' Simion asked, as a single vein bulged in his temple. 'Has it been found?'

'I don't doubt it will.' Leska shifted in her seat; arms crossed over her chest. 'There was a *token* left at the armoury. We will know soon if another was left at the library. Then we can confidently confirm the Hawthorns have joined forces with the South. They've finally found the means to suffocate the Council.'

'This will not only affect Beatrice. It is my name they use, and my aunt's. This is bad for us all.'

'Which is why Leia will look for her escape route as soon as possible,' Leska confirmed, although it seemed even she struggled with this concept. 'With you, Max, being the South's sworn King, and Simion here being a Hawthorn by name... You didn't hear it from me, but my father said the Council are beginning to look to Leia and Simion as suspects.'

Simion was lost to his storm, his gaze detached and distant. I knew him, I knew his silence, and the way his stare seemed to disappear to something unseen, meant he was working out a solution. 'They'll ruin everything.'

'I'm simply telling you how it appears,' Leska replied curtly. 'The *Hawthorns* have returned. And if it is not the Hawthorns, then whoever it is wishes to use the rebellion as an excuse to free those who are possessed. To use them as a means to exploit the tensions in the Council, or just burn everything to the ground.'

'Simion,' I pleaded, thumb running across the broken flesh of his knuckles. His hand shook in mine, the tips of his fingers cold as ice. When he finally levelled his eyes with mine, I felt the force of his anxiety like a blade to the gut. 'You don't need to fix this alone.'

'It doesn't take a scholar to see how this will end.'

Simion was right, if what Leska said was true, then the rekindling of a rebellion starting after Beatrice returned North only incriminated her more. And me, being the husband to Camron Calzmir and the Southern King. It didn't look good for either of us.

It didn't matter what else was said, only one thought mattered now. Mother. I had to get her away from the city, away from stares and interrogations. If Leia wanted to blame me, she would look at my mother too.

I had to get her away from prying eyes.

I had to get home. *Now.*

The carriage stopped, and I opened the door without a second thought. I needed fresh air. Distance. Escape. My gaze swept up the unfamiliar street, panic surging through me. I could run, but Simion would follow. If not Simion, Leska would. And I was right, because I heard his familiar gait from behind me.

'I am trying to free you from these burdens, Max.' His voice echoed across the walled street, until the message of what he said became too heavy to bear. 'I am trying to give you a life with nothing to worry about.'

I turned hard on his, pushing at his chest, forcing him back a step. 'I don't need you! I don't need anyone to protect me, or what is mine.'

Simion winced, but this time he refused to look away. There was no lie to greet me as he spoke. 'I can't just let you get hurt, Maximus. I *won't.*'

I stepped in close, aware Leska watched from inside the carriage. 'Then get me out of this city. Help me.'

My chest heaved with each inhale, the tension only building as I exhaled. I felt as though I was close to exploding, unable to hold it in anymore. Leska was watching, scrutinising from her seat in the carriage as the show unfurled before her.

'Is that what you want?' Rain fell from his face, tracing the lines of his jaw before slipping into the neckline of his dirtied shirt.

Even though lying was a shared skill, this was one time I couldn't form one. 'Yes.'

He didn't ask me why. He didn't push me for answers. Instead, he nodded. I watched Simion's shoulders relax, the tension slipping from him. 'Okay.'

One single word and my entire world seemed to crumble.

'But first you need a warm bath and fresh, clean clothes, then we can face this. Together, remember?'

Exhaustion overwhelmed me. I couldn't push him to do it now, not without revealing everything. But Leska was listening.

The second I said anything about my mother, it would be solid evidence against me.

'Simion—' My body refused me, forcing my mouth to close and teeth to sink into my tongue to stifle my words. I almost told him everything, spilled my soul in the middle of an empty street, as the downpour threatened to wash us both away.

'What is it?' Simion asked, eyes flickering across my rain-coated face.

'I don't want to feel like this anymore. Use your magic. Take it away.' I had longed to say those words for weeks. Needing Simion to clear my emotions, to smother them so I could think clearly, be free from the burdens of grief, panic, guilt.

Finally, I gave in.

His exhale was tempered and desperate. 'I would never refuse you.'

'It really was easier when you didn't like me,' I said, repeating the sentiment I shared during the Ball.

Simion's confident touch comforted me, his fingers drumming across my upper arm as he guided me towards the side street lined with white stone buildings. When he replied, his voice was warm. 'Believe me, Maximus, I am far beyond simply liking you now.'

CHAPTER 13

I am far beyond simply liking you.

Those seven words repeated in my mind, warming me from the inside out, tickling like a feather. It eased me from the inside as Simion opened himself up to his magic and ebbed it over my skin like a smattering of rain.

He filled me with his calming essence until I couldn't think of anything else. I didn't care when the carriage began to move, leaving us alone on the street. Nor did I care for where Leska was going.

All that mattered was that we were finally alone, and Simion stole every single haunting emotion from my body. He didn't stop until I felt nothing more than a numb, empty shell of a being.

It was easier this way.

'Come,' he said softly as he withdrew his magic, 'I have somewhere I would like you to see.'

I didn't resist. There was no energy left, not as my entire focus was on him, his touch, his closeness, his skin brushing mine. Although his magic had been forced back into its holding, his hand never let go of mine.

Simion guided me from the main road to a smaller side street shrouded in the shadows of buildings. They were a mixture of

Avarian stone and wood, each as grand as the next. We didn't stop, not until we reached a small tavern. A sign announced that it was called the Mad Queen. It was an apt name for a tavern that looked as though it housed renegades and vagrants, rather than honest people looking for a stiff drink.

'Welcome to my home,' he said more to himself than me.

'You live here?' I asked, dumbfounded as I stared at the tavern, set down a seedy alleyway among Wycombe's busiest quarter.

'Are you judging me, Maximus Oaken?' Simion asked, voice lighter than it had been. If he looked exhausted before, the last use of his power had drained him substantially. If I was capable of feeling, I would've felt guilt. That was my doing. Simion released my hand and placed his on the small of my back, fingers continuously drumming their rhythm into me.

'Well.' I swallowed hard. The tavern's hanging sign swung above our heads. It depicted a woman whose head was comically large, riding on the back of a golden dragon. 'Yes, yes, I am.'

Simion released me, moved for the door and pushed it open. 'Just you *wait* until you see the inside.'

'It's...' I searched for the right word. 'Quaint.'

'Quaint or not, this is the only establishment who would let in two people looking like we currently do. Leave the judgement at the door, or it might spoil your experience.'

He was right, of course. One glance down and I was covered in blood and ash. The stench of fire oozed from me. I didn't need a mirror to know I looked terrible. Although when Simion gazed at me, it made me feel the opposite.

I appreciated his attempt for normalcy. That all shattered when I got a good look at what waited beyond the door.

The Mad Queen was no different to the taverns and pubs I'd frequented back in the South. In a way, it felt like home. We entered a bustling, smoke-filled room, air rich with burning herbs and red flagstone floor sticky from years of spilled ale, dirtied mops and dryads knows what else trodden into the ground. Low ceilings gave a suffocating yet comforting feeling, as did the dark-painted walls stained with greasy splashes from ale and other ungodly substances. Simion walked with confidence, the smoke parting around his broad frame as he moved directly for the bar at the far side of the large room. It dominated an entire side, the wall behind covered in shelves, each with glasses, tankards, bottles and other containers filled with liquids I didn't even want to imagine. A burly man waited on the other side, a cloth wrapped around a fist that was currently wrist deep in a glass.

'Master Hawthorn, bit early for you, ain't it?'

Grief all but tickled me, as it always did, at the most unexpected moments. If Simion hadn't smothered my emotions, it would've knocked my feet from under me. This nameless barman reminded me of my father. He had a full, thick beard peppered with strands of silver and grey. Unlike my father's eyes, this man's were a dull brown, set with thick brows that met in the middle. He had wisps of black hair folded over a balding head. His cheeks covered with rosy veins and his temple glittered with sweat.

'Consider it a pleasant surprise, Nicho. Could you please see that a bath is drawn?' Simion said, leaning over the sticky bar. 'Before we offend your well-playing clients with our stench.'

There was an ease to the way they spoke to one another. A familiarity.

The barman—Nicho—continued cleaning the glass with a not-so-clean cloth as he eyed me up. 'Big enough for one, or two?'

I caught my lip between my teeth, stifling a gasp.

Before I could make a comment, Simion answered for me. 'One.'

Nicho shrugged, looked over the tavern and called out towards a tall, reedy-looking woman who fussed between tables. 'Master Hawthorn needs a bath drawn.'

'For one or two?' the woman called back, mimicking Nicho's question as she drew her hands down the stained apron.

I leaned into Simion. 'Is this a common question you're asked?'

He stiffened as the woman moved across the tavern, ignoring

dreary-eyed occupants lounging back in chairs as though their minds belonged to another realm.

'No,' he whispered out the corner of his mouth to me before facing the woman. 'One.'

'Suit yourself,' she replied, extending her hand to me. The faint glow of glass lamps reflected off her calloused hand, which extended past Simion to me. 'What's ya name?'

'Max,' I replied, taking it. Her grip was firm and steady, the power in her long, spindly arms impressive.

'Oh yes, we've 'eard all about you, haven't we love.'

'Indeed, we 'ave,' Nicho replied, smirking out the corner of my eye. 'Iria 'ere will sort you out that bath.'

'Looks like you both could do with one,' Iria said, turning her nose up at the foul smell of smoke and flesh lingering on us. 'What about a massage, or a four-course meal, a goose that would lay ya a golden egg?'

'Nothing I cannot settle with the end of the month's bill, Iria.'

At that, Iria smiled proudly, tapping Simion on the shoulder with some affection. 'Oh, you always do. Favourite customer of ours, isn't he, my love.'

Nicho slammed the glass down, more streaked with grease than it likely was when he washed it. 'Indeed, he is.'

It was as though we had walked into another world. One where worries were left at the door. Or perhaps it was the smoke that diluted my mind.

'That is because I'm the only one who pays double the price you charge everyone else,' Simion said, offering them both a sly grin before turning to me. Perhaps it was my quietness, or the look in my eyes, but being left alone didn't sit right with me. 'You're in good hands, trust me. Then I will take you home, okay?'

Home. The feeling of needing to be there was barely a spark now. Clear-headed, I knew the sooner we were done, the sooner I got home.

'Come with me then.' Iria wrapped her arm around my shoulders, pulling me in tight to her side. There was something motherly about it, almost distracting from the fact she smelled rotten. 'Good 'ands? He means the best. Now, since Simion is paying, I suggest you dry him out of pocket. Soup, bath salts, lavender, you name it, we got it.'

Holding Simion's gaze, I replied to Iria. 'I'll take it all.'

His smile was the most honest thing I had seen since the attack.

Iria slapped my back, causing a cough of surprise from the strength of her single hand. 'Just what I like to hear, now let's see you cleaned up before questions start flying amongst my customers.'

'I'll sort some clothes for you,' Simion said, already slipping towards the arched doorway to the side of the bar. When he looked back to Iria, there was the faint glint of warning set into his amber eyes. 'Take care of him.'

She pressed a hand to her chest. 'Be gone with you, Simion. I'll spike your supper if you question my integrity again.'

It seemed all Simion needed to do was wink, and the tension faded, forgotten.

'That man,' Iria said, guiding me towards another set of stairs, these leading down into the dark pits beneath the bar. 'He thinks his handsome face is going to distract me, *bleurgh*.'

As the floorboards above us creaked, a deep voice called out. 'I heard that.'

Iria groaned under her breath. 'Cock.'

Simion's voice rose over the noise of the tavern. 'Heard that too.'

I couldn't help but smile.

A stone basin waited in the cellar of the tavern. The water inside was a milky pale colour even before Iria tipped countless herbs and salts into it. There wasn't much conversation as she got to work, but I watched her movements, reminiscing how familiar they were. It hadn't been long enough for me to forget when I was the one drawing baths and serving. Most of my life had been under the oppressive thumb of the Gathrax Kingdom, and I still couldn't shake the discomfort I had when allowing others to do such tasks for me. When the bath was prepared, Iria produced a towel and handed it to me.

'The water has only been over the coals for a short while, so the heat won't last long. Make the most of it before it cools.'

'Thank you,' I said, meaning both words with such intent.

Iria stopped, as though it was strange to hear such thanks. She paused before she left, eyeing me up and down.

'We see little of Simion these days, but when he shows his face, it is usually with your name in his mouth.'

I paused, cheeks filling with heat. 'Really?'

Her cheeky, knowing smile was confirmation enough. After offloading a number of rules for the bath, Iria left me. I hadn't had it in me to tell her I had drawn many a bath in my time—even if it felt like a lifetime ago.

Finally alone, I peeled the clothes from my body, leaving them in a heap on the floor. Even simple movements made the terrible scent of fire and death billow from my skin. I climbed into the basin, skin melting against the comforting warmth of water. Slipping inside, I didn't stop until I was entirely emerged, staring up at the ceiling through the distorting water.

I thought of Simion's words, his touch, the knowledge I had to leave it all behind. His magic usually lasted longer than this, but it was already fading, giving room for all my emotions to return. My urgency.

There were so many reasons I longed to hold my head beneath the water, resisting the urge to come up for air. It was easier to forget it all when the need to breathe became a visceral scream.

Time slipped away from me, the water growing cooler with every passing minute. I stared at a spot on the wall, replaying everything whilst trying to conjure a plan. No matter how hard I thought, I couldn't comprehend what I had to do.

Footsteps sounded in the direction of the door and Simion

walked into the room. There was a look of relief as his eyes fell on me.

'You've been down here a while. I thought I'd check to see if you hadn't run away from me.'

I double-checked the shield around my thoughts, worried he could read them. It had not dropped—it was still iron strong. If it had, he would've seen those exact plans. To run. Not from him, from everyone.

'Sorry to disappoint,' I said, water rippling around my chin, 'but I'm still here.'

Simion's eyes quickly fell to the pile of clothing he held in his hands. Simion turned to leave. 'Then I'll leave you to finish up.'

'No,' I sat up, shouting out before my mind could think. 'Stay. Please.'

I expected to feel embarrassment at Simion seeing me so exposed, but I didn't. Perhaps it was because I had far greater things to concern myself with.

It had been weeks of dancing around one another. I had been careful not to let him get too close. But here, separated by the steam of water and the heavy scent of lavender, I couldn't push him away.

Not this time.

Simion kept his gaze diverted from me but did as I asked.

I slipped back down into the milky water until only my head poked out of it. 'Shame there isn't sponge for you to assist with this time.'

Dryads, I should learn to think before I spoke.

Simion winced, the memory hard for him to contemplate. This wasn't the first time Simion had seen me exposed—but the circumstances were so different it felt like a first.

I watched as he chewed on my comment. To his benefit, Simion did everything to look anywhere else but me. He placed the spare clothes on the edge of a sideboard before moving back towards the stairs where he took a seat on the bottom step.

'Careful, Max, if you say that too loud, I'm sure Iria would happily find us a sponge if it meant billing me extra for it.'

For the second time, I wanted to drown myself in the tub, if only to save myself from myself.

'Now would be the perfect time to explain why you choose to live in a tavern, of all places?' I asked.

Simion was just out of view, but I could hear the emotion in his voice when he spoke. 'If I told you it was because they serve the best ale in Wycombe, would you believe me?'

'Maybe,' I replied, feeling the grit of salts scratch beneath my bare thighs. 'But then it would only open more questions. So, to save us the time, get to the point.'

I positioned myself so I could see him, just in time to watch the corner of his lip quirked up. The profile of his face was illuminated by the flame burning in the glass lamp just above him. 'After my family was taken from me, I wasn't the easiest child to be around. Leia passed me off to the Academy's boarding accommodations, but that didn't end well. Barely thirteen and I'd already been kicked out of the halls, no elder wanted me in their sections. So that meant I was forced to move back in with Leia.'

'Sounds terrible, poor you,' I added, attempting some light-hearted banter but failing miserably.

'More like poor her,' Simion said. 'If my time in the Academy's boarding rooms didn't last long, the short stint with Leia lasted no time at all. I walked out, found this place, got drunk and never really left. That's the short version of events.'

There was a sadness lurking beneath his tale, but, as always, Simion made an effort to keep his face as void of emotion as possible. He recounted it as though the story was one big joke, when in truth it wasn't.

'Life must've been tough for you to end up in a place like this,' I added.

'Iria and Nicho are family now. They looked after me, kept me fed and warm. I think it worked because they gave me space, and

I also enjoyed knowing Leia was forced to pay for me, which she did gladly if it meant keeping me out of her way.'

The water rushed around me as I lifted my arms out the basin, hoisted myself up, just so I could get a better look at him. Simion's eyes traced over my bare chest, the moment fleeting, but I felt his stare settle over my skin as though his finger had drawn across it.

'And here I was thinking you were the golden child,' I said, immediately regretting it for the sorrowful frown his face drew into. 'Shit, that was insensitive, wasn't it?'

'I was hardly the golden child, Max. I was the only child.'

'Sorry,' I repeated.

He shook his head, running a hand down the back of it. I noticed Simion did it a lot, brushing over the scar across the back of his head as though he required a reminder of the day he gained it. When Camron knocked him back with a force of power, splitting his skull open on the edge of a step.

'My sister was in exile, and now everyone believes she's a criminal. I could shit from the top of Saylam Academy and still no one would think badly of me. It is a curse and a blessing.'

The water was already cooling, but I didn't want to stop talking. As soon as we were done, I would leave here, get my mother and find a way out of the North. But selfishly I wanted to hide myself away here and pester Simion with questions, just so I didn't need to think about the ominous ones that lingered in the back of my mind. Because I would leave him, just like his family did.

'I imagine it was hard for you,' I said, surprised by the lump of sadness that filled the back of my throat. I had to swallow it down hard, just to keep it from showing in my voice. 'I can't imagine being alone like that, I don't think I could ever cope with it.'

I had buried my father's death to the deepest parts of me. It was easier to hide the grief than face it. It snuck up at me in moments, but life had been too busy to truly allow myself to face what I had lost.

Not in the way my mind desired.

Simion caught my eyes, the force of his attention a physical, visceral thing. 'We make good with what we can. Even when you feel as though everything has been taken from you, there is always something else to fight for. Always.'

I swallowed the words down, embedding them in my gut.

He was right, there was always something to fight for.

'Simion Hawthorn, the poet.' I drank him in, eyes peering over the lip of the bath at him. He had done a job at cleaning the grime from his body, but I still saw flecks of it across his forehead and knuckles. 'You should have asked for one big enough for two.'

Simion narrowed his amber eyes, tilting his head to the side. 'Why would that be?'

'Well, you are not exactly clean.' I shifted, bringing my knees up to my chest and wrapping my arms around them to keep myself in place.

He gazed down. 'And here I was thinking the bird bath I just subjected myself to would have been good enough.'

I spoke up before I could regret it. 'Simion, come here. *Please.*'

He stood abruptly, his face serious, the clothes dropped and forgotten on the floor before him. 'Do you know what you are asking me?'

'I do.'

Dryads, I needed this. I needed him. My mind was a storm, and I didn't want to ignore it any longer. I was weak, but I wanted him. Not to take away my emotions, not to distract me from what I would do as soon as I left. I simply wanted *him.* If he didn't, I may not have survived the rest of the day.

This was more than just a need, it was a farewell. But I couldn't leave, not without one final memory of him.

'What do you want from me, Max?'

I held my breath, giving myself a moment to be sure. Even though I didn't need it. I knew, without a doubt; I spoke my desires without regret. 'Get in the bath, Simion.'

His hesitation lasted only a moment.

I watched, breath lodged in my throat, heart thumping in my chest as Simion paced towards me with careful steps. There was something hungry in his eyes—all seeing and all devouring.

'Have we not already come to the conclusion that this bath will only fit one person?' he asked, voice warm as a newly lit hearth.

My cheeks warmed, a blush betraying me. 'Forget I said it.'

'Impossible,' Simion replied quickly.

He stood there, watching me as though I was the only thing in the room. He leaned over the bath, with a view to the outlines of body beneath the water. There was nothing but the clasp of my hands and the milky glaze of water to hide myself from him. Yet he didn't look. He kept his eyes level—respectful. 'Ask me again.'

'Get in the bath,' I repeated, more self-assured this time.

'Are you sure?' His question meant more than checking if I wanted him to strip his clothes and join me with nothing but water as concealment. It meant, are you sure you want to risk it? Risk the potential for pain, the possibility of proving your greatest fear. With the phoenix-possessed attack, the spreading of the plague and the mention of a rebellion using the South to infiltrate Wycombe, there was more to fear than the memory of Camron Calzmir. I couldn't hide from him forever, in death or life.

I scoffed, almost fumbling over my words. 'More sure than anything else, I promise you.'

It was as though my words, or perhaps the meaning behind them, gave Simion the consent he waited for. His eyes diverted from mine, trailing my body. Where the warm amber of his stare touched, a shiver coursed over me.

'Unless *you* don't want... this?' I asked, voicing my deepest concern. Had I crossed a line? Had I asked for something he didn't want?

To answer me, Simion raised his fingers to the buttons of his shirt and began undoing them, one by one. 'Believe me, it is all I want.'

I watched him undress, attempting to give him some privacy by not letting my eyes wander. I failed, miserably.

Whatever deity created Simion, they'd taken their time crafting his body. First came his chest, broad and defined with sculpted muscles. Those muscles continued down to his torso. I counted them as he continued removing his shirt—six, which was four more mounds of muscle than I ever had on my stomach.

It was miraculous how his clothes could hide such a physique. From the symmetry of his build to the V-shaped lines that rested on either side of his hip.

I sank a little further into the bath, grasping onto my legs as a swell of heat spread over my groin. Simion stood still, his shirt no more than a crumpled pile on the floor by his feet.

There was something shy about the way he reached for his amplifier—a curled dragon hanging on a leather cord—around his neck. He fiddled with it, as though giving himself something to do.

Water sloshed against the stone basin as I repositioned myself. This time, as Simion unbuckled his belt and tugged at the waist-band, I kept my eyes up. It wasn't that he was trying to cover himself—but I controlled my urges.

Simion climbed into the bath, his long legs bending awkwardly to fit, his knees knocking into mine. Even if we did ask for a bath that accommodated us both, I still would've preferred this proximity. This closeness was what I craved.

Water rippled across Simion's beautiful skin, glistening like gems in the flickering of light around us.

'Turn around,' I said, unable to stop myself from being so commanding.

'Isn't it a bit late for decency?'

'I'm not asking out of embarrassment, Simion. Just turn around.' I smiled nervously, each breath feeling tight when I looked at him.

'Why?'

'Repaying the favour you offered me all those weeks ago.'

He eyed me before he turned. Water splashed over the basin and spread in puddles across the floor. I didn't care about the mess, not as I was presented with something far more interesting.

His broad shoulders were laced with muscle, his skin smooth as polished stone. I caught the puckered mark of a scar on the back of his head and had to stop myself from offering him an apology. He got it because of me, because of Camron.

I cupped water in my hands and brought it up to his shoulders. It fell through my fingers, splashing over his back. His muscles rippled. Simion seemed to slouch forward as my fingers melted onto his skin.

We sat like that in silence, slowly easing into one another's presence. Soon enough my legs ached and, as if sensing it, Simion reached back and guided them until they stretched out on either side of him. His fingers trailed, unseen, beneath the water. They caressed the outer side of my leg as I continued washing his back.

Where I touched, his skin prickled in gooseflesh, and Simion couldn't stop a gasp from escaping past his lips. I didn't need to see his face to know his eyes were closed, his mouth parted in relaxation and pleasure.

'Simion?'

'Yes, Maximus.'

I inhaled the scent of bath oils, salts and him. Clean as pine and as fresh as open forest—he invaded my sense and claimed it. 'If I could give you anything, a memory, a moment, what would it be?'

He leaned forward, making me drop the hands from his back. I studied his profile, the perfect line of his nose, the proud bone of his brow, his full lips and prominent jaw.

'Why do you ask?'

'Everyone has wanted something from me.'

Julian wanted me because he couldn't have me. King Gathrax wanted me because of my power. Camron wanted me to help him burn the world.

Simion had to want something too.

'I want nothing from you in the same way I want everything.'

Everything. The word rang out in my mind, my body, my soul.

'And I could ask the same. What is it you want from me, Maximus?'

I considered his question, unsure how to answer it honestly without hurting his feelings and my own.

'I want... I want not to think about anything. I want my mind to be free of anxiety and responsibility,' I said in a single breath. *I want to not leave you with regret festering inside of me.*

'If it is my power you require to do that, then you didn't need to ask me to join you in the—'

'I don't want what your magic can do,' I interrupted, resting my hand back on his shoulder. Dryads, it was like holding rock. He was thick and built, strong yet soft. 'Even in death, Camron has kept us apart. I'm tired of pretending I don't have wants, desires, just because the demon I was forced to call my husband still wraps around my arm in silver chains.'

Simion turned back around to face me, his hands helping move my legs until they were repositioned over his thighs. We sat face to face, nothing but cooling water between us. 'Camron is dead. It is over. The marks... they are just scars, no different to the one he gifted me.'

'But what if it... hurts?' I lifted my fast-marked arm from the water and held it before us. Simion carefully took it in his hands, thumb and fingers tracing cool breezes across my damp skin.

His expression hardened. 'Camron can't hurt you anymore. We will not give him that power.'

'This suggests otherwise.' I turned my arm around, skin flexing and tugging the silver marks. 'With everything that is happening, the attacks, the fire, the plague. It is Camron, I know it is.'

'You do not fear pain, but what that pain means,' he said, as though reading my mind. 'Am I right?'

'Yes,' I exhaled, his words lifting the burden from my shoulders.

'Remember, I have seen Camron's ashes, Max. Only his memory lingers, until we banish it.'

'Then do that.' I slipped forward, water sloshing around our naked bodies. 'Banish him with me.'

When Simion looked at me, I knew, without a doubt, he longed for the same thing as I did. Skin. Touch. Distraction.

The night I kissed Simion beyond the cottage, my body felt as though it was being torn apart. It had taken only the brush of my lips and the fast-mark sought to punish me for my actions. Because Camron was still bonded to me.

But he was dead now. I killed him. There should be nothing stopping me from reaching for Simion and breaking that final barrier between us—the one he placed in my hands to control.

'What frightens you, Max? Tell me, let me protect you from it.'

I feared losing my mother, this life I thought I was finally carving for us. I feared knowing Camron was still alive and what that would mean. I feared taking responsibility, the responsibility the Queen bestowed upon me before she died.

'Nothing,' I lied.

'Then do it,' Simion whispered, staring deep through my eyes into the darkest parts of me. He couldn't help but to allow his magic to spread across the back of my mind. He longed to be in my thoughts, but he didn't need his power to fill them completely. 'Act on the desires in that loud mind of yours and let's see what happens. If it hurts, we figure it out. If it doesn't, well, you can put *him* out of your mind for good. Camron can't haunt you forever.'

Can't he?

'You truly have a way of encouragement,' I said, stomach flipping over.

'Close your eyes,' Simion said, voice as rich as it was deep.

I did it without the need to be told twice. Giving into the dark of my mind, it was as though my thoughts swirled among one another like strands of violent colour. All until Simion gently rested a hand on my jaw and held it in firm but gentle fingers.

Everything stilled.

I focused on the pressure of his fingers, the way his breath brushed over my mouth, revealing just how close he was.

A thumb brushed my lower lip. Instinctively, I parted my mouth, allowing for my tongue to draw it in. Just as his thumb slipped beneath my teeth, I bit down gently and opened my eyes to watch him.

Simion looked at me with such feral desire. It coiled in my stomach and hardened my muscles, all of them. When I released his thumb, Simion didn't pull away at first.

'Eyes. Closed.'

This was exactly what I wanted. To give into Simion and allow him to occupy my mind. I attempted to reach out and think about my anxieties—I failed. Even the events of the day faded to a whisper in the far reaches of my mind.

The anticipation would be my ruin. I couldn't steady my breathing as I waited for Simion to say something—do something.

His lips found mine so suddenly. I moaned, the sound muffled as his mouth closed over mine, pressing the kiss deep, as though leaving an imprint on me for an age after it was finished.

I waited for the pain, but I felt nothing but peace.

When Simion pulled away, I almost lost my temper. Lips tender and tongue poised to strike, I scowled at him. 'Why did you stop?'

His eyes searched my face, frantic and panicked. It took me a moment to realise.

'There is nothing,' I said, looking down at my arm. 'I *feel* nothing.'

That was a lie. I felt everything; excitement, relief, joy, pleasure. It tangled into one ball of energy inside of me, weeks' worth of pent-up tension ready to spill out between us.

'Good,' Simion said, forehead smoothing. 'Now you know.'

I released a rushed laugh. Simion did too. Relief flooded through me as I stared down at the marks on my arm.

I dove forward, water splashing in furious waves. Simion

drew me onto his lap, his length pressing hard beneath my bare ass. One hand coiled around my back, the other lingered beneath the water.

I touched him too. My lips to his, my nails drawing marks down his back.

Our kiss was deep, our tongues exploring one another. Dryads, I wanted it all. I wanted him. My teeth nipped at his lip, tugging it until his breathing laboured. We were rushed and frantic, wanting each other with some desperate nature. Even if I longed for this moment to last, there was no way I would slow down.

Maybe seconds had passed, maybe minutes, but as I began to rock my hips, Simion's grasp falling from my back to my ass, something broke. I broke. Deep inside, far beneath the protection of my ribs, my soul unfurled like a blooming rose in summer. Protections fell around my heart, finally opening up to let Simion in.

And that was when the pain arrived.

Blinding. Boiling. Scorching. Murderous pain. It devoured me. It was as though the bath was filled with shards of glass, not water. It tore at me, ripped me to shreds and left me for dead.

I tried to open my eyes, but I couldn't.

I tried to pull away, my body refused me.

There was only darkness.

Around me, above me, beneath me. In me.

Then, there was nothing.

CHAPTER 14

I woke, gasping and riddled in pain. Hard arms encased me, holding me up at an angle. It was as though I broke through the surface of a dark ocean, to find myself cradled against Simion's body. His mouth was moving, the sound faint and far away. Wide amber eyes hardly blinked, his skin had taken on an ashen hue. Fingers cupped the back of my head, holding me up like a newborn child.

Realisation quickly caught up with me. I knew what this pain meant. How it confirmed my greatest fears. I looked to my arm, expecting to find my skin flayed and the silver marks to be scars. But, as before, my skin was pink and fresh. There were no signs to prove the agony which had assassinated me. All but the resounding thrum that lingered even as I woke.

'I have got you,' Simion whispered, shaking hands grasping my face, brushing tacky hair from my forehead. 'I am here, Max.'

One moment we had been kissing, the next I was drowning in endless pain.

'How… how long?' I croaked, looking around at the different view around me. Blades filled my throat, slicing me open with even the smallest of breaths.

I was outside of the stone basin, a damp sheet wrapped

around my naked body. Dryads, I was cold. I couldn't stop shaking, from the chill and shock combined.

'A few minutes,' Simion replied, water dripping over me as it fell from his damp skin. I felt my heart thunder beneath the pressure of his touch. From the way Simion looked down at me, the undiluted horror in his eyes, I knew those minutes I had lost had been the longest in his life.

Everything ached. My lungs felt as though I had inhaled clouds of smoke, my muscles sore and tender. But above all the discomfort, it was the skin across my arm that pained me the most.

'Camron,' I muttered the name, feeling the urge to retch as I said it. 'He isn't...'

'I know, I know.' Simion looked at me and nothing else. The concern in his eyes was palpable. Guilt and fear swirled with evident ire. 'I'm so sorry, Maximus. I shouldn't have encouraged this—' He stopped himself, tracing his fingers across my face. I felt so cold compared to his warmth. 'I don't want to see you in pain. I don't want to be the reason for it.'

His words tore at me.

But what truly hurt me the most was knowing my greatest fear was true. It was the only thing that explained the pain.

I reached up and palmed Simion's cheek. There wasn't a word I could offer, nothing that would bring him peace. Nor me. All I could do was touch him and hope he understood the blame was not for him to bare.

Simion pinched his eyes closed. He leaned into my hand and held it to him with his own, anchoring me. 'I do not know how to save you from this.'

I felt oddly calm. The confirmation that Camron still haunted me was almost a welcome one. *Better the monster you know.*

Camron had murdered my father, the Queen, countless innocents in Wycombe. His power had possessed my mother and others. There were so many questions I had, so many unanswered thoughts and speculation.

When Simion had removed the bandages from my arm to reveal the unbroken fast-mark, I had known. But the pain I had suffered placed the truth far beyond any doubt.

Camron still lived.

Even as Simion held me to him, grasping me as though one gust of cool wind would blow me away—I simmered in a new desire.

Magic fizzed in my blood, the room lighting with cords of power.

'This is not your job. I will finish him,' I muttered, mouth dry as bone.

Camron had died. His ashes had been gathered and collected in a jar in Elder Leia's office. But the pain, it was so real, so violent and powerful, that I couldn't deny Camron still had ties to the living somehow.

'Careful,' Simion said, as I attempted to sit up. I didn't care that he had pulled me from the bath, naked to the world, before covering me in this sheet. And I didn't care that he was still entirely bare. 'I told you, we will work this out together.'

My mind raced. 'The pain... the punishment was delayed. Before, it happened straight away, but this time it didn't.'

Simion helped me up until I sat on my own. I tugged the damp sheet around my shoulders, hoping it would help settle the tremors that erupted across my skin. As he pulled back, I watched the way he lifted my hand and pressed it to his lips. There was a hesitation to it, as though he ran fingers across the edge of a blade.

'Stop, Simion,' I breathed, slowly regaining my composure. 'I won't allow you to regret this. *He* can't win.'

Simion levelled his eyes with me, amber gold twisting in a multitude of emotions. 'He should be dead. He should not still be hurting you. That... that bond *should* be broken.'

'Maybe it isn't broken, but splintered,' I said, voicing my thoughts aloud.

The discomfort was slowly fading.

I had no doubt Camron had died. My mother had seen it, as had I, as had the battlemages and elders who had been present in the throne room that fateful day. The wytchfire had extinguished as Camron perished beneath my magic. Everything pointed to his death—except the silver thorns and vine marks across my arm.

'There is much we still do not know about the phoenixes. And without the Queen to commune with the dryads, we cannot learn more.'

Footsteps sounded from the stairway. Whoever was coming down was moving quickly.

'Don't tell anyone,' I said, urgency scolding through me. 'Enough people don't trust me, if they find out Camron may still be alive, still connected with me... I cannot let it jeopardise my position in Wycombe. It would destroy the South.'

Simion nodded, his jaw set firm. 'I would never.'

'The Council has requested—' Leska burst into the room; cheeks flushed as she laid eyes on us.

Simion's naked body was covered by mine, whilst my body was mostly covered in a damp sheet. We watched as she came to her own understanding of what was happening.

'—well, this wasn't what I expected.'

Simion growled, practically radiating with unspent fury. He gestured with his eyes for her to leave, teeth bared as he continued to hold me close. 'One would normally knock before entering.'

'I do not have the time for knocking,' Leska said. 'Both of you, get some clothes on. I have received word from Elder Leia that we must go to the Heart Oak immediately.'

'Has there been another attack?' I asked, mind moving straight to Camron once again. Dryads, it never left him. The last time I defied our bond, he had attacked the city the following day. Although he did not unleash his wytchfire as a direct punishment to me, I still felt as though the fury of his visit was a reaction.

If he was still alive, had he felt the same pain I had?

I hoped so.

If Camron did in fact live, the pain he would suffer when I found him again would pale in comparison to what just happened.

And I would find him. Except, this time, I would ensure he met his end.

Leska glanced from me to Simion clearly noting the way he never took his hands off me. 'Not another attack, but the Hawthorns have accepted liability. They have said the attacks will not cease until Beatrice is freed.'

'Shit,' Simion exhaled, his hands falling from me. 'Leia will blame her.'

'That's not all.' Leska cast us both a sharp stare, mouth screwing into a taut line. More footsteps sounded behind her, echoing the beats of my heart. Leska could hardly look up at me as a flood of battlemages entered behind her.

Simion threw himself over me, covering my body with his. A growl built in his chest. 'Someone better explain the meaning of this.'

'Maximus must come with us,' Leska said, her voice lacking its usual tone. Whatever was happening, she was not happy about it either.

I couldn't speak, not beneath the glares of so many powerful mages. And they all looked to me. I could not decide what this was regarding; it could have been one of many options. Leia had found out about my mother, or she knew Camron was still alive. Either option, I dared not speak without giving a secret away.

'He goes nowhere until you tell me what is going on.'

'I am not privy to all Council requests, Simion. But what I know is if Maximus doesn't come willingly, these fine mages will help.' Leska could barely look at me. When she did, her brows pinched and lips screwed together.

Something haunted her. I searched for the answer in her bright eyes, willing her to tell me what was happening. She simply looked away.

Simion buzzed, still shielding me. I knew he would do

anything in his power to keep me out of the Council's grasp. But the more I refused them, the more it would jeopardise everything.

'Am I under arrest, Leska?' I fought to hide any proof of pain in my voice. My expression steeled, masking the pain I still suffered from the aftershocks of the kiss.

'No.' Her answer was final.

Well, that was something at least. Enough for me to steady my breathing and mind.

I placed a hand on Simion's arm, willing him to look at me. 'I'll go. Then you take me home, just as you promised.'

The muscles in Simion's jaw fluttered. His gaze told me that if he had to fight a way out for us, he would. That alone was my motivation.

'Together,' I whispered, 'remember?'

That seemed to calm him enough. He nodded, once and sharp. *Together*.

CHAPTER 15

Elder Leia sat upon her throne, staring down at the object in her hands. Her Council were on either of her side, all waiting in tense silence for her to say something. I caught Elder Cyder's eyes, trying to glean what he knew. All I saw was his concern, but for who I was yet to understand.

There was a terrible chill to the room—gone was the finery and elegance of the Ball. It had all been stripped away, leaving just an arched line of chairs, the burned Heart Oak and pillars of Avarian stone.

We had arrived and been ushered straight into the main chamber. Elder Leia had barely looked up from her hands. In them was a twig—a sprig with luscious green leaves cradling a bunch of small, red berries. Elder Leia had one of the berries between her forefinger and thumb, rolling it between them as she was lost in contemplation.

I didn't need to be told she held the token the Hawthorns had left behind. It was poetic, almost, that they used a cutting from the tree Simion's family name came from.

'If you have brought us here to convince us Beatrice has anything to do with this, you would be wasting your breath.'

Simion's deep voice echoed throughout the room, catching the attention of his aunt.

Leia looked up, the berry popping beneath the sudden force of her grip. Its juices dribbled blood-like gore down her fingers. 'Do you understand what this means? To the Council, to Wycombe? The rebellion seeks to undermine me, to turn our name against us in a plot to take hold of a fragmented city.'

'Beatrice has nothing to do with it,' I said, stepping forward until all eyes landed upon me. 'You know that.'

'Do I?' Elder Leia tilted her head inquisitively. 'Then who? Maximus? Or what about you, Simion? Do you see, if we do not act now, the people of this city will soon determine who is guilty? How many innocent people need to die before we stop this madness?'

'Harming Beatrice will hardly stop the Hawthorns. Do not fuel the flames,' I said.

'Flames,' Elder Leia barked. 'Something you would know all about.'

'We all do,' Simion added, posture straightening beside me.

I was not the only one to glance at the Heart Oak. It looked worse than it had days prior. And there was a smell—the scent of death. Rot.

'What would you suggest I do, oh wise Maximus Oaken?'

'Speak with them,' I replied. 'Everyone has something they want. Find out what it is and use it.'

'If only it was that simple. Not only are we dealing with them freeing the phoenix-possessed, but they have also abducted a number of our novices. This is serious. We are beyond conversation.'

Genuine concern darkened her eyes. The Heart Oak was not the only one suffering—Elder Leia was exhausted. It was clear in the shadows beneath her eyes and the ashen glint to her skin.

'You see,' she continued, 'I must worry about the many, not the few. Parents are missing their children, siblings are missing their siblings. Our focus is not breaking bread with the rebellion. It is stopping them, once and for all. And we know what they want… do we not? They wish to see the Council eradicated. They are working with the South to ruin us, to take power.'

That was what the phoenix-possessed were to Leia. Power. No different to a store of Heart Oak to be used as amplifiers. Except this was a power she could not control.

Simion radiated, practically trembling on the spot. 'That is why you kill them?'

Her gaze shot to Simion, frown deepening. She stood rigid, her eye sharp enough to stab through my body over and over. Fury boiled from her expression. It was the look of a person who was scrambling for control. The same look had crossed Jonathan Gathrax's face before I killed him. 'I did not ask for your audience to discuss politics. Please see that Maximus Oaken is taken to my personal study.'

'What for?' Simion demanded.

She looked at him, then at me, as her smile blossomed. 'Well, for the Claim of course.'

I stepped forward, body moving without thought. 'The Claim isn't for weeks.'

'You are wrong, Maximus Oaken. The Claim has been brought forward in the midst of everything happening in the city.'

Brought forward. The Claim. Beneath my feet the floor jolted. If it wasn't for Simion, I would've fallen to my knees.

'When?' It was all I could imagine.

'Immediately.'

* * *

I had to leave. I had to run. But doing so would mean fighting my way through a guard of battlemages, Leska. Doing so would turn attention to what I was running from, and *who* I was running to. If I had to act, I had to wait for the right moment.

To feign complacency, I did as was asked of me, all the while planning my escape. The clothes provided were much like my training leathers—a form-fitting, black, long-sleeved tunic that hooked around my thumbs and was held together by leather straps around my waist and chest. Slim trousers were tucked into tall boots, the cords tied into tight, thick knots. The only other item I was provided was a satchel with a single strap meant to rest over my shoulder and across my chest. Even as I changed, this didn't feel real. I was a phantom, limbs moving by their own accord, whilst my mind was trained on everything I was being forced to leave behind.

But I had no intention of leaving for the Claim. The second I had a chance to run, I would take it.

Leska leaned against the wall, one leg cocked as her arms crossed over her chest. She had yet to speak a word to me, but I knew she studied my every move. The horror in her stare was now clear. She had known about the Claim when she came to get us from the Mad Queen tavern.

Leia's personal office was modest and plain. Beside the wooden chair, a side cabinet and the pillars entirely encased with the roots from the Heart Oak, there was nothing else to look at. Nothing to distract myself with. No way out but the door at my back and the hallway filled with battlemages.

It seemed Leia knew I was a flight risk. But what she didn't account for was I would barrel anybody down if it meant getting back to my mother.

Time stretched out. I scratched at my legs, nails digging through the material of my trousers. The discomfort I caused myself was enough to slice through the tidal wave of thoughts that threatened to drag me away.

'You are not ready,' Leska said, finally breaking the silence. 'I know what you have to face, and I know you will not survive it.'

'Then stop it,' I hissed, unable to stop myself. 'See that I'm withdrawn.'

'That is not in my power, I am afraid.'

I swallowed the lump in my throat, locking eyes with her. 'Did you get to say goodbye to your father before you went? This is punishment, Leska.'

'Are you suggesting there is something you deserve punishment for?'

It was on the tip of my tongue, to tell her everything. I didn't trust her, not at all. But desperate times called for desperate measures, and I was losing my grip on what was dangerous or worth the risk.

Leska kicked off the wall, azure eyes narrowing beneath the lip of her dark fringe. 'Only your confidence will decide whether you live or die, Max. Make sure you don't put my hard work to waste. If there is one thing about you, it is resilience. Use it.'

I paced across Leia's office. The grand window was set into the inner wall, giving a view of the ruined Heart Oak. It overlooked the main chamber room, a bird's eye view from the upper floor of the castle.

There was no searching for a way out of this. Leska ensured I didn't leave the room, and I was waiting on tenterhooks for Simion to return after his petition to call this off. Even from this room, I could hear his shouts and demands. When it suddenly went quiet, the silence was more frightening than the noise.

Everything rested on him being victorious. He was my final chance before I fought myself free.

'I don't want this,' I said, more to myself than to Leska.

'And what do you want?'

Her question was poised. Loaded. I turned to face her, only to notice that she was fiddling with something, keeping her hands occupied whilst her mind was focused on her anxieties. It took me a moment to realise what it was she held.

A feather.

The blood drained from my face. 'Where did you find that?'

Leska looked down at her fingers, thumb and finger brushing the bright feathers of yellow, orange and red. 'I just—'

'Spit it out.' I stormed towards her, heart thundering out of my ribs. 'Where!'

Leska looked to the desk, Leia's desk.

My body spun. Why would a phoenix feather be on the desk? It didn't make sense.

'It was on that book,' Leska said from behind me, pointing just to my side.

The book sat at the centre of the desk. Its cover had been stained a dark navy, plain and without embellishments. The pages were bent and the spine all but ruined. Opening it, I realised it was a journal. A single name was scrawled on the first page. As I read it, dread, unending and devouring, swallowed me whole.

'Camron Calzmir,' I said aloud, finger tracing over the grooves the penmanship had made in the sun-stained parchment. This ink was not fresh and had likely been written a long time ago. His name had smudged slightly, the page crisp where I touched. I had no doubt it was water damaged, a dark smudge lingering halfway up the parchment. The pages had wrinkled, torn in places. Panic clawed itself up my throat, squeezing and scratching. Breathing became impossible. His name. It imprinted itself into the dark of my mind. No matter how hard I pushed the heels of my palms into my eyes, no matter how many times I slammed my knuckles to my temple, I couldn't rid myself of it.

Noise erupted from beyond the room. It afforded me a moment of distraction, enough to slam the book close and slip it into the satchel.

Simion burst into the study, Elder Cyder following close behind. The door slammed hard into the wall, cracking brick from the force. Battlemages. I counted six of them, each adorned with a curled dragon emblem on their breastplates. They filled the corridor, reminding me of who I would need to pass to get back to my mother.

I barely moved an inch before Simion threw his arms around me and pulled me into him.

'Did it work?' I asked, voice muffled by the hardness of his chest. 'Tell me you fixed this?'

Simion shook, his entire body vibrating with unspent ire. It quickly shifted from him offering me required comfort, to me giving it to him. 'There is nothing we can do. The Claim *has* been brought forward. The other novices are being gathered as we speak.'

The room swayed, shifting beneath my feet.

'Max, we must use these precious moments to prepare you to leave. Leia will be sending an escort to collect you shortly—'

'I can't,' I muttered, no longer caring for those who stood in the room. 'I can't leave her.'

Elder Cyder knew exactly who I spoke about. He held my eyes, looking deep in my soul with a look of powerful regret. 'There is no way out of this, I'm sorry.'

'What are you not telling me?' Simion took my hand in his, thumb dusting his usual circle across the back of my hand. 'Out of what?'

Elder Cyder quickly shut the door, blocking the view of my guards. When he turned back to the room, it was to look directly at me. Although he didn't speak, his eyes said a thousand words.

'I can't leave, Simion,' I said, no longer caring to hide the secret. Magic was boiling beneath my skin. Cords of silver light shone around me, flickering into existence, begging for me to reach out and grasp.

Simion sensed the spike of power and took my hand in his. He didn't mean to, but he sapped the emotions out of me without question. Everything slipped away from me. I snatched my hand back, trying to grasp onto a scrap of my panic, but failing.

'It's my mother,' I hissed. I knew I had to get to her, but the desperation was nothing more than a simmering flame within me.

Simion's face softened, lips pulling back in some forced offering of calm he wished to share with me. 'Deborah will be fine...'

'She is *sick*, Simion.' It came out of me without thought. 'My mother... she has the—'

'Careful,' Elder Cyder warned, the single word drawn out.

There was no room for caring. He either found out the truth now, or after I brought this entire castle down just to get to her. 'She has the burning plague.'

Simion's brow furrowed, his head shaking slightly as if what I said made no sense.

'What did you just say?' It was Leska who spoke whilst Simion continued to stare at me, dumbfounded, expecting me to tell him this was all some big lie.

'She is sick. Like those who attacked the library, just like Queen Romar and the refugees your aunt executed.' I shouted the next part, speaking solely from a place of panic. 'Like Camron.'

'Quiet,' Elder Cyder snapped, looking back to the door as though someone would burst in. 'Before unwanted ears hear this.'

'Father, you knew about this?' Leska moved with breakneck speed, straight towards the door. 'I need to tell...'

'No,' Elder Cyder snapped, slapping his palm upon the door, holding it closed. 'Leska, my daughter, you will keep this to yourself.'

'This is treason!' She looked between her father and me, eyes wide as realisation crested over her. 'You've been keeping this secret for him.'

'I have.'

Fury broke over Leska's face, mixed with panic. 'You know what Leia will do if she finds out.'

'My aunt will kill her,' Simion confirmed, stealing my attention back to him. 'We all know what will happen.'

Hearing it aloud made a rush of bile burn my throat.

'Because they are monsters!' Leska snapped. 'Are we forgetting what happened today?'

'They are our friends, family, neighbours. They are *not* monsters,' Elder Cyder still held his hand clapped over the door, fingers splayed.

The blood had drained from Simion's face, sapping the warmth from his sculpted cheeks.

'Simion is right, Elder Leia will have Deborah killed within moments of her discovering she is plagued.' Elder Cyder slowly retrieved his hand from the door. This time, Leska didn't move towards it. 'Daughter, do this for me. If you say anything, it will not only affect Max, but the whole of Aldian.'

Leska cast me a look, one with the power to see through every layer of my being. Then she was gone, slipping out of the room with the movements of someone who knew what they were doing.

'Stop her,' I shouted, unable to follow her as Simion grasped a hold of me.

Power hummed to life, my connection to the earth spiking to existence.

'Breathe,' Simion said, his face reflected in the misty glow of green that emanated from my wide eyes. He slipped his hand into mine. Magic spoiled the air between us. Then, as quickly as the tide, my anger slipped from my grasp.

For once, I didn't wish him to smother my emotions. They belonged to me, they gave me a sense of purpose, of power. Without them, I felt unprotected and helpless.

'How *dare* you,' I said, attempting to grasp the dregs of my anger. I was too late. Even without it, I understood what Simion did was wrong. He released my hands with little resistance. Then I slammed my palms into his chest and forced him back a step. 'You'll just allow her to storm out of this room and tell Leia?'

'Leska will not jeopardise your mother,' Elder Cyder said, slipping his body between us. 'I promise you.'

'How can I believe that?' *She hates me.*

Elder Cyder reached towards me, resting a hand on my shoulder. 'Because I know my daughter.'

Noise sounded beyond the doors, the beat of quick boots over stone mimicking the trembling of my heart.

'We have no time,' Simion said, glowering with defensive power as he regarded the battlemages as though they were his greatest enemies.

'Take me to her, Simion. You know why I can't leave her, please.'

Simion shot Elder Cyder a look. 'Stall for me.'

I couldn't turn around to see how Cyder responded to the command. He stepped into my side and laid a hand on my shoulder.

'I promise, no harm will come to Deborah,' Elder Cyder whispered.

The door opened and the battlemages entered.

Tears filled my eyes. Simion may have taken my anger, only to give room for my sorrow to overwhelm me.

'This is for Maximus Oaken.' The battlemage who spoke held a wooden box in his hands. It was small, with intricate carvings of ivy across its closed lid.

Simion had stood vigil at my back, tension oozing from him in waves. He now moved towards the battlemage and tore the box from his grasp. 'I will be the one to do it.'

'We have been specifically commanded to—'

'I said I will fucking do it,' Simion bellowed.

The battlemage recoiled a step, eyes dropping to a spot on the floor. 'Yes, sir.'

'Perhaps, we wait outside,' Elder Cyder said, arms wide as he guided the battlemages from the room. 'They deserve a moment of privacy.'

My gaze was fixed on the corridor. I felt every stone, every brick, every inch of earth far beneath. Even the dying Heart Oak heeded my call.

Silver cords flickered back to life as my essence collided with my amplifier. I reached out, ready to pull on one, to bring this entire room down if it meant getting free.

'Maximus.' Elder Cyder stepped before me, the expression he shared was enough to snatch me from the moment of over-whelming magic. 'Do not do it.'

I shook, every inch of my body trembling violently. 'I can't leave her alone.'

'She will not be alone,' he answered, as Simion stiffened behind me. 'Before I leave you, I wish to say one thing, which I also told my daughter before she took part in the Claim.'

I held his gaze, refusing to look away. Selfishly, I looked at this man in a new light, needing fatherly words of wisdom more than I cared to admit.

'To discover one's weakness, we must first recognise one's strengths,' Elder Cyder said, jaw tensing. 'Remember that.'

Elder Cyder left, his words haunting me, beckoning for the guards to follow.

All the while, Simion didn't move. His head bowed over the box in his hands, shoulders rising and falling. Slowly, he looked up. As he did, the box was no longer closed. He had lifted the lid and revealed a strange contraption resting upon a bed of red satin. A glass vial was set atop a thin, pointed needle of metal.

'Help me.'

I reached for Simion, grasping his shirt in my fists so he couldn't look away. 'I just want to go home, Simion. Please, I don't want this anymore. My mother...'

He leaned in, his eyes still overwhelmed with sorrow. 'Nothing is going to happen to her. I promise you.'

I believed him, but that didn't mean he was right. 'Take me to her, please.' I pleaded for a final time.

Simion pinched his eyes closed, unable to look at me as he shook his head.

'Coward,' I spat, fists gripping tighter until I felt the tear of material against my nails. 'You're a coward, Simion.'

He didn't deny me, he didn't give me a reason to prove me wrong. Instead, he just stood there, unmoving in my grasp, eyes pinched closed.

'You were not wrong to keep it from me,' Simion said suddenly, tears brimming in his eyes.

His words gripped my throat and squeezed. I longed to offer him comfort as a single tear slipped down his cheek, but I dared not move.

'Then you know why I must go to her,' I said, trying to keep calm when all I wanted to do was push past him and run. Even if battlemages waited beyond the door, even if there was a city between me and my mother, I would break it all into pieces just to get to her.

'If you do this, it will only draw my aunt's eyes in Deborah's direction. You must complete the Claim. Do it for her, for your mother.' Simion's hand shook as he continued to hold the needle between us. 'Do you trust me, Maximus?'

I bit down on my lip until my mouth tasted of iron. 'That is not fair, Simion.'

'I know.' Simion reached for my hand, pulled back the sleeve until my skin was on show. 'None of this is fair.'

I tilted my head which throbbed with tension. 'Please...'

There was no doubt in my mind what was going to happen when Simion pressed the sharp end of the needle to my arm.

'If Camron is still a threat, you are going to need every arsenal, every possible power, at your disposal. You must complete the Claim, for your sake. This is my way of protecting you, Maximus, by giving you the tools you need to protect yourself. It is what your mother would want. It is what *you* need.'

'I could fail,' I breathed, 'like Leska did. There is nothing saying I will pass this, survive this.'

Simion looked at me, truly looked at me as though he was seeing through every illusion, every layer, vein, muscle and bone. He bore through my being with his wide, amber eyes that glowed with his belief. Belief in me, belief in what he said next.

'You will not fail,' Simion said, pressing the tip of the needle. It rested above the shadow of blue, a vein lingering just beneath the surface. 'That is not in your nature.'

I gasped as the needle broke skin. Blood blossomed as the stripe of metal slipped into my vein. Simion refused to look away from me, muttering under his breath as he threaded his fingers into the metal bow.

'I'm sorry. I'm sorry. I'm sorry.'

Pressure built within my vein, causing me to hiss. Simion's fingers pushed the metal hoops down, which forced the glass vial of liquid to empty into me. When there was no more liquid left, Simion carefully withdrew the needle, dropping it. It smashed on the floor, and he swept me into his arms.

My legs were the first to give out. Tingles spread up my thighs, across my lower back all the way until they reached the top of my spine where it met my skull.

'If anything happens to her,' I said, although it sounded as though I spoke beneath a body of water. 'She has medicine... Elder Cyder gave it to me... you must...'

Simion lowered his mouth and pressed his lips to my forehead.

I blinked and the world slipped from view as the liquid seemed to claim my mind as its own. In the dark, I saw the vial of aqua liquid waiting upon my mother's bedside.

'Focus on your task. Claim what is rightfully yours.' Simion brushed the chestnut curls from my forehead. I focused on his touch as the feeling of it faded. 'I'll keep her safe. I won't fail you.'

PART TWO

THE CLAIM

CHAPTER 16

The dream was different this time—so much so, for the first time, I felt more of a participant than a witness. It was as though I was physically there, my corporeal body standing in the midst of whatever dreamscape my mind had formed.

I stood before a mountain, snow blanketing the piercing tip that speared through the sky. Winds tore around me, frost wetting my feet, ice biting at my fingertips.

Beneath me the ground shuddered, a warning of what was to come. I fell backwards, crashing into the hard body of a tree. Its branches quivered and then I heard them. Roars echoed over stone, claws tore through rock.

Dragons.

I knew then what I was witnessing. Oribon had woken. An age long, ancient fury built within him, growing and growing until the ground shivered against my skin. Then, before me, the mountain split in two, carving apart as Oribon broke free. I recognised him from the procession in Wycombe but couldn't understand why he now ripped himself out of the mountain when it happened hundreds of years ago.

Stone rained down around me. And though my mind told me this was a dream, that didn't stop me from raising an arm to protect my face. Shrapnel scratched over my arm, flesh torn apart followed by pain. Once the world settled and the dream progressed, I looked down to see my jacket was torn and my skin parted by stone. Blood blossomed over stinging flesh, running like a river down my wrist and dripping onto the snowy bed beneath me.

Real pain, real wounds. This was like no nightmare I had ever experienced before.

The once-calm skies quickly filled with a chaos of warring dragons. Hordes of them, claws clashing with jaws, scales tearing until their blood rained down across the world.

They were free, but freedom came at the price of war. Blood was not the only thing to fall from the sky. Bodies of broken dragons rained around me, crashing heavily into the ground. I felt each thud in my bones, every shattered body caught by the snow and ice reverberated beneath my feet.

There was no running. I forced my body back onto the tree, hoping the branches above would shield me. My ears rang with the sound of battle, my tongue almost tasting the death in the air. Above, Oribon cut across the sky, bathing me in the icy winds of his wing beats. Then he seemed to look at me. Powerful and ancient eyes settled on me. Then he changed his path, directly for me, jaws open, teeth on display.

I opened my own mouth, inhaling as I prepared to scream. Ice bit down my throat, scorching my lungs. Something hard wrapped around my waist, limbs of branch and twig. Before Oribon reached me, before my scream could escape, I was tugged backwards and—

I woke beneath a blanket of snow. It weighed heavy on my limbs, covering my legs entirely. The side of my face pressed into a sheet of ice, stinging my skin.

My scream echoed over the barren landscape. Where I expected to see dragons in the sky, there was nothing but grey cloud. With my mind fuzzy from the draught Simion had injected into me, I couldn't fathom where I was, nor what was happening.

Frigid winds tore at my exposed skin. Each inhale scorched my lungs and turned my throat raw. Even my teeth ached. Drifts of fresh snow blew across the expanse around me, for as far as I could see there was nothing but white. Sheets of thick mist clung to the ground, swirling around my ankles like phantom snakes.

I allowed myself a moment to panic before I bit down on my cracked lip and took in the details my mind could manage. As I clawed myself out of the bed of snow, dragging my heavy, tired limbs and willing the tingles to fade, I took in the breathtaking view before me.

The sky was painted in blush pinks and oranges, signalling dawn. I couldn't fathom what had happened between Simion injecting me with the draught and this moment, but what I could understand was I no longer stood in Wycombe.

I had only seen the Avarian Crest—the triplet range of mountains that crowned the North of Aldian—from a distance. Now, I stood before them.

It was the same view the dream had showed me.

Something shifted at my back, and I span to face it. But it was just ice and snow falling from the skeletal limbs of a tree.

Focus. I had to focus. It seemed the effects of the draught lingered in my mind longer than it did in my body. It had been afternoon when I stood before the Council. If morning was now upon me, it meant I had slept for half a day. At least. There was no telling which morning I woke beneath.

I stood in the middle of an open expanse, with a sea of frost-coated pines stretching out before me until they thinned and broke apart as the ground raised towards the bases of the Avarian Crest. I thought I was alone. There was no other novice waking around me. No prints in the snow to suggest anyone else had been here in a while.

But I was wrong, so very wrong. I wasn't alone at all.

The tree moved again, limbs shifting as though blown by a gale.

'Fuck, fuck, fuck.' Snow muffled the sound of my shout. I drew on my magic, preparing myself to face an enemy. Then reality quickly caught up with me. The attack, my mother, the pain that shot through my body after kissing Simion. And then there was the creature standing sentinel before me.

A dryad.

It watched me, wary and familiar, with a face carved into the bark of its trunk. We regarded one another, two strangers who were not strangers at all. I reached out to my magic, recognising the same residual glow around the dryad that I had seen around the Heart Oak.

It creaked and cracked, conversing me with sounds I couldn't understand. But what I knew for a fact was what I had seen was no dream—it was a memory.

'Not a memory. A moment.'

The ancient voice was both everywhere and nowhere.

'Is that what happened here?' I said, blinking and seeing the dream and reality blend into one.

The dryad shifted, snow dusting off its branches. I stumbled backwards, falling onto my hands. A strange pain shuddered up my left arm. To my horror, my jacket was torn and my skin parted—just like it had in the dream.

'Yes,' the dryad answered.

I waited for more, barely able to breathe. Between the wound on my arm and the resounding answer that filled my head, I was lost to confusion. But the dryad closed its eyes and settled, the creaking fading to a low tremble. Then it all stopped, and the tree was once again a tree—the dryad had fallen back into slumber.

Time stilled, as did the world. I don't know how long I stood there, waiting for the dryad to move again.

But I knew, without a doubt, it was real. All of it had been real.

I stood out compared to the expanse of white around me. My clothes were made from the same breathable material I had grown used to in training. It would keep my body heat in, and the cold out—but for that I had to generate heat. Move. I had to move. The woollen cloak was sodden from melted snow and slush. It weighed heavy on my shoulders but kept the chill from my bare neck.

My satchel was buried in a mound of snow beside me. I pulled it free, the brown leather glistening and wet. One look inside and I knew Camron's journal was still there, just where I had put it. But I wasn't brave enough to touch it, let alone think about it.

Why did Elder Leia have it? More importantly, how?

Beside the amplifier around my finger, I had no other weapons. All I had was the clothes on my back and the kindling of determination in my chest. I closed the satchel and drew it over my shoulder.

For now, I had other thoughts to occupy myself with.

Survive.

I remembered what Elder Cyder said about the trials we would face. Perhaps simply surviving long enough to find the dragon eggs was one of them. But dragon eggs were not my concern. I had to get home.

Even if I longed to make my way back to Wycombe, to my mother, I hadn't an idea of where to go.

I didn't think before I tore the walls down around my mind. There was no room for action and consequence, as I opened my mind and screamed for Simion. His name ricocheted across my skull, bouncing from bone to bone. No matter how loud my presence called for him, how demanding my will for him to hear was, Simion didn't respond.

There was nothing but silence, both in me and around me.

I was shaking, but not from the cold. It was my helpless fear. I had been taken from Wycombe, taken from my mother.

Dryads, the thought of her almost had me falling back to the ground. I couldn't steady my breathing as images of her flooded me. But I had to trust Simion to help her. I had to put my belief in Leska and Elder Cyder that they would not turn my mother in to the Council, knowing what they would do to her.

My panic shifted to anger in the blink of an eye.

Now I shook for another reason. Thoughts of my mother in the hands of the Council made me rage.

I had to get to her.

That desire alone moved me.

If I was to find a path back to Wycombe, I needed height. I could waste my time, and risk my life, searching blindly for the direction back to Wycombe, but if I could see it, then I would have a better idea of where to go.

I trudged through the inches of snow, passing into the shadows of the pine forest that was before me. Beneath the protection of the canopy, the snowfall was not as heavy. Walking was easier, as was breathing. Even if each inhale through my nose reminded me of Simion.

His scent was everywhere. It both weakened me and kept me going.

The further I walked, the more I knew I didn't have a reliable plan. With each step, I was either taking myself further from the direction back to Wycombe or closer—I couldn't be sure. What I did know was the Avarian Crest was leagues from the city. There was no way I could get back to Mother by foot—not without weeks on the road.

And I didn't have the time.

If I had to make it to her, I had to pass the Claim. And quickly.

Maybe I could trick them, make them think I found what I was looking for only to then force them to take me back to Wycombe city. Even if they refused me, I knew there was one thing that would ensure my return. The only other way to forfeit would be to find myself in a position that meant I couldn't physically continue.

It was fleeting, the thought. But it haunted me every step I took. The only way out of the Claim was if I could not partake, if my body was in no position to continue.

Could I do it? To protect my mother, to get back to her.

Yes, yes, I could.

CHAPTER 17

I lost my focus. Time fell away and no longer did I think about the trials I would face, or the dangers waiting for me at home. It was Camron Calzmir who poisoned my mind. I walked and walked, boots sodden with snow and ice, skin burned red from the cold until there was minimal light left, the world suddenly bathed in night.

I could barely think straight. I was starving, with griping pains in my stomach that made me feel violently unwell. But they were nothing compared to the thought of Camron. His journal was in the satchel. One part of me demanded to open the pages and find out why Leia would have it. Another part, the louder more demanding part, wanted to throw it into the snow, bury it and never think about it, or him, again.

Somehow, I knew I wasn't strong enough for that.

I heard the stream before I saw it. The song of water cascading over stones, ice cracking beneath the forceful ravine. It drew me towards it until I found crystal-clear water running rapidly down the hill. It cut through the ground, rumbling over the brook. I practically fell before it, cupping my hands into the cool water before bringing it to my mouth and drinking in hearty, desperate gulps.

Icy waters stung my throat. But at least it was something. I didn't have room to care about the pain, not when the water soothed my insides and provided me some clarity.

Snow was beginning to fall again. Although there were trees around me, the cover was not as forgiving as it had been. Eventually, I would need to sleep, but I couldn't risk going back on myself just to find cover.

I had to continue ahead, even if it felt as though I was making no progress at all. Although the forest around me changed, the Avarian Crest never seemed closer. I was walking, endlessly, with no hope to ever leave.

Was this one of the trials? It might have been. Elder Cyder hadn't told me how the trials would appear, only that they would test three things. Selflessness, sanity and sacrifice. And this was certainly testing my sanity.

I drank until I couldn't take any more. The water ran in the direction I had come from, so I knew I had to follow it. It confirmed I was moving up an incline, as did my screaming thigh muscles. At least I would have access to drink, but even if the brook was shallow, there were no fish that I could catch.

Water would do for now. But, eventually, I would need to eat. With night falling and the threat of a snowstorm minutes from hitting, I had to find cover first.

I continued forging ahead, following the stream for hope it would take me to a vantage point to see across the land, where I could see the way back to Wycombe. Large flakes of snow fell around me, blinding my vision and leaving scalding kisses across my face. I'd drawn the hood of my cloak over me, but it muffled the sounds around me, proving how important my senses where in such a place.

My spine screamed for reprieve, my muscles and lungs burning. I raised an arm before me as the snowfall went from gentle to unforgiving. It was so heavy I could hardly see the stream I followed, let alone hear it.

The snowstorm and night became one. It longed to destroy

me. Panic seized at my mind, narrowing my focus on one thing. Survival, even if that concept was becoming harder to grasp.

A bolt flashed overheard, turning the world a stark white. It was so sudden I almost missed it. Then it happened again. And again. Thunder rumbled through the dark skies, followed by another bolt of lightning. Except the snakes of light didn't move naturally as I'd expect from a storm.

It shot downwards, as though it was conjured. And the taste of magic coated my tongue. The lightning was not natural. Another mage was close.

Something was wrong. I felt it in every whip of the stark-blue serpents, in every rumble of thunder. The lightning fell like rain, splitting the night apart until every flake of snow was highlighted. Suddenly, I no longer worried about my survival, but whoever drew magic with such ferocity. Such desperation.

Before another bolt split the dark again, a violent scream lit the air. Then, I was running. Not away from the magic, but towards it.

The heavy air was charged with power. It lifted the hairs on my arms and neck. I fought against the downpour of snow and the deep mounds underfoot that slowed my pace. I reached a sheer wall of rock, a path etched into its side. On quickened feet, I followed it around. It curved as I continued to climb higher. The further I moved, the closer to the screams I got. It was so close I tasted magic in the air. So close the thunderous roar of something monstrous wormed into my bones.

My heart was in my throat, pounding with urgency. There was no knowing what threat lurked ahead, but from the roar it released, my mind painted an image of something large.

It sounded gargantuan and powerful.

'No!' a muffled voice shouted, buried by the crash of stone and the hiss of lighting. 'Sophia. No—*ahh.*'

The stone beneath my hands rumbled. I thought it was from more use of power, but this was different. It echoed the sound of a heavy body moving. *Thud. Thud. Thud.*

More lightning. More screaming.

My feet picked up speed until I was running, blindly, towards the chaos. I turned the final corner, chest thundering with anxiety. My body came to an abrupt stop as I finally saw the cause of the magic, the screams, the air-shattering roars. Everything before me was suddenly bathed in the glow of Avarian stone. I had reached a podium of rock, giving way to a cliff edge. The mouth of a cave was carved into the wall, deep and endless in its shadows.

But it was what stood between me and the cave that had my blood turn to ice, my magic flooding.

A creature stood on its hind legs, hunched over something out of sight, before the dark opening of a cave. Its back was broad and coated in thick white hair. Powerful, long arms, draped on either side of its body, ended in pointed claws. I first thought it was a bear of sorts, but no bear stood over fifteen feet tall, had curling tusks protruding from a hanging jaw.

It didn't seem to have noticed me, not as it unleashed a spittle-loaded roar towards the figure who crouched in the entrance of the cave. As another bolt of lightning cast down from the open skies, crashing before the creature to keep it back, I saw the mage's face.

It was Dayn.

The young novice glowered at the monster, teeth bared. Violet eyes wide with fear, his expression one of a person who faced their impending doom. It wasn't that Dayn cowered before the beast, but that he was bent over something outstretched on the floor before him. A corpse, split in two at the waist. Blood reflected the stark-blue light of Dayn's lightning, a puddle spreading between the two parts of the body.

Bile crept up my throat as my mind pieced together the parts of this story I had missed. I recognised death well—even before I caught the iron tang of blood on the winter winds.

It had been a... girl.

The beast expelled an agonising cry as a bolt of lightning

crashed into its chest. Flesh sizzled, fur scorched, but still it was not felled.

It shook its maw, smashed its foot into the ground, then charged.

Intent. Focus. Power. I reached out for the thick roots that lingered throughout the stone wall. They were mine. They belonged to me.

It was *all* mine.

As the monster ran at Dayn, my roots broke free of the earth and shot towards the beast. Starved serpents encased the monster's body, wrapping around its arms, legs, fur-lined torso, until it was bound entirely in my power.

'Dayn,' I screamed, 'run!' He levelled his eyes with me, brows furrowing after a moment of relief. Time stretched out, sounds muffled and faint.

'No.' Dayn shook his head, offering a glance to the body beneath him. I recognised her then, the body Dayn cowered over. Sophia. The girl who had danced with Dayn during the Ball just days ago. Gold hair, wide blue eyes and a gentle smile.

The memory fled as the monster pulled against my bindings. It was strong. One by one the roots broke apart, allowing for the creature to thrash and jolt.

I hadn't seen its eyes before, but now I couldn't look anywhere but into them. Black as night, they drank in the light and refused to let it go. Its protruding nose was something that belonged on a hog, as were the tusks stained yellow and brown from rotten flesh and blood.

I felt each snap of the roots as though the creature tore at the tendons in my body.

'It killed her,' Dayn shouted, fury in every breathless word, more lightning careless slamming into the ground. 'It killed Sophia!'

It was only brief, but as the monster ripped away at the roots, I saw the white fur around its paws stained with fresh blood. It had splashed across its belly, turning its pelt black.

And it will kill us if we don't run. It was such a hot, sudden thought. But I felt the refusal in Dayn. And I, in some strange way, saw Beatrice in Sophia.

'I will not leave you,' Dayn shouted. It wasn't me he spoke to, but the body laid out in his arms.

If the tables were turned, I would never run.

I hadn't when the worcupines attacked us. Nor did I flee when Camron laid siege to the city.

'Then we finish it,' I said. 'Together.'

Dayn answered with lightning, drawing more from the heavy clouds until the air fizzed with heat and power.

For every root I called upon, the monster snapped another. My teeth bit down into my lip; a feral, desperate growl rumbled from deep within my chest. Even my feet slipped across the stone ground as the creature continued to tug and pull against me.

We threw everything we had at it, but it seemed its body was resistant to magic. Its hide reflected the attempts, its muscles broke through root and stone. It was only when the bolts reached its skull or underbelly that the monster seemed to stumble back.

The final roots I conjured shattered apart, falling around the feet of the monster. It towered, throwing its head back into the night and unleashing a roar that sang with the promise of death.

Its focus was on me.

Behind me was the sheer drop to the ground below. Before me was the monster.

The ground trembled as it dropped onto all fours, front paws padding the ground, claws gouging scars into the stone.

In a blink, it charged.

I threw myself out of its way, landing awkwardly on my side. Pain thundered through my body, arcing up my spine. *Fuck.* More lightning crashed down, crackling across the stone like snakes of fire. Where Dayn's power touched, it charred the stone black.

Before the creature's momentum stole it over the platform's edge, it skidded and turned, tusks shaking violently. Foul mist exploded out of its jaw, followed by a roar of frustration.

It charged again. Still lying on the ground, I saw my death race towards me.

Dayn was suddenly there, hands raised as he unleashed a howl of his own. His palms were stained with blood, fingers tacky and glowing with raw power.

Shards of stone erupted beneath the creature. They tore into its paws as it barrelled towards us, ripping flesh and fur apart like the teeth of small beasts.

The attack didn't stop it, not completely, but Dayn did slow the monster down enough for me to stand and gather myself.

Lightning boiled across my skin, lifting every hair to standing. Winds roared as the storm formed within me. It built and built and built until I felt it press outwards from every inch of skin.

This creature was every person who had stood against me. It was Julian, Jonathan, Aaron, Camron. And it was every unnamed person who continued to plot to do the same.

Anger and fury were powerful, but I had stores of something far more feral.

I had grief.

I reached down, clawing past my shields until I located the emotion I had buried since my father died. It reached up for me too, expectant hands grasping for me to pick it up, like a child to a parent.

A whip of boiling light flashed down atop the creature's back, forcing it into the ground, four limbs splaying outwards on all sides. The might was enough to shatter bone. Where the boiling line touched the creature, fire erupted across its back, casting its broad fur-lined shoulders in wings of red flame.

Immobilising fear stilled me as I focused on the fire.

The kiss of flame licked across my cheeks, tearing me from one horror to another. I couldn't move, I couldn't think. My breathing grew harsh and a wave of sickness crest over me, breaking like a wave and dragging me helplessly into it.

The world blurred as all my focus fixated on the fire. Fixated on the man who haunted me from within the flames.

Camron.

My senses were muted. My understanding of what was happening muffled.

The monster seemed to sink into the ground, except that was not my doing. I no longer had a grasp on my power. It slipped through my fingers, evading me. Betraying me.

'Max.' I turned my head towards the voice, expecting another to be standing beside me. Not Dayn. Heat licked the side of my face, casting us both in a glow of boiling red.

Sweat slipped down Dayn's temple, his mouth curled into a snarl. His chest rose and fell, his hands shook before him. Still, he forced his power into the earth. Then Dayn looked at me with wide eyes, confusion lingering within them, and begged. 'Do something. Please.'

The monster continued to thrash, spittle flying over us, the harsh breath of death lancing through our senses.

'I... I can't.' Even if I wanted to, there was nothing to grasp. No power to aid me. There was only fire, flame, ruin. Camron. Camron. I blinked and saw it. It was everywhere. Across my skin. Across my mind.

'Finish... it!' Dayn shook as he shouted at me, crying like the broken child he was.

I recognised the look on his face, of his inability to hold on for much longer. Whatever this monster was built from, it was pure strength, power and resilience. Even with its back encased in fire, even with its limbs captured beneath the stone, it continued to fight.

Stone broke apart, bone shattered. The monster escaped, thrusting its body out of the confines, its back still ravaged with flame. Dayn threw himself before me, shielding me without thought. The beast thrust out a powerful, flame-coated, limb. One moment Dayn was standing, the next he was thrown backwards as the monster smashed into him.

My body reverberated as Dayn hit the ground with a deafening thump. Time slowed as I waited for him to move, to push himself up.

But he didn't.

My fear extinguished. Like a candle blown out by weak breath, it was gone.

I faced the monster. Its arms and legs were broken, but that didn't stop it from dragging itself over the ground towards me. Saliva and blood dripped from its jaw, trailing the ground beneath it.

It was determined and feral—a creature with no understanding of its own pain. Its weakness paled in comparison to its anger.

My magic sang to me until I was full of it, utterly bursting with untapped potential.

The creature dragged itself behind me, slow but steady. It crawled beneath the shadow of stone that hovered above us both. Not caring for my position, I closed my eyes and thrust my power into the stone above me. Hungry, dark eyes were fixed on me; it didn't see as the stone broke and fell.

Death wasn't painful. If I expected my body to be crushed, my skull to pop beneath the weight of stone or my skin to smash like the skin of fruit between teeth, I was wrong. I heard the thunderous crash and felt the ground shake. Something harsh grabbed the back of my neck and yanked me hard.

My eyes flew open to see the stone I was prepared to bring atop me and the beast fall only on the monster. As the chunk of rock fell on the monster's head, all I heard was the wet pop. Blood misted the air, spraying my legs in a film of warm gore.

'You could've died,' a small voice screamed into my ear. I was on the ground, Dayn's little arms wrapped around my neck as he held me. Rubble rolled over the ground near my boots, so close it only proved that I had nearly faced the same end as the monster.

As the death notch etched itself onto the amplifier around my finger, I felt the score of wood as visceral as if a knife was brought to my bone. I added this creature's life to the tally I was collecting.

'I didn't have a choice,' I expelled, breathless and wide-eyed. It was as though I was both there and not, watching on from some sunken place in my mind. Dayn was right. I was prepared to bring the chunk of stone down on me, if it meant saving him.

There had been no thought, only action. The realisation of this hitting me hard as I stared at the remains of the monster.

Flames continued to slither across the creature's back, devouring it in a blaze. Flesh hissed and sizzled whilst fur melted away until the skin beneath boiled.

There was no coming back from this. The monster was dead.

Above us the sky brightened. We both looked up as beautiful waves of emerald and blue hues filled the night. It cast the mouth of the cave in a beautiful glow, highlighting the horrors around us.

'We've passed…' Dayn muttered, neck craned to the sky.

I didn't need to ask Dayn what he meant. This had been a test, one of the trials.

The knowledge of it sparked my fury once again.

Tearing my eyes from the glowing sky, I looked to my side. The corpse of Sophia lingered, wide blue eyes staring endlessly at the night sky.

Whatever trial this was, we did not all come out victors.

'Sophia…' Dayn said, pain lancing across his face. He called out her name as though it would bring her back to life. 'Sophia!'

'I'm so sorry, Dayn.'

I held my breath as I took him into my arms. He buried his face into me, sobbing beneath the glowing sky.

Dayn didn't hear my apology. His youthful face creased as he unleashed a torrent of tears. In that moment, I remembered just how young he was. This was a child—a child whose friend lay dead. A child who had been left out in the wilderness to complete a trial, a trial no one could possibly be prepared for, sent by the Council.

This was *their* doing.

'I've got you,' I whispered. There was no knowing if Dayn

heard me as his screams reached new pitches. For a second, I fought the urge to tell him to stop, not knowing what other creatures could be lurking—ready to attack.

But I couldn't. I simply held him until my cloak was damp from his tears, my ears ringing with the name Dayn continued to scream.

'Sophia. Sophia. Sophia.'

CHAPTER 18

It seemed as though the lights in the sky were moving towards the Avarian Crest. It held above us, flowing like rivers of emerald among the blanket of darkness. If this was our way out of this dense woodland, we had to take it.

A chill had settled into my bones as I watched Dayn lay his cloak over Sophia's body, until only a puddle of blood could be seen. He was mostly unhurt, beside a slight limp in his ankle, something I had no doubt he could heal when he was ready.

I swallowed a lump in my throat as Dayn placed his hand on Sophia's forehead, bowed over her and offered a moment of silent prayer.

There was an emptiness in his violet-hued eyes, a detached expression that told me he was physically here, but his mind was far off elsewhere. He sat beside me, the blazing fire burning before us as it ate away at the creature.

Dayn had called it a barubore. Unlike the worcupines I had encountered before, the barubore was a solitary creature. Due to their highly volatile and aggressive nature, there wouldn't be another close enough to cause us any problems. Which was why he didn't so much as ask, but tell me, that we were going to see the night through here.

Even in his grief, Dayn still took time to heal my wounds. Perhaps it gave him something else to focus on, which was better than drowning in what he had just experienced—what he had just lost.

To my luck, Dayn didn't question the wound on my arm. The one I received during the dream the dryad had showed me.

Dayn would've put it down to the barubore attack, which was fine by me. I don't think I could explain how I really got it— during a dream, a *moment* the dryad had forced me into.

'This is wrong,' I replied after a moment of silence. 'All of this.'

Dayn wrapped his arms around his legs, bringing his knees beneath his chin. He was so lost to his shock he couldn't utter a word in response. 'Oribon has shown us a way out of the Endless Wood.' Dayn looked skywards until his eyes reflected the brilliant lights in the night sky. 'A reward for passing our trial.'

'We've just nearly died.' I swallowed hard. 'What trial has been passed, how are we to know?'

'Sacrifice.' A tear rolled down his cheek. 'Sophia had to die for me to survive. That was my trial.'

It was the way Dayn said it that suggested he paid a different price to me. 'And mine?'

'You were willing to die to save me,' Dayn answered. 'If I didn't pull you back, you would be…' Dead, he didn't need to say it. 'It was a selfless act. The lights are proof we passed, that we are worthy to be guided to our next trial.'

My mind could hardly grasp what had happened with the barubore, let alone the fact we had just passed a trial.

'How did this happen?' I said, fighting the urge to look back at Sophia's covered corpse.

'It is my fault,' Dayn said, as he brought his knees up to his chest and rested his chin atop them. His eyes flickered with the reflection of the fire before us. 'I thought we would find a dragon egg here. If we had, then maybe we could be the first to get back to Wycombe. Instead, my decision killed her. There is no cheating Oribon's trials.'

Dayn had not needed to explain to me how Sophia died. From the stains of blood across the barubore's clawed paws and the way her body had been separated in two, I knew the creature had torn her apart. The thought alone made it easier to watch as the creature continued to burn before me.

'Blaming yourself will not bring her back,' I said.

'*Nothing* will bring her back,' Dayn hissed, the whites of his eyes red. If he had more tears to shed, he would have. 'I wish it was me, it should've been me.'

His voice as empty of emotion as his tired, red-rimmed eyes. 'Sophia—'

He glanced behind him to the mound of the corpse resting beneath the cloak. '—she couldn't stop it.' He whispered those final words. Dayn lost himself to the memory, wincing as though it replayed in his mind.

There were no words of comfort I could offer. Nothing I could say that could dilute the raw agony Dayn was going through. All I could do was sit beside him, offering my company as a means to remind him he was not alone.

'We need to keep moving,' Dayn said between sobs. 'Before Oribon's lights stop. Without them, there is no escaping the Endless Wood.'

I looked over the edge of the cliff, to the sky spoiled in magic I could not comprehend. This was the power of gods. But what I could see was my way home, to Wycombe. It was nothing but a smudge in the distance, a little mark of stone and light so far away it would've taken days to reach by foot.

'Max?' Dayn's voice croaked as he said my name. It was enough to draw my attention back to him, away from the only thing I had been focused on finding. My way *home*. 'Don't...' he sobbed, unable to get the words out quick enough. 'Don't leave me, Max. Please, don't leave me too.'

Something cracked deep inside of me. Dayn had reached in my mind and drew out my desires. I knelt down, gathering him into my arms whilst resting my chin on his head. Dayn grasped my shirt, nails scratching the skin beneath as he clung to me.

'Dayn, I promise, I am not going to leave you.'

'Thank you,' he muttered beneath his breath, before crumbling into a fit of tears. I offered him a hand, doing everything in my power not to look towards Wycombe again.

He took it.

'Let's keep moving, before more barubores come looking.'

* * *

We walked for what felt like an eternity. I hated the silence. I hated the little broken sobs that would fill it as Dayn followed at my side. He hadn't said a word to me since we left Sophia's corpse, covered in his cloak. But I knew each step away from her body was painful. As every step further into the Avarian Crest was for me.

'How does it work?' I said, attempting conversation with Dayn. Anything was better than this silence for another moment. 'Oribon lights the skies, and we follow? Could we not just walk aimlessly until we find a way out?'

Dayn took a moment to gather himself. The forest around us was coated in the iridescent glow of the brightened sky. It should've been night, but it was more like dawn.

'It's not Oribon's light that guides us out the Endless Forest, but a signal to the dryads who comprise it. Legend said Oribon only gives the dryads a signal when he is ready for us to move on. Then it is the dryads who clear the path out.'

The forest had thinned the further we walked. Every now and then we would hear creaks and groans. Was that the dryads moving to provide us with a clear path? My answer came quickly as the tree line stopped, giving way to a stretch of snow-coated hills and far-off mountains.

All at once, the sky faded, the light drawn away, returning it to the sheet of obsidian sky.

Seeing the world no longer bathed in Oribon's magic made it seem ominous. Dangerous. Bathed in the thick darkness of night, the moment we stepped outside of the forest, there was no hiding.

'We should get some rest,' I said. 'It is better to do it under-cover than out there.'

Dayn didn't refuse. 'We just passed a small cave. If we turn back, we can use it?'

Snow was beginning to fall heavier. It was as though Oribon had helped us, and now wished to test us again. 'That sounds like the best option.'

Dayn didn't need to be asked to lead the way. Without a word, he turned back and guided me to the cave he had found. It was close, only a few minutes back in the direction we had come. It waited beside the flat surface of a small lake. A narrow path led towards it, enough room to walk one at a time.

I used my power to make sure the area was clear. What we didn't need was more barubores to reveal themselves. Even using my magic, I knew I was depleted. I connected my essence to the earth, feeling inside for movement. But it was empty, beside the odd scuttling creature.

'If we can get some sleep, then we can be moving by first light.' We could still see the break in trees from here, the way out of the forest evident. I didn't want to tell Dayn that I trusted the dryads to help me.

It was so dark inside the cave I called upon my dragon-blessed power to guide me. I took a branch left outside of the cave and lifted it skywards. A burst of lightning shot downwards, crashing into the end of the wood. Fire burst to life, momentarily freezing me.

If it wasn't for the glow of flame reflecting off Dayn's face, I may not have pulled myself out of the suffocating fear.

He was my focus now. I did this for *him*.

Light bounced off the walls of our resting place. It was cold, freezing to the bone, but it was safe.

'This will do,' I said, offering my flame to another branch Dayn had picked up. Both buds of fire helped us navigate the cave. It was shallow, ending not that far in. Which was good, because it meant nothing could sneak in from behind. So I took up residence, facing the entrance.

'I'm not tired,' Dayn's lie echoed around the cavernous space. 'I'll keep first watch.'

'You may not be now, but if you don't get some rest, by tomorrow there is no way you'll survive what is to come.'

'I don't want to do this anymore,' Dayn said so quickly it snatched my breath away. 'I promised Sophia we would overcome the Claim. I promised her, Max. What is the point of trying if she is not here?'

'Dayn.' There was no hiding the command in my tone. It came from a place of caring, one that longed for him to close his eyes and give into the peace his mind could offer in sleep. 'All those questions you have asked, you will be able to answer for yourself once you have a clear head. Please. For Sophia, get some rest. You have a promise to keep, and you cannot do that unless you allow your body and magic to renew with sleep.'

Between the exhaustion from trekking all day, the use of magic, my hunger and now the emotional turmoil of facing my fear, which almost resulted in Dayn's name joining the list of those who died because of me—I felt as though I was on the verge of passing out.

Dayn stood still, body trembling from unspent emotion. I expected him to refuse me. He didn't.

'Here, have this.' I removed my cloak and offered it to him. His was currently shielding Sophia's corpse where we had left her. 'I'll take first watch. You sleep.'

'What if I can't?' Dayn questioned, his voice shaking in tandem with his hands.

'Put can't in your pocket, and pull out try,' I replied. 'That is all I'm asking. Just try.'

It became clear that we found cover at just the right time.

Drifts of snow fell outside, hissing as fat flakes smothered the view beyond. Between the screaming winds and the violent drop in temperature, a snowstorm was passing overhead. There was no telling what time of night it was, beside the deep-rooted exhaustion confirming it was late.

I took a seat against the far wall, pressing my back into the jagged stone in hopes the discomfort would keep me awake.

Dayn took himself to the other side of the cave, laid out my cloak across the ground and curled upon it. His back was to me, shoulders rising and falling as he cried beneath his breath.

We stayed like that for a while, sadness hanging over us in a heavy blanket. Soon enough the storm grew so vicious that I couldn't see an inch before the mouth of the cave. Dayn rolled over, his face tense as he attempted to keep his eyes closed. I could see he warred with the desire for sleep, although his body refused him it.

I began to hum. It was a soft tune that my mother had offered me in times when sleep evaded me.

Dayn opened his eyes, the lines across his forehead smoothing. He didn't say anything to me but shared a look that sang of his thanks. When he closed his eyes again, it was with ease. This time, he didn't struggle against sleep—he allowed it to take him.

Even when his round cheeks dried and his chest rose and fell in a steady rhythm, I didn't stop. I continued humming the lulling tune until my lips felt numb from the constant vibrations.

I didn't stop because I feared what I would think about if I didn't have something to focus on. Simion, Camron, my mother. They all lingered in the far reaches of my mind, willing to fill the void of silence at any given moment.

There was no room to think of them, not when Dayn was laid out before me. I felt an overwhelming sense of protection as I regarded him. He was only a child. A boy who had hardly seen the world, let alone experienced life, yet he had already faced death and stared it deep in its ugly maw.

If there was ever a reason to see the Claim through—I was looking at it.

Careful not to make noise, I reached my hand into my satchel and pulled free the journal that haunted me. I couldn't let him win. I wouldn't fear him anymore.

Whatever awaited me within the pages, I thirsted for the distraction.

A shiver coursed down my spine as my touch explored the cover. I ran my fingers gently across its face, sensing the phantom marks left by Camron's touch—the same marks that still tingled across my skin.

I cracked it open, pages crisp from old water damage. The first few were empty of writing, except for his name. My heart rose in my throat as I turned the yellowed sun-stained pages over. I found it again, nestled in the bottom corner.

Camron Calzmir.

I traced my finger over his name. Camron's writing was neat enough to read, but expressive. Proof of his privileged life of education, of wealth.

A few more turns of the crisp pages and I finally found more writing. I drew my eyes to the first line of his entry and began reading the words.

No, I *devoured* them.

And so my story begins. Mother, this is the start of a life, one I pick. Not one handed to me, but one I can earn. A story of my own, written by my hand, not yours.

I will never forget today, not for as long as I live. I have stolen this moment to write down the happenings, but, in truth, I wish I was up on deck with them all now. It does not feel right to be sat down here, in my chamber of plush fabrics and wealth, when I should be sharing an ale with my crew, celebrating the start of our journey.

Mother, you said I would empty the contents of my stomach the moment the ship set sail. Was it so hard to believe in me? I wish I could tell you how wrong you are. What I feel is far from sickness. The feeling inside my stomach is elation and freedom.

The smell of salt and warm wood, I hope it stays with me until the end of my days. If I could bottle up the scent and send it back to you, I would. Dryads, I would keep it in a vial around my neck and smell it whenever I needed reminding of this day.

Not that it will be forgotten.

I feel as though my life has only just begun. My life, Mother, not the one you wanted for me, but the one I found for myself.

There may be more time to journal tomorrow, but I must join the brave souls above deck.

Tonight, we drink. Tomorrow, we journey.

CHAPTER 19

Everything was blanketed in snow by the time morning arrived. Although the storm had passed, the air held a crisp bite that bore into my exposed skin. I blinked back the bright light, taking my time to come around.

I felt oddly rested. The type of feeling that makes waking up a slog. Usually, my mind would be racing from the nightmare I had been lost to, but this time there was nothing but quiet in my thoughts. No nightmare, no haunting visions. Of course, the peace didn't last long.

I had woken with Camron's journal laid out across my lap, my back aching and my neck stiff from sitting up all night. Seeing it, feeling its weight on my numb legs, was enough to tighten my lungs. Part of me longed to pick it up and throw it, the other part wanted me to gather it to my chest and never let go.

As my senses came to, I heard the telltale sound of breaking ice somewhere outside the cave. My head snapped in Dayn's direction, but the place he had slept was empty.

'Dayn?' I shouted, jumping up and shoving the journal back in my satchel.

It only took a few seconds for a reply, but dryads, they felt like the longest seconds of my life. 'I'm outside.'

A cool rush of relief flooded over my shoulders.

I found Dayn near the cave, standing over the ice-coated lake. A fixed frown of concentration was etched into his face as his hands moved back and forth. He controlled a large rock, hovering it over the icy layer of the water. Small fish swam beneath, toying with him. From the jagged hole already in the ice, the noise that I had heard was clearly a missed attempt to catch one.

'Do you want some help?' I offered.

Dayn's lip curled into a snarl, his teeth gritted as he replied. 'No. I can do it. I can—'

The boulder slipped from his control, smashing through the ice. He erupted in a howl of frustration, his emotions fuelling a far-off rumble of thunder.

'It's okay,' I said, pressing a hand to his shoulder. '*You're* okay.'

He slumped to the ground, defeated. I got my first good look at just how exhausted Dayn was. His skin had taken on a pale sheen, his eyes circled with deeply etched shadows. The smile I had grown used to seeing him with had completely faded, replaced by tears that began to fall from his eyes. And from his red-tipped nose, I could tell he had not long stopped.

'Take your time,' I offered, taking a seat next to him. Dayn gathered himself into a tight ball, legs drawn up to his chest with his arms wrapped around him.

'You don't look like you slept much,' I said, noticing the dark circles beneath his violet eyes.

'I didn't. Every time I closed my eyes, I saw Sophia. She was there, waiting to punish me...' Dayn turned and looked at me, his face ruined by his grief. 'My choices killed her, Max. I killed her—'

'Keep your mind on the task.' I wrapped an arm around his shoulders, reminding him I was there. There was something about the way he spoke of Sophia that made it seem like he was fading into another realm. 'None of this is your fault.'

He sniffed, clearing his nose with the back of his hand. 'Have you ever felt like you've lost a friend?'

The question floored me. My mind took me back to a cold cell, one I had been in myself. Except it was Beatrice who waited within it now, someone I had evaded for weeks. 'I have.'

'And did you feel like your world was ruined?'

'I did.'

Dayn slumped forward, head in his hands. 'Then you know that I can't do this. Not without her. She was my—'

'Dayn, you need to listen. I need you to do this, because dryads know I am not prepared. But you... *you* are. Focus on the steps before you, not those you took to get here. Dwelling on the past will only inhibit you from moving forward.'

Dayn bowed his head, tears falling between his parted legs. 'I can't just leave her there. Alone.'

I didn't know the young girl, but it pained me to know her corpse was left beyond the barubore's cave for the weather to claim her. 'I think I can say with confidence that Sophia wouldn't want you to stumble now. She would want you to focus, to complete this, if not for her in life, but in her memory.'

'What about her family?' Dayn looked up, breath fogging beyond his thin lips in a pale cloud. 'I failed them. I promised them I would look after her, but now she is...'

Dead. Dayn couldn't say it, and I didn't blame him.

'You're a child,' I said, feeling a swell of anger at the situation he was put into. 'Your responsibility should be protecting yourself. No one is going to blame you for what has happened.'

'But the Council—'

'*Fuck* the Council,' I repeated the same words Dayn had spat the night prior. 'They did this. They put you here to test you. If anyone's decisions killed Sophia, it is theirs, not yours. What is stopping them from gifting eggs to those who require them? I have no doubt they have the means to do so. Instead, they send children into the wild, knowing the dangers they might face.'

'This is Oribon's will. A way of testing us with trials, to prove that he made the right decision when he first blessed us as infants.'

'So we've been told,' I said, gazing out across the snow-coated forest. It hadn't changed during the night, the way out still clear as day. 'It's easier to hate the Council than an ancient dragon god.'

Dayn huffed a laugh, so brief I almost missed it.

I stood, offering a hand for him to take. 'Come on. We are going to finish this. We are going to get back and stand before them and see that *they* answer for Sophia's death.'

Dayn gazed defiantly at my hand. 'I *will* go back for her. When I have my egg, when I have my dragon, I will fly back here, find her and I *will* bring her home.'

His hand clasped into mine, and I pulled him from the ground with ease. His rosy cheeks were a deeper shade of red from the intense chill of the air.

'That's more like it,' I said, as something tugged in my chest, a tether pulling from my heart to a person far away, locked in a room in Saylam Academy. Beatrice filled my mind and refused to release me. For a moment, I was transported to a time before all of this, when it was Beatrice and I, blissfully unaware of each other's truths and lies.

'All right then,' I said, forcing those painful memories to the back of my skull. 'Which way do we go?'

Dayn wiped his face with the back of his sleeve, rolled back his shoulders and exhaled a tense breath. For the first time, I sensed his will in its attempt to keep him from looking back towards where we had buried Sophia. He turned his back on me, faced the same pathway that led away from the platform. It was etched into the stone wall, only enough for one to walk on it at a time.

'*Forwards*,' he repeated my early sentiment. 'Keep up, Max.'

Dread dropped in my stomach like a stone. 'I'll do my best.'

CHAPTER 20

The Thassalic Ocean despises us.

Not a day from the Calzmir coastline, and we have faced nothing but storm after storm. I almost think it is your doing, Mother, your desire to see me fail so I return to you with my tail between my legs.

But I would rather throw myself into the ocean before that becomes a reality.

I have not had a spare moment to document what has occurred because all hands have been required on deck to simply get us this far. The Unknown Isles are a week or two away and, if the turbulent seas this far from our destination are anything to go by, we may not make it.

There is a young lad aboard, perhaps no more than nine winters—his name is Ruhen. Maybe one day you will meet him. In a way, he reminds me of what I may have been if you had not suffocated me with your wants and aspirations. I was reluctant to allow him to join this journey, but how could I take away his desire for adventure? It would have made me no different than you, would it, Mother?

He has been working for our captain for almost two years and, after little conversation with him, I have discovered we both share an equal dream. A dream of adventure and freedom. The Unknown Isles are nameless, but I have promised Ruhen that when we discover them, I will name an island after him. I may even name one after you, would you like that? I already know you would, your ego has always been bloated.

Last night was the first time in almost eight days that we could all rest. The Thassalic went from violent to docile in a matter of hours, but I am not complaining. I am just happy to be alive.

Gosh, it is thrilling. I was not unaware of the risks of this journey, but nothing could have prepared me for the swaying and shouting, the camaraderie of the crew.

Ruhen is sleeping in my quarters whilst I write. He needs rest.

He believes he saw a person in the water. But this person he saw had hair of seaweed, a tail made of water and eyes as pale as milk. Ruhen said he heard them crying and looked overboard. He was hysterical. By the time we reached him, the person was gone, of course it was.

Madness is coming for us.

Do you know what he said to me, before sleep claimed him?

He said that we had displeased the gods of the sea. The nymphs do not welcome us in their domain. Between the pissing of sailors overboard and the vomiting, no ocean-bound creature would be happy to have us sailing over them.

I shall keep my eyes peeled, though, Mother. If only I can come back and tell you I saw one myself. Now, wouldn't that be a story? Perhaps it would even make you proud.

Hopefully, it will not be another nine days until I write to you. I missed you. Can you believe that?

When you read this, know I will be sleeping beneath the stars. There are so many out here. The sky is full of them.

It is beauty beyond compare.

I closed Camron's journal, feeling as though I could breathe for the first time since starting to read. It was so distracting, so alluring. As I read Camron's own words, written by his hand, it was as though he whispered into my ear. I shouldn't want to know more, to continue turning the pages and devouring this story. But I couldn't stop myself. Yes, I hated him. But this person on the page, the one who filled my mind whether I was reading it or not, felt different. Another person, someone familiar yet not. Someone I had only met in moments.

The man before the monster.

I sensed Dayn, who watched me from the corner of his eye, not once asking what I was doing. But I recognised his wariness, as though he could read the atmosphere that oozed from the pages.

We had stopped for a break when we found a stream of water. Blisters had erupted across every one of my toes. I didn't dare complain as Dayn forged ahead, head bowed against the torrent of winds that sliced around us. But when I suggested we find something to drink, he didn't argue.

The terrain changed frequently, from harsh rock faces to shrouded expanses of icy forests. Regardless of where we walked, the ground beneath our feet was always sloped upwards.

I cupped mouthfuls of the spring, drinking until I was gasping for breath. Then I splashed the cold water across my face, waking my senses from the hours of our trek. We ate from the strips of meat Dayn had prepared, allowing ourselves a short moment to rest before we continued.

A pack of worcupines passed us later in the afternoon. They chased through the forest, in the valley below us, bounding over roots, in pursuit of something unseen. Their presence confirmed we were on the right track. After my last encounter with the poison-tipped creatures, I knew that they were feral for the flesh of a dragon. If there were worcupines, there were dragons close by. If there were dragons, there would be eggs.

And we could hear them. The song of large-winged creatures echoing over the barren landscape. The winds carried the sound, growing louder the closer we gained on the three points of the Avarian Crest.

The sun was setting, disappearing over the top of the snow-covered hill. Night would be upon us soon, and it was best we found somewhere to make camp until morning.

'Dayn,' I said, chasing up a step until I was beside him. 'We should think about finding a place to see the night through.'

He shot me a confused look. 'Look around you, Max. There is nothing but hill and open sky. Unless you want to head back into the forest and curl up next to the worcupines, we keep moving.'

Something had bothered him, but I hadn't placed my finger on it yet. His entire demeanour had changed from when we had woken. I put it down to exhaustion, but I knew that wasn't entirely the reason for it.

'We keep moving until we reach the top of this hill,' I said sharply. A day of walking and silence had taken its toll on my patience. 'Then we find a place to stop.'

'But we are so close—'

He wasn't wrong. The further we travelled, the closer we gained to the base of the Avarian Crest. It almost felt too easy. After every step we took, I expected another trial, another test. There were two to go, but so far, nothing had happened.

'Dayn,' I snapped. 'I'm not asking, I'm telling.'

He rolled his eyes, scoffing beneath his breath. 'Fine.'

I had always wondered what having a younger sibling was like. Now I imagined it was no different to this. Youth made someone feel invincible as the thorns of a rose, age reminded us that we were as delicate as the petals those thorns protected.

The skin around my nails ached. I didn't know I was chewing them until the skin bled and I tasted it on my tongue. If I wasn't reading Camron's journal, I was thinking about my mother. Two nights had passed since I last saw her, and my imagination could conjure countless scenarios of what was happening to her.

'Something is bothering you,' Dayn said, breaking the silence. 'You might as well talk about it, we've got the time.'

'It's nothing,' I said, brushing him off with a forced smile. 'Although I could say the same for you. Care to share?'

How could I tell Dayn that my mother was phoenix-possessed? I had no way of knowing if she was still okay or not;

no matter how many times I reached out for Simion with my mind, there was only silence.

I longed for him. It was a physical reaction. There hadn't been a moment to truly contemplate his body climbing in the bath with me, his skin touching mine, his lips… In those quiet moments, Simion's memory filled them. It was easier to think of Simion than everything else I had been forced to leave behind.

'I'll offer a trade. One thought for another.' Dayn gave me a look riddled with pleading. 'Give my mind something else to think about, something other than…'

He didn't need to say her name, I saw the way Sophia had haunted him every step we took from her resting place.

'Nosey, you are.' I knocked into his shoulder with my elbow. 'If you are so inquisitive, I was thinking about what I was forced to leave behind.'

There was a moment of pause, the quiet filled by the crunching sounds of boots on the snow-covered ground.

'I heard you calling for *him*, you know,' Dayn said. 'This morning you were shouting in your sleep. It's what woke me.'

'Was I?' I don't remember dreaming, but that didn't mean I wasn't haunted by something. In fact, since the Claim began, I hadn't dreamt of anything beside the memory the dryad had shown me.

'Yes,' Dayn said, kicking at the inches of snow we waded through. 'I was going to wake you, but I thought you calmed down and I didn't want to disturb you.'

'I'm sorry if I frightened you.'

'I was awake anyway.' Dayn shrugged, screwing his mouth. 'Plus, I'm used to it. Before the Claim, I was put on nightshifts at the infirmary, I was used to hearing people shouting out for the ones they loved. In a way I think it is beautiful, to have something to occupy your mind even in times of sleep, or suffering.'

'Elder Cyder did tell me you were moved to the city infirmary. After the… incident at the Academy with the missing novices.'

The look Dayn shot to me was one of surprise. 'You know about that?'

I nodded, watching the tension ease from Dayn within seconds. 'I don't think I am supposed to, but I do.'

'Dryads, it has been terrible.' His shoulders slumped forward. 'We were sworn by the Council to keep it to ourselves.'

Sworn to secrecy? Was that because Elder Leia didn't want everyone knowing that people were disappearing under her nose? 'I met with Elder Cyder at the Academy when I came looking for you to fix my—'

'She broke your nose again, didn't she?' If Dayn wasn't walking, he would've popped a hip and raised his brows at me. 'Of course, Leska did.'

'Yes, but you weren't there to fix me up. Cyder did it instead, he... he told me about the abducted mages.'

'Abducted.' Dayn scoffed at the word, although his face was nothing but serious. 'That is what they told us too.'

'You don't believe it?'

Dayn looked at me, truly looked at me, as though he was trying to discern if he could trust me enough to answer the question. When he finally spoke, he clearly made his mind up. 'We gossip. There isn't much else to do between lessons. But I saw Leia, she visited the Academy before the Ball and hand-picked a small group to stay behind... something about needing gleamers for a task. Then suddenly'—Dayn lifted his fist before him and flicked his fingers out—'*Poof.* Gone.'

My blood pressure dropped, rushing from my skull to my feet. 'You... you think Leia has something to do with it?'

Cyder had said Leia had visited my mother the morning of the Ball.

Dayn nodded, face set in a grimace. 'Maybe.'

A sharp pain shot through my skull, enough for me to lift a finger to my temple and massage the area. 'What did she want from those who were asked to stay behind at the Academy?'

I was waiting, holding onto a thread for Dayn to answer me. 'I'm not sure.'

My mind was racing. It twisted and turned, building a story that involved Elder Leia and the missing mages. Then there was Camron's journal. All the anomalies felt connected.

I was so lost to my thoughts that I didn't notice when Dayn came to an abrupt stop. We had been walking up the face of the bulbous hill, pushing against the flurries of snow that blew across the landscape. By the time we reached the top, my lungs burned with every breath, whereas Dayn didn't seem as badly affected. He just stood, looking out across the world from our vantage point.

'Max, you really should see this.'

'What is it...' I trailed off, as my eyes fell upon what Dayn saw.

A corpse. It was half-buried by snow, glassy brown eyes staring up at the sky, skin as pale as the ice around it. The dead body wore the same dark clothing that me and Dayn had on. Except it was sodden with blood, fresh blood that still dribbled from the angry gash around their neck.

I could hardly move. 'Do you think a barubore did that?'

'No,' Dayn answered, his light voice cracking. 'This was a trial.'

Tearing my eyes from the body, I cast them out across the world. We stood on the top of a hill, with a view as far as we could see in every direction. The Avarian Crest stood proud, a sentinel of rock and stone. Its mountainous form was as tall as the sky itself; its snow-coated tip piercing the veil between the earth and air.

It was a god in its own right, leagues wide and far taller than anything I could ever imagine. It made Saylam Academy look like a humble cottage in comparison. But what drew our attention was something else. It was as though the mountain had cracked in two. From the side angle, no one would have known there was anything untoward about the mountain. But seeing it this close, it was like a blade had arched down from the heavens and cleaved the earth in two.

A glow of light oozed from the belly of the mountain, as though a star had fallen into the earth and burned. I had no doubt it was the same light that threaded through the stone in veins—drawing in the light of day and emitting it during the night. It could act as a beacon, keeping us going in the right direction, no matter the time of day.

An old poem came to mind, filling me with a sense of wonder as I looked on at the broken mountain. 'When the earth first moved, and the mountains cracked in two...'

'Out birthed dragons in their hordes, who claimed the skies as their new domain.' Dayn finished for me, his eyes lost to the view before us. 'We all know the story.'

'So, the South and the North agree on something,' I said, breathless from the beauty of the mountain. A cry sliced through the night, faint but impossible to ignore. I squinted, my heart thundering in my throat, as dragons flew from the pits of the mountain and danced in the air around it. Reds, blues, greys and blacks. A patchwork of scale and talons and it was... amazing.

Dayn nodded, reluctantly taking his gaze from the wonder ahead of us. 'Every mage born is brought to Oribon's domain. You would've been brought here, as was I. It is where he decides who is worthy of his blessing.'

When I looked back to the mountain range, I saw it in a different light. 'Oribon, the father dragon, he dwells inside there?'

'Yes,' Dayn said. 'He was believed to be the first dragon who broke free when the mountain split apart. Some even say it was his size alone that forced the mountain to break, freeing him and his children to fill the skies they belonged to.'

'The way you say it, you make it seem as though he was imprisoned there.'

'No one knows, but I can't help but wonder.' Dayn chewed his lip, lost in thought. 'Someone must have put the gods of air inside. How else would they be below the earth when they don't belong in it?'

I'd never thought about it as more than a myth. Dragons were real, of course, but mountains cracking in two, that was something out of stories.

Except, it wasn't.

'What trial is this?' I gestured back to the dead body at our feet.

Dayn lifted a finger and pointed out across the open landscape. I followed it, something catching my eyes, far off in the distance. Along the very path we stood on, flames bobbed in a line.

'The others,' I breathed, feeling a swell of relief. 'If we catch up with them—'

'No,' Dayn said, grasping my arm so suddenly his fingers pinched my skin. 'It was their trial, Max. Sacrifice.'

My mouth dried, my chest pained. 'They... they did this?'

He nodded his head once in confirmation.

'But why would Oribon want his chosen to kill others—'

'Oribon wouldn't,' Dayn answered. 'But there are no rules in his domain. It is not said how we prove our sanity, our selflessness or provide our sacrifice... only that we do it.'

'They would kill one of their own, just to get an egg?'

Dayn held my stare, his presence reaching deep inside. 'What would you do for something you've wanted all your life?'

The answer was simple. I thought of my mother, how I would give my life to protect hers. 'Anything.'

A shadow passed beneath Dayn's eyes as he contemplated my answer. 'We should keep at a distance. Let them test the path for us, where they walk, we know it is safe to go.'

There was something else Dayn was not telling me, I knew it just from looking at him. But I also knew if I asked him, he would conjure a lie.

Whatever he was hiding from me, he did so for a reason.

It strained my body to call upon my power. The reserves of it had dwindled from the constant moving and the exhaustion our travel had put me in. Without a clear mind, it was hard to grasp hold of my intention and focus on the intricacies of the magic. After burying the dead novice with their split neck and lifeless eyes, I was exhausted. As was Dayn.

Once the frozen ground had opened enough for the body to be buried deep within, we conjured four perfectly cut slabs of stone. They rose around us like walls, blocking out the world from view. Within the concealment of our stone-made tent, the sounds beyond were muffled.

It was as good as our protection from the weather could get.

I leaned against the slab of cold stone, wondering how I could offer him reprieve from the thoughts that haunted him when I was busy drowning in my own. My stomach cramped in hunger, my throat desperate for something to drink.

'You don't need to protect me from them,' I said finally. 'The other novices, that is what this is about, isn't it? Why you don't want us to get close to them.'

I expected Dayn to lie to me, to tell me I was wrong. He didn't. He looked up slowly, unable to hide his inner thoughts from his face.

'Do you remember I told you about the bets others place on you?' he asked, voice barely a whisper. 'Every day when you turn up for me to tend to your wounds, they all win coin on what will be broken and bruised.'

It didn't bother me before. I cared little for the games children played, especially if it involved me and my well-being. 'Let me guess, the same applies for me passing the Claim?'

'Not passing,' Dayn said, dropping the meat and crossing his arms over his chest. 'Surviving. When you turned up and saved me from the barubore, I was both elated and horrified. But if they find out you are here...'

A shiver passed over my skin and it had nothing to do with the drop in temperature at night.

Dayn's lips thinned, pulled into a taut, pale line. 'It was planned. Even before the Claim began, it was always what was going to happen. When you didn't wake with us on the first day, I thought it was because you were not partaking. I never felt relief like it. But now… now I know someone was protecting you. And that body we just buried… they were the price paid in your absence.'

A warmth filled my chest; knowing I had someone as loyal as Dayn to stand beside me made this easier. 'Don't waste your energy worrying about me, Dayn. I've faced worse than some young students. I'm not frightened of them, nor should you be.'

Wasn't I?

Dayn kept his hand outstretched, an offering for me. 'Believe me, I am not scared of them. Not for my sake.'

'Then all is fine.' I took his hand, squeezing firm. 'We rest here tonight, let the others complete the Claim. Then we will swing in after them, get our eggs, go home and make the Council answer for what has been lost—'

'Max,' Dayn interrupted, fingers cold as ice to the touch. 'Can I ask you something?'

I nodded. 'Go ahead.'

'Why do you call out for *him*?'

My mind flew back to Simion, as it had during the hours of the day. He was always there, lurking and waiting, ready to distract me.

'Simion is…' Is what? I had to toy with the concept, attempting to find the right word to voice aloud how I felt about him. 'Simion is… important to me.'

Dayn's eyes widened as he shook his head. 'Not Mage Hawthorn. The other one…'

'Who?' I tried to pull away, but his grip was firm.

'Camron,' Dayn said, grimacing as he spoke the name. 'You shouted the name of the man who destroyed my home. You called for him as though you wanted him to answer. Why?'

'I didn't…' Words slipped just out of my grasp.

Dayn's hardened mask melted into one of sorrow. Regret. 'Do you know that Sophia's sister died during the attacks? So did the parents of some of the novices who place bets on your life. She didn't blame you, but they do. Here, far from the Council, far from anything, there is nothing stopping them from seeking revenge. I know you're not scared of them, but I am.'

Nothing mattered, but the knowledge that I cried out for Camron in my sleep. The mention alone made me sick, turned my stomach in knots and made breathing close to impossible.

His voice grew hazy as the sudden tiredness sapped at my mind, my body.

'I couldn't protect Sophia, but I can protect you. Let me do this for you. I owe you my life.'

I blinked, unable to resist a wave of weakness that built in my mind.

'Dayn, what are you…' I couldn't finish. My mouth grew heavy, my tongue leaden and mind foggy.

A cool rush of tingles spread down across my skull, flooding across the rest of my body, all towards my connection with Dayn. His eyes glowed with a purple-misted hue as he drew on his power, grasped my tiredness and fuelled it.

The undulating wave of darkness enveloped me. It smothered my senses until I couldn't see, couldn't hear or speak.

'I suppose this is my next trial,' Dayn said, his outline blurring the heavier my eyes grew. 'It is my turn to be selfless and protect you.'

Dayn released my hand.

Then there was nothing.

I was alone.

Until *he* stepped into my mind.

CHAPTER 21

Camron waited for me in the dark.

He lurked in the shadows, his obsidian eyes scratching over my skin. There was some relief in finding Camron in this dreamscape, and not the monstrous creature with the army of shadows. Then again, whilst Camron might have looked like a beauty, he was more a monster than anything else.

I was no longer in the midst of the Avarian Crest, but back in Gathrax manor. Around me was the haunting red of Julian's bedchamber. And there Camron was, entering Julian's room, dark bleary eyes that drank in the light. Eyes that then burned with fire, furious strands of red and orange, twisting in a cyclone as he exposed the truth of himself to me.

I knew I was dreaming, but that didn't dilute the fear of seeing him. Nor the anger.

He presented himself before me, golden-blonde hair, strong-boned face shadowed by a well-trimmed beard. Freckles lining his lips. My mind had memorised this man to the finest detail, and it punished me with him.

He didn't speak, he didn't move. He just stood and watched me expectantly.

I screamed at him to do something, to say something. Over

and over, I cried his name until the darkness vibrated with it.

Then I woke, gagging on Camron's name as I broke myself free.

Stone shattered around me, every slab that had been erected for protection exploded outwards, forced by my power. Magic oozed from every one of my pores, slipping free of my ability to control it.

Breathless, I stood and scanned the dark. Aldian was engulfed in the shroud of night, there was no knowing how long it had been since Dayn had used his power to put me under. What I did know was I felt rejuvenated, as though I had slept deeply for days.

Which meant the reserves of power inside me were practically overflowing. I could feel it, pushing outwards, demanding release.

And Dayn was nowhere to be seen. But there was only one place he could have gone.

Before I could truly think, I was running. I forced my will and determination into every limb, vein, bone and vessel. My focus was on searching the dark landscape for a sign of him, but it was lightless. The only beacon that called to me was the Avarian Crest —the split mountain that was our destination.

That was where he had gone, I knew. So I would follow.

Magic slammed within my chest, synchronised with the pounding of my legs, the beat of my frantic heart. It begged for release. I held it in, for now.

I screamed Dayn's name at the top of my lungs until my throat burned. But the night swallowed the sound. Winds tore at the open skies, catching snow whilst attempting to blind me. Head down, my entire focus on my destination, I barrelled forward.

The hill gave way to a ridge, a narrow path that wound up and down across the landscape, leading to the mountain ahead. It glowed as a beacon, emitting the stores of light it had collected, bathing the view before me in an unnatural incandescent glow. The light was my guide. I focused on it, pushing myself to run faster, harder.

Dawn soon spread its dusky pink coat across the sky. So, I had been sleeping for longer than I had hoped. With morning, a frozen wind sliced across the sky, threatening to throw me down the sheer drop beside me.

Strange shapes soon revealed themselves as winds tore snow from the ground. Bones. They were everywhere. Large skulls gave way to long spines, half-exposed. Slithering pale snakes of skeletons, and what once must have been leather-bound wings.

It soon became clear the Avarian Crest was not only the birthplace of the dragons—it was their graveyard. Just as the dryad had shown me. When the dragons clawed themselves from their prison of stone, they tore at one another.

But why? War had a reason, I could not fathom what theirs had been.

It was not stone or rock that my boots crunched over but scales and teeth, small shards of bone and the shattered remnants of old gods.

The closer I gained on the mountain, the harsher the elements became. It seemed they, too, wished to keep me away. Winds buffeted against me, forceful pushes. My eyes stung, fat flakes of snow blinding me as clouds filled the sky and unleashed their fury. Blinded by the elements, I forged ahead through the dark.

Then it all stopped.

I stood at the precipice of a bridge made of stone. It glowed beneath my feet, veins of light thrumming through it, guiding me towards the arched opening set into the mountain.

Turning back, I watched as the snowstorm buffeted an invisible veil, falling outside of it, as though a curtain had been raised between me and the world.

I raised a hand, pushed it at the veil until the frozen bite of ice pinched at my fingers. *Magic.* I felt it, familiar yet entirely different. It was old—a presence so ancient it tickled across my skin; whispers of the unknown past. It was a feeling I had felt only once, when I grasped the Heart Oak and called upon its essence.

This was not dryad-born magic, this was the power of the dragons. It was ice and air, wind and song.

And I heard them, as if my thought alone conjured them into existence. Deep within the archway ahead, a chorus of sounds reached me. I had no doubt this would be where I would find Dayn, where I would discover the eggs.

It felt like a warning—a dangerous place. As though I was intruding on something.

It was then I felt the shifting of the earth, as though the mountain moved. A deep cawing sound came from within. Not inside the mountain's flesh as much as it *was* the mountain. Breathing. Slithering. It was as though something large lingered within the very walls I walked towards.

Oribon. The father of the dragons welcomed me into his domain, whilst warning me all the same.

I moved forward, feeling weightless as I peered over the side of the bridge. Teeth of ice and stone awaited to shred the poor soul who fell into the mountain's belly. The chasm was a gaping maw, ready to devour me whole.

One step and everything changed.

* * *

I fell forward on my hands and knees, rocked by a force that shattered my perspective. But when I looked back up, it wasn't to see the mouth of the Avarian Crest. It was to see a room, with familiar crimson wallpaper, plush furnishings and a crowd of people around me.

'My son, my son,' a voice drawled as a figure stepped free of the shadows. Orange wisps of hair clung to a balding skull, jewelled fingers twisted a thin beard, as piercing bright eyes looked down at me. 'Here is my son, I have found him.'

'King Gathrax?' I stammered, blinking away the vision. But it didn't fade, it didn't falter.

'It is I.' He opened his arms, beckoning me into him. 'And you have found your way back to me.'

'But...' Defiance unfurled in my stomach. 'I killed you.'

'Killed me?' His face turned down into a frown, his brow furrowing with deep lines, shadows stretching out beneath his haunting eyes. 'Oh dear, it would seem you need yet another reminder as to how my son behaves. As you know, compliance is the key.'

'This isn't real,' I said, looking around at Julian Gathrax's bedroom. There was the same hearth Simion had lit, the bed I had been chained to, the window that Beatrice had made me leave open.

King Gathrax laid his hand on my shoulder. The weight of it pressed down on me. I felt the bite of his nails through my jacket... my red velvet jacket. I lifted my arms, inspecting the impossible, only to find my skin was newly cleaned and smelled of lavender. I searched for the silver ink marks, but there was nothing but freckles and fine hair.

It should've filled me with relief; it didn't.

'I am very displeased with you, my son,' King Gathrax whispered into my ear, foul breath invading my nose. 'I give you everything you could want, wealth, power, comfort, and yet you throw it back in my face.'

I looked him dead in the eyes, growling with bared teeth. 'You are not real. You are dead.'

His laugh scratched over my skin, as did his scent and his touch. If he was dead, how did he feel so real? Cold fingers and a sickly scent of lavender like rot itching my nose.

'Because I *am* real,' King Gathrax answered, patting my shoulder before finally letting me go. 'Silas, bring in Julian's next test.'

My head snapped towards the door, to find it occupied with two people. People I never thought I would see again.

'Dad?' I watched, frozen to the spot, as my father walked into the room. His hands were bound before him, smile spread over his familiar face, blue-grey eyes, sun-kissed skin. It was him. His very aura felt as real as the floor beneath my feet. I took a step towards him, desperate to hear his deep, rumbling voice.

But it was another who answered for him.

'*Husband.*'

Camron Calzmir walked into the room, his hands also bound before him. It was as though he had been plucked out of my last dream, except he spoke. A breeze brushed in from the darkened corridor at his back, tickling the sea-salt smell of him. It was... pleasant. Horrifyingly pleasant.

This was a reunion of everyone I had killed. A meeting of ghosts, returned to torment me, ruin my mind.

Silas hobbled behind them, cane tapping the floor in a sickly rhythm. He gestured to the stone-slabbed floor, silently commanding both my father and Camron to kneel before me.

I was so focused on them that I hadn't noticed a new weight added to my hand. Glancing down, it was to find a knife, the handle carved from the antlers of a stag. It was the knife Julian Gathrax had showed me in the library on that fateful night—the knife he had chased me with through the grounds of his manor, promising pain, before I granted him death.

It was cold to the touch, firm against my fingers and as real as everything else around me.

'Which one will it be?' King Gathrax said, gesturing to the kneeling men before me. 'Who will you pick, the man you call father or your husband?'

Sweat bled across my palm. The knife slipped free, metal clattered against the floor, skipping to a stop before Camron. I watched, breath hitching in my throat, as he reached down with bound hands, his navy-blue jacket straining against the muscles of his arm.

'This belongs to you,' Camron said, awkwardly lifting the knife back to me in offering. His steady hands held it firm as he looked up at me through pale lashes. For a moment, I lost myself in his eyes once more.

'This is not real,' I said again, although less convinced.

Then why did sweat roll down the side of my face? How could

I feel the hot breath of King Gathrax brush the hairs across my neck?

'It is,' Camron said.

'Maximus, take the knife,' my real father said.

I didn't move, I couldn't.

'Take—it.' King Gathrax loomed over my shoulder, his presence a haunting shadow. 'Or I decide for you.'

That was enough for me to reach and take it. My fingers brushed Camron's skin, feeling his warmth just as I remembered it.

'What do you want from me?'

The question was for my father, for Camron, for King Gathrax—dryads, it was for the universe.

They all answered in unison. 'Prove your sanity.'

Something rang familiar about the answer, but the horror of everything before me diluted to it. I locked eyes with my father, begging for him to give me the answers.

'Go to him,' King Gathrax said, lifting my desire from my mind. 'I will give you a moment, then you must pick whose life is worth taking. Or I will be the one to choose for you.'

I didn't need to be told twice. My bones jolted as I threw myself to the ground before my father. Even if he wished to throw his arms around me, he couldn't. They were bound before him. But that didn't stop me from falling across him, holding onto his solid frame as though my life depended on it.

'Father?' I cried into the crook of his neck. 'Tell me this is a dream. Please, tell me this isn't real.'

'I am here, Maximus. You feel me, do you not?'

I sobbed. 'I do.'

'And I will always be here.' He leaned his face into mine, pressing a firm kiss to my forehead. The connection broke me. Something deep inside of my chest cracked, allowing the feral serpent of grief to finally consume me. As Father leaned back, the coarse hairs of his beard scratched my skin. 'I love you, my son.'

'Would you like a moment with your husband?' King Gathrax

almost laughed as he spat the final word.

My neck twisted back towards Camron. Not once had he removed his eyes from me. There was something so unfamiliar about him, as though I was looking at someone I never knew. His arm, like mine, was without the fasting mark. The sun had yet to bring out the freckles across the bridge of his nose, nor had it lightened his golden hair from its darker hues. There was something younger about him too, the way his posture slouched forward. Was this the Camron who had set out for a first adventure at sea and written a diary for his mother?

'Do you know who I am?' I asked.

The question hung between us. To my surprise, Camron looked around the room as though searching for the answer. I blinked and the scene flickered. Stars burst behind my eyes as I rubbed them with the heel of my hand, unsure what was happening. By the time I opened them again, Camron was leaning forward, fingers grasping the bottom of my velveteen trousers. I was not the only one scared in that moment. Camron was terrified.

'Please,' Camron begged, his eyes stained red with tears, 'free me. Don't send me back to her.'

Camron was not the man I thought he was. He was a broken child, shattered into a million pieces, tears flowing down his face.

'Who?' I asked, the single word echoing around Julian's room as though I stood in the middle of a mountain.

'My keeper.' Camron stopped shaking enough to answer. His cheeks were flushed crimson, his dark eyes wide with dread. 'My mother.'

King Gathrax was behind me, drawing me away from them both. 'So, Julian, who will it be?'

I was Julian, he spoke to me. It was happening so quickly, the knife trembling in my fist.

'Son,' Father joined the chorus with his deep, resounding voice. 'Me. Pick me.'

'No. Free me,' Camron shouted, eyes bulging. 'I beg you.'

I longed to clap hands over my ears, to block out the noises. There was no focusing, no discerning what was being asked of me.

'Compliance is the key, my heir. Choose who dies.' King Gathrax was behind me again, guiding my arm by my elbow, moving me like a puppet until the knife was raised. I became a pendulum, shifting from left to right, deciding on whose death would free me from this hellscape.

'I can't... I can't do this. I *won't*.' But no matter how many times I left the knife fall to my feet, it materialised back in my hand as though it had never left.

'Me,' Camron shouted now, pale face broken in a petrifying mask. Spittle flew beyond his lips. 'Save me from her. Pick me.'

'You are Maximus Oaken. You are my son. Do not let them make you a monster. Kill me,' my father shouted too, veins bulging in his neck and head.

'Quickly,' King Gathrax sang. 'Or they both die.'

I pinched my eyes closed, refusing to watch this nightmare. In the dark, the sounds of desperate pleas grew louder, so much so they pained my ears, thundering against my skull until the pressure felt as though it would simply pop.

'No. No. No.'

'Maximus,' Father scolded now, angry as a vengeful storm. 'I am dead anyway. It has to be me.'

A tempest raged in my mind, paining me from the inside out.

'Husband, I cannot bear to live in this life. Please, free me.' Camron joined, screaming, demanding, angry.

'No.' I slammed my fist into my head, wishing for it all to stop. 'No.'

'Compliance is the key,' King Gathrax chuckled into my ear. Of course, he was enjoying this. 'If you wish to free yourself of this nightmare, you must make your choice. Who will die for you this time?'

The noise was so loud it invaded every part of me. Camron's horrified desperation, my father's angered demanding, King

Gathrax's enjoyment. I didn't dare open my eyes, not as the knife continued to move from each man as though my body decided the answer.

'No,' I said for a final time.

My eyes flew open, inspecting the now calm scene. Both men stared at me, waiting to find out my decision. Both were so equally hopeful, it broke me.

I turned the knife on myself, watching as both men's eyes flew open in understanding. But before anyone could do anything, say anything more, I thrust it into my chest, burying the blade to the hilt.

There was no pain. There was only peace. When I looked down, readying myself to see blood pump from an open wound, it was to find something else. Not a knife in my chest, but a key. An old brass key inserted into a lock.

'It seems your mind is strong, just as I first believed it would be,' a strange voice said from the darkness. There was something primordial about the voice, as though it belonged to another place, in another time. As though my mind made sense of a series of sounds, forming them into something I could understand. It was both human, and not.

'Who are you?' I asked the dark. Something large slithered before me, dissipating the view like smoke. '*What* are you?'

'Two trials completed,' the voice replied beneath the subtle click of scales over stone. 'One more to go.'

I blinked and I was transported. No longer was I faced with Julian's room or the two men kneeling before me, pleading for their death. Icy winds whipped around me, twisting my hair. I stared back into the face of the Avarian Crest, only the faint murmuring of voices lingering in the far reaches of my mind.

Carried on the wind, the voice finally answered my question. Although it was faint, a whisper almost out of reach, there was no denying it.

'For I am Oribon, father of the dragons, and you Maximus Oaken, are close to discovering *all*.'

CHAPTER 22

The vision had flayed my mind apart. It twisted my sanity into knots, so much so that I could barely free myself from it as I walked across the bridge towards the mouth of the mountain. Cut from smooth Avarian stone, the bridge spanned across a sheer drop. There was no rail on either side to stop a traveller from falling to their death. But falling was not the problem.

I was halfway over the bridge when I found a mound of material beside the edge. Two shoes had been removed, left neatly beside one another. A cloak, like the one I had worn, was folded neatly to the side, the satchel weighing it down. I peered over the edge, looking down into the jaws of darkness and rock. There was no need for explanation as to what had happened to this unfortunate novice. Whoever these items had belonged to had not passed the Oribon's test.

Sanity. That was the trial. Whatever magic lingered around the mountain, the veil I had pierced had reached into my mind, created a scene of the worst magnitude and tested me with it. I had passed, barely. Whoever these belonged to had not.

Dayn? It crossed my mind if these shoes belonged to him. That panic alone was enough for me to push the vision to the back of my head and forge on.

The entrance of the mountain was a large open doorway. Carvings etched themselves into the rockface, as though large claws had attempted to leave beautiful designs, when all it did was make the place look as ominous as it felt.

Inside, veins of light emitted from the stone, leading the way. If I thought the bridge beyond was terrifying to navigate, it was nothing compared to the narrow rock path that greeted me inside. It hugged the wall adjacent to a drop that seemed to have no end. If I looked up, I could see the sky, exposed from where the mountain was cleaved in two.

Movement caught in the corner of my eyes. Shapes cut across it, dark smudges with open wings. Dragons. They were everywhere. Lurking in the shadows, eyes glowing up at me as though they were snakes lingering in their nests. Some crawled across the stone walls, nails gripping on as thin, unformed wings which could not yet to take flight.

Unlike with Glamora, I didn't feel safe with these beasts. They were wild, hungry. I saw it in the way they glowered at me, hissing with long tongues, warning me not to get too close. I heard it in the clicking of jaws.

Everywhere I walked, I was watched.

If anything kept me from moving, it was the dragons lurking in the walls, protecting their offspring from me.

I didn't blame their distrust; I was here to take one.

A terrible cry lanced through the air, disrupting creatures from their nests. As suddenly as a flock of birds broke from a tree, dragons exploded through dark holes in the rock face. Not flying towards the sound, but away from it.

My heart rose to my throat, skin crawling with every soul-destroying scream. As it echoed across the mountain's innards, I felt the emotion. Pain. Desperation. Ire. Each was as clear as if it was my own.

I continued forward, urged by the cry. Soon enough it was muffled to a faint whimper. As I rounded the corner, I saw why.

The cavern opened up into a large, rounded dome. It was as

though a god took a spoon and carved a nook into the mountain's wall. Figures stood around it. Out of them all, I rested my attention on Dayn. But my relief was short-lived.

Power radiated around them, cords of earthen magic tainting the air as they each called on their power. The force of so many mages working as one was both beautiful and terrible. As was what they used their power against.

Bands of stone encased a dragon, scales crafted of tarnished gold. She cawed out, long snout resisting the manacle of stone that had been forced around her. She was the size of two warhorses, although compared to Glamora, this dragon was slighter.

That didn't take away from her might, her ferocity. She snapped her jaw, trying to fight against the mages. But the more she fought, the more bands of rock and stone encased her body, imprisoning her just as the old stories told.

The mages forced the dragon onto her belly, wings forced down by boulders they'd torn from the wall behind her. I felt each tear in the leathery hide as the dragon continued to struggle, only to be smothered by more of the mages' power.

This was wrong. Awful. These creatures were gods, not something to be tied down and smothered. And there was Dayn, helping them.

More bands of conjured stone rose like liquid from the ground beneath the dragon, only to harden around her armoured body. I was reminded of Julian Gathrax's bed, where I had been bound with iron around my ankle.

And then bound to Camron by magic I could never understand.

'Stop,' I screamed, releasing my power into the air until it crackled with bolts of hot light.

Their magic released, if only a fraction. Faces snapped around to see me. I barely focused on any of them but the beating, demanding magic that warred in me.

The dragon took her chance, rising from the ground, stone

bindings shattering. She smashed her long, muscled neck into one of the nameless mages. He was torn from the ground, thrown with such a force that his head cracked against stone and his body fell over the edge of the platform. Dead. I could almost hear the continuous slam of the corpse buried the gold dragon's roar.

Just like that, one second and another life was lost.

But where was my guilt? Where was my grief?

Pain exploded in my ankle, the bone bending to an unnatural angle. I had been distracted and didn't notice as one of the mages sank my foot beneath the ground until it shattered the bones in my ankle. I flew forward, falling on my hands and knees. Debris cut into my palms, tearing flesh. And then the ground moved, and I sank further into it.

'The dragon,' one of the novices screamed above my pain. 'Restrain her, quickly. *He...* is mine.'

I looked up, knowing they spoke about me.

Chaos engulfed the scene as the remaining novices attempted to restraint the golden-scaled dragon. Instead of forcing her to the floor, they used the creature's momentum and pinned her to the wall like a butterfly to a cork board.

Dayn was the only one not helping the others. His violet eyes glistened with power, his hand outstretched and pointed at me. 'You shouldn't have followed.'

His four words cut into me. Their presence weighed heavier than the encasing of earth around my feet and hands. Dayn's pale skin reflected the glow of the Avarian stone, making him look sickly. Exhausted. His eyes were red-rimmed and heavy, his brow creased in concentration as he fuelled his power with more of his intention.

'And you shouldn't have left me,' I hissed, shoulders aching as I continued my attempt to pull free. 'I came for you, Dayn.'

Agony broke over his face, pulling down at his lips, extenuating the internal struggle he warred with. I saw it, a familiar battle like a shadow behind his eyes. He was doing this, not because he wanted to. Because he *had* to.

The dragon released a whine that sang of her defeat. Spears of stone protruded through her wings, severing the leathery membrane. Just as they had with me, the mages had willed the rocks to devour the creature, coating her powerful legs, her torso and part of her neck.

They left her face uncovered. It was as though the novices wanted the dragon to bear witness to what they came to accomplish.

'Kill the Traitor Mage, Dayn,' one of the novices hissed, scooping something from the ground. An egg. It was as large as her torso, curved and coated in a skin of scale. Where the deep-maroon scales overlapped, it seemed the egg pulsated with a light from within.

This is what they came for. This is why the novices restrained the dragon and acted so brutally. They wanted her eggs, to pass the Claim, but hurting the dragon was not necessary.

'We've got what we need,' Dayn replied, voice breaking. 'Leave him for the dragons.'

'No. We do it like we planned. That bastard just had Liam killed.'

'It was the dragon…' I hissed, trying to fight out of my bindings. My bones ached in their sockets, but the more I struggled, the more I sank. I was not the only one to try.

The dragon fought on, not for her life but for the life of her offspring. I understood her pain. It was as if I could hear the truth behind her whimper, which intensified as the remaining novices each collected one for themselves.

'Dayn lied,' another novice said, pointing at Dayn, an egg held beneath the crook of his arm. 'He said he had already killed him.'

Dayn refused to reply; his silence spoke of volumes. He continued to stare down at me, face twisted into a scowl. 'I thought I did—'

'Do it then, Dayn,' the first girl said, goading Dayn beyond his shoulder. 'Finish him for good. He killed Sophia, and now Liam.

Not to mention our families, our friends, when his husband was let into Wycombe. It will be worth it. No one will ever know.'

Dayn had lied to them, to save me. My breath lodged in my throat, sweat trickling down my temple.

'Dayn,' I said, boring my eyes through him. 'I understand—'

A boot smashed into my jaw, blinding me. My teeth cut into the flesh of my mouth until blood pooled in my cheeks. Rough hands gripped my hair and tugged my head back.

'Traitor Mage,' the young girl said.

I opened my eyes, the dull light harsh compared to the pounding in my head. She was young, too young to carry so much anger. 'Because of you, my parents died. Because of you, there is no one to greet me when I return home with my egg. And because of you, those who wait for your return will be sourly disappointed. This is your fault.'

'You don't need to do this,' I hissed, blood splattering down my chin.

The girl smiled, her eyes narrowing. 'Oh, yes, I do.'

Her fist smashed into my head. Skin split across my brow, red gore dribbling freely into my eyes. I tasted blood; I saw blood. Through the river of it, the dragon spat ice across the stone, dropping the temperature of the cavern dramatically.

'It isn't just pain I will give you. It will be death, just as you deserve. It is a surprise the Council didn't do it sooner—'

My scalp burned as her hand was torn away. A blur of bodies moved before me. One moment she was hovering over me, the next she was pinned beneath Dayn as he straddled her hips, snarling like a feral beast.

'Don't. Touch. Him,' Dayn screamed, eyes pinched closed as he rained his hands down upon her.

'My egg!' The girl's panicked cry proved she cared of one thing and one thing only. The dragon egg that lay shattered at her side.

It took little effort for Dayn to be removed from her. The rest of the novices grasped him, drawing him back as he screamed.

It was my time to plead for him. 'If you hurt him, I will give you a reason to hate me.'

No one seemed to hear me. Although, the gold-scaled dragon rumbled, spitting more ice across the rocks above, as though she understood the truth in my warning.

The girl picked the pieces of her egg from the floor, fingers stained with the liquid that spilled from within. She stood, face flushed red with fury and punched Dayn once. His head snapped to the side. If he had not been held up by the hands of the other novices, he would've fallen.

The magic forcing down upon me lessened during the distraction. I used it to my benefit. All around me, stone shivered as I expelled magic from beneath my hands.

The mage slammed her fist into Dayn's head again. Blood sprayed; a tooth shattered. Dayn expelled a breathy moan, his eyes overflowing with fear.

Crack.

Fissures spread across the walls, spreading from beneath my hands until my presence lingered everywhere. The dragon purred, no longer fighting but watching. Watching me. Waiting.

Two of the novices noticed. They were the lucky ones to escape.

The girl knocked her bloodied and broken fist into Dayn's face for a final time. He fell, no longer held by the others, as they took their eggs and fled from the shattering cavern.

'I'll have your egg, Dayn,' she cried, 'you can fail. You will leave without one.'

Even if Dayn wanted to reply, he couldn't. Blood filled his cheeks, his face swollen and bruised. He moved to attack again but was met by the back-handed smack of a hand. It was such a simple touch, one I was familiar with. But I felt the slam of his face into the ground as if I, too, had been knocked to the floor. My bones echoed it.

Unlike the first time, Dayn didn't get back up.

'Get up, you liar,' she shouted, eyes wide and spittle coating her chin. 'You deserve this.'

Was this the kind of mage the Council longed for? Powerful beings who harboured deadly thoughts and equally frightening actions?

Dayn didn't move.

'Come on,' I said, as tears of knowing cut down my face. I repeated the girl's command, except mine came from a different place. It was hope, because I supposed even I knew it was wasted. 'Move, Dayn.'

I studied his body, searching for signs of breathing or twitching.

Crack. Dust rained down around us, clogging my nose, my throat.

'Dayn,' I whispered, but he didn't respond.

The girl was continuing to scream. 'Now! Stand and face me, you liar. Did he even kill your little friend, or did you lie about that too?'

Crack.

I dared not give reason to why Dayn had not answered. Speaking it aloud would only make it more real.

'Dayn?' When she spoke again, it was not with the same fury. She said his name in question, as though wondering why he was so still. Wondering why his glassy eyes seemed to stare endlessly at the sky, why the puddle of dark blood spread beneath his broken skull.

Dayn didn't get up, not because he refused. It was because he was dead.

Crack.

I broke free, as did the golden dragon.

The girl barely looked up as the creature's jaw spread wide, flashing rows of spear-edged teeth. The dragon engulfed her where she stood. In one violent swing of her neck, the dragon snatched the girl from standing, threw her skywards as a herring would to a fish, only to catch her helpless body between rows of sharpened teeth.

Bone crunched. Flesh burst like ripe fruit between teeth. And just like that, she perished too. Devoured beneath the serrated jaw of the monster she had imprisoned.

Free from my earthen bindings, I crawled over to Dayn, not caring for the pain in my ankle. Not caring for the dragon that chewed on the novice until her scaled snout glistened with the girl's blood.

I scooped him into my arms, his body limp, his chest still. My fingers trailed over the broken bone protruding through his skull. They came back coated in thick blood and the vile gore of brain matter.

The silence lasted only a moment before the dragon slammed her four limbs into the ground, claws gouging scars into stone, and unleashed a roar, her foul, ice cool breath exploding over me.

Tears blurred my eyes, burned the back of my throat. All my emotion, all my sudden understanding as to what happened came flooding out of me at once. And I roared too. I released a cry so deadly, so violent, even the dragon recoiled. Her serpentine eyes narrowed as though she recognised something in me.

This was my sacrifice. My final trial. If I had not followed after Dayn, he would still be alive. But I did. And it led to his death.

CHAPTER 23

I don't know how long we were left like that, two grieving creatures, shedding tears over what had been lost—what had been taken from us. Whereas I refused to let Dayn's limp body go, the dragon cowered over shattered shells and an empty nest, her whimpering blending in symphony with mine.

It was only when the dragon shifted her attention to me that reality seemed to catch up. The dragon stared at me with storm-grey eyes, a rumbling growl building in her chest. I expected her to open her jaw and engulf me. I felt fury flowing from her in waves, so powerful that it was hard to separate from my own.

She looked to Dayn, nostrils flaring as she took in the scent of fresh blood. A forked tongue slipped between her curling lips, brushing over rows of teeth the size of blades.

'You can't have him,' I screamed, unable to separate my emotions from the creature's.

The dragon didn't attack, not as I expected she would. Instead, she watched as I shed my pain, cradling Dayn to my chest, his blood soaking my shirt. I supposed the dragon recognised my suffering. She recognised death. In a way, I saw it reflected in her ancient eyes.

Her offspring had been torn from their nest, never to return.

Not only did the creature share in the internal agony, but her body was also riddled with wounds. Gashes marred her belly and hide; her wings ruined with tears. Dark blood slithered across brass-gold scales, marks left from the mages' restraints.

She shifted closer, expelling a drawn-out whimper from deep within her throat.

My hold on Dayn tightened, my lips drawing back into a snarl. 'Go away.'

I wondered if she understood me. The dragon pulled back and shook her long neck. Her features smoothed as she blinked both her eyelids, coating the sorrow in her serpentine eyes. No, not sorrow. It was understanding. I would recognise it anywhere.

When the dragon lowered her head towards us again, I didn't refuse. She pressed her snout into Dayn's side, nudging him as she had with the shattered egg. A puff of frozen air expelled beyond the slits of her nostrils, casting a gust of wind over me.

A single tear jewelled on my cheek, crystalising.

The kiss of ice shocked me enough to raise blood-soaked fingers and touch my face. The dragon followed, inquisitively watching my every move. She slipped closer, placing her wolfen-shaped head before me.

Instinct took over and I placed my hand atop her crown. The puckered scars of my mage-mark shivered as I brushed my palm across the cold, hard casing of scales. Resistance pushed against my touch as the dragon nuzzled into me. Then I saw it, a single tear escaping her storm-grey eyes—mirroring the one she had frozen upon my face.

We were bound together by loss, by grief. With the smashed egg to my side, Dayn's broken skull bleeding on my lap—this creature and I were no different from one another.

Two beings bound as one.

The dragon growled, eyes narrowing as though communi-cating something to me. I looked her dead in the eyes, refusing to show fear. Then it seemed the atmosphere changed. New emotions bloomed in my mind. They were both familiar and strange, as though placed inside by another... by the dragon.

'I understand,' I said, pleading with everything in me for the dragon to understand. 'I know your loss as you know mine. I know what it feels to have your family torn away.'

I thought of my father, knelt before me as he begged for me to kill him over Camron. I thought of my mother, bedbound as the burning plague destroyed her from the inside out.

The dragon recoiled, swan-like neck shivering as another whimper broke out of her maw. It sounded like water rushing down a creek of pebbles.

I took in the details of the creature, marvelling at her. Even coated in blood, even poisoned with grief, she was beautiful. Rich golden scales; four ivory horns protruding from the crown of her head, two on either side; long tail with a spearhead point at its end; powerful limbs and a body thick with muscles, protected by an armour as rough as stone and as shiny as a newly forged coin.

To complete the Claim, we were meant to obtain an egg. Pass the trials and walk away with our bounty. But I would rather fail than leave Dayn for a moment. Even if I found an egg of my own, I wasn't prepared to leave Dayn—alone. How could I continue when he was dead? How could I continue knowing I was returning to Wycombe, and his family would never see him again?

There was no egg for me to take, nothing left to claim. The rules were simple, but simple was dull. Simple didn't save lives. I hadn't failed yet.

I stared at the dragon, knowing little of the bond required between a dragon-blessed and the beast itself. But what I shared with this creature was stronger than time.

I had freed her, saved her with my power, but that was not why she was indebted to me.

Selflessness, sanity and... sacrifice.

Gently, I rested Dayn on the ground. He was my sacrifice. I couldn't pay mind to the puddle of blood that covered the floor, which soddened my clothes and stained my skin pink. There would come a time when I would let it haunt me, but not now. Now I had to find a way to Wycombe, with Dayn.

The dragon—no, my dragon. She was mine, as I belonged to her.

I stood awkwardly, the weight on one leg, as the dragon paced forward. She unfurled her wings as I stepped closer towards her, my mage-marked palm lifted for her to see.

'Take us to them,' I said, carefully moving closer, one step at a time. I was hesitant to move quickly. 'Help me return him to his family.'

There was no explaining how I knew it, but the dragon understood me. She bowed her head, pressing her hard temple into my hand again, coaxing a cold shiver to spread beneath where it touched.

She reared up on her hind legs, wings spreading on either side. In parts they had torn. The golden beast flapped them as though testing, checking to see if the damage was minor. When she slammed back onto the ground, shaking the cave, I knew she had made her decision.

No. I *felt* it. Deep inside, as though we shared something I couldn't explain.

It was a bond, one that left no scar, left no mark of silver ink. It was a common connection, tethering us together. Dryads, I grasped it and held on firm. Invisible tethers, binding the dragon's scales to my flesh.

I sensed the dragon's encouragement in my mind, a far-off call that spurred me on. So I reached for my magic, not stopping until the silver cords connected my amplifier to the earth around me. And there it was. Something new, something I had not seen before. A cord of gold speared from my heart to the dragon's chest.

I might not have claimed an egg, but I claimed a dragon instead.

When I rode upon Glamora's horned back, there was enough

room for three of us, with space for more. On this dragon, only I could sit on her back. She only needed to lower to her belly for me to climb a leg over, there was no need to scramble up wings and use my muscles as leverage.

It was as though this creature was made for me. My body fit the dragon's frame like a glove, perfectly forming against one another. My thighs ached as they gripped onto the body of the creature. I wrapped my hands around her horns, fingers paling beneath the tension. The muscles in my stomach tightened as the dragon shifted to standing, testing the weight on her back.

Dayn lay out across the stone, surrounded in his blood.

'Be careful with him,' I urged, knowing the dragon understood my intention.

She released a click in agreement, shaking her powerful neck. *I shall.*

The dragon scooped him up, carefully wrapping her claws around his body. Dayn dangled in the dragon's grasp, head lolling backwards, stoic face looking skywards. I swallowed a lump of sorrow and focused ahead, patting the dragon on her side.

Deep inside my lungs I felt a sudden weightless feeling. A feeling of freedom. The promise of open skies. The shield in my mind was strong as iron, but something new had penetrated it. A presence that was as much my own as it wasn't.

I supposed I had felt it when I first touched the dragon, as though it claimed me long before that moment. There was no keeping the dragon out, nor was there a need to invite her in.

Unlike when Simion infiltrated my mind, this was different. It was emotion, not words. It was feeling, not thoughts. It pulled on the deep-rooted pain I felt, pain that spiked every time I looked at Dayn, pain that tripled when the dragon looked back at her emptied nest and the single smashed egg.

'Fly,' I said, pressing my forehead to the cool kiss of gold scale.

The dragon grumbled, bellowing clouds of mist between her snarls. She sprang ahead, careful not to put weight on the claws that held Dayn. I pinched my eyes closed and gave into the comfort the dragon offered, as she threw her lithe body over the same edge the novice had fallen over. Wings splayed out, wind catching as it did in the sails of a ship—a torn sail but they would do.

Nothing would stop this god—determination pierced the veil of the world with every building roar she expelled. And as the dragon threw herself into the air, wings pounding with vigour, I conjured images in my mind. A destination. Castle ruins; the Heart Oak. I didn't so much as tell the dragon where to take me but showed it.

Another face filled my mind and I felt nothing but boiling red fury. Elder Leia. Her Council.

This was their doing and I would see that they paid.

CHAPTER 24

We reached Wycombe city beneath the cover of night. If anyone had looked skywards, it would have been only to see the flash of shadow passing through the already onyx sky.

My dragon knew where to take me.

Against the backdrop of the starless expansive, the Heart Oak looked every inch the corpse it had become. Bare branches more like the reaching limbs of burned bones. It clawed the night, begging for someone to save it.

For *me* to save it.

When we landed beyond the steps of the castle, there was no one to greet me. I didn't see so much as feel the dragon perch herself on a building at my back. In my mind's eye, my skin was scales. It was as though it was my own golden tail wrapped around stone walls, whilst talons grasped onto them for leverage.

We were one and the same. And I was drunk on this power as much as the fury coiling through me. What I couldn't discern, was whose anger was it? Mine, or the dragon's?

It was an ever-present comfort to have the creature linger within me. If I needed her, she would come. The creature was protective, as though she had lost her eggs only to find a new offspring in me.

I hobbled forward, my mind barely registering the pain from my shattered ankle. The agony in my chest was far too overwhelming. I carried Dayn, his stiff corpse cold and awkward in my arms. If it wasn't for my dragon lending me her strength, I would never have made it a step.

It didn't take long for people to sense my arrival. All it took was for me to rip down the shield in my mind and called out to Leska. I no longer needed to shield my thoughts, not as I had a dragon to protect them.

A crowd rushed out from the castle's main entrance, cloaks gliding across the stone steps as they flooded down to greet me. My dragon exhaled a rumbling growl from her perch, the perfect warning.

Then my eyes settled on the only person I wanted to see, my lip drawing back in a snarl.

'Maximus Oaken, what is the meaning of this?' Elder Leia said, leading the crowd of Council members and guards at her back like wings. Her silver hair billowed in icy winds, an oversized jacket draped over her shoulders. It was clear she had not expected this, and why would she?

'He is dead because of you.' I could barely look down at the body, how his skin looked blue beneath the night sky, his lips silver and eyes yellowed. 'All of you.'

Her gaze fell to Dayn, his body splayed across my arms, eyes continuing to look endlessly at the sky. There was something peaceful about him. If I didn't focus on the divot at the back of his skull, I might have just believed he was sleeping.

Leia's hand clapped over her mouth, stifling the broken cry. It was not the reaction I expected, but the shock of it nearly snatched my ire away. One of the Council members rushed forward, arms outstretched. 'Let me take him, Mage Oaken.'

A growl broke out of me, spittle flying out between me and the Council member. I didn't take my eyes off them as they cautiously took the body. One wrong move, one misstep, and I would've destroyed them.

To their luck, they treated the dead with the respect he didn't get during life. That was always the way, I supposed.

'His blood… is on your hands,' I spat, my dragon expelling a loud rumble from the shadows at my back. Elder Leia looked from the corpse to over my shoulder, narrowing her eyes, searching for the beast that lingered not too far.

She couldn't see her, but she certainly sensed her.

'Look at *him*,' I shouted, pointing to Dayn's cold, stiff corpse. Wycombe was so still, so quiet, my words echoed across buildings and filled the very air. 'Look at him, Leia. He was only a child. A child you sent into the belly of the beast, knowing the dangers that would await him.'

'The Claim began years before I was even a concept in my parent's futures. This is not my sole doing.' Leia grimaced, jaw set firm as she held my stare. Another Council member knelt before the body, placing fingers to Dayn's neck and wrist. 'His blood is on the hands of history and tradition. Not mine.'

Bile crept up my throat, scorching it with a sickly burn. I had to spit on the floor just to stop it from gathering in my cheeks. 'You preach about saving your people and yet you send the most innocent into that terrain, knowing the dangers, knowing the possibility of death.'

'Maximus.' She used my name as my own parents would, attempting to calm me. 'This child… is not the first to die during the Claim,' Elder Leia said firmly. Her white hair tumbled over her shoulders, softening her face in a way I had not seen before. She was exhausted, dark circles pronounced beneath her golden eyes. 'He will not be the last. Those deemed unworthy are…'

'He was the best of us,' I bellowed, the night full of my ire. 'You know nothing about worthiness.'

There was no denying the sadness etched into her face. It felt wrong, misplaced almost. How dare Leia grieve over Dayn?

'How can you protect the North from monsters, if it is run by them?'

Her eyes flayed wide, her lips paling with tension. But even I knew she didn't have the answer for me.

'Fuck—you,' I shouted, unable to catch a breath. Everything was beating. My heart; my lungs; my head and my power.

'Careful, Maximus Oaken—'

I stepped forward, seething. Pain ricocheted through my ankle and up my leg. It only fuelled me. Blinded by dark desires I could hardly think straight. Magic flooded through me, brightening the dark landscape in cords of pure power.

'Guards,' Elder Leia said, voice breaking, hands raised before her as though that had the power to calm me. 'Please see that Maximus doesn't do anything he will regret.'

The ground shuddered with the force of pure muscle and scale. I didn't need to turn to know the dragon had landed on the street, prowling lower to the ground, teeth bared and the promise of ice in the air around her.

'That dragon.' Elder Leia's eyes widened, chest swelling with breath, 'has claimed *you*?'

My dragon leaned forward, and parting her powerful jaw, erupted a roar so violent they all stumbled back. I held firm, feeling the brush of frigid air on the side of my face.

'We've claimed each other,' I replied.

'Not by the rules in which you should have adhered to.'

'Fuck the rules.' Anger rose in me, higher and higher. 'Rules should be put in place to protect. Not control. Not maim and kill.'

Perhaps it was the proximity to the Heart Oak, or maybe it was just the tidal wave of anger which finally broke in me, but I felt magic everywhere. My amplifier connected me to the earth. The air around me, it shivered with energy and the promise of storms.

This magic, it was different. Intensified.

It's claimed you.

It was the dragon—she fuelled me with her emotion, her power. It scratched across my skin like nails, except the feeling was not terrible or painful. It was pleasure. It was power. And it was mine.

Before I let it break and wash away everything before me, before Leia could act on the ominous thoughts that lurked behind her eyes, I reached for the dragon and clambered onto her back.

'You are not leaving,' Leia shouted, as her guards fanned out around me, magic spoiling the air. 'You have lied to the Council, you have lied to this city. Maximus Oaken, you are under arrest,' Elder Leia said, tongue sharp as a blade.

Lied? She was speaking in riddles.

'Desperate. You are desperate to find a way to criminalise me when you are the ones killing innocent people. Not me, *you.*'

The ground rumbled, magic spoiled the air. 'Your actions are seen as open rebellion against the North.'

My lips pulled over my teeth, baring every one of them in a snarl to rival the beast's I now sat upon.

'Your threats no longer have power over me. The last man who tried died. I have nothing... nothing you can use against me, nothing with that power,' I shouted above the grumbling roars from the dragon. *My* dragon. 'There is nothing more dangerous than someone with nothing to lose.'

To my surprise, Elder Leia's face broke into a smile. 'You are wrong,' she said, eyes narrowing. 'More so than you could even imagine.'

I paused, struck into silence by the way she looked at me, an expression that told me she held something back.

'I am not arresting you for your actions during the Claim.' Elder Leia shook her head slowly. 'You are under arrest for harbouring a phoenix-possessed.'

My blood spiked, then dropped with vigour. If I was not holding onto my dragon's horns, I would've tipped sideways from her back.

'Yes, I know all about Deborah. You see, I knew not to trust you. And it has now been proven that you are involved with the South's attempts to harm us...'

'You could flee all the way to the isle of Voltar and I would get you, Maximus Oaken. Test it, test me.' Elder Leia stood firm, refusing to look away, as the dragon beat her torn wings. The force of wind blew the white hair from her face until there was no hiding the expression across it. *Run, little rabbit. Run.* It was the look of someone who had won.

The rest of what Elder Leia had to say made little sense. Her lips were moving, but all I could hear was the thunderous crash of my heart. The dragon released a final scream, the air splitting with a torrent of winds.

I pushed an image of the cottage. The dragon didn't need further explanation, I sensed she knew where to take me.

Home.

* * *

Where the cottage once stood was now a smudge of ash, charred earth and ruin. Parts of the ground still twisted in flame, singeing everything to black. I clutched onto my golden dragon. It was the only thing keeping me from falling. There was nothing left. It was as though the colour had been drained away. A small pile of rubble, blackened stone that still seeped with smoke and complete ruin.

No matter what I felt until this moment, no matter what loss and grief I believed I was familiar with—looking down at the destroyed cottage beneath the glare of stars, I knew my world had ended.

My dragon cast pillars of frozen air across the burning ground, burying the cliff's edge in jagged teeth of ice. I screamed out into the abyss, clawing at my throat as though I couldn't get the emotion out soon enough.

My mother—I had left her and this…

I couldn't begin to fathom what it meant. I wasn't strong enough to discover it.

A chorus of roars sounded at our back. I barely had the energy to turn my attention, but when I did, it was to see dragons. A riot of them. Too many to count. They flew through the sky, dark smudges of power far larger than my dragon was. Moonlight caught off the silver armour of battlemages on their backs.

Leia's promise. She had come for me. I knew it with complete certainty. Lightning flashed through the onyx sky, casting everything in harsh, brilliant light.

Winds ripped the silent tears from my face, snatching sobs from my throat. I leaned into the dragon, part of me wishing to give up, the other part of me refusing myself that luxury. This time the dragon didn't require a command. She acted from her innate understanding that we were bound, connected. She shared my emotions, my heartbreak, just as I took on her burdens.

She would do anything to protect me. Deep in my core I sensed the dragon's desire to tear into those that flew towards us. She wanted the skies to rain with blood and scale. But, unlike me, she knew her strengths, and more importantly, her weaknesses.

The dragon sensed what I desired most and that was to survive long enough to find my mother. She circled the cottage a final time, faced the endless ocean that seamlessly joined the night sky and flew towards the horizon.

If Leia wanted to chase me to Voltar, dryads I would make her.

Torn wings beat with vigour as the line of dragons gained on us. I looked back only to find them closing the gap. It was desperation that drove me to level my magic towards them. It was the not knowing of my mother's well-being that made me pull on my power. It was the idea of losing everything that called upon the bolt of lightning.

Clouds parted. Serpents of lightning lashed across the sky, breaking apart the stars. It whipped towards Leia's battlemages and their dragons, breaking their formation. I screamed into the night, unleashing volleys of power over and over.

Still, it didn't deter them.

A shadow passed overheard, blocking out the minimal light

from the moon and stars. I looked up to find a gargantuan shape
of a dragon gliding above.

Move.

As my dragon dove down, my stomach jolted up. The ocean
was so close beneath us, water sprayed from waves, soaking my
skin, my hair, my clothes. The dragon's pointed claws disturbed
the ocean's surface, rippling the endless obsidian, tail thrashing.

I couldn't call upon the lightning, not so close to the body of
water. It would kill us before it had a chance to hurt anyone else.

I inhaled deeply, filling my panicked lungs. We were
surrounded by ocean and dragons, no earth to command and
claim. Beneath the body of water, I felt the remnants of my
power, but it was so far away I couldn't reach for it.

Frost bit at my skin. It was the only warning before the
monstrous dragon atop us opened its jaws and spewed winter
beneath it. My dragon reared back as the dragon's breath crashed
into the ocean. Pillars of ice rose, freezing waves in place. I
pressed my face into the cool gold scales, gasping on a scream as
it jerked again. Side to side, it wove around the downpour of ice,
missing the power by inches.

As quickly as it came, it stopped.

I heard a roar from out across the ocean. Another warning,
except this one wasn't for me.

Another riot of dragons flew towards us. It seemed they were
conjured from thin air, parting from a far-off cloud as though it
birthed them. These were not decorated in the silver armour of
Leia's regiment. The riders were almost invisible, wearing
leathers and dark burgundy clothing. Two dragons led the horde,
both monstrous and deadly as the next. From their claws, they
carried a banner, just as my golden dragon had carried Dayn's
body.

'Hawthorns!' A battlemage cried from beside me, pulling up
fast on its brown-scaled dragon.

'Rebels!' Another shout caught on the winds.

One moment I was looking outwards, the next I was snatched

into the mind of another. My dragon showed me the scene, gifting me her eyesight. It brightened the worlds, dialling the contrast and composure until the finer details were easier to make out.

Painted onto the banners of material in white paint was the symbol of the Hawthorns. A sprig of leaf and berry, the same Leia had held in her hand, the token left after the attacks in Wycombe.

And they flew directly towards us.

Forced back into my mind, I knew how this would end. I was caught between two enemies. Leia's soldiers at my back, the Hawthorn rebellion—the very people who had Aaron attempt to kill me—at my front.

I was doomed. But if that was the case, I wouldn't go down without a fight. And plus, I had elevated magic to try out.

It didn't take long for the dragons to reach us. The closer they gained, the harder my heart beat in my throat. Black scales shot ahead, flying past the front line of the Hawthorns. On its back I caught the glint of silver.

Glamora.

She shot through the sky, breaking formation, powerful jaw separated as it careered directly into the dragon who flew above me. The force of the two beasts connecting rippled through the air. Then teeth ripped into its neck, raining a wash of warm blood down over me and my dragon. Talons scorned flesh, tearing chunks of muscle away with ease.

My mind couldn't understand what I was watching. There wasn't time.

Another dragon shot towards us, blue as the summer skies. It nipped at my dragon's tail, teeth missing by inches. I saw the battlemage over its horned shoulders, staff raised as winter winds and lashes of lightning danced in the air around it.

I braced myself, ready to meet my end.

Crash. The dragon behind was forced into the ocean, buried beneath water as another landed atop it.

Ice spread across the water's surface, burying the other dragon beneath frozen waves. I waited, breath lodged in my throat, for the battlemage to emerge. They didn't.

Dragons turned on dragons, battlemages on Hawthorns.

Glamora continued tearing into the giant of a dragon. Her obsidian jaw glistened with blood. Entrails dangled from her enemy's torn belly, ropes and gore so large other dragons tangled helplessly in it.

My dragon dove us to the side, wings beating viciously, lifting back away from the ocean. Just in time before Glamora took one final rake of her claws over the thick neck of the dragon, killing it, sending it down into the watery depths of its grave.

There was no room for thinking about my mother, not as the skies rained with dragon blood, their flesh feeding the monsters of the deep. My thoughts blended with my dragon again, mixing as one.

Move. Dip. Wings. Higher. Side. Survive.

It was chaos, the screams of dragons and humans filling the night sky.

Glamora flew into place beside us, her large frame blending in with the sky around her. Two figures rode on her back, both armoured in silver. I squinted, unsure if her presence should scare me or comfort me.

My answer came in the form of a feeling. A cold brush of ice crept across the back of my mind. I knew who it was before the mage on Glamora's saddle tore the helmet from his head, revealing the truth beneath.

Simion. And he wasn't alone. Sat behind him, black hair whipping before vibrant blue eyes, was Leska.

They had come amongst the rebels. Not to kill me.

To *save* me.

CHAPTER 25

I tore down the steel barrier around my mind. Simion's presence was there, waiting and poised. His power filled my thoughts. I kept my eyes on him, enthralled by disbelief at what I saw.

In my distraction, one of Leia's battlemages flew in close to our side. Bolts of stone shot out from concealed parts of their armour, directly towards me. My dragon spun, almost forcing me off her side. Her cry of agony was bone-shattering as the stone spears smashed against her scales. Pain radiated off my stomach, mimicking the few that had gone deep into her flesh.

Silver cords burst to life, connecting my power to the shards within my dragon. The battlemage continued his connection, worming them in deeper. But I was stronger. I didn't simply rely on my ring to fuel me when the right of magic was in my blood.

I wrapped my intention around the shards of stone, pulled them free of my dragon's flesh and cast them back out to the battlemage who first shot them.

Stone cut into his face, piercing eyes until he was blinded. My dragon then took the chance to raise up, claws outstretched, and snatch the flailing battlemage from his dragon's back. There was nothing that could be done to stop him from being thrown into the sea. I looked back, expecting another to attack, but the war between dragons and mages settled. They had been the last, another notch to my amplifier. There was no more fighting because so many were dead, left to sink in the belly of the ocean.

Maximus. My name was an exhale, a breath filled with relief. It was so distracting I didn't care to watch as the remaining dragon settled into a new formation, around me.

All this time, you were with them... the rebels? I forced the question out to Simion with our mind-speak.

No. There wasn't a pause before he replied. *That has been forced upon us. Desperate times call for desperate measures. This is all for you.*

I caught Leska's scowl, knowing she would never align herself with the rebels. Yet here she was, using her power against Leia's mages.

Keep flying, Max. Don't stop until you can't see Aldian. Leia will send more.

Leska pointed a finger out to sea in the direction they had just flown from.

Go. Simion fuelled his words with his desperation and command. *Now.*

It seemed my dragon recognised his authority, but it was still ignored. Only I gave the commands, and I was not prepared to do as he asked. Not without answers.

I filled my mind with images of the cottage. It was easier to show Simion rather than ask him the burning question that lingered. Even in my mind, I couldn't form the words for fear of the answer. Then he filled my thoughts with three words beholding the power to undo me.

Deborah is safe. But unless you get away, you won't be. I can't save you if you stay in the line of danger.

My dragon beneath me expelled a cry that sang in symphony with the one in my chest. It was riddled with my heartache, my anger and fury. We were two entities, but we were also one. A single unit, flesh and scale, united in more than just choice.

'Where is she?' I shouted out into the nightly winds, waves

breaking and thrashing beneath me. Ice crackled beyond my
dragon's jaw, thickening the air in bouts of frozen clouds.

I will take you to her, Maximus. I promise she is safe; I promise that
you *are safe.*

His words etched themselves into my bones. The death, the
blood-stained ocean, the rebellion we flew among.

There is no returning from this, is there? I forced the question out
from the caverns of my mind even though I knew the answer.

Never.

There *was* no going back from this. Blood stained our hands
red. But there was one person who would take the brunt of this
crime, someone who didn't fly in the skies as we escaped
Wycombe city.

What about Beatrice?

Simion's silence was answer enough. He didn't retreat from
my mind but kept at the edges, as though he wasn't strong enough
to answer me.

I looked beyond my shoulder, eyes falling upon the spindle of
stone that pierced the veil of night out in the distance. Saylam
Academy stood proud, a beacon, beckoning me towards it. If we
left, there was no coming back from this, but Beatrice would be
tied to this in some twisted way, and she would be punished.

My dragon knew what I longed to do before I filled my mind
with the images.

Simion finally entered my mind again. *We will find a way back
for her.*

I didn't answer Simion with my own thoughts but filled them
with something he had said in passing in the library, the day
before the Claim. *I do not exactly have a dragon I could fly on and
break her out.*

Maximus, Simion's mind-speak was a scream, *don't!*

I threw the wall back up around my mind, cutting Simion's
plea off. There was nothing that could stop me from completing
my personal trial. I would not fail.

I showed my dragon what I required from her. We were both

weak, both broken and wounded. But there was one thing I needed with such a burning desire.

Beatrice. Academy. Go.

My dragon dipped low to the thrashing ocean. Sprays of salt crashed against her underbelly, sharing with me the pleasant sensation through our connection. She extended her wings out like the sail of a ship, catching the momentum and changing course.

We shot through the night, turning back towards the very place we were escaping. Roars filled the air behind me, whilst Simion continued to gain entry into my thoughts. I wouldn't lose my focus; I wouldn't turn my back on my friend a day longer.

Dayn would've given anything to save Sophia. He faced a barubore, prepared to use his body as a shield over hers. It was my turn to be Beatrice's shield. Her life had suffered because of my name. She had been criminalised, used, exiled and all the while I had longed to find a life whilst she waited for her impending judgement.

No more. I wouldn't leave without her.

It took little effort for Glamora to catch up, black scales blending seamlessly with the night. She was far larger than my dragon, more powerful and experienced. Any moment I expected her to stop us, to put her body before us and block the path. Instead, she kept pace. Soon enough, more of the rebellion's dragons flew into step.

My golden dragon speared through the night, uncontrolled, determination filling each powerful roar. I couldn't hear Simion's shouts, but his mouth moved frantically, hands pounding on the dragon's neck as though it would help him regain control.

It was futile. Because Glamora was not his to command.

She belonged to Beatrice.

In that moment, I knew Glamora sensed the same desire that boiled through me. This was why Glamora had been locked away —to keep her from clawing through stone to get to her bonded. To get to Beatrice.

I smiled into the night, weightless with relief, as I knew I was not the only one prepared to do anything to save Beatrice.

My dragon sensed my elation and drank from it. Wings flapped with verve; legs pounded into the sky as though it would speed us towards our destination. Every second drew out as I focused on the tower whilst my mind was pinned to the woman locked within it.

We reached Saylam Academy in minutes with Glamora leading ahead, and a rebellion at our back.

The trident spires that crowned the top of the Academy glowed like spears, catching the moonlight whilst oozing light from veins lingered throughout the stone. I remembered the awe it captured me in when I saw it for the first time. In a way, I shared the same feeling now but for different reasons.

I pushed out a command, fuelling my dragon with it.

Follow Glamora, she will find Beatrice.

There was no knowing where Beatrice was kept. But that was not a concern, because Glamora would find her through their bond.

And she did.

We flew around the spire of the tower twice before Glamora unleashed a growl so violent the night seemed to shiver, the stars hiding themselves behind ominous clouds. She held herself, wings pounding with vigour just to keep her in place. With a world-rocking inhale, Glamora unleashed a river of ice from her jaw.

It crashed into the tower's side. Silver spread over stone, webs of ice cracked and devoured everything beneath it. I urged my dragon to assist. She was not as large as Glamora, nor was her power as matured. But she helped. Frozen winds nipped at my face and knuckles as I held onto the horns down my dragon's spine, drunk on the shared power she spewed from her bowls.

Simion no longer fought against Glamora. It was pointless, he knew that. His sword was drawn, Leska held her mace ready, earthen cords of magic crackling from her eyes in a mist. The rebellion flew around, shielding us. There was no doubt that others would come to stop us.

Glamora ceased her ice-breath; my dragon followed. Saliva froze into shards of frozen death beneath her black-scaled mouth. She landed on the Academy's wall and began tearing at the ice-coated stone with her talons, like a child tore into a wrapped present during yule.

We were all left to watch. It was my dragon who sensed the danger, her focus hypervigilant on the silence around us. That quiet shattered apart by a noise from beneath us. I looked over the edge of my dragon, to watch a red-scaled dragon expel a screeching hiss. It shot out the layer of clouds clinging to the tower's wall, slithering up the Academy like a vengeful serpent. Silver flashed on its back. A battlemage, staff drawn, lightning crackling around its tip.

Leia's soldiers were here, just as Simion promised.

I thrust my awareness out, grasping my power. Before I could pull on my magic, stone cracked like a storm breaking. Glamora tore a section of the wall away, talons bleeding beneath the force. She lifted away from the wall and allowed the chunk to fall directly in the path of the red dragon and its battlemage.

Bones shattered and scales cracked. The force of broken wall caught the slithering beast in the maw, knocking it dead before it peeled from the wall and fell into the pits of cloud.

I held my breath until I heard the far-off thud of a body hitting the ground below. In my mind, I saw the smattered body laid out across the steps of the Academy, bodies crushed beneath it, steps shattered by the force.

Lightning cut across the night sky, illuminating everything. I saw more shapes beneath the clouds, more dragons clambering up towards us. A swarm of them.

If I thought the ruin was over, it had only just begun.

But nothing mattered as my eyes settled on the woman I had come for.

Beatrice stumbled out of the shadows, wind tearing her dark

hair until it whipped around her face like vipers. She moved towards the torn wall, hands gripping the jagged edges as she looked out at the sky full of dragons, blood and magic.

A bolt of lightning crashed into the wall beside her, casting her face in stark light. Through it all, she didn't scream. She didn't flinch.

Glamora roared with her success, knowing she had found what she had been longing to locate. Then she twisted in the air and shot towards the battlemage who had attempted to hurt Beatrice with their lightning. In seconds, their flesh was caught between the rows of her teeth.

Amber eyes settled on me. They found me through it all, tracing over my dragon, over me, from a distance. Beatrice's fist held firm at her sides, winds coiling around her as though her demeanour controlled the element.

The golden dragon beneath me didn't need a command. What I felt, she shared. We flew towards the torn away wall, giving view to the cell of dark stone within. Gravity pulled me back as my dragon settled on the wall, her compact body small enough to settle in the space Glamora had made.

There was so much I longed to say to Beatrice, but I knew she wouldn't have heard me over the ruckus of battle.

I extended a hand to her, eyes singing with the two words that burned through me.

I came.

Beatrice wasted no time in closing the space between my dragon and her. She threw herself behind me, arms wrapping around my middle and squeezing for dear life. There was hardly room for her body, but the weeks of imprisonment had made her look smaller, thinner. We made do with what he had. Beatrice buried her face into my back as I looked to the chaos of the skies.

There really was no coming back from this. I knew that. It was uncontested.

All I longed to do was get away from Wycombe and never look back. It was a common theme, always running from the place that held the title of 'home'. Then I remembered, it was not the place but the people. And with Beatrice's arms anchored around me, and the promise of seeing my mother, I had everything I needed.

A storm gathered above me as I drew upon my power. I wrapped my mental fists around every cord I could sense until my presence was in the sky, in the earth, in my dragon.

This magic was unlike anything I had experienced before. In fact, it was not mine at all. It was a gift, given by the creature who I clung to, the creature I had bonded with. My dragon's magic was mine in that moment, the winds, the air, the ice, the force. And I used it, just as I used the gifts given by my dryad blood.

I was formidable, for my family.

I thrust the magic outwards, clearing a path before me. Winds cast forward, lightning and ice with it. My dragon shot amongst it, passing by reaching talons and teeth, rebellion and soldiers, until there was nothing but the endless sea and wall of night before us.

When there was only ocean beneath us, I risked a glance back to find only a handful of dragons at our back. Glamora led them, eyes pinned to the woman clinging to me.

It was not nearly the number that had followed before. Many had fallen whilst we had freed Beatrice. Many more had died, names scrawled on a never-ending list. Names I never knew. Names I didn't care for.

All that mattered was escape. To put distance between me and the home I thought I'd carve for myself.

Except home was not a place, but a people. Beatrice taught me the very concept. One I had lost sight of and paid the price. I wouldn't forget it again.

PART THREE

OF MYTHS AND RUIN

CHAPTER 26

I kept my magic close. Although the earth was buried far beneath the ocean, I could still feel it. It was faint, the cords no more than streams of dust caught in the sunlight through a window. If I had to use it, I would, no matter the cost.

My golden dragon rumbled, rows of teeth flashing at the dragons around us, in warning, in promise. Behind me, Beatrice held on for dear life. There was barely room for her, but if she fell, I went with her—and my dragon wasn't going to allow that to happen.

The further we flew out across the Thassalic, the stronger the winds became. Thick clouds passed over the night sky, blocking out the stars. The waters beneath us crashed, mirroring the storm of emotion I was battered with.

So much had happened, and I feared it was far from over.

Simion's gaze passed over me continuously. His eyes glowed with relief and disbelief, but I sensed his thanks. I kept my gaze pinned forward, knowing if I looked at him for too long, I would lose my focus.

My thighs ached against the rippling muscles of my dragon's sides. I squeezed them tighter, knuckles paled as I grasped onto the ivory horns for leverage. Sea-salt spray slapped into my face, dampening my skin and hair until I looked as though I had swum in it. I was drenched, wet to the bone and cold.

A vicious boom split the night in two. I looked around, searching for the dragon who expelled it. But no one else seemed to react. When it came again, I was drawn back to the view ahead of me.

It was impossible to discern what I saw when the roar happened for a third time. It looked as though the night had thickened ahead, rising in a wall before us. My blood chilled to ice as I quickly realised what I witnessed. It was a wave, rolling in our direction, as tall as a Heart Oak, as wide as the Avarian Crest we had left behind. A frothing white crest at its tip, like a barrier of horses racing in a line—it readied to crash headfirst with us.

The gold-scaled dragon reacted to my sudden panic. She banked to the right, attempting to break free of the formation of dragons. But she failed. No one let us go, no one changed course. Glamora flew in close to our side, black wings beating with vigour. There wasn't the time to allow Simion back into my mind, not before the wave overcame us.

I pinched my eyes closed, sucking in a final breath. The night was impenetrable and black, but beneath the shadow of this towering wave, there was no light at all.

It rumbled, the ire of the water filling my ears with its demanding cry.

Then, just like that, it was over.

There was no water. There was no powerful force knocking us from the skies and into the ocean. My ears popped; my stomach jolted violently. As I had when I entered the Avarian Crest, I felt a wave of magic pass over my skin, as though I had pierced a veil.

I opened my eyes to watch my impending doom. Instead, I saw light. Fire light. Stretched out before us was a body of land, an island.

Rocks penetrated the waters around it like sentinels. Wrapping around the edge of the island was a barricade, built from glowing stone. I caught figures upon it, some standing behind strange weapons that looked like bows, so large they would take many hands to use. Burning torches reflected the light of the monstrous arrows set into the weapons, bolts that looked as though they were made for giants.

The dragons surrounding me changed course, forcing mine to follow. We flew around the length of wall, passing closer to the island's boundary. For as far as I could see, there were canopies of tents stretching across the land. It was as though a sea of material had been erected around a singular stone building with a flat roof and thick walls in its centre. A system of what had to be caves waited close to the northern shoreline of the island, shrouded in dark and secrets.

Flags billowed in the nightly wind, banners of deep purple with a painted spring of berries upon it. It was the very same I had seen—the sprig of hawthorn berries that had been left after the attack on the library. The same one the rebels had flaunted when they flew in and saved me from Leia's mages.

I had no doubt I was looking at the base of the rebellion. The Hawthorns.

My heart lodged in my throat as my earthen power burst to life. I felt my presence in every stone beneath me, every spec of dirt and blade of grass that stretched the expanse of the island.

There were so many people. Faces looked up and watched, hands raised to their brow, as we flew towards a stretch of clear land. I looked back out to sea to find an impenetrable mist that hung around the island like a curtain. There wasn't a tidal wave to be seen. The water was mostly calm, steady and glass-like.

The wave I had seen was real—real enough for me to prepare to meet my end. One moment I was ready to be swallowed by the ocean, the next I was here. This island was nowhere to be seen until it was. Magic, it had to be. Except this was magic that I was not familiar with. Whatever gods favoured the rebellion were not ones I was familiar with. It was not the cooling kiss of dragon power, or the solid, grounding draw of the dryads, or the burning passion of the phoenix.

It had been different.

The lower was gained to a stretched of clear ground, my anxiety had grown hands and squeezed my throat. If it wasn't for Simion who, the moment we landed, threw himself from Glamora's side, landing smoothly and reached us in a few powerful strides.

Beatrice tumbled from my dragon's side, falling directly into her brother's arms. I longed to do the same. Instead, I just watched, unable to move. It was Beatrice who consoled her brother as he sobbed into the crook of her neck, face buried in her hair.

It was both heartbreaking and joyful, watching the siblings hold each other as though they never thought it would happen.

Then golden-hued eyes raised to me, and Simion extended a hand, beckoning me to join them. There were no words, no request. Just the look he gave me sang of his want, whilst simultaneously making me act upon it.

I fell, willingly, from my dragon's back, into his waiting arms. Partly from over-exhaustion but more from the reality that we had made it. Together. Pain jolted up my broken ankle, reminding me I was in no position to fight. Perhaps my dragon sensed it. It wasn't that I watched the golden dragon curl around us, I felt it. A press of cool gold scales on my skin, a brush of her protective presence. Glamora did the same, covering us with her shadow, a hiss breaking out of her jaw in warning to the growing crowd of rebels around us.

'I've got you, Maximus. Beatrice.' Simion spoke in hushed, breathless words. Each one sounding as hard to expel as the next. 'Nothing bad will happen, I swear it.'

It was as though he spoke more to convince himself than us.

Simion's fingers reached for my ankle, brushing carefully over the snapped bone within. I hadn't needed to tell him I had broken it—Simion knew my body well enough to sense a problem even amongst such chaos.

He fixed my shattered ankle as more people bustled around us. The bones formed together, carefully mending the damage. I know he did it quietly to keep me ready, prepared. For *anything*.

Metal sang against leather as Simion withdrew the sword at his belt, levelling it towards the crowd who encircled us. Even my gilded dragon snarled her teeth, tail whipping. Distrust rolled off Simion in waves.

'Not one more step!' He sneered, glaring down the edge of his blade.

The crowd hesitated. Leska was there too, placing her body between us, joining Simion in his threat. 'You heard him, lads. Keep your distance.'

If I thought they trusted the rebellion, it was proved otherwise in that moment.

A stab of Simion's power slammed across the barrier around my mind. The ground rumbled beneath Leska. Glamora and my dragon slithered like snakes, wings caught to the back, teeth flashing to anyone who got close enough.

Then the crowd parted, splitting into two sections to allow for someone to walk through the middle.

The phantom hands of anxiety around my throat loosened but slammed hard into my gut.

'Elder Cyder?' I looked, dumbfounded, at the man walking swiftly towards us.

'Hello, Maximus.' Relief softened his brow. 'I admit, this was not how I saw this going.'

Leska didn't lower her amplifier, not as her father stepped into view. Her face pinched into a scowl, her own teeth flashing as though she was more dragon than human. 'The warning stays the same, Father.' She spat the title at him. 'Keep your distance.'

'We have lost many brave soldiers today.' He shifted his blue eyes from me to the dragons, Beatrice and then back. 'Do you know the damage you have done? Breaking someone out of Saylam Academy... this was not the order I gave you.'

I felt as though we were being reprimanded by a parent.

'We are not yours to command, Cyder.' Hate filled every word Simion spat.

I broke free of his hold, standing alongside my dragon as I gave into the anger within me. As though the emotion was a monster unto itself, the anger cracked an eye open and looked directly in the face of Elder Cyder. 'Don't talk to me about loss. You can't begin to understand the meaning of the word.'

'Oh, but I do.' He lifted a finger, pointing directly at Beatrice. 'How can I protect you? How, if you are going to ruin everything, I have worked towards... by bringing her.'

'Beatrice Hawthorn,' Leska spat, fingers wringing around the handle of her amplifier. 'Say her name, Father. I would have thought it would be easy for you to say it, since it's the very name your little rebellion goes by.'

Elder Cyder took a deep breath, filling his chest whilst attempting to regain composure. The countless faces of rebels seemed to shift around. 'I would not exactly call it little, daughter. Look around you, see for yourself.'

Leska refused to take her eyes off her father. 'Your numbers still pale in comparison to Leia's battlemages, and you know it.'

'All this time, and it was you.' My brain imploded, detaching me from the world. 'The rebellion, the attacks on Wycombe. It was you.'

I trusted you.

I waited for him to dispel the accusation—instead Cyder confirmed it. 'Maximus, we prefer the term resistance.'

'You wanted me dead.' My dragon thrust her head over us, jaws snapping inches from where Elder Cyder stood. His beard tugged to the side beneath the force of my dragon's frozen winds. '*You* sent Aaron to the South to kill me!'

The ground shuddered, but it wasn't from me. It was Leska who reacted, her magic flaring at the mention of Aaron. Her reaction stilled her father. He looked at her, grimacing as though he stared at a festering wound, instead of his daughter.

There was one thing that cut deeper than a knife; secrets. And Elder Cyder had an abundance of them.

He lifted a hand to my dragon's snout. As his fingers graced her cool gold scales, I felt my ire slip away.

'Now Maximus,' Elder Cyder said, stroking my dragon as though she was some household pet and not a vicious god, 'if that was *still* the case, we wouldn't have risked our inside agents by rescuing you from Elder Leia's grasp. The tides have changed, alliances have shifted. Allies are simply enemies who share a common cause.'

'Is that what I am to you, your enemy?' My lip curled over my teeth.

Cyder's expression softened, his lips turning down, bright eyes dulling. He either couldn't find the words or didn't want to voice them.

'Answer him, Cyder, so I know what to do with this.' Simion lowered his sword only when Elder Cyder brushed it away with the back of his fingers.

'I am afraid that is all perspective. Only you can answer that.' Cyder's reply was not what I expected but still clear enough. 'It would seem we have lots of issues to smooth out in the meantime. Starting with Mistress Hawthorn, she will need to be seen by a healer.'

'No,' Simion growled. 'No one touches her.'

'I can speak for myself, brother,' Beatrice snapped, voice as dry as stone. She pushed herself free, stood and placed herself beside me. 'Or have you forgotten this in the past weeks?'

'But Beatrice—'

There was something harder about her. Beatrice was still my friend, but recent events had chipped away at her bit by bit. 'I have survived this far without you, Simion. I have faced the treatment of our aunt; I am sure what Cyder here has to offer will seem like luxury in comparison.'

There was nothing he could say back to that. Beatrice was right and that reality hurt tremendously.

'Please,' Elder Cyder said, hands raised to his side in surrender. 'I understand you all have questions. Some more than others.' His eyes cut to his daughter whose eyes glowed with power—poised and ready to use it. 'We have dragons who need seeing to, wounded to heal and deaths to respect. It has been a long night, an even longer few days for some and weeks for others.'

'I'll go with you,' Beatrice said, gesturing to those around her. 'Wouldn't want to upset you any further... since you made it clear I am such a burden.'

'Not a burden, Beatrice. Simply a surprise. And we don't like surprises, makes keeping up our secretive pretences rather difficult.'

Simion locked eyes with me, a question lingering in the furrow of his brow and the narrowing of his amber eyes. I nodded, knowing exactly what he wished to ask me. He was searching for permission to leave me.

'Leska,' Simion called out without removing his eyes from me. 'Will you stay with him?'

Him. Me.

When I looked to Leska, I was surprised to hear her agree. 'Yes.'

Beatrice was already walking away with her escort, head held high and shoulders back. Simion looked between us, the tension of choice evident in every creased line over his face.

'Go,' I mouthed, when I silently harboured the truth of what I wanted.

Don't leave me, never leave me. I can't do this without you.

Simion shot one more look to Cyder, his expression hardening into one of warning and promise. 'Harm him, and I swear I will destroy everything you've worked towards, Cyder.'

To my surprise, Cyder smiled and spoke. 'I do not doubt it for a second. If I wanted Maximus harmed, I wouldn't have wasted valuable soldiers saving him.'

Glamora lifted into the skies, battering winds down upon us. Then she was gone, black scales blending with the night as she followed Beatrice.

'Maximus, I am sure you have many questions to ask me, but shall we begin by visiting your mother?' Elder Cyder called out, gesturing for me to join him.

'What have you done to her?' I simmered in the thoughts of her suffering, her pain. The cottage was destroyed, Leia had learned of my mother's sickness.

'Nothing you haven't asked of me. And I take my promises very seriously, Maximus. Deborah is safe and in better hands than she would have been if—'

'Where?' I refused to blink, refused to look away as I stared at the man I trusted.

He gestured north, in the direction where I had seen the formation of caves when we flew over the island. 'Deborah is currently being cared for by the only *beings* with the power to stifle the possession she is suffering.'

'I saw the cottage,' I spat, the image of destruction filling my mind. 'I saw the destruction…'

'Your mother didn't react well to the news of your departure to the Claim. From our understanding, those who suffer from the burning plague have their passions amplified, and hers were practically overspilling,' Elder Cyder said, hands clasped before the swell of his stomach. 'No matter the light you see me in now, I am a man of my word. Deborah, you, Simion, Beatrice, my daughter. You are safe whilst you are here.'

A deranged, bubbling laugh broke out of me. I scanned the crowd, faces alight by the glow of firelight. 'It is always those you think you can trust, who turn out to be the ones you can't.' I shot my gaze to Leska. 'Did you know about this?'

'No.' Leska held my gaze, her jaw tense. I could practically hear her teeth grind with tension. 'I did not.'

I believed her implicitly.

'It was safer if my daughter did not know about my dealings,'

Elder Cyder said, genuine concern dripping from his tongue. 'Believe it or not, but I do not wish to jeopardise her, nor any of you. This was my last resort, one I was forced to take.'

'So, you don't deny it?' I said, my dragon hissing, magic thrashing in my veins. 'It was you, behind the abductions, the missing novices, the attacks of the phoenix-possessed. Using the South against the North. All this time...'

'Not everything is as it seems, Maximus Oaken. You should know this. What picture Elder Leia and her Council paints of us is simply to aid her own wants. Yes, I have lied to you all, but not about everything.' Elder Cyder cut his gaze across me. 'You will get your answers soon, I promise.'

'What does this mean for us?' I asked the question I feared I already knew the answer.

Elder Cyder paused, hands wringing together before me. It was as though every soul on the island held a collective breath. Then he opened his mouth and spat the words out I never believed I would hear. 'Welcome, all of you, to the resistance.'

CHAPTER 27

The moment my eyes fell upon my mother, I felt all the tension seep from my body. Days of pent-up anxiety ebbed out of me as the azure waters around her gauze-wrapped body rippled and shifted.

She floated in a pool of glowing water. It was one of many pockets of water buried into the stone floor, in this strange network of caves beneath the island. In each one of them, another body floated, face peaceful, eyes closed. It was as though a star was buried beneath the water, because it glowed with a shimmering silver light. Ethereal.

'Is she…' I couldn't face to speak the word aloud.

Dead.

Dryads, she looked it. Wrapped in white cloth, floating without aid in a pool of water, eyes closed and face void of haunting emotion or pain.

'Deborah is currently in a stasis state. It isn't so much as healing her but keeping the burning plague from causing her suffering and pain.' Elder Cyder's voice echoed across the low stone walls. He rubbed his hand up his arm, pushing the sleeve away enough for me to notice a glint of metal around it. He caught me looking and quickly rolled down his sleeve, covering the cuff of silver inset with blue gems. Although, I got the impression he longed for me to see it. 'It is the same for all of the unfortunate souls we are looking after here.'

I looked across the cave, unable to count the number of bodies that floated in little pockets of glowing water. There were so many of them. 'All these people are... phoenix-possessed?'

'Do you know, I petitioned for Leia to let me continue my research. I believed I had a way of helping those in need, but you know she was not open to such concepts.' Elder Cyder placed a hand on my shoulder. It was a gentle gesture, familiar. 'It has been a challenge getting these people here from the South. Some have slipped through our nets, but mostly we have been successful. Leia would say we are using them, when all I have been trying to do is save them. It is my job. Something Leia prevented me from doing.'

'And the novices? The missing students who were abducted?'

'*My* students wanted to help. You cannot ask a healer to stand back and watch those in need suffer and perish, or worse... slaughtered like sick animals. Leia called it abduction, we prefer seeing it as using all possible means to do what we must. To save innocent lives. With some unfortunate mishaps on the way, as you are aware, our goal is and has been about preventing the deaths of innocents. I fear there is more in the city we will not be able to save, not now Leia will know I have betrayed her.'

'The library, was that one of the mishaps?' I asked, unable to fathom how Cyder wanted nothing more than to help the South. Separated by Galloway Forest, the North and South never worked together, until now. Until him.

'No, Max. The attack on library was planned, however it seemed the phoenix-possessed were still drawn to you. I wouldn't have chosen it if I knew Leska was not training you. Just as the attack on Leia's armoury was planned.'

My mouth dried at the new information. 'Why?'

'Because you asked it of me. When we saw one another in the infirmary, you asked me to stop Leia from attacking the South. So

I did what I could, with what I had.' Cyder bit down on his thin lip, the skin around it paling.

'The library was a distraction, whilst you attacked the armoury?'

'Indeed. And it worked, didn't it? Leia has yet to send her numbers to the South, it has not stopped the inevitable attack, but postponed it.'

You asked me to stop Leia. I did what I could.

Elder Cyder shifted, standing almost too close to my side. But it wasn't disconcerting, it was oddly comforting. 'When Queen Romar entered the North, I had hoped Leia would see the need to finally help our siblings in the South. Sadly, you witnessed how that went. I am simply taking what was given to us and using it to help a cause.'

My breath hitched in my throat at the memory of the Southern Queen's death. 'I have so many questions.'

'And I have many answers, Maximus Oaken.' He raised a hand to my shoulder. I fought the urge to shrug it off. That didn't stop Cyder from reading my body language and removing it. 'I am going to ask that you trust me, Maximus. As you did before. Nothing has changed, only that you have found out my secret. I still long to help *you*.'

That single word soured in my mouth, even though I didn't speak it. Yes, I did trust Elder Cyder. But trust was a blind thing, something I clearly handed out too freely. 'How do I trust the man who sent his soldier to kill me?'

'I admit, Aaron was a mistake,' Elder Cyder said, clearing his throat. 'One I have regretted deeply since.'

'I'm surprised you don't deny it,' I snapped. 'It would be easy for you to lie; after all, you've had plenty of practice.'

He raised a single brow in contest. 'Haven't we all?'

Beyond the cave, wrapped around a pillar of rock, I sensed my gilded dragon erupt in a growl. She waited outside the system of caverns beneath the island, as did Leska. She was at Elder Cyder's order. Although I had no doubt that if I required my dragon's aid, she would claw through rock to get to me.

'Then why did you want me dead?' The question was clear, ricocheting off the cave's walls, rippling over the honeycomb pools throughout it.

'You were important to the Queen.'

'As simple as that?'

He nodded once, eyes falling to his boots. 'Since Celia Hawthorn was exiled, we have been working in the shadows, attempting to dismantle the Queen and Council. You were simply one of them. Not only were you important to the Queen, but you were also the reason why Celia was punished, as with Beatrice's exile. It wasn't personal, it was simply our attempt to hurt the Queen by taking something important from her. You could call it a lesson.'

'One ruined when Camron killed her for you?'

Elder Cyder chewed on the question, toying with his careful answer. 'I admit we never wished death on the Queen, but Camron's actions saved us a lot of trouble. Does that make me a monster?'

'It makes you honest,' I replied, because there was nothing else I could think of to say. I attempted to steady my expression, worried I would give my inner thoughts away, my secrets. 'And do you know why I was important to the Queen?'

Elder Cyder's brow furrowed, lines creasing across his bald head. 'That, I am not confident enough to answer. Nor am I going to ask you as to why, or petition for warrant into your thoughts as Elder Leia has been working towards these past weeks. I'm sure, in time, you will tell me, once you learn to trust me again.'

'If you think I will allow you to use me against *her*, you are wrong.' My fist clenched, cords of power brightening around me. I was surrounded by earth, it was everywhere, reminding me it would heed my call if required. 'All I want is to live, with my mother. No battles, no burdens, not secrets and lurking threats.'

Out of everything I said, it was the first comment that Cyder latched onto. 'Are you suggesting you are a tool to be used, Maximus?'

I swallowed hard, studying the man before me, searching for a reason not to break the spike of rock and drop it on him. 'That would depend.'

'I understand being used is something you are used to. Perhaps you even expect it.' Elder Cyder stepped away from me, robes shifting around him as he knelt before my mother's pool of water and dipped his fingers into it. Ripples cast away from his hand, each one glowing with the bright blue sheen. 'That is not the case here. Although my words are just words to you at this time.'

He lifted his hand up to the waters, as though calling something forth from it. I didn't know what he was doing until I caught a ripple at my mother's side. I blinked, unsure what I was seeing, when an opaque hand lifted out of the waters in return. My feet drew me closer to the water's edge, peering beneath the clear waters. There was nothing to be seen. Was I so tired my mind was conjuring illusions?

When my eyes rested on my mother, there was nothing else in the world that mattered.

'Is she going to be okay?' I asked, gaze fixed on her smooth face. Unlike the last time I saw her, she didn't look as though she suffered. She was finally at peace.

'She will not die,' Elder Cyder answered, 'if that is what you are asking.'

'But living through the possession is as bad as death. I know what she will become.'

The fast-marks beneath my sleeve shivered, as though the thought of Camron caused a physical reaction. He hadn't filled my mind since the vision Oribon tested me with. So much had happened since to keep me occupied.

Until now. Now he stepped out of the darkness again, lurking in the far reaches, reminding me of the possibility of him. The satchel had made it to the island with me, his journal still inside.

There was no ignoring that when Cyder looked to my mother, his expression softened. A glint of emotion seemed to cause him great discomfort, and yet he couldn't tear his eyes off her. 'With the help of the waters, your mother will survive the burning plague, but it will not cure her of it.'

'What good can these waters do if it cannot exorcise the monster that is mutating her?'

As I asked the question, something else materialised at my mother's side. A face. It was made from water, features solidifying into a mask that looked almost human. I blinked, lowering my fingers to disrupt the reflection that looked back at me.

'It can ensure her body is strong enough to survive the possession. That is half the battle. And, as you can see, Deborah is in very good hands.'

The face lifted out of the pool until I saw a neck, a torso, a body made from the same blue expanse my mother bathed in. Pale eyes like pools of milk set in a face without skin or bones; hair of sea-foam and weed, cascading and rippling.

'Nymph,' I breathed, unable to move away. 'They are working with you.'

'I had the same reaction when I saw a god of water for the first time,' Elder Cyder said, although he sounded far away, as ringing filled my ears. 'Solitary creatures, they usually keep to themselves. Like you, they do not trust easily. So take their presence here as yet more confirmation that we are on the right side of this fight. We, too, have gods behind us.'

I couldn't fathom what I witnessed. The nymph rose upwards, body crafted from azure liquid, features clear yet wavering, shifting. When it opened its mouth, it wasn't words that came out, but the sound of water against rocks, the bubbling of a brook, the rush of a stream. It shifted like a wave, moving swiftly behind my mother, where it lifted its strange hand to her lips, droplets falling from its liquid-skin into her parted mouth.

Protective panic had me reaching forward, ready to disrupt

the creature and get it away from my mother. Elder Cyder stopped me with a firm hand. 'Allow the god to do what it must.'

'But—'

'Do you remember the vial I gave to you? The liquid inside was an offering from the nymphs. They have power to combat the devouring burn of the phoenix. It cannot eradicate the creature from the host, but it can smother it. Prolonging the possession whilst we continue to search for a permanent cure.'

I blinked, unable to take my eyes off the god. The noise that bubbled out of its mouth filled the cave like a song. Soon more voices joined as the nymphs revealed themselves in each of the glowing pools, caring for the bodies of those floating in them.

'And do you believe there is a cure?' I said, unable to blink, unable to remove my eyes from the vision before me.

'I believe so. I just need time to discover it. Something which is proving difficult with all these recent distractions.' Elder Cyder nudged my shoulder, shooting me a sideways glance.

It was me, I was the distraction.

Hope swelled in my chest—then came crashing down. 'But Leia,' I spat, suddenly breathless. 'She will send an army to the South if we—'

A hand rested on my shoulder again, fatherly and calming. 'We have the time to plan our next move. And I hope you will do so beside me. After all, you are their rightful King. No matter what you have learned to believe about the Hawthorns, our goals are very similar.'

My skin itched at the title he had used, but this time I didn't refuse it. There was no point; he was right. 'Cyder, if you want me to trust you, then you will need to be honest. No lies, no misleading illusions.'

'I will, but you must rest first. There is nothing you can do now, not in the state you are in. And believe me, after what you orchestrated with Beatrice's breakout, Leia and the Council's focus will be on retrieving you. The South will be safe, for now.'

I caught my fingernails between my teeth. In the far reaches of my mind, my dragon paced and moved, sharing the pent-up energy. 'That should calm me, but it doesn't.'

'Breathe, Maximus. You have faced more than any of us. Moving straight from the Claim to tonight's events, it is a miracle you are still standing.' He pointed towards the end of the cave were the azure glow of water reflected off the rockface walls. 'There is a pool of water spare that you can bathe in. Clean clothes will be provided, followed by a meal, then sleep. Then perhaps I can share my plans, and you can share how you obtained that dragon of yours...'

'You know how.' Tears pricked at the back of my eyes. 'I passed the trials where others didn't.'

He sensed the sadness, the pain that lingered behind the fact I had bonded with a dragon.

'You are safe,' Elder Cyder said, head nodding towards the nymph who floated around my mother's still body. 'As is Deborah. This base has been here for many years, Maximus. Elder Leia will not be able to locate us, and, if she does, you saw what she must pass through to reach us.'

The tidal wave. 'It was real, the wave I saw.'

'It was an illusion, but it could have been real if required.' Cyder lifted a hand and rubbed it over his sleeve, to the beautiful cuff hidden beneath it. 'The nymphs were always known to be the tricksters of the four elemental gods. They can conjure deceptions, much like the ones surrounding this island. Ways of diverting gazes, keeping unwanted visitors away. But they, too, can make those illusions real, if required. Nothing would stop them from rising a wave so great it would wash half of Aldian away in an instant. I hardly imagine Elder Leia has the power to combat a god, don't you agree, Max?'

'They have dragons,' I said, jaw set firm. 'And they have the support of the dryads.'

'Ah, but they don't.' He wagged his finger, clicking his tongue as though he was pleased to reveal that to me. 'Since the Queen died, the dryads departed the city. That is part of Elder Leia's desperation. She is unable to commune with the very gods that helped create us. Leia feels as though they have turned their back on us. And they have, I am sure.'

'And where are we exactly, am I privy to know that?'

Elder Cyder smiled. 'The first step to trust is honesty. We are concealed far from Wycombe, in the midst of the Unknown Isles.'

My mind went directly to the journal. Camron had depicted his journey to the Unknown Isles; hearing it from Elder Cyder made his story visceral and real. My hand went to my satchel, pressing against the journal lingering within. It hadn't left me since I departed the Avarian Crest. Since...

Dayn

I blinked and saw his body, felt the pressure of his limp form in my arms until I handed him over to the Council member. I hadn't noticed it until now, but a brown stain had worn into my tunic. It was Dayn's blood. But instead of staying with him, I had left him, forgotten, as I fled to find my mother.

'You are haunted,' Elder Cyder spoke softly, his gaze over-spilling with worry. 'I can see it in your eyes.'

I opened my mouth to tell him what had happened during the Claim. Something stopped me.

'Take some time to be with your mother,' he said instead, offering me a kind smile that faded as he gazed towards the cave's exit. 'Bathing in the waters will help restore some energy to your body. In the meantime, I must go and speak with my daughter. As you can imagine my lies haven't only affected you. She deserves an explanation now she knows I am the one responsible for Aaron's death.'

I swallowed hard, seeing the torment and guilt Elder Cyder suffered. One touch and it seemed he longed for me to sense the emotion, forcing a hint of it into my mind. 'Do not blame her for hating you.'

'However Leska views me now, she knows the truth, I deserve it.' Elder Cyder said, drawing his hand away. 'Oh, and Maximus, one more thing before I leave.'

'Yes?'

'There is a rule I must ask that you follow during your stay here.'

A strange feeling swelled within me.

'Curfew. From dusk to dawn, please stay in your provided tent. Camping with so many around is difficult as it is, it is best we respect each other's need for rest.'

'Of course,' I said, glancing back to my mother. 'But what about tonight?'

'Tonight is a *special* expectation. But once you are done here, someone will be ready to escort you to your tent.' A heavy hand patted my shoulder. 'Your compliance is truly appreciated.'

CHAPTER 28

I stared at the candle's flame, wondering when it would devour me. It was only a small thing, a wick no bigger than my thumb, yet it still conjured such a deep-rooted fear I couldn't ignore it. Even now, Camron had so much power over me.

I hated it. I hated *him*.

The beeswax candle was set upon a small table in the centre of the tent. The glow reflected off the dull metal of a tankard beside it whilst illuminating the crumbs left on the plate of food I had just devoured. And then there was Camron's journal. It waited before me, a semi-conscious presence, begging me to take it in my hands and open it. And a part of me longed to open the pages, to devour Camron's story. Another part of me, the louder more vicious part, wanted to rip it to shreds and allow the pages to wither in flame.

But I wouldn't, because I was weak. Even after everything, I couldn't give up on his story. Not until I understood what he went through. This journal could hold the secrets to saving my mother, it could hold the key to understanding how the plague was spreading—and how to stop it.

As promised, Elder Cyder had provided me with a small tent in the heart of the camp. It was a modest dwelling, enough room for two people, three at a push. No matter its comforts or lack of, I couldn't sleep.

Dawn fast approached; I hadn't slept in a day, but my mind no longer suffered. Since climbing from the nymph's water, I felt alert. It had to be magic, a result of bathing in the waters of a god. If I lifted my skin to my nose, I could almost smell it. Faint and sweet. Clear-minded and rested. Reassured that if I could feel like this after bathing in their magic, my mother would be okay.

My dragon didn't experience the same struggles. She waited beyond the tent's entrance, curled up in a ball of gilded scales. Her wings were still torn from the attack in the Avarian Crest, although her deepest wound was the grief I sensed across the cord that tethered us.

I had promised to return her to her eggs, but instead I had criminalised her the moment she flew over Wycombe. There was no denying I didn't deserve the dragon's respect, yet she hadn't left me. Nor did she allow anyone to heal her.

It was through our bond that I sensed a disturbance beyond the tent. A presence, it woke the dragon, and warned me of the visitor. If it wasn't for the familiar trace of ice against my mental shields that followed the dragon's warning, I wouldn't have allowed her to let them pass.

It was Simion, someone I could never refuse.

I stood abruptly, smoothing the creases from the brown training leathers Cyder had provided to me. The form-fitting top and trousers hugged the lines of my body, straps tightened around my waist, with empty holders for weapons I had not been provided with. It was strange, but it felt odd to have Simion see me dressed in the same uniform of the rebellion, especially with the symbol of the Hawthorn berry stitched over my heart.

Although it was the perfect place to put his family crest.

Simion entered, pushing the tent flaps aside with the sweep of his hand. Before his eyes settled on me, he swept them over the tent—searching. Silence stretched out between us, unspoken words that had built over the days we had been separated. He didn't know what I had faced, nor did I know what had happened to him. But in that silence was a mutual understanding, patience and the need for careful, gentle hands.

The *need* for one another.

'Looking for something?' I asked, unable to take my eyes from him.

'Yes, and I found him,' Simion responded calmly, offering me a smile that didn't quite reach his eyes. He looked tired, as though a deep-rooted exhaustion had burrowed itself into his very bones.

I hadn't seen him since we arrived on the island. Part of me longed for him to find me, the other wished for him to stay with Beatrice. At least she was safe... at least she was free.

'Not to say I don't want you here, but you *shouldn't* be here' I said, catching a glimpse of the still dark sky. 'The curfew.'

'Fuck the curfew,' Simion said. 'I would have come sooner but—'

I raised a hand, cutting his excuse off. 'I understand. Beatrice, how is she?'

Simion closed his eyes, bowing his head. 'She will be fine. My sister is resilient. It will take more to break her, but that still does not suggest she has not suffered minor wounds.'

'You could've stayed with her,' I said, finding my eyes falling to his chest. It was easier to look at his body than hold his stare. 'She needs you right now.'

'And what about your needs?'

The question knocked the wind out of my lungs; it was as though he reached inside of me and found that desire, exposing it. 'Stop worrying about everyone else but yourself, Simion.'

'All right.' He stepped into the tent, bringing with him the scent of pine, open forest and earth. 'Allow me to rephrase what I said. What if *I* need you?'

I wanted nothing more than to throw myself into his arms, but there were still thorns keeping us apart. The same thorns that had punished me when we had last tested the fast-mark bond between Camron and me.

The few days we had been separated felt more akin to a century.

'You know that isn't wise.'

'Then I would happily be a fool,' Simion replied, candlelight reflecting off his skin, hardening the edges of his powerful jaw. 'I can't help myself around you. The moment you left me... I... you've never left my mind.'

A deep-chested growl rolled out of my dragon, her outline shifting outside the tent's walls, re-curling back into her ball of gold.

'You're not the only one,' I whispered, a blush creeping over my face.

'I am glad you don't deny it.' Simion looked behind me, to the glint of golden scales through the gap of the tent's entrance. 'You know, Glamora won't leave Beatrice's side either. If what the dragon did to free Beatrice is anything to go by, then nothing will happen to her. She has a god protecting her. Same goes for you. It is a bond I will never experience, but I have enough knowledge to revere it.'

'Then that is more evidence that you don't need to waste energy worrying about me.'

Simion puffed out a laugh. 'As if that would ever be a possibility. I will sleep better knowing your dragon is close.'

My chest warmed. Since bonding with the creature, I had felt more at ease. As though a shield was constantly strapped to my back. 'We've been through a lot together, in a short period of time,' I said, feeling the weight of these words on my shoulders. 'I can't explain it... but I feel as though I have always known her.'

The memory was painful. The loss we had endured.

'Do you want to talk about it?' Simion asked, pulling up a chair and sitting at the table with me. I fought the urge to reach for Camron's journal and conceal it. But I had nothing to hide. Not from him. 'I suppose rules do not matter, not here. If you want to off-load what you went through in the Claim, I will listen.'

'Not yet.'

Honestly, I wanted to bury the memory of the trials. Of what was lost.

Simion rubbed his jaw, fingers bristling over days' worth of growth. I couldn't help but think how it suited him, the dark hairs framing his sculpted face, hollowing his cheekbones and sharpening his jawline. 'I understand. When you are ready, I am here. Always.'

Always. Dryads, that one word was far too powerful on his tongue.

'What happened, Simion?' I asked, finally brave enough to hear the truth of what I had missed. 'How did I come back to this?'

He took a deep breath in. His shoulders hunched forward as though the weight of the world rested on them. His discomfort at the question drove me forward; I pulled my chair until I sat directly beside him. There was nothing but inches between us, which was a risk. One I selfishly was willing to take.

'Where do I start?'

'The beginning,' I whispered.

Simion narrowed his eyes at my sarcasm, although I could tell he enjoyed it. I seemed to find strength the closer I was to him. It took effort not to reach out and touch him.

'Elder Cyder sent me directly to your mother after I gave you the injection,' Simion began, gaze drifting off as he revisited the memory. 'I promised I would keep her safe, no matter the cost. Deborah was unconscious and suffering, but I think my presence gave her some comfort. I did not tell her why I was here, Cyder told me not to. But by the time Cyder arrived, she...'

I blinked and saw the ruin left in the place the cottage once was. Now there was nothing but the charred remains of a cliff ravaged by wytchfire.

'He was able to subdue her with a draught he brought, the same one he had provided to you before. But the damage was done, he had to get her away from Wycombe before my aunt got to her. It was then his involvement in the rebellion was revealed to me, he had no choice if it meant getting Deborah to safety.'

I caught the way he looked at me, as though he was disappointed in something.

'Are you angry with me for not telling you about my mother being sick?'

'No,' Simion said, face softening as though he didn't realise his reaction gave away his internal thoughts. 'No, because you were right not to tell me. I knew what my aunt was doing to the phoenix-possessed. How can I be angry at you, Max, when I am furious at myself. It proves only that I continuously fail you. Only I am to blame. You should have been able to trust me with your secrets. Dryads, I should be worthy of them, but I am not. I have been helping the wrong side of this...'

'None of it matters.' Unable to resist him, I took Simion's hand and squeezed it, allowing him a moment to calm himself. 'Carry on, Simion. I need to know it all. What happened next?'

'Glamora. Cyder instructed me and Leska to free her. Cyder sensed we would need her, and he was right. He then called back all his rebels from their placements within the city, even from within the Council. He was preparing for the inevitable, without it I fear the worst would have already come.'

'I've turned everything on its head,' I exhaled, a sudden jolt of pain stabbing through my skull. 'And now we have become enemies to the Council. You have gone against your own family...'

'To save my family.' Simion winced, turning his head away at the mention of his sister's name. 'To save Beatrice and *you*.'

'Do you trust Cyder?' I asked, gazing down at our entwined fingers, refusing to focus on the way he was looking at me as if I was the only soul in the world.

'Do you?' Simion replied, forehead furrowing with harsh worry lines.

I took a deep breath in, allowing the time I had missed to

slowly piece together in my mind. 'There isn't much choice. But yes... I do.'

'Then that is enough for me. Where you go, I go. What you do, I do.'

It was so easy, almost too easy, to lose myself in Simion's gilded eyes. I had to snatch myself back, just to stop myself from closing those final inches between us. 'Leia is going to use every tool, every power at her disposal, to find us. And we are going to need to decide to help when she does.'

'Leia can't reach us here,' he said. 'Her control is strong, but not indestructible. The Hawthorns have evaded prying eyes for years. That isn't going to change now. You are safe here.'

'*We* are safe.'

It was almost impossible to believe, but I had to. If I didn't, then there was nothing stopping the pain from rising like a tidal wave once again.

'Elder Cyder has called a meeting to begin after daybreak, to discuss our plans and ensure everyone has the same understanding.' Simion's brow furrowed, his hand rubbing the back of his head. 'Between the threat of an army in the South, and Elder Leia's intentions to execute every person suffering from the burning plague, there is much to prepare for.'

I turned my attention towards the journal left on the table. It weighed heavy in my fingers as I lifted it, still warm to the touch, as though Camron's presence had worn itself into the cover.

'Then there is the other matter we must worry about.'

'What is it?' Simion took it carefully from me. As his finger traced over the leather binding, my skin shivered as though he touched me.

'Camron's journal,' I said.

If Simion's eyes had held the power of destruction, he would've ruined the journal simply by looking at it. Before he could ask any questions, I gave him what little answers I had. 'Before the Claim, I found it in Leia's study. I took it with me...'

Simion refused to touch it, handing it back to me, his face screwed in disgust. 'Did you read it?'

'The real question is, why did Leia have it? Or how.' It wore heavy in my hands, reminding me of the burden inked on the skin of my arm. 'I read it for answers. He was my husband, after all.'

Simion's handsome face broke into a feral snarl. 'He never deserved that title.'

'You speak of him as if he is dead, when we both know that is not the case.'

Simion looked everywhere but at me. I searched his face, waiting for him to level his gaze with mine again, but he didn't. He refused no matter how I silently urged him.

'I have seen his ashes, Max.'

'Only in death shall you part. The rules are simple as the magic is old. It should be broken... but it is not. Many people died that day, what is to say Leia is using someone else's remains in Camron's place.'

'You think she has lied all this time?'

I shrugged, hating the tension that thrummed between us. 'It wouldn't have been the first time.'

When I reached for his hand again, Simion pulled away. His reflex was lightning fast; he grimaced at his own reaction, knowing what it would mean to me.

There was a barrier between Simion and me, a double-edged blade as sharp as lightning, conjured in the days we had been kept apart. We both knew what would happen if we got too close, if we gave into the desires we equally shared.

No matter how I physically longed for him, it could never happen.

'So, you don't wish to touch me anymore?' I snapped, eyes narrowed as a torrent of anger burst out of me.

Simion stood and stepped back, eyes lowered to the floor. 'I'm sorry, Maximus. I should really leave you to—'

'No!' I shouted, scraping my chair back, not caring if I woke the entire fucking island up. 'If you dare take a step outside of this tent, Simion Hawthorn, I swear I will make you regret the day you left me.' When he looked back at me, his amber eyes glowered with sorrow. It was a beautiful thing, to watch a strong man present emotion. Simion didn't just wear his heart on his sleeve, he held it in two hands and extended it for me.

'How can I be what you need, when one wrong touch causes you immense pain? How can I possibly stay close knowing I can make you suffer? What happened back at the Mad Queen, it has haunted me. Every day, every hour, every *fucking* second. Your scream rings in my skull, but it was the silence after... that will never leave me. I want to be the one to bring you peace, not suffering, Maximus.'

I paced to him until there was hardly an inch between us. Simion gazed down at me, chest heaving, eyes wide. I couldn't steady my breathing, chest aching with each violent slam of my heart against my ribs.

'Camron cannot win,' I said, feigning calm, refusing to look away. 'I won't let him ruin my choices when they are finally mine to make.'

'What is your choice, Max?' Simion questioned, his voice barely a whisper.

'You, Simion. I choose you.'

Emotion swirled in his eyes, causing them to gleam with held back tears. 'I want you more than I could ever begin to explain. There are not enough words to depict the burning desire that aches within me when I look at you.' Simion bared his soul to me, offering it up entirely. It was both beautiful and haunting.

I took a deep, shaking breath in before reply. 'Then we are under a mutual understanding.'

Simion flinched as I laid my hands on his chest. It wasn't that I hurt him, but that he expected me to suffer.

'Do we wait for a time when that is our reality, or do we make it?' I asked.

Simion was quick to respond. 'Make it.'

'Then I should tell Cyder,' I said.

Simion's chin dropped to his chest, his hands laying atop mine. 'Do you think that is wise?'

He didn't tell me it was a bad idea, because Simion always had a way of relying on my decisions. There was no telling me how to think; he always encouraged me. Although, in some instances, I wished he would make these decisions.

It would be one less weight to bear.

'I do. I'm tired of the secrets and lies. And if Camron is still alive, it would explain why the burning plague is continuing to spread. Cyder is trying to help those who suffer. All this… everything he has risked, is because he wants to help. He deserves to know what he is working against.'

Simion's eyes fell back on the journal. 'If that is what you want to do, I will stand by you.'

I stiffened, spine forming to steel as I remembered the last entry I had read. Ruhen, the young boy Camron had travelled with, had thought he had seen a person in the water. Face made of water and eyes pale as milk. After seeing what I had in the caves beneath this island, I knew Ruhen had encountered a nymph. But that was not what set me at unease. It was how human Camron was.

His words, his story—it humanised him.

It showed me the man I had met in Oribon's test of my sanity. That was the Camron before, the one before the plague. The one I saw in glimpses before he tore my family apart.

The journal blurred lines in my mind. No matter how I wished his entries would only make me hate him more, it only reminded me that Camron was once simply a man thirsting for escape from his life.

He had run from one monster and found himself in the jaws of another.

Simion's gaze settled on the pallet at the far side of the tent. A thin mattress was rolled out across it, a woollen blanket folded and waiting at the end. 'There is much we must fix, and I promise we will do it together. But first, you need to sleep. You look…'

'Terrible?'

'Exhausted,' he corrected.

'I don't think I can,' I said, finding there was no point in lying. 'I've tried, but every time I close my eyes, I replay it all over in my head.'

Simion peeled my fingers from his chest, took them in his hand and guided me to the pallet. The journal was placed back on the table, beneath the glow of candlelight. Forgotten, for now. It surprised me when Simion sat down on the pallet, scooting back until his broad body was nestled on the edge.

'What are you doing?' I asked, amused at how his feet fell off the end. He was far too tall for such a bed.

'I can help you sleep.'

'By laying in the bed when there is hardly enough room for one?'

Simion rested his arm behind his head, welcoming me into the crook of his body. 'Where there is a will, there is a way. Come, Maximus, lay with me.'

'This wasn't exactly how I imagined we would first share a bed together,' I said, instantly regretting it when Simion's eyes raised and his mouth slipped open, tongue flashing.

'You've imagined sharing a bed with me?'

I held my tongue, refusing to allow the telltale creep of crimson across my cheeks to expose me. 'Maybe.'

'Good.' Simion said with a smile.

I sat on the edge with my back to him. The wood creaked as hands slipped over my shoulders, urging me backwards. Simion guided me carefully, gently. He didn't stop until I was nestled into him, my spine pressed to his chest, my ass perfectly placed within his crotch. I didn't know how this would help me sleep when my mind was racing every time I moved an inch and brushed against him.

But this was the comfort I had longed for. No, not longed for but *craved*. And now I had it, I refused to ruin the moment.

'Close your eyes,' Simion urged, deep voice dripping with sultry tones.

'Okay,' I replied, quietly as his arms encased my body, anchoring me to him. Cool breath tickled the back of my neck as full lips settled themselves a hair's breadth away.

'Focus on my breathing.' Simion leaned in closer, hips nudging against my ass. Dryads, I hungered for him in ways I didn't dare admit. How could I focus on his breathing when I felt every inch of him pressing against me?

It took more effort to stop myself from pressing into him deeper, but the warning of punishment and pain kept my desires at bay. All my thoughts drifted away, slipping like sand through open fingers. Because this is what I had wanted after sleeping in caves and on rocky terrain. My mind closed off, focusing only on Simion—then there was nothing.

* * *

Noise of morning broke beyond the tent. It woke me from my light slumber, but, then again, a pin drop could've disturbed me.

Simion's light snoring settled at my back, his shirt ruffled up the hard form of his exposed navel. It had taken iron will not to stay curled up beside him, leeching the warmth from his body. But the longer I stared at Camron's journal, the more the siren song of its call beckoned me to open it.

Not wanting to wake Simion, I took the journal, fingers trailing over the warmth of the leather, and sat myself at the table carefully.

As I lifted it, I caught the waft of pungent sea-salt. My body warmed at the scent as I opened the page and found the last entry I had read.

I cannot recall how long it has been since we entered the maze of the Unknown Isles. Truly, it is a miracle I am writing to you. Our ship is damaged beyond repair, we have lost over half of the crew. The captain was confident he could navigate around the stretch of whirlpools, but, as soon as we saw thick cloud pass over the sky, we knew our chances were limited.

I begged him to turn around. He did not listen. I want you to know that I tried, Mother.

You were right. I dare write this, to make it real. But you were right about me—I am nothing if not the harbinger of disappointment and failure. I am destined for those words, a prince only to them.

Ruhen is dead.

The Thassalic claimed him the night before last. I have not had a moment to grieve the boy, not until now.

I blame myself. Mother, I killed him all because of my desire for escape—for purpose. Ruhen and many others drowned when our ship crashed into the rocks that surround one of the islands. There was nothing we could do to stop it from happening. Between the whirlpools and violent winds, we were pushed off course...

I am going to die here.

I suppose I should document what I can see, just in case you one day find it in your heart to send another scouting ship to search for us. For me. We will be nothing but bones by then, but I find comfort in knowing you might understand how that came to be.

Our ship sinks just off the coast of one of the islands. I named it Ruhen, after the boy who drowned before he got to see it.

There is no sun here. The sky is black with plumes of smoke that seep from the mountain I see in the distance. I think it is Voltar, but I cannot be sure. If it is, the continent has won. If we do not starve to death first, the heat that lingers in the air will surely kill us.

At least it is beautiful. From the tip of the mountain, I see flashes of orange-red flame. I thought it was snowing when we pulled ourselves from the water. But it was ash. I am covered in it.

I do not want to die, Mother, I am scared. I would never wish to admit something like that to you, but I am. Father was wrong, and you were right.

I am no fighter.

I ran from you. Now I wish I could run to you.

My mind filled with images, painted in vivid colour, conjured by Camron's words. I tore my eyes from his writing, desperate for reprieve. Yet still I touched it, unable to let go. My thumb ran over the paper, understanding why its pages were stained with dried patches of water and smelled like salt. It had met the Thassalic Ocean, just as Camron had.

There was no room for thought, not as the need to know what happened next overcame me. Camron must have survived—but how? He was weeks away from Aldian land, with no ship and the dregs of a crew.

How did one go from expecting death to defying it?

I turned through a couple more water-crusted pages until I found his next entry. Without taking a breath, I dove back into his story, longing for answers.

Five more souls lost. Good people. They died because I failed them. I wish to cry, but there is nothing left to shed.

I cannot see the ship anymore. The creatures at the bottom of the Thassalic have claimed it. All I see is the fire-spitting mountain and I curse it, over and over.

I will not stay and wait for my end. I will not let these women and men die for nothing.

Ruhen. I promised him.

'How,' I whispered, flickering through more blank pages, trying to locate the next part of his story, as a question broke out of me. 'How did you survive, Camron?'

CHAPTER 29

I sat on a verge, fingers combing through damp strands of grass. Salt air danced around me; a constant reminder of Camron. It seemed even the slightest of things drew him to the forefront of my mind. Or perhaps he just never left it.

To stop myself from drowning in the last entry I had read, I watched as the resistance's gleamers got to work on repairing my dragon's wings. It was a miracle she let them close enough to help. Unless I filled our shared tether with the feelings of trust, I was confident some of them would've come away with one less hand.

As their power seeped into my dragon's body, I felt it unfurl over my skin as though I was the one being healed.

Simion was with them, treating the dragon as the wild creature she was. He would catch my eyes, a knowing smile spread across his face. It hadn't been long since he had woken and, by that point, I had already nestled myself back into his body before he noticed I had left to read the journal. But I didn't sleep again, not with Camron's story haunting me. There was something about the death of Ruhen that lingered with me. It reminded me of Dayn, and how there had been little time to grieve.

If Camron had felt an ounce of what I did now, it was no

wonder he was broken enough to allow a darkness to fill the cracks.

Unlike the rest of the dragons that had been reared since hatchlings, mine had only ever known the cruel touch of the Avarian Crest. It would take some time to learn trust, as it would take time to rely on the bond that had formed between us.

Sunlight glinted off gilded scales, flashing fragments of light across the faces captured in concentration. The ocean was calm as glass, lapping gently across the black sands that covered the beach.

On the outcrops of rocks jutting out the sea, more dragons lingered and watched, assessing both my dragon and me. However, they were not the only one watching. I *felt* the azure eyes score over my skin, before I saw them.

Leska paced across the beach, body garbed in the same brown leathers I wore. We hadn't spoken, not more than a few words since arriving, but I knew it was only a matter of time before we faced one another.

Sensing the spike of concern in me, my dragon raised her long neck, following Leska with her silver-grey eyes.

I would've told the dragon that it was fine, but that was yet to be seen.

'If anyone would've taken the rules set for them and completely disregarded them,' Leska said, blocking out the glare of sun with her frame, 'of course, it would've been you.'

'Hello to you too,' I replied, patting the sand beside me in an effort to feign friendliness.

To my surprise, Leska sat, drawing her legs up and wrapping strong arms around them. Not before removing her amplifier from her belt and resting it on the ground between us. It almost seemed like she was reminding me of our past, present and potential future.

'How did you do it?' she asked softly.

I followed her lightning-blue eyes to my dragon. My mind

slipped back to the mountain, as I lost one life and gained another. 'I don't think I could begin to explain.'

'I know the trials all too well.' I hadn't realised it, but there was a mutual understanding between Leska and me now. Shared experience. We had both faced the horrors of the Claim. 'You don't think you can, or don't want to share how fucked up it all is? Which one is it, Maximus?'

I took a deep breath as a cool spread of phantom hands brushed over my back. It echoed Simion as he inspected the wounds across my dragon, wounds made when the novices restrained it with stone bindings.

'Option number two. Me and the dragon, we both lost something in that mountain,' I said, chest aching at the memory of Dayn. 'Sacrifice was paid in full. When we had nothing left but each other, it seemed the bond clicked into place.'

'As easy as that,' Leska said. 'It gives me hope, I suppose. When this is all over, I may just go there myself. Face Oribon and prove I *am* worthy. Might even claim Oribon himself, he owes me as much.'

'You both would make a formidable pair.'

'Is that a compliment?' Leska shot me a look, brow pinched over tired eyes. There was no denying the grimace that passed over her face.

'It is.'

She nudged my shoulder, without offering a smile.

I replied with my own, except it never reached my eyes. 'Are you… okay with all of this?' The island. The rebellion. Her father.

Leska chewed on her lower lip, looking away from me. 'I have just found out my father is the head of the Hawthorn rebellion. That he was the one who signed Aaron's fate in blood. I don't think I have the luxury to answer your question.'

'I can sympathise with that,' I replied, because using the word understand was both insensitive and wrong. I would never know the pain of a parent sending the person I loved to their death.

Or would I?

A stab of discomfort raced up my arm, drawing my attention back to my dragon. She had snapped her jaws towards a gleamer, sending her flat on her behind as my dragon tried to scramble away.

Simion was there, placing his body in the line of danger, arms raised to steady my bonded. Perhaps it was because it was Simion, or maybe it was the way I reacted to seeing him, that calmed my dragon immediately.

'Only you would find a dragon with teeth as sharp as you,' Leska said, her focus entrapped on my golden mount.

We had never shared a friendly comment like this before. There was something forced about the relaxed nature of it. I could see Leska was trying hard with me, even though it was not easy.

'Wow, even I get a compliment.'

'Consider us even,' Leska said, her sudden smile fleeting. I sensed her words meant more than she was letting on. There was pain behind her bright eyes as though it snuck upon her and pounced. I recognised it for what it was.

'Your father told me about Aaron,' I said, breaking the barrier that had formed between us. 'Back before all of this, he told me what he meant to you, Leska. And if I could go back and change what happened, I want you to know I would.'

Her gaze settled back out across the horizon, lower lip caught between her teeth, the skin paling beneath the pressure she held it with. 'And I believe you. Aaron's death is no longer your sole responsibility. My father...' Leska choked, eyes widening in surprise. When she spoke again, her voice was as hard as stone. 'My father gave him the orders. You may have been the one to kill him, but it was my father who signed his fate.'

We weren't friends, not in a matter of words. With every broken nose Leska had gifted me in the past weeks, with every gruelling minute of training, she had punished me in her own way. But without that, I may not have survived the Claim. She had taken me and forged me into steel—even if that wasn't her intention.

'You've sacrificed a lot to save me, Leska.'

She laughed, clearing the snot with the back of her hand. I hadn't noticed she had started to cry until the silent tears streaked down her face. 'I didn't do it for you. I did it for Aaron, because he believed in the rebellion's goals even if I don't.'

Even if I don't. Her words settled over me like ash.

'You don't?'

'There is a reason my father didn't reveal his deceptions until he didn't have the choice. He knew where my loyalties lie. He says he kept me in the dark to protect me, but all he did was take my heart, break it and lie in hopes to fix it. It's a hard pill to swallow.'

'It seems that pill has been forced into your mouth,' I replied, sensing the tension oozing from her.

'Yes, I suppose it has.'

'What happens next then?' I asked, gazing at her profile as though studying it for the first time. 'Who do we betray, family or Council?'

'That line is blurred for the both of us.' Leska turned to look at me, eyes burning with determination. 'I may not agree with my father's rebellion and their goals to dismantle the Council, but I do believe a war is coming. Not between people, between gods.'

'A war between gods,' I repeated, thinking back to the vision of dragons fighting one another after clawing themselves free of the Avarian mountains.

'Yes,' Leska said, eyes falling to her amplifier as though she'd need it at any moment. 'My father believes Leia is preparing a major assault on the South. And she plans to do so by fighting fire with fire.'

I lost myself to the ocean view, mind whirling with the knowledge of what Leska had just revealed. 'How? How does she plan to do it?'

'By learning from the mistakes of battles past. The last time we invaded the South, it was to eradicate the four ruling mages. This time, it will be to destroy all of them. Every last one, phoenix-possessed or not. That is why I am here. Because my father has found a way of saving lives, not taking them.'

'We... *I* have to stop her.' I spoke without truly thinking. My nails dug into the sand beneath me, every muscle tensing until I was more stone than flesh. Tears pricked in my eyes.

'I know,' Leska replied solemnly. I didn't realise I scratched at the silver fast-marks until she levelled her eyes with the raw skin. She placed a cool hand upon mine and stopped me without words.

'My father wants the meeting to begin shortly,' Leska said, standing so suddenly it was as though the tension between us had returned. 'But if we are to fly with him to protect *your* people, you should really have a name for your dragon.'

I was so distracted by the concept of naming the golden creature, I almost didn't notice Leska's use of the word *your* when referring to the South and its people. At least this time it wasn't with the same poison I was used to.

'There is far too much to worry about than that,' I replied.

Leska nodded in the direction of my gilded creature as she pounded across the black-sand beach and shot up into the sky, roaring with renewed vigour. 'A dragon is never nameless. We learn early on that a dragon will reveal its name to the rider, if they feel the rider is worthy. It solidifies not only the bond, but trust between god and mage.'

I was unable to move past thoughts of a ruined South and what that would look like. 'I wouldn't even know where to start.'

The exhale Leska expelled was full of unspoken emotion. 'One of the pleasures of bonding to a dragon is the ability to share your truths. She will see you, just as you will see her. Allow her to tell you. Aaron once told me that it is a sign of eternal connection both in life and death for a dragon to give its bonded its true name. I like to think he still rides on the back of his, even now.'

Leska left me, gazing at the sky as though Aaron would cut

through the wisps of clouds on the back of his ruby-scaled dragon.

I locked eyes with mine, picturing the tether that bound us together as a rope forged of the strongest of metals. In that moment, it was only the two of us. Everything else disappeared, fading into the background, as the dragon's presence came to the front of my mind.

Who you are?

There was no hesitation as my dragon shared her true name. It came as a whisper on the winds, the kiss of ice against my cheek, the brush of scales over my skin.

Inyris.

I spoke it aloud, eyes flying open. 'Inyris?'

My golden-scaled dragon, Inyris, breathed a pillar of ice and wind, crystallising the surface of the ocean she flew over. It was both an acceptance of me, and confirmation that she trusted me with her most trusted secret.

Her power belonged to me, just as I belonged to her. This bond was not forged by silver ink over skin, or scarred marks on my palm. It was made from the proudest mark of all. *Trust.*

CHAPTER 30

My bones thudded with every hack of Beatrice's axe. What had been a wooden dummy was now a mess of severed limbs. The head was on the ground, discarded and hardly recognisable. One of its arms was hanging on by a splinter.

But still she fought it as though it was a living, breathing person. At one point, she slammed the axe with such force, it embedded into the dummy's side. It took a foot for leverage to pull it out.

The training yard was set in the busy island's centre, in the courtyard of a guarded stone building. We were on the way to the meeting with Elder Cyder when I heard the grunts and followed them.

I was surprised to hear she had already been dismissed by the healers, but not surprised to find her with her favourite things. Weapons. Sharp steel, folded metal.

'I've had my time with her. You should too. I'll meet you inside,' Simion had said moments ago when he left me. Even now, I still felt the reassuring squeeze on my shoulder.

Part of me had longed for him to stay, but another part desired some time alone with Beatrice. After all, the last time I had spoken to her was as she betrayed me under Camron's control.

Beatrice's hair had been braided from her face, pulled back in a sleek ponytail that ran down her spine. For someone who had been locked in a stone box for weeks, you wouldn't know by watching her. A bead of sweat rolled down her temple, tracing the proud lines of bones protruding after weeks of reduced food.

I stood there, watching like some lurking creep, hoping she was notice me. But she was so focused on ruining her dummy, Beatrice didn't know I was there until I called her name.

'Bea, it's good to see you are—'

I regretted it instantly. Beatrice spun on a beat, axe pulled back, amber eyes wide and glassy. The axe left her hand so suddenly, spinning viciously towards us. Whatever trance she was in quickly passed as she realised who called her name.

But it was too late.

I raised my hand, pulling on the cords of power. My essence entered the wooden handle of the axe. Somewhere above us, slicing through the skies, Inyris unleashed a cry of panic. Before the axe hit its unintended mark, I stilled the momentum, thrust my will towards it, and sent it spiralling off at the last moment.

'Shit, Max!' Beatrice shouted, crossing the training yard with a mixture of panic and anger. 'Don't come sneaking up on me like that!'

'Think I was someone else?' I said, brushing off the incident with a smile, whilst my chest ached with the pounding of my heart.

There was something distant about her stare. As though she was looking through me. Beatrice brushed a hand over her forehead. Her knuckles were covered in bruised, torn skin. Before I could question it, she hid them behind her back. 'Who would I have been thinking about?'

I nodded to the ruined wooden remains of what was once a dummy. 'I could hazard a guess. The same woman who is willing to murder countless people instead of helping them? Or maybe the man who used us both, in differing ways.'

Beatrice swallowed hard, rubbing her sweaty palms down her

form-fitting leathers. 'So my aunt has been using her time as Head of the Council well?'

'A little too well.' I tipped my head towards the remains of the wooden dummy. 'Is there another one of those, I have some pent-up energy to expel.'

'Sorry,' Beatrice shrugged, 'the rest of them look worse than that.'

I wanted nothing more than to throw my arms around her. It was a selfish desire, to offer myself comfort by hugging her. But she had been through a lot; I wasn't prepared to overstep a boundary.

Beatrice gripped her belly as though she suffered a deep-rooted ache there. Her wince only confirmed it. My eyes scanned her—fingers, wrist, arm, belt. I couldn't see an amplifier, nor sense her power.

'Cyder has offered to give me a new staff,' Beatrice said, reading my mind, 'but I refused.'

'Why?'

I watched her move for the discarded axe, flipping it with her boot and catching it mid-air. 'Relying on magic isn't always the answer. Plus, I have a rather intense connection to my original staff. I'm going to personally retrieve it from Leia when we next see each other.'

A tempest brewed behind her eyes. I practically heard the wooden handle of the axe scream for reprieve as her bruised knuckles tightened.

'Did the dummy suffer your fists before you picked up the axe?' I asked.

She looked down at them with some sense of pride. 'No. These came with me from Saylam Academy.'

'But Simion told me the resistance's gleamers had already seen to you.'

The urge to march into Elder Cyder's tent, and demand he saw to Beatrice's wounds immediately, was almost too hard to quell.

'Max,' Beatrice scolded me into silence with a single look. 'I don't need anything from these people. I don't need their healers, I don't need their help. Simion offered the same thing, but I refused because I can. It is my choice. Just because I'm no longer a prisoner, doesn't mean I am free. None of us are.'

Choice. This reaction wasn't only about her imprisonment, but her lack of will when Camron used her for his plans. I understood that even without the need to voice it aloud. I gritted my teeth until my jaw ached. Beatrice was right. Of course, she was.

'I'm sorry I never visited you.' The apology had been in the forefront of my mind since we arrived. I had thought about all the different ways of saying it, but spurting it out was certainly not what I had planned.

'You don't need to apologise to me, Max. Not now, not ever.' Guilt hung heavy in her stare, it deepened the lines across her forehead. 'I know why, and I understand.'

A shadow passed overhead. I didn't need to look up to know it was Glamora. Another followed quickly, a smudge of gold against blue sky. Inyris.

'We got you out in the end.'

'With some help,' Beatrice said, looking up at her dragon dancing with mine.

'Even if I wanted to, I would never have been able to claw through stone to reach you.'

'No,' Beatrice said, retuning her eyes to me. 'But from what Simion admitted, it was you that turned back for me. It wasn't my brother; it wasn't the Hawthorns. It was you.'

'Home.' The word cracked out of me. 'You taught me that.'

Beatrice closed her eyes as if the single word pained her. 'Home.'

My mind flicked through memories, back to that time we shared all those weeks ago. 'It is a people, not a place. I couldn't leave you knowing what would happen if we did.'

Beatrice allowed the words to settle over her, the sentiment to follow like an aftertaste. Her shoulders seemed to relax, not completely, but enough to see the woman I knew.

'Every day,' Beatrice paused, taking a deep inhale, 'I go over what happened. How Camron was able to use me. Take those deep desires and twist them into something of his own. And every day I remind myself of who was lost because of it. What my actions took from you...'

I couldn't see her through the tears. Although I refused to let them spill. I reached out and grasped her hand, careful not to cause her ruined knuckles discomfort.

'You don't need to say it,' I choked out. 'And anyway, you lost a life because of me, consider us equal.'

'I do,' Beatrice snapped, almost shouted. Not out of anger, but desperation. The burning need to get the words out, to lift the weight of her conscience. 'Your father's death is as much my fault as it is Camron's. I know the pain of losing a parent. I blame myself and I will, always.'

One look at Beatrice and the grief I had locked away began to slither out like roots through stone.

'I don't blame you,' I said, unable to resist the urge for distance another moment. I laid my hand on her shoulder, praying I had the ability to share the truth of my admission. 'Not now, not anymore.'

'Well, I do. And I am not saying this to get an apology from you. I am saying it because you deserve to hear it.'

I pulled her close, body trembling as sobs heaved in my chest. 'I know what it is to be used. I know the choices we make, or the choices made for us. He used us both.'

Beatrice whispered her wish, as she, too, lost herself to tears. 'I wish he was still alive. I would be the first to kill him.'

There it was. The opening to reveal the truth to her.

I stepped back, cool tears slicing down my face. As I rolled my sleeve up, Glamora and Inyris danced in the sky. Beatrice didn't need me to say it. She looked down at my arm, to the silver vines that twisted like manacles of ink across my skin. Unbroken. As bright as the day they were made.

'Only in death shall you part.' It was all I needed to say. Between the horror in my eyes and the silver marks on my arms, Beatrice worked out the rest.

Her lip curled, face pinching in a mask of horror. Gone was her sadness, it faded quickly. 'Are you certain?'

'I am.'

Beatrice looked out across the ocean, eyes cutting through the shroud of mist that blocked this island away from the world. 'Then we find him. No matter where he is hiding, and when we do… we finish him.'

I expected the weight of the world to lift from my shoulders, but it didn't. Before Camron became a demon who split my life in two, he was simply a man. Where the line was, I couldn't work out.

'We should go,' I said, rolling my sleeve back down again, not wanting to speak about Camron for another moment. 'Wouldn't want to keep our humble hosts waiting.'

Beatrice grimaced when she looked behind me, to the tent we had been asked to meet at. 'Do they know about… Camron?'

Even she struggled to speak his name out loud.

'Not yet, but I will.'

Her body tensed, mirroring my own. 'They might see you as a threat, knowing you kept this from them.'

'They might,' I said, not able to say otherwise.

'It could affect how gracious they are with keeping us here.'

'Not us. Me.'

Beatrice placed a firm hand on my shoulder, broken skin flexing in the daylight. 'No. I meant what I said. There are hard choices left to face, but we will make them.'

Inyris screeched above us, Glamora chasing through the sky, nipping playfully at her tail.

'You're right,' I said, straightening my spine. 'Sometimes half the battle is making choices.'

Like whose side we stood on. It seemed like a simple choice for me. If Elder Cyder was prepared to use his resistance to stand with the South, I would stand with him. I knew history, I knew the past. I wouldn't allow history to repeat itself.

'We've done it before, we will do it again.' Beatrice wrapped her arm around me, partly healed knuckles dribbling blood where they had opened. 'Together.'

'Together,' I echoed.

CHAPTER 31

Elder Cyder was the last to sit at the table in the middle of his tent. Mismatched rugs were laid out beneath it, covering the mud-trodden ground. Not a single chair matched. The thick material walls did well to block natural light from seeping in. If it wasn't for the white-pillar candles set across the table, we may not have been able to see each other.

It took effort not to lose myself to the fires. Simion sensed my discomfort and placed a hand on my knee, squeezing softly, just out of view.

Members of the Hawthorn resistance stood around the outskirts, each equally decorated with weapons. It wasn't the steel I was worried about, but their amplifiers. Like me, they each left a hand resting on their conduit if magic was required. It wasn't that I didn't trust them, not when these very men and women fought next to me in the skies not long ago. But I was wary. And from their stoic glances, they shared the same sentiment.

Cyder had gone around the table, offering us each a drink in turn. I couldn't help but pick the tankard up and down the contents. My urgency had little to do with thirst and everything to do with the requirement of liquid courage with the many eyes on me.

Simion sat to my left, Beatrice to my right. Leska stood at the tent's entrance, arms folded over her chest, refusing her father's offer to take a seat. He didn't press her to join us, because he knew it would be a wasted effort.

'I trust your stay thus far has been comfortable,' Elder Cyder said, offering us each a careful smile as he passed his gaze across the tent. 'It pales in comparison to a four-poster bed, but you soon get used to it—'

'Get to the point, *Father*,' Leska grumbled, voice as sharp as the blades at her hip.

I cringed at her tone, which clearly sang of the distance formed between them. A distrust. And it was clear from the way his eyes fell to his fidgeting hands that his daughter's reaction to his deceit was a stab to the gut. I felt somewhat guilty being the cause of this tethered relationship. If I hadn't begged Elder Cyder for his help, we may never have been in this position.

But better the devil you know.

'When does Leia plan her attack on the South?' I asked the only question I cared to hear him answer.

He raised his gentle eyes to me, thick brows furrowing over them. 'In a matter of weeks, perhaps sooner. It all depends on how fast she can recoup after our attack on the armoury.'

'You must feel proud of yourself. This is what you have always wanted, isn't it?' Simion straightened in his chair, hands splaying out across the table. 'Finally, a cause worthy enough for the rebellion to justify their attacks on the Council.'

'I will not deny that completely, Simion Hawthorn, because doing so will offend your intelligence. How long have I known you? Years—'

'And what about me, Cyder,' Beatrice called out, leaning back until her leg swayed. 'Could you say the same?'

Tension thickened to Leska's enjoyment. I watched a smile crease over her shadowed face, bright blue eyes narrowing like the gaze of a serpent.

'She deserves to hear an answer.' Leska stepped forward,

prowling until she stood behind Beatrice's chair. 'In fact, I am sure we all want to know why the very rebellion who used her mother's name didn't bother to save Beatrice from the South during all the years she was exiled?'

Was I the only one who wanted to lower the tension? There was some part of me that owed Elder Cyder a lot for his help with my mother. There was another part of me that longed to hear his answer.

'It was under my authority that we were to leave Beatrice. It was safer for her to stay clear of the North and their oppressive, controlling regimes. If I had it my way, she would still be there now.'

Beatrice shot forward, lips pulled back in a snarl. 'You use my family name. You flaunt it around, waving it like a banner and yet you do little for us. What gave you the right?'

Before I could offer her comfort, it was Leska who placed a hand on Beatrice's shoulder and eased her back into her chair.

'This was never my decision,' Elder Cyder said. 'I did not create the Hawthorn rebellion. Believe it or not, but it was Celia, your mother, who began all of this.' Arms waved to the tent around him, but I understood the gesture stretched further beyond this place.

'It is convenient you say such a thing when she is not around to confirm or deny her involvement,' Simion growled, jaw gritted, eyes wide. His palms slapped down on the table, shuddering the empty tankards in a symphony of clinks. 'I suggest you keep the references of my mother to a minimum for the duration of this conversation. Instead, do what you wanted us here for and convince us why we should help you dismantle the Council, once and for all.'

Elder Cyder looked directly at me, as if no one else mattered. 'I do not think it is convincing you need.'

Every set of eyes fell on me. 'Cyder is right. There is little persuasion needed,' I added gently, simply wishing to get to the bottom of this. 'You all may need it, but I don't.'

'Thank you,' Elder Cyder whispered, looking at me through his lashes. 'Maximus.'

'Whether we support the South or not,' Leska said, 'we will all be crushed by Leia and the power she holds. Dragons, magic, training, knowledge. All things the South do not have, or you father. I have seen your numbers, you hardly have an abundance of people to stand in Leia's way.'

She was right. Cyder had the numbers to cause some discomfort, but certainly not to sway the tide of war.

'Ask yourself, what does Leia fear most?' Elder Cyder asked.

The question hung across the tent. As the silence drew on, the tension grew so thick not even a knife would cut through it.

'Power,' Elder Cyder finally replied. 'She fears what she cannot control. Like you, Beatrice. Shunned, locked away, all because you have a mind of your own, one not moulded or affected by the North and their teachings. That is what she fears, so, like any successful resistance, we use that very thing against her. Harold, please step forward.'

To my surprise, it was one of the guards who followed the command. There was something rehearsed about his movements. The man had dark eyes, a head of tight blonde curls and skin as pale as Inyris's horns.

'Harold, please can you tell us where you are originally from?'

Without so much as looking at us, Harold answered. 'A small bordering town between Romar and Zendina.'

He was a Southerner.

Elder Cyder continued, waving encouragingly with a hand. 'And what brought you here, to the North?'

The entire room hung on every word. Simion's hand found mine beneath the table and held on, unsure if he was offering me comfort or if I was doing it for him.

'To be saved.'

'Good,' Elder Cyder said, encouraging with a kind tone. 'And do you feel as though you have been?'

'I do.'

Everything stilled. No one made a sound, no one dared move, as we watched Harold's every move.

'Please, show them what you mean.'

He peeled off a glove to reveal a hand completely encapsulated with twisted flesh. Burns. I would recognise them anywhere. With his scarred hand, he undid his jacket until it pooled at his feet like a puddle of darkness. Then, one button at a time, he removed his shirt until he stood bare-chested before us.

'A strip tease,' Beatrice barked, 'wasn't exactly what I expected.'

Dread rose in my stomach as I got a full view of the scars across his back. I blinked and, in the darkness, it was another man I saw. Wings of scarred flesh, warm skin, silver-inked marks up his arm.

A memory of Camron haunted the dark of my mind. One of him sitting on the edge of my bed, skin exposed, his story laid bare.

'Over the weeks, the Hawthorns have been working to remove from the South as many victims of this possession as possible. Harold here was one of them.'

I reached for my power, readying it. Simion's hand grasped the pommel of his sword. Leska opened herself up to her magic, spoiling the air with the taste of pine and soil. Not a single one of us sat back and watched, not in the face of a phoenix-possessed.

'There will be no need for that,' Elder Cyder dismissed, waving our reactions away. 'Harold is in complete control.'

'Over what?' Leska hissed, eyes glowing with the mist of power.

'The phoenix inside of him,' I answered, as Harold turned back around. I could see it then, in his dark eyes. It was a glint of light, of warmth.

This was what Leia would go to war for. This is what she feared the most.

A brush of ice passed over my mental shield. By the time I focused back on Simion, it was to see his face pressed in concentration. Power itched over my skin as I watched him delve into Harold's mind.

His amber eyes widened. Simion's gaze seemed to settle on something else as he leaned back, fingers pressed to his temple, mumbling words beneath his breath.

'Simion,' I grasped his hand. The moment my fingers touched his, he snapped out of his trance. 'What do you see?'

He raised his eyes to Elder Cyder, his expression placid, distant. 'It is true. Harold has an entity inside of him, but it is...'

'Caged,' Elder Cyder answered. 'We discovered the nymphs' power has the ability to smother the phoenix, using the host as a means of possession. With regular dosages of their essence, we are able to sever the bond, allowing the host to remain in control whilst still calling upon the... *gifts* provided by the possession.'

'Gifts?' I asked, unable to move.

'Power.' Harold raised his palm out before him as though catching a snowflake. But it was not snow he wished to catch. It was fire. I flinched as a spark burst from his skin, furious tongues of orange-red fire unfurling like a bud.

I was blinded by fear. Caught in a landslide of horror as the flame licked over skin as though coated in oil. It grew and grew, spreading from a single bud to an inferno of life-scorching death.

My mind barely registered the breathless call of my name until I was entirely lost to it.

Simion stood, chair knocking to the floor. He snatched the tankard from the table and thrust the contents out towards the burning hand. Water splashed over them, extinguishing it all in a moment. Only when the trails of grey smoke curling from his sodden hand dispersed did I allow myself to inhale.

'That's more than enough,' Simion snapped, leaning over the table as though he longed to throw it out of his way and pounce on Elder Cyder. 'We get your point.'

'No, we don't,' Leska snapped. 'You told us there was no cure.'

'There isn't. This, what you have seen, is as close as we can get to a cure,' Elder Cyder said. From the folds of his cloak, he withdrew a vial. It was the same he had given to me, filled with an azure liquid that caught the light. He dropped it on the table and rolled it away from him. Simion snatched it before the vial fell from the table. 'This is simply a means of weakening a bond between parasite and host. To sever it entirely, we must root out the phoenix and destroy it. My gleamers are still studying, working endlessly on finding a finite solution. Only then will those plagued by the phoenix be truly free. Simion, I may need your help explaining this next part...'

My mind was still reeling from the display of flames; I almost missed the way Simion's entire demeanour hardened to stone.

'This isn't the first time I have seen into the mind of a phoenix-possessed,' Simion began, eyes lost to something on the table. 'When I did, it was chaos. Loud, messy, violent. But this... Harold's mind is his own. Deep in the shadows I sense something, but it is out of reach. Kept at bay.'

Silence thrummed across the room. Whilst I languished in it, all I could think about was my mother. When I looked to Elder Cyder, his eyes were already on me. Expectant, patiently waiting for the question he knew I would ask.

'My mother, will she be like... like him?'

A small smile lifted Cyder's thin lips. 'Yes. Deborah will not only survive, changed, but she will be in control. As will everyone who suffers in the South.'

'But if the phoenix is inside of Deborah, how do we destroy it without...' Beatrice carefully stopped herself from saying what lingered on the tip of her tongue. 'How do we destroy it without harming Deborah?'

'You mean killing,' I corrected my friend, mind numb to the truth.

Beatrice's jaw tensed, her eyes dropping to her hands.

'I'm afraid my knowledge is limited. Mages are bonded to the dryads by the amplifiers we use to connect to their earthen power, the marks left on our skin is proof of that. Mages like Maximus, like Beatrice, are able to bond with dragons—'

Leska's expression softened, her eyes trailing off. She, too, was dragon-blessed but had not passed the Claim.

'—the phoenix is simply another god tying themselves to us. Their magic is only compatible if they dwell within their host's body. Essence joining essence. But with every bond, there must be a weakness. Without an amplifier, a mage cannot access their power. Weakness. Once a dragon-blessed loses its dragon, their soul is sheared in two, never to be whole again. Although these possessions are new, it is only a matter of time before we understand them. And that is exactly what we need— we *need* time.'

'Then this is what we show Leia,' Leska snapped, hands splayed out on the table as though she desperately held on to prevent war. 'We show her what you can do, prove that death is not the answer. We prevent a war, we prevent death.'

'If she is willing to listen, then yes, that would be the best outcome. But there is something different about Leia, her desires are shifting ever constantly.'

It was as though the seed that had planted in my mind finally sprouted.

'To discover one's weakness, we must first recognise their strengths.' I repeated something Elder Cyder had said to me before I began the Claim.

'Precisely.'

'Leia is right to fear them,' I said, 'and I think I know why... I know *how* this plague is spreading.'

Simion placed a hand over mine, coating the silver marks on the back of my hand. Beatrice leaned in too, knowing what was to come.

'You do?' Elder Cyder said, almost shocked I had the answer.

I swallowed hard. 'I believe Camron Calzmir is still alive.'

Elder Cyder's bright eyes flashed. It was impressive, to watch so many emotions flood over someone's face in such quick succession. There was panic, disbelief, wonder, fear.

'That is a bold theory,' he said, eyes drifting to the guards around him. 'And belief admits doubt. To believe you must acknowledge that something is not necessarily real. So, tell me, do you *believe* Camron Calzmir lives, or do you know?'

I looked to my hand, barely seeing the silver lines beneath Simion's grasp. 'I believe he is alive. I think, I...'

I held my breath, expecting Elder Cyder to ask how I thought such a thing. When he didn't, I sagged forward, relieved I didn't have to conjure a lie to avoid describing the bath, Simion, me, our naked skin.

'Then you have doubt,' Elder Cyder confirmed, almost relieved. I could understand where this relief came from. Camron had almost destroyed Wycombe; he had killed many innocents and ruined the Heart Oak.

Camron was destruction incarnate.

'I think we should consider what Max is saying,' Leska said, side-eyeing me. 'Before the Claim, we found something in her study.'

The colour drained from Elder Cyder's face. 'What was it that you found, daughter?'

'Camron's journal and a... feather,' I said, noticing Beatrice stiffen beside me. 'It looked the same as the one used to let Camron into Wycombe.'

Elder Cyder waved his hand, dusting off my accusation as though it was a lie. 'It must be something Queen Romar brought with her to the city. Perhaps a token. It doesn't suggest Camron is alive. So many saw him die.'

'You can have it,' I said, feeling almost pained by the idea of being away from the journal. 'It might have the answers you need to find a cure. But what it does reveal is that Camron, he... he gave the plague to his father. And he offered it to me. That is to say he isn't spreading it around now. If what Stephine Romar said is true, his Kingdom in the South is riddled with it.'

I could hear Camron, whispering his promise in my ear as though he stood behind me now. I almost turned and looked over my shoulder. *The power I will gift you shall be unlike anything you could possibly imagine. It will hurt, it will leave your body scarred as*

*mine is, but the rebirth you will experience on the other side will be
unlike anything you could ever imagine.*

My mind had been made up. In that moment, I had no doubt
that Camron was involved in this. He had to be.

And I will be there, by your side, aiding you through it all.

Bile crept up the back of my throat. 'When was the last time
that any of you saw his supposed ashes?'

Simion mumbled to himself for a moment. 'Weeks ago.'

'And you?' I asked, looking directly at Cyder, who looked
more uncomfortable at the notion this could be true. Camron
was not only responsible for sparking fear in me, but in everyone.

'Leia was very protective over Camron Calzmir's remains—'

'*From the ashes, we rise,*' I said, reciting the excerpt I read from
the book before the attack on the library.

'Pardon?' Elder Cyder said, skin ashen and eyes wide.

'Dacraire, the story about the dragon who killed the first
Phoenix King. It had a part about the phoenixes rising from the
ashes of their own destruction.'

I searched the man's familiar face, looking for proof that he
knew. Just when I believed I caught something in his unwavering
stare, he looked elsewhere.

'Is it possible?' Simion added, also looking expectantly
towards Elder Cyder.

'Anything is possible. We do not understand phoenix magic.
But speculating will not change the issue at hand. First, we must
stop Leia from completely eradicating the South from Aldian's
future. Then we can worry about Prince Calzmir.'

'When?' I asked. 'When do we act?'

We all waited, with a collective breath, for the answer.

'Tomorrow. Before Leia can make her first move.'

'Tomorrow,' I repeated. 'We end this before it truly begins.'

A smile crept over Elder Cyder's face. It was so sharp that it
almost felt misplaced on his face. 'I understand the decision may
be hard, but I promise, all of you, it is the right one.'

CHAPTER 32

Curfew was hours away, and I was far from ready to settle in the tent for another long night. Knowing what was to come tomorrow, not only did the thought create a knot of unease to settle in my chest, it took that bastard knot and spun it into a web of iron.

Hope was a strange thing. It was a double-edged blade. Hope either gave someone something to fight for or reminded them they had something to lose. This was how it felt knowing Mother was currently in the hands of gods trying to heal her.

A storm was building in the darkening skies. The far-off rumbles raced over my skin, the sporadic flashes of lightning casting the insides of my tent in its stark glow. I reached out to Inyris, pulling at the unseen cord that bound us.

She was curled up on the outcrop of rocks just shy of the island's shoreline. Rain tapped across her golden scales. The sensation was so real, it was as though I was led beneath the rain. Inyris was sleeping, dreaming of her eggs, her family. Sorrow didn't fade, no matter the creature, no matter the time.

I made a promise to my dragon. A deal that I would see through. Tomorrow, we were not only going to put an end to Elder Leia's plans. We would save those who suffer and offer them the same chance that my mother and Harold had. And I would find Inyris's hatchlings, that was one promise I would not forget.

Then there was Camron, my third bonded.

His journal was already on my lap, my hands brushing over the leather as they had his shoulders not so long ago. By morning I would give it to Cyder, so I would make the most of the last hours I had with Camron's story.

I thumbed through the stiff pages, searching for the last page I had read. It took longer to find it because the entries were separated by many blank pages. It was as if Camron forgot to finish this tale. I fought down the pang of worry that there was nothing else to find—that he had given into the possession and forgotten the man he was before.

But somehow, I didn't believe it.

The man who I had first met was not the monster I had last seen. Not completely. He fought for life; I knew that now. It was just a sadness that he failed.

What I found, nestled on the final pages of his journal, turned my blood to ice.

An entire page was covered in the same word, over and over. Camron had written it into the paper so vigorously, it had ripped and scratched in places, smearing ink across the pages beneath it.

Burn. Burn. Burn.

Insanity oozed from the page beneath my fingers. There was nothing neat about his writing. It was childish and rushed, the words big and small. I could see towards the bottom of the page, where the ink was beginning to run out, because Camron had overwritten *burn* in the same place, the lines frantic and desperate. As I ran my finger over the page, I felt the grooves the word had made in the parchment. I could almost sense the chaos of Camron's mind in the overlapping abundance of that single word.

At first glance, the single world blurred together, forming a page almost entirely black with ink. I was wrong. Because in the middle, etched beneath the ink were other words—buried beneath his frantic scrawl.

From the ashes, we rise.

They were the same words I had read before, the very same I had shared with Elder Cyder. It was as though Camron was haunting me even now. An icy chill raced down my neck as I looked around the darkening corners of the tent, expecting him to be lurking there. He wasn't, of course, but his memory had never felt so corporeal as it had now.

The rest of the journal was empty. I flipped through the pages, all blurring into one, as I longed to find out what happened next. It wasn't until the last page that I found something, written in handwriting I didn't recognise, in ink that didn't match the rest.

Mother is coming.

Camron hadn't written this. I knew it, deep in my core. This was not done by his hand.

Then who?

Thunder crashed, echoing in my chest. I snapped the journal shut, knowing I had heard those three words before.

'Mother is coming?' I asked the darkness, repeating the words aloud. They were familiar, terrifying and real. 'Mother is coming.'

My nightmares taunted me, the one that had gripped me in the depths of night, even poisoning my mind during my waking hours.

A sky covered in flames. Withering life. Piles of bones. Buildings buried by rolling waves. Ruin. Death. A woman. An army of darkness. Coiling shadows. Monsters.

The Heart Oak had sung this very sentiment to me. My own mother had repeated that chant, as though she had been the one to pluck it from my mind. Now it was here, before me, scored into the book.

'Mother is coming,' I said for a final time.

'Who is coming, Max?'

I looked up to find Simion standing in the entrance to my tent. Lightning flashed at his back, illuminating him in a halo of silver. Seeing him snatched me back to reality, although it did little to rid me of the strange aftertaste of Camron's final journal entry.

'I don't know,' I replied, as I closed the journal.

'Just a touch of light reading to take your mind off tomorrow?' Simion asked, trying to inject some humour into the moment. I appreciated his attempt, but it was misplaced and awkward. 'Find anything useful?'

'No. Nothing.' *Had I?*

Looking beyond Simion, I longed to leave the tent now and give the journal away. I promised Cyder he could have it, but that didn't mean I wasn't prepared to finish it first. 'I should really get it to Cyder before—'

'Maximus, you do not need to hide from me. Curiousness is a trait I admire in you. It isn't a crime to want to know more about *him.*'

A shiver passed over my skin. 'Even if it is curiosity about the man who was known as my husband?'

'Yes, Maximus. Even that.'

Dryads, the way he looked at me was my undoing. How his eyes glowed as though a star encompassed them.

'How long have you been standing there?' I asked, longing for a distraction.

Simion was soaked through. Dark curls were tight and heavy, his skin glistening with a sheen of rain. Where he stood a puddle of water formed beneath him, soaking the mismatched rugs through. Even in this state, he was breathtaking.

'Not long.' Simion answered, gesturing behind him, smirking. 'If there was a door, I would've knocked.'

'You never need to knock. Not with me.' I set the journal down, a sense of finality in doing so. I would've been lying to myself if I pretended that I hadn't wanted Simion to find me tonight. Sleep was easy to find when our breathing synchronised and his warmth comforted me.

'You may regret giving me that permission one day.'

I shook my head, a blush creeping over my cheeks. 'Come here, Simion. You're shivering.'

'Am I?' Simion replied, hardly taking his eyes off me for a second. 'Oh, so I am.'

I paced towards him, laying my hands on his jacket. If I squeezed, it would've cast rivulets of water down my wrist. 'You'll catch your death. Take your clothes off, I should have some spare clothes around—'

Simion stopped me from walking away, grasping my wrist with careful but sure hands. 'Maximus.'

The use of my name sang of a thousand unsaid emotions. I looked back to him, carefully studying his gaze.

'What?'

Simion took my hand and rested it upon his chest. I thought it was just to show me how wet he was, as though I wasn't already demanding he remove his clothes so I could wrap him in blankets. There was a shape within his pocket, a small bulge of something hard.

'Simion, use those words you are so talented with and say what it is that you wish to.'

He took his hand and dove it into his pocket. 'Elder Cyder gave me this. For you.'

My eyes veered from Simion's stoic expression to the vial he held between his finger and thumb. It was the same Elder Cyder had shown us during the meeting. The same he had given me to use on my mother.

'If Camron is still alive—'

'He is,' I snapped almost urgently. 'You know he is.'

Simion bowed his head, eyes closing as though the knowledge was far too much for him to bear. 'This might just help dampen the bond between you. Just as the nymph's essence is helping those suffering with the possession, Cyder believes it will help you with yours.'

My possession, the fast-mark, Camron. It was all the same, nor was Cyder wrong.

Perhaps I should've felt wronged for knowing Elder Cyder had worked out my suffering. It didn't take a scholar to understand that I was only punished by the fast-mark when I betrayed it.

Hope. There it was again, bottled up in a small vial made of glass, no bigger than the heart of my palm. I grasped it, holding on for dear life, until the smooth edges caused a semblance of discomfort.

'It doesn't mean you need to take it, Max,' Simion urged, eyes a caress as they drifted over me. 'There is no comprehending what side effects it could have.'

'We know it smothers the bond set between a phoenix and its host. We know it is currently helping my mother. You have seen what it has done for Harold.' I began listing off the reasons as to why I knew what I was to do. It was a selfish desire, to have something of my own choosing.

And that was what Simion was.

He was a choice.

A choice I could make.

He was mine.

And he was someone I had craved for weeks.

'Why else did you bring this to me, if you didn't hope for the same thing?'

Simion rocked back a step; fingers pressed to his chest. 'Because it wasn't my choice to decide whether you took this risk or not. I should help support you through decisions, not make them for you.'

'And this is one of them?'

He nodded, eyes refusing to drop mine. 'Seeing what happened to you before… it was terrifying.'

'It wasn't so bad,' I said, closing the space between us until we stood chest to chest. 'Might even say it was worth the pain, waking up in your arms.'

'Don't tease me, Maximus. Nothing was worth seeing you like that…'

'Not even what came before it?' I said, pouting, brows furrowed. Those moments between us, mouths touching, skin to skin, were the best I had experienced in a long while. I wanted more. Not minutes of bliss, but hours, days, centuries.

Simion held his serious stare, his face not allowing anything but refusal to show. I gave him props for effort, because there was no concealing the shiver of his eyebrow that gave him away. 'What do you want, Maximus Oaken?'

'I want you, Simion. Just as me taking this vial is a choice, so are you. Look me in my eye and tell me you don't want me back?'

As always, when Simion looked at me, he truly looked at me, as though nothing else mattered in the world. 'I want you too, Maximus. *Desperately.*'

I couldn't help the childish giggle erupting from me. 'For someone so known for his lyrical words, I'm surprised you put it so plainly.'

Simion's eyes darkened, his lips curled into a starved snarl. It was almost a surprise he didn't shoot forward and snap his teeth deliciously at me. 'There is not any other way for me to say it.'

I laid both hands on his hardened chest. 'Then have me if that is what you want.'

Simion didn't need to be told twice. His arms wrapped around my waist, muscles hardening around me so I couldn't pull away. Not that I would. This thrill, the danger of his proximity and the desire in his eyes, made my stomach jolt. It was as though I stood on the precipice of a cliff and stared over the edge.

'*Want* is a pathetic word used to describe how I feel when it comes to you, Maximus Oaken.'

'Do you desire me?' I whispered, breathy with anticipation.

'Desire, it hardly touches the truth of my feelings. It is a need. One so visceral, it is as if I couldn't survive without you. Like air that feeds a fire. Like water that nourishes the earth. How I have gotten this far in life without experiencing someone like you is beyond me. Perhaps the universe was simply telling me to be patient, perhaps I was not worthy. But whatever I am, whatever I have done to become worthy of you, the gods know I will not ruin it.'

I was stunned, blinking rapidly, his words invading my body, my mind, my spirit, and latching on with feverish determination.

'Well,' I whispered, entirely engrossed in the trance Simion placed me under. 'You truly rose to the task.'

A hand stroked up the side of my face, palm cupping my cheek, fingers drawing over my scalp. 'I could continue, if you like.'

'Yes,' I exhaled. I wanted to hear it all. I wanted him to never stop talking about me in ways that made me feel exposed and raw. 'But first, let me take a precaution.'

'Max, since when are you the cautious type?' Simion asked, so distracted by me he hardly paid mind to the vial I still held onto.

I lifted it before him, twisting the vial around so the blue liquid exploded with light as another bolt shot across the sky.

'Because this time, I'm not going to allow bonds to ruin what I *need*.'

Simion's eyes glowed at the way I took his words and cast them back at him.

'And what do you need?'

It was the easiest answer to give. 'You. All of you.'

CHAPTER 33

I lifted the vial to my lips and tipped the contents into my mouth. The draught was sweet, coating my tongue like melted sugar. All the while, Simion just looked at me. It was as though I was entirely exposed, skin as bare as my soul.

The dribble that fell over my lip was quickly caught by my tongue, drawing it into my mouth. His gilded gaze followed the sweep of my tongue. It seemed I was so absorbed with Simion that I missed a bit, until his thumb rose, drew the drop from my chin and brought it to my mouth.

'Open,' Simion said, eyes boring through me. *'Please.'*

He didn't need to say please, he knew I would have done it even without the soft command. I parted my mouth, allowing his thumb to slip inside. My tongue wrapped around him, sucking him in, teeth grazing his skin. Simion released a tempered groan.

I freed his thumb, although there was resistance before he drew it out, the firelight catching across the spit that glistened across it.

'Are you certain this is what you want?' Simion asked, chest heaving with laboured breaths. 'If you want to stop, at any point, we can.'

There was something so delicious about Simion's care for my

consent. It showed his respect, his careful and tender nature. Even if the answer was simple for me, hearing him ask the question was as exciting as what I was about to say.

I raised my hands and brushed them over his chest. His shirt ruffled beneath my fingers, lifting until his navel flashed. Beneath my fingers, his muscles tensed to stone.

'Yes,' I said, the word soft and tender. 'I am.'

Simion took my chin between his thumb and forefinger, lifting my head up so I couldn't look anywhere but him. 'If this is going to work, I am going to need you to be vocal with me.'

Vocal. I don't think there would be anything stopping me from vocalising once his hands explored me. Once his mouth was on me, devouring my skin, tongue exploring every inch, there would be no controlling what came out of my mouth.

'You'll regret saying that when the entire camp can hear me,' I said, eyes narrowing.

'Let them,' Simion said, shrugging as a mixture of excitement and pride twisted in his gaze. 'Let them all hear.'

Inyris grumbled far beyond the tent, sensing the elation I felt at Simion's words. I couldn't face what was to come knowing the dragon shared everything. So, I sent her away with a thought, urging her to stretch her wings and explore the island. It was bad enough risking the potential pain that came when giving into my temptations, but knowing my dragon could hear, let alone sense what I was to experience…

I expected her to resist the command. Then again, it was Simion she left me with. If there was anyone else with the ability of a god to protect me, it was him.

'One step at a time, Maximus,' Simion whispered, lowering his mouth to mine. His lips were a hair's breadth away, eyes roaming my face, breath tickling my senses. 'If you feel anything, we stop. Any sign that the draught hasn't worked, we stop.'

How did I tell him that I didn't think I could? Not if I truly gave into him.

'I'll be fine,' I said, reading the worry in his amber eyes.

'I am not taking chances, Max. Not with you.'

'But risks?' I said, voicing exactly what this was. The draught would either block the pain my bond to Camron created, or it wouldn't. It was a risk; we both knew that.

'Maximus Oaken. For you, I would risk it all.'

Our mouths found each other, melding together in a gentle caress. Simion's fingers flattened on the side of my face, nails brushing over my scalp as he lost himself in my hair. My hands caught between the press of our bodies.

There was no holding back my groan, not as my body delighted in every part of our connection. Deep down I waited for the pain to come and ruin the moment. I knew there would be no warning, only agony unlike anything I could truly describe.

But there was no pain. For now, at least.

Simion's tongue slipped free of its confines, brushing against mine, encouraging, enticing. I met it, sharing the sweet taste of the draught with him.

When he tried to pull away, I sank my teeth into the soft flesh of his lower lip. A shiver broke over my neck at the sound it elicited from him. It was deep, feral. It sang of his hunger.

He took my refusal of distance and dove back into me.

Simion's greedy hands dropped to my thighs. One movement as I was lifted from standing, my ass pressed onto the table. He lowered himself over me until my spine was laid flat against the hard wood, my leg drawn up to my side, his hand holding it in place.

'More?' he asked between breaths.

I wrapped my arms behind his neck, locking him in place. Refusing to let him move away.

His lips broke into a smile against mine. 'I shall take that as a yes.'

There was a part of me who longed to rush this. If the fast-mark would ruin it, by the dryads, I would get all I wanted from this moment before it shattered. But with Simion on me, his hips pressed into mine, his hands and mouth relinquishing any thought of anything but him, I knew time didn't matter.

We had it, time in an abundance. Tonight was for the taking. We were hidden away on an island, far from the grip of his aunt. Beatrice was safe. My mother was healing. There was nothing stopping me from enjoying every last *fucking* moment.

Simion rose from my mouth before I could stop him with my teeth again. Disappointment lasted a second before he dove into my neck, paying the tender skin there the same attention he gave my mouth. I arched into him, my back rising from the table. He pushed deep, hips forging with mine so perfectly it was as though we were made from one another.

'Don't you dare stop,' I moaned, eyes rolling into my skull as his kiss undid me. I began to undress him, urgent fingers tugging the buttons from his shirt. A few came undone with ease, the others I ripped from the thread.

The material slipped from his limbs, falling to the floor. When he retrieved himself from my neck, Simion leaned back so he could watch me looking at him. My eyes widened as they raced over his bronze skin.

Where my eyes graced, his muscles hardened. My fingers reached up, brushing over the puckered lines of his mage-mark, which painted the skin above his heart. His amplifier—the carved dragon of wood—hung forward as he leaned back over me.

'I was not finished,' I whispered, suddenly shy beneath his attention.

'With what?' he asked, mouthing the question against my neck again.

'Seeing you.'

A blush exploded across Simion's cheeks, his mouth parting as though my words were ice traced down his spine. This time, when he pulled back, it was different. He did it to give me exactly what I wanted.

'Where do you think you are going?' I scolded, leaning up on my elbows to watch him.

'You wanted to see me,' Simion said, half-exposed before me, hands falling to the leather belt around his waist. 'Then watch. And when I am done, I wish for the same thing from you, if I am deserving.'

His words froze me. All I could do was offer him a nod.

Simion wasted no time in undressing. He didn't remove his eyes from mine, not once. His fingers plucked at the leather belt. When it was discarded atop his forgotten shirt, he moved to his trousers. Long fingers slipped beneath his waistband, shuffling them down his hips.

I didn't dare move, didn't dare blink for fear of missing out.

This wasn't the first time I had seen him naked to the world, but dryads it felt like it. Heat dripped through my insides, pooling in my crotch, spreading like wytchfire until I was entirely consumed by it. I longed to slip my hand and grasp it, to stifle the hardening of my length, or to encourage it.

He was indescribable. Utterly beyond words. 'You're beautiful.'

I counted his muscles, one at a time. Strong arms, broad chest that tapered to a narrowed waist. Simion was a god cut from stone. Modest undershorts were all that was left, pitched at the centre from his own arousal.

My stomach flipped as he rearranged himself, the press of his length visible through the thin material keeping it concealed.

'What do you see?' Simion asked, his voice a breathy whisper. He stood still, allowing me to take in every part of him. I contemplated my answer, unsure if I should complement his hardened stomach, his long limbs, his devilish eyes or kiss-swollen lips.

'I see you,' I said, longing to reach out for him. 'I see you, Simion.'

He exhaled a long breath from his nose, body rippling as he tensed. 'Then I think it is your turn. Undress for me, Max. Let me see all of you.'

The fear of pain was slowly fading away. Even if I wasn't touching Simion, physically betraying the fasting bond, the thoughts that filled my mind were detailed and raw. Those alone should've flayed my body apart in punishment.

I was giddy, bubbles of thrill popping within my chest. Whatever was in the draught, whatever magic was contained in the waters of a nymph, it was protecting me. It made me invincible.

Simion's fingers drummed on his waist as he watched me take off each item of clothing. I was slow, not because I wanted to draw this out, but because my fingers were fumbling and awkward. But he didn't help. He enjoyed the show as I slipped my shirt over my shoulders, one at a time. As I undid the buttons of my trousers and as I kicked off my boots.

Soon enough I stood in the cool tent, Simion's eyes brushing my skin alongside the nightly winds. The island seemed utterly silent for the first time. Peaceful, almost. Although I could admire it, I knew it wouldn't last.

Simion closed the space, eyes roaming my body. His fingers reached for me first, brushing tenderly over skin. Knuckles traced over my nipples, hardening them. His hand wound around my neck, flowing like water down my shoulder, my arm, until he reached my hand and held me.

'This,' Simion said, 'this is a privilege. I want you to know, I do not take it for granted.'

I wished to come up with something sarcastic to combat my sudden shyness, but there was nothing to aid me.

Concern flashed over his face. 'How do you feel?'

'I'm not suffering if that is what you are asking,' I replied, looking up at him through my lashes. 'I'm quiet because how can I possibly offer you words when you speak to me with such poetic integrity. I wish I could say something so beautiful to you.'

Simion brushed his finger over my lower lip. 'Your silence is beautiful. Your breathing is beautiful. Your existence is beautiful.'

'See,' I laughed, nesting into his chest whilst he engulfed me in his arms. 'You did it again.'

'You inspire me,' Simion chuckled, his deep voice rasping.

'Kiss me,' I demanded, nails digging into his chest, as though I needed to anchor myself to him.

'With pleasure.'

This was it. I knew what was to come. The world became an afterthought as we fell to the sheep-skin rug. I straddled his waist, thighs gripping hard to his sides. At some point, he had tugged my undershorts off, ripping them at the seams.

Simion groaned into my mouth as I rocked on his hardening cock. His sounds encouraged me, as did the guiding force of his large hands on either side of my hips. He pinched the fleshy skin of my ass, toying with the line of pain and desire.

I littered kisses down his body, moving from his mouth to his navel. My tongue roamed over mounds of muscle, licking the salt from his skin, trailing the lines of his mage-mark. Curls of coarse hair spread up his navel, surrounded his perfectly formed belly-button in shadows.

When I took his undershorts off, it was with careful hands. This time my fingers didn't shake. They were calm, sure in knowing what they wanted.

Exposed, I took him in my palm, wrapping my fingers around his hilt. They didn't touch around the hard width.

Every part of him was impressive, every inch hypnotised me.

The world stilled as Simion looked down his body at me, eyes wide with anticipation. His parted mouth, his hearty exhales, the thunderous clash of his heart beating with mine.

I brought his tip to my lips, pressed the curve of his cock to my tongue, then engulfed it.

His taste burst across my tongue, sticky and sweet. I spread the wetness of my mouth around him, making sure he was covered with me. Simion fell back on the rug, back arching as he pushed himself deeper into my mouth. I took him in until I couldn't anymore. A gag crawled up my throat, pleasing him, pleasing me. Then I pulled him free, yanking him out as I gasped for breath, spit linking my glistening mouth to his tip.

'Dryads,' I swore, eyes and mouth watering with levelled excitement and hunger.

'You did well,' Simion encouraged, laughing to himself, pride brightening his cheeks. 'Good boy.'

Fuck.

Before he could say another word, I took him back in, hand moving in tandem with my tongue. I ravaged him to a breathless creature. He was so blessed with words until now. Suddenly, I held the power. Fingers slipped into my hair. I thought it was to keep me in place, keep me in pace—but I was proved otherwise when he tugged me back. Not before some of his seed slipped into my mouth, exploding my cheeks with his sweetness.

Forget my amplifier, forget my dragon bonded—this was power.

Simion growled as he lifted me back to his lap, smashing his lips into mine. His tongue shared in his taste. He kissed me with desperation. I returned it with equal vigour. When he pulled back to catch his breath, he looked me dead in the eye. 'My jacket, in the pocket. Now.'

'Pardon?' I said, delighting in his sudden commanding tone.

'Go, see what you find.'

I did as he asked. His eyes followed me, tingling across my back, as I walked over and picked up his jacket. My hand dove into the inside pocket and retrieved a vial. This one was not filled with the blue liquid I had taken. It was different, clear and thick lubrication.

'You planned for this, didn't you?' I said, leaning on my hip as I waggled the vial at him.

'I wasn't going to come unprepared. Just in case.'

Thank the dryads he did; looking down at his cock I knew that spit wasn't going to help. Just seeing the size of it made my stomach leap.

I padded over the tent to him, settling back on his waist as though he was my throne.

'It was not too presumptive, was it?' Simion asked, as I proceeded to rock on his groin. Firm hands grasped my thighs, nails pinching into fleshy skin.

'Not at all,' I giggled, placing my spare hand over his mouth. Simion's tongue caressed it, teeth grazing. I quickly replaced my hand with my mouth. Simion tore the vial from my grasp. 'In fact, there is something rather sexy about your ability to think ahead.'

'My ability to think ahead?' Simion laughed. 'Is that what makes you hard for me?'

I glanced down, following where his eyes looked, his hands touched. A rumbling breath exploded out of me as he wrapped his fingers and began shifting up and down my cock.

'And many other things,' I mumbled, lost to the pleasure of him.

The pop of a cork sounded at my back as he rushed to empty the contents of the vial onto his cock. I didn't see it, not with my face pressed to his. But I sensed the anticipation as he prepared himself for me.

Before our excitement stole us, his kiss softened. I melted into the sensual change, allowing my body to calm, my muscles to relax. He guided himself into position, whispering into my lips.

'Take your time,' Simion said, kissing me over and over.

He entered me slowly. The burn wasn't uncomfortable, not entirely. It was warm and filling, settling over my skin until he was entirely within.

No longer needing the guidance of his hand, he returned them to my face, brushing the hair from my eyes. His brow had softened, his eyes roaming my features, his mouth open, his tongue littered with a thousand unsaid things.

He started slowly, pulling in and out, allowing my body to familiarise itself with him. I leaned over him, stomach fluttering as his tip pressed into the pleasure deep inside of me. It was my undoing. My forehead pressed into his, my eyes closed, my breathing laboured.

As Simion's pace picked up, my pleasure built and built, doubling over until the world fell away and I was caught in a river of euphoria.

I let it take me.

It was fire and ice. It was ruin and repair. As Simion drove himself inside of me, his steady rhythm wreaking havoc with my soul, there was no stopping the truth from breaking free.

'More,' I demanded through gritted teeth.

Simion worked faster, harder. He kissed my mouth, my neck. Teeth pinched me, fingers dug into my ass and pulled it apart, easing his entry.

For once, he had no words of wisdom to share. There was nothing he could conjure as he gave into the divinity my body offered.

Simion was so careful with me, even when I longed for him not to be.

Far in the reaches of my mind, I knew there should be pain. But it never revealed itself. I opened my eyes long enough to look at the silver marks on my arm. There was no splitting skin, no blood, no ruin or destruction. Not with him. Never again with him.

Simion looked me dead in the eyes, sweat racing down his temple, catching on the proud bones of his jaw. 'Open your mind—'

He had to pause for breath, to catch himself. His eyes rolled back into his skull as I tensed my pleasure for him.

'—open your mind, for me.'

I did as he asked. The steel walls around my thoughts were now paper thin, tearing apart as Simion entered.

With his presence came an overwhelming wave of emotion. It snatched at me, clawing me away in its powerful gush.

Pleasure. Joy. Happiness. Relief. Love.

Love. It was without bounds, without rules and justification.

Tears filled my eyes, falling over my smile and dripping onto the beautiful man beneath me. I felt everything he had to offer, I accepted it and gathered it in a place within me so I could covet it long after this would end.

It wasn't that Simion longed to change my emotions, my feelings. No. He showed me his and they matched mine like the piece of a puzzle slotting into place.

We raced to the precipice together, two bodies as one, two minds joined. Every feeling heightened, it was intoxicating. It was magic. There was once a time I hated magic. Now I kissed magic's feet in thanks for offering such a moment.

Simion held me to him as he planted his seed within me. Mine splashed across his stomach, pooling in a puddle of milky white in his belly button. There was no care for the mess, not when he pulled me on top of him, exhausted and sweaty.

Cold winds brushed over our warm, sticky bodies as we laid with each other. Breathless and gripped in the afterglow of gratification, he slowly regained composure. It was like clawing up the riverbed after being torn down a ravine—a ravine one would willingly drown in.

'I feel as though I should thank you,' I said, breaking the heavy-breathing-filled silence. 'For that. Is that embarrassing?'

'The feeling is mutual,' Simion replied, planting a kiss on my hand, arms refusing to let me go.

One of the moment's joys was knowing we didn't need to speak about anything. What we had experienced was beyond words. Beyond explanation. It was a long time coming and, dryads, it was worth it. I had never felt so weak in the knees without the need to stand.

'You deserve it and more.' Simion held me close. 'And I long to be the one to give it to you, over and over.'

I closed my heavy eyes, allowing the dark to fill with the images of his body on mine. It was painted in clear colours, highlighted by strands of brilliant light.

'We will,' I promised, knowing this would happen again without the need for medicine to quell the bond between me and Camron. Tomorrow. Day break. It would be over. All of this would be over.

'Simion,' I said, delighting in the slam of his heart through his chest, banging against the side of my face.

'Yes?' he said softly, tired from his performance. I peered up at him to see his eyes closed, the most breathtaking smile sliced across his face.

'I love you too.'

He peered down at me, neck pressed to his chest at the awkward angle. 'Say it again. Louder.'

It was on the tip of my tongue, waiting and ready to spill. My ears tickled to another sound, one far away from the beat of his heart, the rasp of his breathing. It was a cry, a scream perhaps, caught on the wind.

I turned my head to the tent's exit. 'Did you hear that?'

It came around, whistling through the tent's entrance. 'It's just the wind, Max.' His eyes narrowed, his grin widening. 'Are you trying to distract me from what you just said?'

Concern flickered through my chest, filling a void I hadn't realised was there until this moment. I turned my mind from the noise, wondering why the wind would cry out as though it suffered from agony.

'No,' I said, finding it easy to lose myself when I looked back to him.

Simion couldn't hold his eyes open long enough, but his smile never faltered. 'Sleep with me, Max. Just like this. One night, just me and you, before the inevitable.'

How could I refuse him? 'You're in my tent, or did you forget?'

'Do I require permission to stay?'

'Never,' I replied.

I lowered my ear back to his chest, glad to hear his heart over the far-off scream of... wind. Simion pressed a final kiss to the top of my head, lingering as he exhaled. We slept like that, with nothing but skin to warm each other as we settled into the silence of the camp. I slept to his heartbeat and the crying winds for company.

CHAPTER 34

I remembered a time when Simion's snores had irritated me. Now the sound was a symphony—something I would give anything to listen to. Luckily for me, he was a heavy sleeper. Because of that and the energy we had spent last night, his eyes fluttered, his lips flickering into a smile.

We had woken in the early hours of the morning, clumsily grabbing one another. The second time we made love was almost more euphoric than the first. There was no speaking, no words. Only the sense of rushing before the vial faded out of my system.

I had slept better than I had in weeks.

I dressed carefully, not wanting to wake him. He looked so peaceful, so calm. If I could've climbed back onto the pallet, nestled up beside him and pushed all other thoughts from my mind, I would've. Instead, I prepared to break Elder Cyder's only rule. Considering everything that had transpired, I barely imagined he would care. Especially not when all I wanted to do was see my mother—that was my right, after all.

Curfew was only a matter of hours from lifting with daybreak. And I wasn't planning on disturbing the camp, but on visiting the caves beneath it.

I was so focused on being quiet that I didn't notice the sentinel guards standing just outside of the tent.

'Mage Oaken.' I recognised the speaker immediately. It was Harold, the phoenix-possessed rebel who stood beyond my tent, strong arms folded over his chest.

'Harold. Can I help you?' I said, veering my gaze from one guard to the next. It had been weeks since I was guarded. And it was never for my safety.

'I think I should ask you the same thing,' Harold replied, his kind smile almost too kind. Forced. His eyes traced over me, fully dressed, boots tied up. Certainly not dressed for sleeping. 'May I suggest you go and get some more rest. We have a big day ahead of us all.'

'Am I not permitted to visit my mother?'

Harold hardly moved a muscle, but his eyes lifted to the deep-navy skies as though reminding dawn had not arrived. 'During *reasonable* hours.'

What he meant was, *during hours outside the curfew.* Unease enveloped me. It strangled fingers around my throat and squeezed. I was forced to fake a smile of my own, rolling my eyes as though shocked at myself. 'Dryads, the time gets away from me! Am I that early?'

'Yes,' Harold responded, smile still in place but voice wary. 'Sleep well, Mage Oaken.'

I nodded, trying my best not to show unease in my expression. 'Of course.'

By the time I slipped back into my tent, my heart was cantering like a stampede of wild horses. After everything I had been through, I trusted my instincts. And, in that moment, they screamed like the bells of danger.

Something was wrong, I just couldn't place my finger on it. It was as though the world was too quiet after being loud for so long.

How long had they been outside? More importantly, why? Did they take Inyris's distance as an opportunity to fill her space?

I toyed with waking Simion, but I didn't want to ruin the morning after the night before. He deserved to experience the bliss I had woken to, not have it destroyed with my suspicions. It was nothing, just a way for Elder Cyder to uphold the curfew. Even as I attempted to convince myself, it still didn't take away from the fact that this has been the first night we had been guarded.

Determination lit my blood vessels with lightning. I wasn't prepared to wait and allow my distrust to build.

What were the point of rules, if not for breaking?

It was surprisingly easy to escape out of a tent. All it took was finding a couple of iron pegs that stabbed the material into the dewy ground, lifting them out and slipping beneath the heavy sheet. I kept as quiet as possible, careful not to alert the guards who waited beyond the main entrance.

The storm had saturated the ground, turning hardened mud to a bog beneath my feet. My jacket was all but ruined by the time I stood. My hands caked in dirt, my knees sodden with earth.

Looking around, there were no other tents with guards outside. Noticing that didn't help my paranoia.

I slipped through camp, keeping to the back of the sea of tents. Every now and then, a patrol of rebels passed through the main streets, eyes cast over the camp in search. But in search for what?

The air was charged. Each inhale was filled with the scent of a storm. Clear skies hung above me, whisps of clouds barely formed. The world was bathed in a dusky glow, muting every-thing, only aiding to the strange tension.

It was so quiet even my breathing sounded as loud as a thun-derous boom. When I heard the struggling, muffled shouts in the opposite direction of the caves, it shattered the calm.

The cry was so brief I almost passed it off as the same screaming winds from the night prior. But then I watched the patrol of rebels run in the direction, pointing towards the stone building in the distance.

It reminded me of the scream I had heard last night, the one

Simion blamed on the winds. Except the air was still, there was barely even a gust. So, I followed it. And if I was caught, I would simply use the scream as an excuse.

My heart lodged in my throat, making every breath ragged. I kept low, sometimes stopping if I heard noise.

Inyris was quiet in my mind. I couldn't sense the dragon's presence and praised the dryads that I didn't. If she felt my panic, there would've been no stopping her from ruining my need for secrecy.

I rounded the large stone building—the only one of the island —and noticed a swell of rebels outside. It struck me then that the curfew was certainly a one-sided rule. It seemingly applied only to visitors, not to those who lived there.

And it conspired I was not the only one who broke the rules, after all.

Leska was on her knees, held by the hands of guards, her mace on the muddied ground just out of reach. My blood spiked as I watched one rebel kick her amplifier further out of the way.

There was no room for thoughts. The guards gagged her, bound her arms in chains and hoisted her from the ground. All the while, Leska didn't stop fighting against them. She kicked out her legs, smacking her boots into the jaw of one of the rebels. Then her skull cracked into a nose, shattering it.

Soon enough the crowd of rebels swarmed her. My nails bit into my palms as I watched on from my hidden perch. I went to move, ready to shout out and stop whatever was happening, when an arm wrapped around me from behind, a hand clasped over my mouth to stop me from shouting.

I was spun around before I could call upon my magic, faced with familiar amber eyes.

Beatrice glared at me, face inches from mine, her eyes wide with panic, the whites bloodshot and the skin around them concealed with shadows. My breath fogged against her hand, dampening my lips. It took a few moments of heavy breathing for her to release me. Not before she lifted a finger to her mouth in a clear signal.

Quiet.

She took my hand in hers and drew me away from the scene. By the time I looked back, Leska was no longer fighting. Blood trickled down her temple, casting a river over her closed eyes. There was no more fight left in her as the sea of rebels dragged her body into the stone building, closing the door behind her as if nothing untoward had occurred.

Beatrice didn't stop guiding me away. We didn't stop moving, not until we were in the shadows of the great wall erected around the island's exterior. We had to be careful when moving from the stone building's exterior to the wall; rebels patrolled the parapets, not watching out across the ocean, but looking over camp.

'Beatrice,' I pulled back, breathless, legs aching as wildly at my chest, 'what the fuck is going on?'

She threw her stare around, voice kept to a low whisper as she spoke. But it wasn't in reply to my question. 'Did you take a vial of liquid last night?'

'I don't understand—'

She grasped my shoulders, her face a mask of horror. 'Tell me. Did you ingest anything Cyder gave you?'

Well, technically Simion gave it to me.

'Yes,' I replied, hardly blinking.

'Fuck,' Beatrice scolded to herself. When she looked back at me, I knew what she was going to reveal before she said it. 'So did I.'

'Why?' I didn't have it in me to ask exactly what I was wondering. Why take the vial to smother a bond, if she wasn't affected by one? Only I was handfasted, only I wished to tempt the boundaries with Simion.

Beatrice raised a thick brow. 'Elder Cyder gave it to me, said it would help with my healing.'

'As did I.'

I could tell she didn't believe me, but that didn't matter. I couldn't voice why I had taken it. Not without revealing what I had done with her brother last night.

'Maximus, I can't feel Glamora.'

It was the urgency in her gaze that had me reaching out to Inyris. I suddenly had an answer to the silence to our bond. It was not because Inyris slept, it was because I couldn't feel her.

'Fuck,' I echoed Beatrice. 'I don't sense Inyris either.'

'Your magic, Maximus. Can you use it?'

I filled my mind with intent, opening myself up to the cords of power that linked me to my earthen abilities. The world stayed dull. No cords revealed themselves, I was severed from them. 'No, I can't feel... anything.'

Suddenly, the quiet nature of the world made sense. It wasn't simply dawn, it was the lack of Inyris in my mind, the lack of magic in my veins.

Beatrice dropped to her haunches, burying her face in her hands. 'That vial, the nymph's essence, it doesn't simply sever the bond between a phoenix and its host. It severs all bonds, Max. It cuts it all off. They've drugged us.'

CHAPTER 35

They've drugged us.

I didn't need to question Beatrice's accusation. I knew she spoke the truth from the lack of magic inside of me. I was empty, longing for something constantly out of reach.

A blaring horn exploded across the island, shattering the quiet in a matter of seconds.

We ducked low to the ground, pressing into the shadows of the wall. I glanced up to see the rebels rushing across the parapet, weapons drawn. I watched as amplifiers were raised, but still I sensed nothing. No telltale draw of magic. My connection was entirely severed. Whatever was in that vial, whatever magic Elder Cyder had given us, had done this.

I stretched out my mind, searching for Simion, knowing he would've woken to the noise. I hoped to feel his icy presence brushing over my mind. My open, explorable thoughts. Even without my abilities, I knew that the wall around it wasn't standing.

A new wave of panic gripped me. The kind that came from knowing all my secrets were laid out on a silver platter.

'Why would he do this?' I asked aloud, as the island was suddenly alive with people. 'It doesn't make sense!'

'There is no time. We need to get off this island, Max. Now.'

Iron fingers gripped my arm, bruising skin. Beatrice pulled me along in the outskirts of the wall, forging forward.

'Simion,' I snapped her brother's name, unable to pull out of her grasp. 'We can't just leave him—and Leska!'

'We'll come back for them.' There was hesitation in her voice, but it was faint. 'Leska told me to get Leia, to tell her what is happening here. This has all been—'

If I believed the horn to be loud, the sound paled in comparison to the roars that split the sky. Dragons flooded over us, swimming through the dull dawn. They flew over the wall in a tight formation, a multitude of shapes, sizes and colours. I had no doubt they searched for us.

My heart pained at the thought of Inyris unable to sense me.

Beatrice stopped suddenly, tearing me away from an archway as rebels flooded out. She had a weapon drawn in her hand, a dagger the length of her forearm. We had only but a moment to catch our breath. Beatrice saw me looking at the blade with the same starving gaze a sailor would to land.

'Here,' Beatrice said, passing it to me. I didn't refuse. It was well-balanced, the edges sharp enough to slice the very air apart. 'I have another.'

And she did. Beatrice had many weapons on her person. She reached into her boot and withdrew another similar blade. I caught the flash of steel against her forearm, her hip, her thigh.

'Steel cuts deeper than magic anyway,' Beatrice muttered. 'Leska told me she trained you. You know how to use it?'

I glanced down at the blade, testing the balance, sweeping it through the air as if holding something so deadly would steady the raging storm inside of me. 'I'll do my best.'

She hardly taught me to use my magic, let alone a blade.

'Let's hope that is enough to get us off this island.'

'Bea,' I said. She stopped, pulled back not by my hand but the hitching in my voice. 'What's going on?'

Her panicked gaze changed before my eyes into something else. Something darker. 'If I tell you, you won't come.'

She could've lied, but she didn't.

'They have my mother. They have Simion and Leska. Whatever you have to say to me isn't going to be the reason I don't want to leave. I already have enough to keep me here.'

Light exploded in my peripheral, distracting me. Out in the distance, one by one, the tents exploded with flame. Deep red tongues devoured the material, boiling so hot it destroyed them in a second.

'Simion.' We exhaled in tandem.

My body buzzed. I stared at Beatrice; this time she regarded me with a knowing she hadn't dared reveal yet.

'Go,' I said to her, gripping the blade. 'Find Glamora and get away. I can't leave.'

'It isn't safe,' Beatrice said, urgency burning in her eyes—or perhaps it was the reflection of fire as it engulfed the tents, dark clouds of smoke curling skywards, blocking out the brightening sky. 'For *you*.'

I hardly heard her, over the names repeating in a list in my head.

Beatrice grasped me hard, pinching my upper arms this time. 'Listen to me, Max. Elder Cyder has been lying. He thought he could rely on Leska, but she betrayed him. She told me... everything.'

An arrow whizzed through the air, cutting us apart. It embedded into the wall beside us, feather tip shuddering just between our faces.

'Go!' I pushed Beatrice hard, forcing her away just as another arrow shot forward, missing her side by inches. 'Now.'

I didn't have a choice but to run.

We pelted along the outskirts of the wall, dodging arrows. If I had connection to my magic, I would've felt the air spoil in warning. But there was no preparing as the rebels forced power into the ground, shuddering it beneath our feet.

Beatrice leaped over the fissure that split the earth in two, mud splattering like the splashing of waves against a rock. I pushed all my confusion, all my panic as to what was happening, to the back of my mind and forged ahead.

Survive now, think later.

'Get—onto—the—wall.' Beatrice pointed ahead to the archway embedded in the wall's base. 'Cut them... off.'

A ball of flame tore across the sky, arching at its peak before falling towards us. I didn't need to look to know it was conjured fire. Nor did I need to wonder where it came from. Harold was not the only phoenix-possessed rebel on this island.

They *all* were.

Beatrice shot into the shadowed opening first. I followed a second before fire exploded at our backs. Heat blistered my neck, sizzling hair. I looked back to see the entrance of the wall completely engulfed in tongues of red fire.

With fire at our back, and enemies before us, I forced down the fear and focused on my fight.

I gave into my body, fuelled by muscle memory, as we met our resistance. Beatrice charged at the rebels, barrelling into them with her blade drawn. I followed, allowing no room for hesitation.

If Leska had taught me anything, it was to handle pain and deal it out. That is what I did. My fist cracked into bone. My blade drew across flesh.

Beatrice was a whirlwind of muscle and steel. A wraith of shadow she barrelled through the narrow corridor, flames at her back. Bodies crumpled beneath us. Blood sloshed at our feet, soaking into the wooden panels, staining the air with a rusty tang.

So much death. It littered the ground, soaking the earth and poisoning the air. And still I drew the blade, unable to focus on the faces of the lives I took one by one.

Beatrice inspired me in that moment. Her choice to refuse the Heart Oak from Elder Cyder was suddenly clear. Years of her life had been spent dealing with the loss of magic. Like her family, it had been torn from her. Instead of failing beneath the lack of power, she took that weakness and made it a strength.

I would do the same, if it meant saving ourselves.

I drove the blade into the chest of a rebel, forcing my weight into the thrust. We fell to the ground, their spine popping beneath me as I landed, legs a straddle, over their waist. Blood spluttered past their paling lips, casting crimson across their chin.

If I allowed myself to contemplate every life I took, I wouldn't have been able to focus on what this all meant.

Strong arms suddenly wrapped around my throat, squeezing. I was yanked backwards, unable to remove my blade from the chest of my victim.

I forced out a rasped cry, but it was buried beneath the sound of battle. Beatrice forged ahead, not knowing that a rebel held me.

'You should have followed the rules,' a harsh voice sang into my ear. Warm lips brushed my skin, sickening me. I couldn't see the face of my attacker, but I sensed something familiar.

'You caught me, Harold,' I said before his warm hand clamped over my mouth. I bit down hard, breaking flesh until blood gushed down my throat. I swallowed it, refusing to choke, refusing to fail. Then I smashed my head backwards, cracking my skull against something equally hard. The shout of agony behind me was my prize.

Beatrice turned at the sound. Her eyes fell on me, wide and wild. Then they narrowed on my assailant. There was a clear warning in her gaze. *Keep still.*

Heat erupted across me, blinding my senses. I barely had time to turn my head away as flames slithered across the arms that bound me, searing through clothes and skin, working their way to me.

I lost myself to the fire. It still had the power to disarm me. My weakness, one I didn't think I could ever turn into a strength.

The air hissed. I couldn't close my eyes as I prepared myself to be devoured by the conjured flames. I exhaled a heavy breath, chest aching, mind screaming, but the fire extinguished. It was as if I blew it out, like a candle on a cake.

The grip on me relaxed, unravelling like limp rope. I fell free, just in time to see Harold slump backwards, a dagger embedded between his eyes. Beatrice was locked in the throwing position, her breathing shallow as fear painted her expression.

He was dead before he hit the ground.

'More will come,' she said, flushed, as she stood among a mound of fallen rebels. Blood dripped from the weapon she still held.

I nodded, refusing to look back at Harold. He had found his peace. His *cure* from the possession.

We forged ahead, shouts following at our backs. The stairs were narrow and steep. We climbed them, two at a time, before exploding out onto the top of the wall. It gave view across the oceans, to the barrier of mist that clung around the island. But it also had the perfect view over the camp—a camp consumed in fire. Rebels flooded through the land, racing around charred mounds, screaming orders.

I searched for Simion, frantically, last night's memory waning with every passing second.

Like bees to honey, the rebels hovered around the main stone building—the one Leska had been taken into. I could barely see the faces of those standing before it, but I did recognise one body. Elder Cyder, stout and short, his bald head catching the rays of dawn, his cloak of ivory falling around him in a shawl.

Dragons circled the stone building like vultures, cawing out in warning, splitting the sky with pillars of ice. A riot of them seemed to be fighting something else, all scaled bodies writhing in the air around... gold.

'Inyris,' I choked, arm stretched out across the sky as if I could reach her.

It was her, amidst the riot, trying to fight her way to me. I knew it deep in my bones, like an ache I would never forget.

'There's no time,' Beatrice shouted, peeling me away from the scene. 'I'm sorry!'

Beneath the noise, I could hear her. Not in my mind, but her caws of agony and desperation.

On either side of the curved wall, two crowds of rebels pincered us in place. There was nowhere to go...

'We have to jump,' Beatrice shouted. Wind caught her hair, whipping dark strands around her like serpents. 'If we can get in the water, we can swim until Glamora finds us. She *will* find us.'

I looked back to the dragons fighting Inyris. Glamora was nowhere to be seen. Even if I had hoped the black-scaled dragon would help mine, I was wrong.

As I had countless times, I stretched out my mind to my dragon, but it was pointless. The draught still clung to my being, severing my bond to my magic, my dragon.

Camron. This was the price I had paid to remove him from my body, all for my selfish desires.

'The fall will kill us,' I said, tears filling my eyes, desperation in my chest. Beneath the opposite side of the wall was the raging ocean. Jagged rocks pierced the frothing surface like teeth of a hidden giant. If we didn't land upon one, the crashing waves would surely devour us.

'Death waits for us if we stand around and wait for it to come.' Beatrice cast her gaze from each end of the wall, watching as the gaggle of rebels gained closer. 'We jump, Max, together!'

Beatrice pulled herself up onto the wall's edge, toes lingering over the abyss. I pulled back, catching her off balance. Where I expected resistance in her hand, there was none. My fingers slipped away with ease as I stepped away.

'Bea, I can't,' I said, not caring for the storm of shouts that grew on either side.

Beatrice's jaw tightened; her eyes refused to blink. Sea-spray glistened across her cheeks, coating them with a glossy kiss. Perhaps our powers were returning, because I tasted the magic the moment before it was used. Although faint, there was no disguising the pine-fresh ooze of earthen magic.

Inyris cried out, filling my mind with her despair and pain. A shadow separated from the wall, black wings beating, powerful body slicing towards us. Glamora. She was here.

'Jump, now!' Beatrice cried, reaching for me.

Glamora screamed, knowing our chance was seconds from reaching us.

Shouts grew closer, the ground shuddering with the countless boots that ran towards us.

'I can't,' I said, frozen to the spot, watching my window of escape growing smaller and smaller.

Beatrice snarled, reaching out for me. 'Max, come on—'

The stone shook violently, cracking beneath Beatrice's feet. Time slowed as she slipped, arms pinwheeling as though she could grasp the very air to stop her fall. I broke out of my trance, reaching out to grasp her. My fingers barely brushed her before it was too late.

Beatrice fell. Then she was gone from view. I screamed her name as hands grabbed me, yanking me back. Everything was happening too fast. Cords of power flickered to life around me. I grasped out, plucking the strings as a musician would an instrument. My magic was there, but it was weak. A tired beast waking from a heavy slumber.

A roar split the world in two. A spark filled my chest as a presence reared its head. But the rebels overwhelmed me, pinning me to the ground as I strained my gaze out for a sign Beatrice had made it.

A fist cracked into my face; boots knocked the wind out of my chest. I was held down by uncaring hands as Inyris unleashed another roar. She was closer this time. So was my magic. Just out of reach, close enough for my fingers to brush over but not for them to grasp.

Bodies continued to bundle on top of me, smothering the world from view. I reached out to every cord, to every possible chance I had, and I grasped it. The wall cracked in two, throwing rebels from my back. The world swayed, but it was not the world but the wall, as my power ripped at it like the claws of a dragon.

Something scratched my neck and it all disappeared.

My power. My dragon. My chance. Gone, just like that, before I ever truly had it back.

I could barely move, but I managed to raise a hand to my neck, to the needle that was left protruding from it. I tore it free, a wave of numbness cresting over me. Thrashing in the vial, at the needle's top, was the same azure liquid I had taken the night before.

If I focused, I could almost feel it overwhelm me from the inside out.

'Dragon!' One of the rebels screamed as a shadow cast over the sky, sending a bout of frozen wind us. The force was so great it tore rebels off me, some falling over the wall, screaming before their bodies broke against rock.

I looked up, expecting Inyris to have reached me. What I saw was the dark of obsidian scales rising before the wall, wings spread wide, blocking out the view of the great Thassalic.

Glamora. She rose, higher and higher and higher. An empty saddle rested on her back, but she was certainly not alone. Dangling from her claws was a limp body. Sodden with the ocean water, arms and legs falling awkwardly to the ground, Beatrice was no more a ragdoll than a human.

'Shoot it down,' someone screamed the order. Hands released me; bodies raced around. I was not a threat now, not compared to the creature who turned the skies against the island, battering wind over the wall until bodies toppled over the edge.

I couldn't do anything but watch as rebels ran to the turrets, climbed atop the mechanical bows set onto the wall. It took countless bodies to use the monstrous weapon.

'Stop,' I rasped, face pressed to the ruined ground, not daring to blink, to miss a single moment. It was a futile attempt, I knew that. But I couldn't just watch. I screamed and screamed, but it was as though no one heard me, or cared.

The bows turned into position, levelling the steel-tipped arrow in the direction of Glamora. No matter how I kicked, how I knocked my head back, there was no breaking free.

'You'll kill her—'

My cheekbone screamed as the rebel atop me grasped my hair, pulled my scalp and slammed my face to the ground. I saw double; triple. Stars filled my vision, refusing to clear.

Glamora soon became a speck in the distance, weaving through the sky towards the boundary of mist. Arrows twice the length of the dragon's chest tore through the skies after her, falling into the ocean, missing by mere inches.

'More,' the screams continued. 'Bring it down.'

It took six of them to reload the weapons. Three to move the bow into position. And one to press down on the pedal that sent the arrow flying.

The rebellion's dragons couldn't go after Glamora. With the sky full of powerful bolts of steel and wood, it wasn't safe for the other dragons to follow. As more arrows filled the sky in a swarm, it was the battlemages who steered them in hopes to hit their target. And they did.

Even from a distance I could hear the leather tear apart as the arrow hit its mark. It tore through Glamora's wing, just as she reached the nymph's mist, breaking her apart with ease. Her scream broke me, tearing one from my chest. It ripped out of my throat, scoring the flesh until I filled with blood and horror.

Then she was gone, falling from the sky, through the barrier of cloud, out of sight.

I would've hoped she made it through, but the eruption of cheers from those around me proved otherwise. It was over.

Tears blinded me as sobs wracked my chest. I couldn't breathe, not with my mind playing over and over what had happened.

Hope may have been a double-edged blade, but it was still a blade. Sharp and deadly.

Fuelled by the hot poker of grief, I reared up and used the little fight I had left. I didn't care who I attacked, I swung my limbs, hoping to break bones and cause pain. Nothing I could do, nothing I could offer, would compare to the feeling that tore through me. But dryads, I would use it. I would use it all until they all felt even a hint of what I did.

My fist cracked against bone, crunching it. I blinked to see blood spray from the nose of a rebel, only to see their gaze harden. Something hard smacked into the side of my head, knocking me back against the ground. My skull bounced over stone.

Then there was nothing but darkness.

CHAPTER 36

I woke to find my body bound to a chair, rope burning skin as I tugged against it. Before my eyes burst open, I sensed the presence before me. It started as an ache at the back of my mind. It wasn't the caress of Simion's presence, or the scratching nail of Leia's magic.

This was the brush of scales, as a snake languished over stone.

'Do you have a death wish, Maximus?' Elder Cyder sat on a chair before me, watching me.

I shot forward, exhausted, but granted strength by my fury. My arms resisted behind me, but that didn't stop me from trying until my skin tore. The pain mattered little when all I could focus on was this man and his betrayal.

'Fuck you.' My teeth snapped inches from his face. Cyder didn't flinch.

'Settle yourself, Maximus. I am not your enemy.'

'Are you not?' My arms were strapped to a chair with thick leather bands. I attempted to move my feet, but I knew they were held down too. As was my waist. Cyder's power still blew through my mind, opening doors I had no power to close. No matter how I focused on the steel wall, I couldn't raise it.

'No, I am not.'

'Get out of my head,' I hissed, spittle crashing against the side of his face.

To my surprise, he retreated. The intrigue in his blue eyes dimmed but didn't fade entirely. Although my mind no longer felt the presence of his serpentine scales, I recognised the danger of a lurking viper just out of reach.

'This truly is an unfortunate turn of events, Max.' Elder Cyder leaned back in his chair, looking down at his hands. 'I never wanted for this to happen.'

'For what?' I spat, unable to grasp a single coherent thought. 'Drugging us? Lying to us?'

'All necessary steps, as I am sure you will understand.'

I blinked and in the dark I saw Glamora tumble into the frothing ocean, wing torn apart by the arrow, Beatrice with her. 'She is *dead* because of *you*.'

'Beatrice's choices led to her death.' Elder Cyder snapped his head back to me, eyes flying wide. 'If you had not attempted to flee, she would be sitting in this very room with you. Alive. Her death will not scar my conscious, Maximus. Not as it has yours.'

He might as well have driven a dagger into my chest and twisted. There were no words I could use; no sentence I could string together to offer or ease the very thing he had just exposed me for. Because I felt it. Deep in my gut, the all too familiar grasp of grief pulled apart a wound I had begun to heal. 'We trusted you... *I* trusted you.'

'And you still can.' He laid a hand atop mine. 'No harm is going to come to you. I promise—'

A tear slipped down my cheek, caught by a gentle thumb he reached towards me. I stiffened beneath his soft touch. It didn't make sense.

'—you are pivotal to my plans.'

I gathered spit in my mouth. One hack and I sent it out at him. 'Fuck you, fuck your plans.'

'Now Maximus, that is no way a King should speak, is it?' Cyder reared back, drawing his hand away from me and resting it on his lap. 'Why didn't you tell me the truth of it all? I thought we could trust one another, but I suppose we both have had this proved otherwise.'

I didn't need to ask what he spoke off. Cyder had gleaned the truth from my open mind, reaching in and taking what he wanted out.

The laugh broke out of me. 'Trust has no meaning to you, does it?'

Offence creased his face, layering deep lines over his forehead. 'It means everything to me. This island is built on it. The Hawthorn rebellion started with it. Have I not shown you that you can trust me? I saved your... *mother* from Leia's grasp. I did as you asked and yet still you lied.'

He looked genuinely hurt, which angered me more.'

'All for your own gain, no doubt.'

He rocked back. My words were as much a weapon as the power he had taken from me. 'Perhaps. But now I understand why you were so important to the dearly departed Queen. Because you are her child. Born from her blood. The rightful heir, the dryad-born King.'

'Find anything else in your excavation of my fucking mind?' I shouted, spittle flying between us.

'Yes,' he answered plainly, with an expression that looked closer to fear than anything else. 'Which is why I wished you were honest with me from the start. I'm not going to lie to you, like Deborah has. Like everyone has. I am here to offer you the truth, all of it, nothing more hidden.'

'Don't you dare speak of my mother.' My fingers dug into the wooden chair, nails aching from the force. 'When you had your own daughter harmed.'

'Leska should not have gone against me,' Elder Cyder said so calmly I almost thought he was another man from another time. In that moment, with his bright eyes and soft grin, I saw King Gathrax sat before me. 'The same goes for Beatrice. We had a rule, a curfew. One rule to follow and they couldn't do that.'

'Did you not have their tents guarded as you did mine?' I spat.

'I did,' he replied coldly. 'Those guards were found bleeding out on the ground, throat sliced.'

'Because you poisoned us, Cyder!'

He shook his head. 'No. It is because I was foolish to believe Leska would understand our goals if I showed her the truth behind our perfectly lifted veil. Ensuring you each were given a dosage of Nytraith was necessary after you revealed to us your continued bond with Camron Calzmir. It was a precaution. I explained this to Leska, but my daughter didn't see eye to eye with my reasoning—'

Scales shifted over my skull. There was nothing I could do to stop Elder Cyder from reaching into my thoughts, my memories. I had not heard that name before, but I understood it was what had been in that vial.

'—Nytraith has many properties. It is the product of a nymph, as I have explained before. The physical essence of their power. Except it can be used to sever the bond of magic, open one's mind to those who desire access and—as we have recently discovered—smother the possession of a phoenix and allow the host to gain control over their body.'

Blood drained from my head, flowing down the length of my body until it dissipated at the bottom of my boots. Elder Cyder had been through my mind. He had seen the secrets I had kept hidden.

'Ah, yes, I have. And finally, it makes sense as to why the Queen was so desperate to get you back to Wycombe. All this time you could have fed the Heart Oak. All this time you were the key to providing power back to the North.'

'And you see why I kept it to myself?' I asked, tasting blood from where I had bitten down on the inside of my cheeks. 'Because I do not care if the Heart Oak survives. I do not care if you are without magic or not.'

He winced, the word crashing into his soul like the arm that tore through Glamora's wing. 'I do not believe that Maximus. I believe you do want to help, or at least that is for me to convince you too. In the meantime, know that your secret is safe with me.'

'Is it?' I screamed, muscles aching as I shook in the chair, trying everything to break free. 'If your own daughter doesn't trust you, in what realm do you think I will?'

Something I said affected Elder Cyder. He shot forward, wrapping his stubby hands around my throat to silence me. 'You have no idea what you are talking about. Realms. You are not the only one who hides secrets, Max. Believe me when I tell you that yours are dull in comparison with what the Queen kept from us. What Deborah has been keeping from you. Then again... I have seen into your dreams.'

I gasped for air, throat aching as though it bled from the inside. My skin bruised beneath his fingers. Elder Cyder was lost to his thoughts, so much that he barely blinked, barely looked at me. Whatever occupied his thoughts frightened him.

'You have seen *her*.'

'Who?' I asked, watching as Cyder broke himself out of the grasp of his trance.

'Our damnation. The very reason I am doing this.'

'Which part? Drugging people, or using the phoenix-possessed towards your own gain?'

I waited for him to tell me I was wrong. He didn't.

'Both. The Hawthorn rebellion was set up years before Celia and Beatrice's exile. Before you were taken from Wycombe by Deborah and hidden away. It started before we adopted the name Hawthorn. It was a vision between three friends, friends who uncovered some deadly truths that their home was built on. But you, Max—you are the key to giving us a chance to survive what is to come.'

He was crazed. I saw it in his eyes as he slowly raised them to me. The whites were stained crimson, his pupils dilated to large discs. That didn't take away from the fact that he believed himself.

'I don't want any part of this.'

'And you think I do?' Cyder tilted his head, lip caught between teeth, brow furrowed. 'Do you think any of us would want to continue living mundane lives, knowing the type of hell we are one day to face?'

I saw her then, the monstrous woman with her army of shadows.

'Ah, you see. How can you deny me of what I want, when you too have been shown the truth?'

Cyder held the vision in my head, blinding me with the panic it conjured.

'What… what do you want?' I screamed, trying everything to force him out of my mind, but failing.

'To save us. The Hawthorn plan is the same, although now we have more of a chance in success. We will storm the city, we will take control from the Council, from Elder Leia. Doing so will stop her planned attacks on the South, just as I promised I would help you with. I will need the South for what is to come. And then we will finish the very task the dryads started all those years ago.'

'You're crazy,' I said, unable to blink as the man before me shifted through emotions like changing a mask.

'And you are the child of our Queen, an egg placed in the belly of a woman you now call your mother. We all have a purpose in this world, and you, Maximus, were born to continue fuelling the Heart Oak. Since it was your husband who destroyed it, it is your responsibility, more than ever, to repair it.'

I leaned forward, wild fury oozing from my eyes. It was so potent, it was a surprise that I didn't burst through the barrier keeping me from my power, my dragon.

'You can't make me.'

'I do not intend to *make* you do anything,' Elder Cyder said, pushing on his thighs for leverage as he stood from the chair. 'I am not like those who have come before me. People who used you. I understand you had no choice in this life, just as I had no choice when discovering the truth behind our world. It is a burden. One we will share. I will make you see, make you understand, and then you will help me. Willingly.'

He continued to surprise me. Cyder withdrew a knife from his robe, drew the cold blade beneath the straps at my wrists, and tore upwards in a swift motion. Leather parted and I was free. 'I would have revealed my plans. But you took matters into your own hands and look what has happened... who has been lost.'

I could've stopped him. I wouldn't have needed magic to overwhelm him, take the knife and kill him before he had the chance to scream for help. His own daughter had made sure I learned that. But something stopped me. I kept still as he continued to undo my bindings. When he was finished, he returned his knife into his robe and offered me a hand.

'All this... just to make me feed the Heart Oak?' I asked.

'No, not completely. We all have a motive,' Elder Cyder said, offering me a hand. The same hand that had been wrapped around my throat. 'Yours has never changed. All you have searched for is a home. Everything you have been through, in the South, in the North, that has never wavered. But you will continue searching for it blindly because wherever you set roots, you will find them severed. North, South. No place is safe from who is to come.'

'And pray tell, what is your motive, Cyder?'

His eyes narrowed, but not in anger or displeasure at my question. It was something else. It was fear.

'I'll show you.'

CHAPTER 37

I followed Elder Cyder through the maze of rooms, passing corridors full of rebels, their eyes settling on me with an understanding I had yet to figure out. It was almost easy to allow my mind to settle on the plan that formed—but Elder Cyder's scaled presence reminded me to fill my thoughts with something else.

So, I did. Not wanting him to see into my mind, I thought of something with the power to repulse him.

I thought of Simion.

My head filled with images of him. Clothed, naked. The more I dredged up the images of our bodies entwined, the further Elder Cyder strayed until I could barely sense him. The old man didn't wish to see what had happened between Simion and me, what we used the Nytraith for.

This was my wall to keep him out—one conjured of flesh and bone.

But my *need* for Simion was all encompassing. Soon enough my body was present in this world, but my mind was elsewhere. It was back in the tent before this betrayal. It was back when we had forged our own world together, nothing else mattering but our touch and connection.

Of course, that joy didn't last long. Not when Beatrice slipped into my thoughts. Then I was presented with another concept. One that involved the need to tell Simion what had happened to his sister.

That she was... dead.

My knees buckled. Elder Cyder noticed and, within a second, I was held up by the arms of rebels by his command. This time, they didn't long to hold me down whilst I watched my friend and her dragon fall into the belly of the ocean. It was to hold me up —assist me.

I despised how honest Cyder's concern was for me. It hung as heavy as a storm cloud at the back of his gaze. There was nothing more I longed to do than turn on him—but patience was a virtue I had practised.

'There was a very good reason I had to enforce a curfew,' Cyder said, as he continued to lead the way. 'In an ideal world, we would never have lied to one another. But, like your need for caution, there was something I knew you would not understand.'

We entered a room through two swinging doors. It was so bright it blinded me. I inhaled, my nose overwhelmed by the sterile scent of lemon.

Once my gaze settled, it was to find a large room filled with beds. They were lined up on either side of the room with minimal space on either side of them. Only enough for someone to walk between and check on the people who laid upon them.

There wasn't a single bed that was empty.

Gleamers raced around the infirmary, tending to those who needed it. Children, some as young as ten.

'The missing novices,' I breathed, unable to take my eyes off them.

'Safe and sound. I had a purpose for them, one they would never be able to refuse.'

Blood thundered in my ears as I noticed another peculiarity. The people laying on the beds did so facing down, backs bare.

We walked swiftly through the heart of the room. When I attempted to slow down, the rebels kept me at pace. My eyes fell on one of the gleamers, a straight-faced girl with tired, brown eyes. She raised a metal tray towards the edge of the bed closest to her. It wasn't a scene I had not already seen, but it was what lay across the tray that stole my breath.

It was a feather, strands plucked from ruby reds and furious oranges. The same Leska had found in Leia's office alongside Camron's journal.

'Wait!' I forced weight into my heels, attempting to stop myself from being moved. Hands held harder, bruising my skin. 'What is she doing…'

'I am not simply using the phoenix-possessed, Maximus. I am—'

There was no need to hear what he had to say.

He was *making* them.

Teeth gritted, I forced the little energy I had left into refusing those around me. All the while I watched as the gleamer lifted the feather from the tray and lowered it to the naked shoulder blade of the person in the bed.

My mind raced with answers, piecing together everything I would never have believed possible.

The pointed thorn of the feather's base stabbed through brown skin. Blood blossomed, slithering down the curve of their back as the novice gleamer continued to insert the feather beneath flesh. Then, as though pulled inside from unseen fingers, it disappeared. Absorbed by the body as though it thirsted for it.

Fresh skin bubbled and boiled, staining the person's back in a smudge of scars. Scars I had seen on Camron's skin. Scars that covered my mother and all the other phoenix-possessed people I had encountered.

'It was all you,' I stammered over the word, looking back to Elder Cyder. 'You never wanted to save the phoenix-possessed. You… you wanted to make more of them. An army of magic that would finally combat the Council.'

'Yes.' He stood, watching me, hands held carefully before him.

'Well done. But, Maximus, I would appreciate if we kept this room as peaceful as possible.'

'You're a monster!' I shouted louder, screaming to the point my throat burned. 'It was you, not Camron!'

Pride flashed over Elder Cyder's face. It was short-lived. When he spoke, it wasn't to me. 'Mage Oaken requires some assistance. Please—'

I threw my head back, skull connecting with bone. The rebel gasped out; something wet splashed against the back of my neck. Blood. Their grip loosened, enough for me to pull away. Other hands grasped pathetically for me, but I slipped through them with ease, slamming my knuckles into the sneering faces of any who dared get close.

Part of me wished Leska was here to see me. She would have been proud.

The novice who had placed the feather into the man's back stumbled backwards, gasping. It was that moment I knew they were not working with the rebels, but *for* them. Fear clouded over her eyes.

I tore the tray from her weak grasp and threw it with all my might. Metal cracked into the side of a rebel's face, splitting skin. Before they could round back, I drove the air from their lungs with a slam of my knee. As they doubled over, I used their shock and shoved them. As they fell, they took another rebel down with them, a mess of tangled limbs.

Breathless, the girl cowering at my back, the newly infected man motionless beside me.

'Not another step,' I screamed, 'any of you.'

Not a single soul looked elsewhere. Every set of eyes were on me.

Elder Cyder ignored me and took one step forward. His hands were raised beside him, giving the illusion of defeat. Except the glint in his eyes told me otherwise. 'Stand down. I will handle this.'

His rebels calmed, fanning out around me in a semi-circle of warning.

The infirmary was filled with the silence of unconscious bodies and the chaos of panicked gleamers.

'Maximus, please,' Elder Cyder said, feigning a soft tone, the one he had already tricked me with. 'I will explain everything. Perspective is important, and until you understand why I am doing this, you will think me cruel.'

His serpentine presence slipped over my mind. Cyder had the power to disable me, but he needed to touch me for that. Let him have my thoughts, let him see exactly the dark things that filled my mind.

'Is this what you showed Leska?' I asked, my voice reining the room. 'She discovered her father is behind the plague and, what a shock, she didn't stand by it.'

He bowed his head, eyes closing briefly. It was enough of a confirmation. 'It was, in part.'

Bile and spit gathered in my cheeks as the knowledge of what this meant filled my mind.

'My mother...' Ire crashed within me; a storm so great I could barely breathe through it.

Cyder had done it, he had infected her. 'You said that Leia visited my mother the morning of the Ball, but that was a lie, wasn't it?'

I waited for him to tell me I was wrong, but Elder Cyder didn't refute my accusation. Suddenly, my thoughts were filled with the images of a cottage ruined by wytchfire and I saw the destruction from a new vantage point. 'Deborah and I have... history. I visited her to see if she was prepared to continue helping the Hawthorns' cause. When she refused me... I, well, I gave her a reason that meant she had to help.'

The wytchfire was my mother's reaction to Elder Cyder. It was not her losing control, it was her protecting herself from the man who did this to her.

'See my thoughts, Cyder,' I growled, unspent anger in every

vein. 'Witness what will become of you the moment I get the chance.'

'I will not stand here and lie to you anymore, Max. Honesty is important, and we are both going to need to practise honesty if we are going to succeed in what is to come. Yes, I did this, and I deserve this reaction.'

'Why did she not—'

'Tell you?' His head bent at an angle. 'Because I ensured she would not be able to. Same with Queen Romar not remembering who allowed her into Wycombe. It was me. But, knowing Leia would see into their minds to get the answers, I had to scramble reality for them enough to keep eyes from looking my way. I have been doing it for years.'

Cyder was proud of himself, the emotion glowed from his eyes.

'If you think I will help you,' I screamed, temper so high the air around me seemed to boil, 'you are sorely mistaken.'

As sharp as the arrow that tore Glamora from the skies, Elder Cyder shot into my mind and withdrew something from it.

'Compliance is the key,' he said with a smile. 'Is that what you wish for me to tell you?'

All that bile and spit, all the disgust, fear, hate, refusal, gathered in my cheeks. I spat at his feet, the glob splashing against the bottom of his cloak. Elder Cyder looked down, disgust breaking across his face. When he looked back to me, it wasn't with the kind, understanding eyes I had become used to. It was with the punishing glare of a displeased father.

'Put the tray down. Now.'

My fingers tightened, the novice's wails rising behind me. 'No.'

'You have a choice now. Come with me peacefully and we will figure this all out. Or, I will be forced to start using the things you care about against you. From what I have gleaned, that seems to work in regards to stifling your behaviour.'

I laughed. It was a deranged reaction to his threat, but perhaps that was because I was numb to it. 'And did you also *glean* what happened to those who controlled me?'

'I did.'

My smile was as honest and winning as Elder Cyder's. 'Then you will know what I will do if you threaten me or mine.'

All emotion drained from his face. Colour seeped away like dusk to night. 'You are right, Maximus. Maybe I should offer you a third choice. If you come with me peacefully, I will allow you to see Simion. That is what you desire, is it not? That is why you took the Nytraith with little encouragement?'

'You're lying,' I said, refusing to acknowledge the swell in my chest. 'Scrambling for something to use against me, pathetic.'

Cyder gestured to the body beside me. The one lying face down. The one whose shoulder blade bubbled and cracked where the feather had been inserted.

The tray slipped from my fingers, clattering to the floor. Everything became a blur, sounds muffling as my eyes settled on the face of the man at my side. A face I had not noticed until now.

Simion. It was him.

Hard hands grasped me. This time I didn't fight. I had nothing left. All I could do was keep my eyes pinned to Simion's relaxed face squashed into the pillow, his closed eyes and slightly parted mouth.

'Simion, like your mother, will be fine. I will give them power, power to the evil we are to face. This is not a bad thing, Maximus. It is a necessary thing.'

I didn't stop looking at Simion as I was dragged away. Only when I was taken through the next set of doors did I let out my breath. But it was not a breath, but a gathered collection of broken-hearted sobs that tore out of me.

Elder Cyder knelt before me, bending down so he could meet my gaze and hold it. 'You've seen what I can do for those who are possessed. I can offer them power and control. Deborah, Simion, they will all come through it. I promise you—'

I promise. Two words that shouldn't have meant anything in that moment, except Elder Cyder's honesty bled into my mind, my skin, my bones and muscles, until I was riddled with it.

'—We need them. And more. I will create an endless army of powerful beings; it is our only chance of survival. Do you understand? Together we will take over the city. You will heal the Heart Oak and strengthen our bonds to the dryads. I will offer a new power between humans and the phoenix. Controlled for our benefit...'

Cyder's mouth was moving, his eyes wide and unblinking. This time I didn't hear him. It was all crazed words. Even if he believed them, I couldn't. All I could think about was what I had witnessed. A room full of people ready to be infected with a burning plague.

'How?' I said, cutting him off. 'Tell me how you've done it.'

Deep down I knew the answer. But I longed to hear it from him.

Elder Cyder straightened, knees cracking as he stood. Until now I had not focused on the new room I had been brought into. My mind was entirely lost to Simion, to the burning plague; nothing else mattered.

'I think what I must show you will, once again, take us back to a mutual understanding. You may think I am a monster now, but I am merely a man wishing to save the world. You'll understand, I know you will, because you are clever. You are your mother's son, whether she was only the carrier or not.' He leaned in until his lips were so close to my ear his breath tickled over skin. 'I have been into your mind, Maximus. I know you have seen her, you have seen our fate. In dreams, in visions. You know who is coming.'

Mother is coming. The chant echoed in my mind, magnified by Cyder's power. *Mother is coming.*

'Mother... is coming.'

'That is right,' Cyder whispered, turning my body so I faced what was before me—a detail of the room I had yet to notice. 'She is coming, and we must be ready to face her... no matter the cost.'

A pained groan lifted over Elder Cyder's words. I thought it was born from me, an audible reflection of how I felt inside. That was until he moved out of the way, allowing my eyes to settle on the view behind him.

If I thought my chest had cracked before, now it shattered entirely. And this time, when I fell to my knees, no one was there to catch me. I barely registered the pain as I looked towards the large cage hanging above the floor. It was made from thick bands of wood and stone. Large enough to hold Inyris, wide enough for my dragon to extend her golden wings to full width.

But it wasn't Inyris who occupied the cage.

A naked body, cowering with knees drawn up to a thin chest. Golden-blonde hair dirtied and limp, hanging over obsidian eyes. Skeletal, bloodied stalks, which were once full wings, now bald and thinned. Plucked of feathers and left as nothing but bloodied bones.

Even if my mind refused to believe what I saw, it was the smell that filled the room, coating the sterile scent of lemon. It was open oceans, sea-salt and sun-bleached wood. It was the scent of adventure, the scent of danger.

It was the scent of my husband.

CHAPTER 38

Camron Calzmir hunched over himself in a cage, broken and bloodied. My breath caught in my throat as he turned his head, limp blonde hair covering one of his eyes entirely. I felt his gaze on me, his attention scored over my skin, flaying me to the core.

His dark eyes drank me in the minimal light of the room. The last time I had seen them, they had swirled with the fire of the creature inside of him; now they were empty.

He was empty.

If I thought seeing him would conjure fear, hate, fury—I was wrong. The silver marks on my arms seemed to shiver, as though they were living things. His skin was thin and pale, stretched over the bone. It distorted the fast-mark on his arm, an arm that once was full and strong, an arm that ended in a stump of ruined, scarred flesh.

This was not the man who ruined my life. This was not the man who used me. This was merely a fragment of what I had come to know. A broken body encompassing a broken soul.

He looked at me through the bars of his cage as though he didn't recognise me. He leaned closer, his only hand grasping a bar for leverage. The tips of his fingers were bloodied and torn, not a single nail left in place. Then his mouth opened, and a gargling sound rumbled out. I didn't recognise what he said at first. Not until he repeated it, louder and more desperate.

'Maximus, please.' My name fell from his paled lips, ruining me.

Conflicted, my mind refused to accept what I saw whilst another part of me told me exactly what it was. This was no illusion. It was real. He was real.

'Camron will not harm you,' Elder Cyder said, believing that it was fear that caused my reaction.

'I… killed him.'

'Weakened, yes. Killed, clearly not.' Elder Cyder's voice sang from beside me, but I didn't turn to look at him. I couldn't tear my eyes from Camron. 'The phoenix is an immortal creature. One cannot simply kill a phoenix, not when their death is meaningless.'

From the ashes, we rise.

'He… he isn't…' I couldn't find the right words. 'He is phoenix-possessed, how did he—'

'Camron Calzmir was far more than phoenix-possessed, Maximus. Look at him, look at his wings. Camron is the product of what happens to a body when the parasite entirely claims the host. We still know little of what this new power means. What I do know, by killing Camron you simply allowed for the phoenix to win.'

'Maximus,' Camron called out again, bars creaking beneath his hardening grip. 'Save me.'

I turned to Elder Cyder, eyes blurred with tears of pity and horror. 'What have you done to him?'

Confusion clouded the old man's face, drawing the lines across his forehead into deeper etchings. 'What was required—'

'Answer the question,' I screamed, my voice echoing over the barren room.

'I admit I am surprised you care for *it*,' he spat, barely gesturing towards Camron and his cage. 'It murdered your father, as well as many other innocents. I kept this from you because I need it alive and could not afford for you to find out and seek your revenge.'

Cyder lied because he believed I would kill Camron again. Would I? Camron had murdered my father, he had hurt me, used Beatrice. But how did looking at him then make me feel as though it was someone else I saw? My mind was not filled with images of his crimes, it was filled with the story I had read in his journal.

A man seeking freedom. A man seeking escape from his family.

Thin strips of dirtied material covered Camron's privates. Gone was the muscle I remembered, the mounds my touch had explored. Whatever was left was a shell. Besides his obvious malnourishment, his dirtied skin and wide, fearful eyes, it was the mess of feather and bone protruding from his back that sickened me. There were hardly feathers left. Downy sprigs of red and orange had grown back over red-raw flesh, but they were not the beautiful plumage I had seen before.

Because I knew, without the need for explanation, what Camron was required for.

'You're using him, to make others. To spread the plague. It was never in the South was it—'

'Yes, the plague surely spreads in the South. Queen Romar confirmed that during her... brief visit. Instead of fearing it, like Leia, I harnessed it. Power is power, neither good nor inherently bad. It is what we do with it that determines which. I can offer the phoenix-possessed the chance of control, allowing the plague to spread until they, too, become one with the phoenix. Image the power we could harness...'

Tears fell down my face, uncontrolled and violent. 'This is wrong, Cyder.'

'Is it? A dryad's power is within their physical form. We snap their limbs and call them amplifiers. A nymph's power is in their waters. Nytraith is a name given to its physical embodiment. But a phoenix, their power lingers within the feathers of their wings.

Those possessed in the South are spreading the sickness through the embedding of a feather to flesh. That is how the transmission completes. Embedded into their skin, left to grow and bond to the birds of fire until the human becomes them, in flesh and blood. Then, in time, they will become the very thing which possess them. A god. Imagine, that power, an army of gods at our control.'

A sob choked me as Simion's bare back came to mind. Then I blinked and saw my mother's scarred flesh. All of this was caused from a feather inserted into their skin. My stomach cramped, squeezing tight as a retch broke out of me.

My adrenaline had finally left me, not a single scrap was left. All the pain and aches my body endured during my fight came barrelling into me.

'Help me understand,' I said, pleading. If I hoped Elder Cyder would believe me, his straight expression told me he didn't.

'I commend the attempt,' he replied, almost disappointed, 'but it will take more effort than that.'

I snarled, teeth snapping. 'You're deranged.'

'Maybe. But you would be too if you knew what I know. For someone who has seen the impending doom to our world, you surely do not see the severity of it? Maximus, *Mother is coming.*' The smile he gave me was brilliant and horrifying. 'We must be prepared.'

My blood spiked, causing my head to rush and the room to sway. 'Camron, will you do me the honours and tell Maximus here everything you have told me?' Elder Cyder didn't take his eyes off me as he asked Camron the question. 'It will help him understand that those dreams he has, the visions the Heart Oak has shown him, is more than a fabricated warning. It is *real.*'

I almost expected there not to be a reply, until a broken voice rasped from the cage. 'I will.'

'Good,' Elder Cyder exhaled with a smile. 'Perhaps then you will understand my motives, Maximus. And I am sure you have a lot of questions, so I am going to leave you to reacquaint yourself with your husband.'

Panic rose in me, breaking over in a tidal wave. I reached out, grasping the loose sleeve of Cyder's robe. 'Don't leave me... with him.'

'But I must.'

'No,' I said, body trembling. 'Please...'

Elder Cyder lowered himself before me, taking my hands with a fatherly tenderness. I hated to beg him. 'Oh Maximus, he will not harm you. Although the same cannot be said for him, can it?'

I shook my head, heart thundering in my chest. 'Pardon?'

Cyder leaned in, holding the back of my head with his hand, keeping me close to him. 'Last night, the entire island heard Camron's screams. You were so willing to break this bond that you took little encouragement to drink the Nytraith. Whilst you reaped the benefits of the draught, your husband suffered *greatly* for you.'

My memories flooded to the surface, replaying the noise I had heard. The noise Simion had blamed on the winds.

But it was never wind, it was... it was...

I sagged forward, knees hitting the floor, hands pressed against the stone, chest heaving with breath as though my lungs couldn't hold it.

It was Camron. I had heard Camron, suffering the pain from me going against our bond.

'You're lying,' I shouted, mind racing, seeking an excuse to make me feel less like a monster. 'How would Camron have been punished by the fast-mark, if he has Nytraith rendering him powerless? It would smother the bond in him as it did me.'

The laugh was slow. It bubbled out of the old man's chest, one barking yip at a time, until he doubled over with hacking chuckles. I watched, dumbfounded, as Elder Cyder completely lost himself to hysteria.

'Camron Calzmir hasn't a lick of Nytraith in his system,' he said finally, cheeks flushed crimson, a single joyful tear rolling down his cheek. He cleared it away with the back of his hand, still not entirely released from the laughter's grip. 'He is here by choice, Maximus.'

I lifted my eyes back to Camron, finding that he had not yet looked away from me.

'This looks like no choice a person would make in their right mind.'

'Camron wishes to repent his sins. He rejects his past and wishes to aid with securing our future. He is doing this... for Aldian. He is doing this for *you*.'

CHAPTER 39

I was left in the room with the monster who had haunted me. For weeks, Camron had filled my thoughts, burning my mind to cinders, just as he had my father's flesh. Even before I learned he was still alive, Camron held fear over my neck like a blade. I was powerless to face him—my magic smothered by Nytraith, my amplifier taken as a precaution—before Elder Cyder departed.

There was no place to hide. I stood, exposed, beneath his obsidian gaze.

'I deserve your hate,' Camron said, breaking the silence with his shattered voice. 'I deserve the pain you granted me.'

There was no stopping the tears from spoiling my illusion of strength. Even with him locked in a cage, stripped back to dirtied flesh and draped wings, I still couldn't move.

'Who am I talking to?' I asked, nails cutting crescent moons in my palm.

'Me,' Camron pleaded, knuckles paling as he gripped the bar tighter. My eyes continued to fall back to the stump of his hand, the one Father took off with Simion's sword.

A hand for a life.

'The Camron who tricked and used me, or the Camron

before? Or is this the one who ran from home, from his life, in search for something better?'

Silence stretched out between us. I was vaguely aware of noise beyond the door, muffled and quiet. Simion was out there, one of Camron's feathers infecting his body. I wouldn't allow this disease to take anyone else from me. That thought alone had me taking a step towards the cage.

All the while Camron was silent.

'Answer me,' I demanded, slamming my palm into the metal bar.

'I am sorry I did not stay dead, Maximus. Believe me, I wish I had.'

His words struck a chord within me. 'Then why didn't you?'

'Because I was not worthy of the peace death afforded.' Camron bowed his head, finally releasing me from his stare. 'Maximus, I am sorry—'

'Don't you dare,' I shouted desperately. 'Don't you dare use those words against me. You are undeserving.'

When he looked back to me, tears cut paths through the dirt caked to his face. They slipped over his mouth, distorting the freckles that lined his lips, before disappearing on his tongue. 'I was not in control. I am now.'

I didn't want to believe him, but I did. When Camron had murdered my father, his eyes had twisted with molten flame, his voice had overlapped with another as the creature inside of him took over. But I couldn't wrap my hands around the neck of the phoenix for what it took from me.

It was easier to blame something corporeal, something with a face.

'I won't accept your apology, Camron.' It was my turn to capture him with my eyes. I refused to let him look away. And he showed no sign that there was anything else in this room, this world, that he would rather look at than me. 'It won't bring back what you took from me. What you did—what you are still doing.'

The howl that broke out of him was poisoned with emotion.

Like it had festered in his broken soul, twisting in rot until Camron finally let it free.

Camron began tearing at the newly sprouted feathers. His bloodied fingers smudged over the skeletal wings. He tore clumps away at a time, throwing the feathers out of the cage where they floated to the ground.

'Stop it,' I snapped, eyes burning with tears.

He didn't hear me. It was as though I felt the feathers tear as I heard them. Blood blossomed over raw flesh, but still Camron didn't stop. He kept ripping them free, mumbling his apology over and over.

'I am sorry, I am sorry.'

'Camron, stop!' I ran to him, reaching through the iron bars until my fingers grasped his wrist. It was thin and frail, like handling glass.

He lacked the strength to resist me. Skin smudged with gore, it leaked down his arm and flowed over my grasp. The silver of our handfasting mark practically glowed in comparison to the crimson.

'This isn't how you seek my forgiveness,' I hissed, refusing to let go.

There was no pulling back as Camron reached from the cage and grasped me. His blood-wet hands were gentle as they graced my face. 'How. Tell me how.'

The scent of copper overwhelmed me, as did his warmth and the underlying kiss of sea-salt that never left him.

'You have your power,' I said, shivering beneath his touch. 'Use it. Help me.'

Just when I relied on hope, it reminded me what a wasted emotion it was.

'No, no,' Camron repeated, eyes pinned to me, but clearly his mind was elsewhere. When he withdrew his hands, it took great effort not to scratch the feeling of him from my skin. Camron fisted his hands and slammed them into his temple, over and over.

I was wrong. This was not the man who used me, nor the man I learned about with his journal. This was a shattered soul that had been broken, put together, broken, put together—so many times the pieces no longer matched.

'I have to do this,' he said, eyes wide and unblinking, lips taut until I could no longer discern their colour from the pale sheen of his skin. 'Mother is coming. Mother is coming. I must protect you. Mother is coming.'

Gone was his calm demeanour. He was screaming now, shouting out over and over. There was nothing I could do or say that would offer Camron comfort. His head was bruised from where he had hit himself. His screams shred his voice to a painful rasp.

'Who?' I asked. '*Who*, Camron. Tell me who!'

It all stopped as suddenly as it began. Camron was breathless, veins bulging in his forehead, the whites of his eyes red-rimmed. He scrambled to the middle of his cage, far out of reach. Knees brought up to his chest, his bloodied, wings hanging limp at his side, he rocked himself in a puddle of torn feathers.

'Answer me,' I screamed, slamming my palms onto the bars. Who was the frantic one now?

'*Lilyth.*'

The world ceased to exist as the strange name filled my mind.

'Her name filled my fucking head the moment the phoenix infected my body. A being unlike anything we could comprehend. Mother of all, mother of monsters. Mother is coming. Mother is coming.' When Camron spoke, it wasn't to me but to the unseen phantom standing over my shoulder. 'Lilyth is coming.'

When he finally settled his eyes back on me, it snatched the breath from my lungs. The same fear that had settled in Elder Cyder's eyes shone back at me from Camron. He was a broken little boy, alone in a world where every shadow scared him.

'No,' I said, refusing to believe him. 'Do not allow Cyder to use you for some false theory—'

'Damnation,' Camron howled, teeth shredding his bottom lip. 'She will ruin this world just as she has hundreds before.'

I stumbled back from the cage, putting as much distance between us as possible. Only when the hard press of the door was forced against my spine did I stop. Camron continued to scream. He tore at his feathers, howling that name over and over.

Lilyth. Lilyth.

I screamed too, pleading for someone to let me out. My knuckles tore as I slammed fists into the door, begging for someone to help me. Eventually, when they heeded my pleas, Camron was still screaming. He didn't stop, not as I was snatched from the ground and carried from the room. I heard him all the way through the maze of the building, that single name echoing off every wall.

The guards forced me into a dimly lit room. I had my hands clapped over my ears, blocking out sound. My eyes had been closed up until the point they pushed me forward. Pinwheeling my arms, I fell, only to be caught in waiting hands.

'Get yourself together, Max!'

The shock of blue eyes scared me at first. It wasn't Cyder who caught me, but his daughter.

'Leska.' I replaced her name with the one ringing in my head. 'Thank the dryads, *you* are alive.'

Blood had dried on the side of her head, tacky in her black hair. Her skin was parchment white, shadows clinging beneath her eyes. Firm hands grasped my upper arms, but I didn't mind the pain. It was enough to draw me out of my mind and cement me in reality.

'Why wouldn't I be?' Leska looked to me, then around me, as though expecting someone else to be standing at my side.

My heart snapped when I realised who she expected to find.

I couldn't answer. All I could manage was to throw my arms around her and hold on. To my surprise, a single arm took me in, locking me in place. 'Hysterics aren't going to save us. Get this out of your system and focus.'

'I saw you.' The words were tumbling out of me. 'Beatrice stopped me from helping—'

'Where *is* Beatrice?' Leska interrupted, narrowing her bright eyes, daring to move from where she stood against the far wall. 'Did she get out like I told her?'

I shook my head. 'She's dead...'

Everything stilled for a single moment. It was as though the world held in a breath. Then Leska spun around and slammed her fist into the wall. If she had access to her power, I was certain the stone would've imploded beneath her force.

'No. No!' Leska slammed her fist countless times into the wall, tearing skin. When there wasn't anything left, she sagged forward.

'We should never have trusted him. I should have followed my instinct.'

I stepped in behind her, placing a shaking hand on her shoulder. 'No one was to know your father is behind the burning plague.' Saying it aloud made it more real.

Leska growled, her head against the wall, shoulders rising and falling vigorously. 'He believes he is saving the world from...'

'Damnation,' I answered, repeating the very word that had been echoing in my mind since leaving Camron. 'And he is using Camron to do it. Leska, he has infected Simion.'

She knew about Camron, I could see that in her lack of reaction. 'And he will not stop until everyone North or South of Galloway Forest meet the same fate.' When she looked around, it was with an expression of calm determination. 'We need to get out of this, Max. Together. We must find a way to warn Elder Leia and the Council before he uses his army to change them all.'

'There is no training that will help us,' I said, trembling. 'We've lost.'

'No,' Leska snapped, pacing back and forth, mind lost to thought. 'He hasn't given me any more Nytraith. If I can make him believe I am on his side, he might give me back my amplifier. The second he does, I will end him.'

Deadly promise glittered in her gaze.

'But he is your father.' I couldn't stop myself from saying it.

'He lost the right to that title a long time ago. Shared blood doesn't equate to family.' Leska's attention settled on the wooden stool to her side. In seconds, she had picked it up and threw it across the room. Upon impact with the door it shattered, clattering over the floor in countless splinters and parts.

There was no escaping this. Beatrice was dead. Simion was plagued. My mother was once again being used against me. And I was alone. Powerless. It was a position I had been in before, one I felt familiar with.

Once again, I felt like I was on the ground of Galloway Forest, with Julian Gathrax straddling my waist. I had been powerless then... until I wasn't. I had searched blindly for an escape from that moment and found my power when I needed it. No—it found me. Except there was no clawing my way out of this.

My eyes settled on the broken stool. A plan formed in my mind, unfurling like a bud beneath a beam of light. They could sever my magic, take my amplifier. But what Elder Cyder couldn't dampen was my truth.

'I have an idea,' I said, so quietly I was surprised Leska heard me.

I wasn't merely a mage using an amplifier. There was dryad blood in my veins. Cyder had confirmed it. Galloway and his dryad lover, their story was written beneath my flesh. I was born from it. Just like the dryad had made the first Heart Oak, and their child made the second—could I do the same?

My power didn't come from bonds, it came from blood.

The night Julian Gathrax chased me, I had filled a mundane stick with my essence, creating Heart Oak without knowing. And there was nothing stopping me from doing it again.

'I am all ears,' Leska said, one brow peaked as I moved towards the shattered stool.

'It is a big ask, to turn you against him.' I lifted the leg of the broken stool, dusting my fingers over the smooth, polished wood.

My nails scratched over the body, familiarising myself with its shape, its form.

'Bludgeoning him to death with that isn't going to work, Max.'

'Look at me. Tell me you can fight him.'

'He signed his fate when he took mine from me,' Leska said, fury creased over her face. There was something else, though, another emotion that I recognised with clarity. Grief. 'Aaron did more for me than my own father ever did, and he sent him to his death.'

I nodded, swallowing hard as I remembered the rebel I had killed.

'My father... he had always been quick to fantasies. This damnation, it is simply one of them. He thought he could let me into his world, show me the monstrosities he was creating, and I would just accept his delusion with open arms. He is crazed. There is nothing out there that will ruin this world, nothing but him...'

Was it a delusion, though? Even now I heard the name in my mind as though it was innately familiar.

Lilyth.

'What if it isn't?' I said, lifting my gaze from the wood to Leska. 'What if there is something else—'

'Then we will need more than that stool's leg as a weapon,' she replied.

My grip on it tightened. 'You're right. But you are going to be the one to use it.'

'Has my father wormed his delusion into you, Maximus? Or did I smack you in the head one too many times?'

There was nothing humorous about this situation, but I laughed anyway. 'Elder Leia was right. I have been hiding something from her.'

'Of course, you have.' Her brow furrowed, eyes narrowing as she regarded me. 'Well, spit it out.'

Instead of saying it out loud, I opened my heart to the wood, allowing the essence inside of me to leak out of my skin. As it poured into the wood, there was no flashing lights or exhales of power. It was merely a feeling. Weightless. This wasn't magic, not to me. This was as normal as breathing. As existing.

It was me.

I extended the stool leg to Leska. 'For you.'

Her expression didn't soften until she grasped the wood. Magic hung in the air. Leska's eyes widened, the blue brightening as they spilled with the use of magic.

I may not have been able to use it, not with the Nytraith in my system. But *she* could.

'An amplifier,' Leska said in disbelief, as the magic flooded her system. 'But you're not...'

Whatever she was going to say, died in her throat.

'I'm dryad-born,' I replied, refusing to look away from her. 'I'm the product of the Queen. My mother carried me, but I was never hers. Celia Hawthorn helped my mother get me away from Wycombe because she knew I was born for the sole purpose of feeding the Heart Oak.'

I could see the questions rumbling behind Leska's expression as the reality of what I shared settled over her. But when she opened her mouth, it was not to ask what she longed to know.

'Out of all the things I imagined, this was never one of them. And you may have just given us the chance we needed,' Leska said, drunk on power, devious grin sliced across her face. 'Let's not waste it.'

CHAPTER 40

I screamed until my throat scraped and lungs burned. I didn't stop, not until the heavy beats of running sounded beyond the locked door. My spine was pressed against the floor, my breathing thunderous as I looked, empty-gazed, at the ceiling. Leska stood above me, the leg of the stool raised.

It felt as though I was counting the seconds, waiting for this single chance to get free.

A cool breeze rushed into the room as the door was thrown open. Out the corner of my eye I recognised four, maybe five of the rebels enter.

'She's attacked him—' It was clear, from the panic in their tone, this was not supposed to happen. I was important to Cyder's plans, after all, and here I was strewn across the floor amongst the remnants of a shattered chair.

As four rebels prepared to overwhelm Leska, who hissed like a wild cat, I waited for the right moment. A shadow passed over-head as one of them leaned over me. I reared up, thrusting the hard part of my skull into their nose.

'Now, Leska!'

Stone melted to liquid beneath the rebels' feet. It trapped them in place whilst Leska finished the job. Bone shattered with a *thwack*; bodies crumpled before they even registered what had happened. The tip of her new amplifier glistened with blood, like ruby jewels decorating its end.

'That was almost too easy,' I said, snapping Leska out of the trance she had just lost herself to. She stared at her blood-slicked amplifier, wonder and disbelief glittering in her azure eyes. 'This will only afford us a short window of time. We've got to move.'

'Get into their clothes,' she commanded, already pulling the shirt off one of the unconscious bodies. 'Better to be looked over, then focused on.'

'Hurry.'

We both undressed a rebel each. The guard I chose had a stature that was broader than me, but the height was an almost perfect match. If that wasn't a divine sign that their deaths were justified, I don't know what was.

Dressed as a rebel, armed to the teeth with their blades, we left the room under our disguises. The corridor beyond was quiet and unfamiliar. I surveyed each end, checking for sound or movement that would guide us in the right direction. Leska sealed the door, conjuring the wood to splinter and reform until the naked bodies left inside were barricaded in. An act like that would give us the time we needed.

'Recognise any of it?' I asked, breathless from anxiety.

She hesitated, looking both ways down the corridor before settling on one direction. 'That way.'

'Are you sure?'

'No. But there is only one way to find out.'

We moved quickly, footsteps echoing over the barren corridor. Soon enough I recognised our location. I pointed ahead to a double-doored room that smelled of citrus. The infirmary. The way my heart leaped in my throat confirmed as much.

'We get in, we get out,' Leska repeated what we had agreed. 'If I think we risk our position, we give up and run.'

I gritted my teeth until my jaw ached. It was easier to nod as though I agreed, but deep down I knew I was not prepared to leave empty-handed. Leska saw right through it, setting her face into a scowl. I turned away to ignore it but stopped when she grasped my hand.

'This is bigger than Simion,' Leska growled, reading my thoughts.

I snatched my arm back. Even if Leska wished to look away from me, she couldn't. I had her trapped in my stare. 'With him, or not at all. That was the deal. I'm not leaving Simion behind.'

'Dryads,' Leska swore, rolling her eyes. 'If only you had this determination during our training sessions.'

'Sometimes, we don't know what we are fighting for, until it is taken from us.'

If I was a gleamer, I would've heard a single name repeat in Leska's mind. *Aaron.* Her fate, her lifeline, the one taken from her.

'I've lost Beatrice,' I choked, eyes welling with tears. I bit down on my tongue, refusing to shed a single one. Focus. Now was not the time to drown in grief, even as it lurked like an assassin in my mind. 'I can't lose him too.'

'Keep behind me,' Leska said firmly. 'Head down and quiet.'

'Yes, captain,' I replied, slipping behind her shoulder as she pushed the doors wide open.

The infirmary was the same as it had when I first saw it. Abducted novices raced between beds full of bodies. There wasn't a single one empty. I suddenly realised why it smelled so heavily of citrus; it was to bury the scent of burned flesh. My eyes first fell on the doors at the far end, mind drifting to the man locked in his cage. Two rebels stood before it, eyes barely noticing as we entered. My gaze veered to the beacon of light that was Simion. Seeing him sparked something in my chest. I dared not name the emotion for fear it would let me down again.

Novices still worked on the many bodies sprawled out on the beds. It was so quiet I could hear my heartbeat in my chest. Leska led us to the nearest novice, who practically jumped out their skin when they were spoken to.

'We have come for the Hawthorn heir,' Leska said, requiring

little effort to come off commanding. The stool leg was slipped into the back of her belt, keeping it in place but in arm's reach. 'If you would be so kind as to prepare his body for transfer.'

'But... he must stay with us for monitoring until the fever breaks. Then he will be taken to the pools,' the young novice said, practically shaking in her boots. 'He isn't ready, his body will not cope with it.'

Her words made the sickness in me thrash violently.

Leska leaned in, smiling wide but showing almost every tooth on display. 'It isn't a request, nor is it up for debate.'

To my surprise, the novice showed signs of refusal. 'You keep us here, force us to do this terrible thing and now you throw demands? They are under our care until we feel they are strong enough for the transfer...'

My eyes moved back to the rebels who overheard the commotion. They shared a look before leaving their posts to uncover the cause. All the while Leska was attempting to defuse the situation with the exhausted novice.

'Change of plans,' I muttered, noticing the distrusting glares from the other novices. Then I saw the one who had infected Simion with the feather, and I knew she recognised me from the widening of her eyes, the paling of her skin.

'Don't you dare—' Leska couldn't finish before I sprang into action.

I moved into sight of the rebel guards, drawing my blade swiftly. They shot forward, grasping for their magic. Heat flared in the air, sizzling it with anticipation of an attack. As one's eyes glowed umber, I buried a blade into their stomach. I released the handle, throwing myself out the way of a ball of flame that spilled from the second rebel's fingers like molten gold.

Phoenix-possessed, both of them.

I held my breath, burying the fear until it simmered rather than overspilled. He raised his hand, marvelling at this new-found power, a power that never belonged to him. Firelight reflected off his porcelain skin, highlighting the pride in his eyes.

It was the last thing to fade as a pellet of stone shot through his skull, embedding in the wall behind him. I turned back to see Leska, new amplifier raised, magic pooling from her eyes.

Then chaos erupted.

Novices raced towards the doors, ready to flee. Leska stopped them, raising the broken stool before her as though it was a sword of great myth. 'We're here to help. We're not with them!'

No one listened. And why would they? We were dressed in rebel clothes, death left in our wake.

'Help us,' I shouted, knowing we had failed our chance to escape without the need for a fight. 'Please!'

'It's the Traitor Mage,' someone shouted back. My eyes fell on the novice who'd infected Simion. They pointed directly at me. 'They aren't with the rebels.'

'We are here to help you.' I raised my empty hands at my sides, praying they would listen. Novices lingered around me, the ones who had refused to heal my broken noses. Novices who had placed bets on how many marks Leska would leave on my body— those who had been abducted by Elder Cyder.

'You've all been forced here, against your will,' I said, looking at each and every one of them. 'Fight beside us and I promise—'

'They'll kill us!' someone wailed.

'Cyder will turn us into monsters,' another added. 'Our families will be punished.'

'No,' I said, refusing them. 'No.'

They were all so young. Children. Taken by someone they trusted. Their exhausted faces, eyes ringed with shadows, skin ashen from the overuse of power. This could've been Dayn if he was never taken to the Claim. Except he did and he died, and they all had a chance to fight and survive.

What fate would have been kinder?

'Maximus, we need to leave,' Leska warned beneath the bustle. 'Now.'

I ignored her, grasping onto this final chance. Simion was so close I could almost reach him. I wasn't prepared to turn my back on him, not now. Not ever. 'You are mages. You have magic. What is stopping you from fighting back?'

'Maximus,' Leska scolded, reaching for my shoulder. Her fingers didn't reach me before thundering footsteps and shouts sounded from outside the infirmary.

'Shit,' I spat, fumbling at loose strings. We were so close, we couldn't give up now.

'You're telling me!' Leska snapped before thrusting her power out. Perhaps the Nytraith was wearing off again, but I could sense the magic as though it lathered my tongue. Beyond the doors, more rebels were coming.

'Fight them,' I shouted, this time louder, more desperate. 'Protect those around you. Protect yourselves.'

Gleamers were passive in power, but I had known enough of their magic to know they could disarm someone mentally. If we were going to find a way off this island, it would be together.

Power was in numbers—Elder Cyder taught me that himself.

I felt the atmosphere change, just as the doors burst open and the first wave of rebels entered. Like pins, they fell as the mental wall lashed out across the room. As one, the gleamers speared their power out against their captors. Rebels writhed on the ground, like worms on the end of a hook. Some cried out as pain riddled their minds; others were in fits of laughter as gleamers forced humour into them and turned it into a blade.

Any that were missed, Leska and I took out. It was refreshing not to rely on magic. I had spent more of my life without it than with it. It had become a support, but I was quickly reminded that I had the power to rely on myself.

'We need to get everyone outside,' I said, sidestepping a fist. I drove my elbow into ribs, brought my knee up into the crotch of a rebel. They stumbled into the back of a novice who grasped their head and used their power to knock them out. In seconds, the rebel was sleeping on the piled-up floor of bodies.

'And once we get outside, what then?' Leska growled, expelling bouts of power out, swinging the stool leg around as though it was her mace. 'I don't think your dragon can carry three of us, let alone close to thirty.'

Inyris. I hadn't stopped reaching out to her, praying she would respond. Still, she was quiet. I hoped it was because of the Nytraith, and not what the rebel dragons did to her.

'Then we find another way—' The wind was knocked out of my lungs, silencing me. I fell, dragged down by the weight of something heavy. My head knocked into the floor, and I saw stars, dancing in the dark of my mind. There was pain, but it was muffled by the disorientating spin of the room.

A fist drove into the side of my face, bouncing my skull back over the floor. I barely saw the deranged snarl of the rebel atop me. But I did see the sign of fire in their eyes just before their skin erupted with it.

Even above the screaming and shouting, I heard the pop. I looked up, seeing double, as the rebel atop me tumbled to their side, fingers crawling at their face.

Then there was a new face in their place, one less vicious. I was helped up by the novice who I had, hours before, used to threaten Elder Cyder. She extended a hand to me, the room a blur of bodies behind her. The rebel who was prepared to kill me was left on their side; a syringe embedded into their eye, blue Nytraith seeping into their brain from the glass capsule at the end.

'Thank you,' I exhaled, not needing to touch my head to know it was bleeding.

'I'm sorry for what I did,' the young girl said, pale face stricken with horror. 'We don't have a choice... Elder Cyder, he threatens us, our families. We thought we were doing the right thing but... this is wrong.'

'He can't hurt you anymore,' I said, although I could see in her eyes that she didn't believe me. 'I won't allow it.'

Leska, breathless and coated in sweat, stepped in close. 'How did he get you here?'

'There was fire. It came over us at the Academy. He... Elder

Cyder had a feather, he threw it into a fire, and it opened a portal. If we didn't walk through it… if we didn't do as he asked, he was going to unleash hell on Wycombe. Many of us had already lost family, we didn't want to be the reason more lost theirs.' She choked, hand grasping at her throat. 'We came to save our people, instead we are forced to make more of the monsters who threaten us.'

I remembered the smell of burning that oozed from Leia and Cyder the night of the Ball. Had it happened then?

Something clicked in the back of my mind, a new plan forming that only encouraged my urgency.

'None of this is your fault. I understand the discomfort of acting out of fear.'

Compliance is the key.

'We are healers,' she cried, 'not makers of demons.'

'Then heal them,' I said with vigour. My eyes settled on Simion, where he lay still as stone. 'Cure him. You can heal what you know, right? Well, now we know how the burning plague is caused. Can you undo it?'

'Maybe, I…'

That was good enough for me. Head throbbing, the room locked in chaos, I found Simion. He was face down on the bed, his back a mess of scars as the burning plague spread.

I urged the gleamer towards him. 'Try, please. Reverse what you have done.'

She looked at me, then back to Simion, and nodded.

My knees almost buckled as she lowered her hands to Simion's back. Leska was suddenly by my side, talking about how the rebels had been dealt with, but more would soon come. No matter what she said, I couldn't focus on anything else but Simion.

I fixated on the scarred flesh, longing to reach out and run my hands over it, to show him I was here.

The novice's face was set into a scowl of concentration. Their brow furrowed, a bead of sweat rolled off their temple and into the neckline of their shirt. Just when I believed nothing would happen, Simion's skin rippled like the disturbed surface of a lake. I leaned in, eyes trained on the very spot the scars seemed to spread from. And there, beneath the surface, slithering like a living creature, was the feather.

'It needs to be cut out,' the novice said through gritted teeth. 'The scarred flesh is hard as stone, I can't separate it—'

I didn't need to be told twice. Drawing a blade from the belt, I brought it to Simion's shoulder. Just beneath the slithering feather, captured by the novice's magic, I cut a small incision. With my spare hand, I pinched the quill with the tips of my nails.

I drew it out.

The feather was limp, the rich colours that once shimmered were now dull and muted. But I didn't care for its beauty, or lack thereof. I cared only for Simion.

'You did it,' I said, grasping the gleamer and drawing her in close. 'Do you know what this means?'

A firm hand landed on my shoulder and squeezed. Leska leaned in. 'It is a chance for the rest, but first we need to get out of here. Alive. Then we can worry about deploying this new cure.'

'Can you wake him?' I said, seeing just how exhausted Simion had become by the sheen of sweat-drenched skin.

'Yes, but I cannot guarantee the state he will be in.'

I looked from Simion, his back still scarred from the short time he was infected by the burning plague, then to Leska. There was a part of my plan I had yet to divulge. Because I knew Leska enough to anticipate her reaction. But she had focus now, a room full of Saylam Academy novices to care for. Even if she longed to follow me, there was no chance she would. 'Barricade this room. Hold it. We leave and we are dead.'

'For how long, Max? Until we are weak enough to fall willingly?' Leska caught how my stare fell back on the room at the far end of the infirmary. She didn't need to read my mind to know what I was to do.

The fast-mark on my arm seemed to pluck, as a string played

by unseen hands. Except the only song it made was one of impending doom. Leska held my gaze, her brows furrowing at what she believed she saw in my eyes.

'We harness the same power Cyder has used against us.' My gaze fell back on the door, to the shell of the man who lingered inside. 'We use Camron.'

CHAPTER 41

The Nytraith ebbed away from my blood, as though leeches drank from me. Magic began to invade my senses, as my body warred with the poison. Nytraith wasn't like a normal draught— it was magic in its purest form. The novice couldn't entirely rid it from my system, but thin it out. Weaken it enough for my natural defences to resist it.

Pulled at my back like a cord, all I wanted to do was turn around and be with Simion when he woke. I wanted to be the first person his eyes landed on. But if I allowed myself that moment, I would've been selfish with my desires.

I couldn't allow for any weakness, not if I wanted to get us out —alive.

Camron Calzmir didn't look up when I entered the adjacent room. He was laid out on his side, plucked wings draped over his body. Bustle from the infirmary raised at my back, and I was sure I heard the deep baritone of a familiar voice.

'Camron,' I spoke the name as though it was a command.

'Have you come to finish me?' There was hope in his tone. He pushed himself up onto his elbows, the minimal weight of his body still causing him to struggle.

'No,' I replied, 'I have come to give you a chance of forgiveness.'

He rose, unfurling to a great height, bones protruding from taut skin drawn across them. His night-black eyes were wide as he regarded me like a dog I held a bone out to. 'Anything.'

'I need to get you out—'

Camron wrapped his fingers around the bars. Black flame erupted beneath his touch, spreading with vigour as the unholy light of wytchfire bathed the room. I stumbled away from the licking tongues, throwing my arm over my eyes to shield them. Stone melted beneath the heat.

It was as though the air folded it on itself, writhing in agony. Then it extinguished, as though blown by the winds of a storm. Camron stepped free.

'All this time, and you could've broken free?'

'I stayed to save you,' Camron said, 'from Lilyth.'

That name was slowly crafting more fear in me than the fire did. Camron noticed my trepidation and took a step towards me. I moved back.

'Get us out of here,' I said, unable to stop looking at the mess of his wings. 'You've opened a portal before, you can do it again.'

'He made me do it,' Camron urged, lips trembling. 'He said he would hurt you—'

Cyder said many things, most utter bollocks. I dared him to hurt me, dryads give me the excuse I need to repay the favour. 'It doesn't matter anymore. Nor will I make you do this. I'll give you the choice to help us. There are innocent lives out there. Regardless of Lilyth, they'll die if you don't help us. Camron, this is your chance. This is your redemption.'

He clutched at his chest, bloodied fingers gouging at prominent ribs. 'I'm not worthy, Maximus.'

I searched his eyes again, still waiting for flecks of gold to show, or his voice to multiply as the phoenix within him spoke.

'Yes, because this is you. The Camron who fled his home, the Camron who traded responsibility for adventure.'

Camron dropped his stare to the floor. 'You freed me, Maximus Oaken. I tore your heart apart, and you freed me. It is not fair.'

I swallowed the lump that formed in my throat. 'It is your turn. Free us, do this for me.'

He grasped me hard, fingers digging into my arms with feral desperation. 'But Lilyth will come. Mother... Mother. This is the only way I can protect you from her.'

I was losing him. His moments of clarity were ever shorter. I grasped onto it and pulled him in, like a mother would a child. Doing so disgusted me, knowing this man murdered my father. But did he? His body was not his to command, he was merely a doll pulled by the strings of a god.

A god he had now become.

'I believe you, Camron.' It was as though the world snapped into place and Camron clawed his way back from deliria to me. 'I've seen Lilyth, in my head. The Heart Oak showed me what is to come. But this isn't the answer. Not here. Not like this. Can you do it?' I asked again, clutching his hand and drawing it into mine. 'Open a portal, that is how you can save me.'

Where his eyes traced my skin, I felt them. Like an unseen finger drawn over my flesh, it prickled, hairs raising. 'I do not think I can—'

'Think of Ruhen. You would have done it for him if given the chance.'

Camron's eyes flared wide at the name. He tugged backwards as though hearing it was a physical blow. As I said it, I sensed another presence rear its muzzle once again. It was faint, but there. My dragon, stirring back into my consciousness as our bond reformed around the Nytraith.

'All of them out there, they are all like Ruhen,' I continued, watching as tears filled his dark eyes. 'All they want is to get home, and you can do it. This time, you can save him. Try, if not for me, do it for him. For the boy you promised to name islands after. To the boy you lost out at sea.'

Resolve hardened in his expression. Camron narrowed his eyes, the muscles in his jaw flexing, as he allowed that name to expose the power it had over him.

'I cannot open a *bridge* to any place. It must be to a fire that burns with my feather. But there is one fire that still lingers, a place I connected myself to.' Camron withdrew another feather from his balding wings. It was small, hardly grown, and billowed with the downy white plumage one would find on a hatchling. But amongst the white, there was no ignoring the faint red and orange.

'Where will it take us?'

'Home.' He stiffened, mouth paling as he contemplated his answer. '*Our* home.'

I was rooted to the spot, unable to move with the weight of his answer bearing down on me. Sparks jetted from his ruined fingers, catching on the feather and turning it to flame. I knew what to expect as the fire spread into a disc, spinning into a portal of red, orange and gold. Hot winds cascaded over the room, brushing the hair from my tacky forehead. I winced but refused to close my eyes.

The disc settled, as tall as Camron and as wide as the cage he had left. A vision solidified in the heart of the portal. My heart skipped a beat so violently I clutched at my chest as though it was seconds from breaking free.

I'd recognise this place anywhere—during anytime. Home, Camron had said. But that was simply one of the many names the place had.

I looked through the portal of flame, directly into a room within the Gathrax manor. Specifically, the room Camron had occupied. There was the table covered in books, there was the sofa we had entangled ourselves upon before the lies, before the betrayal. I never thought seeing the manor would make me feel anything but dread. Oh, how wrong I was.

'Home,' I repeated, remembering a time I would've liked the idea of finding my way back to Camron.

'I... I cannot hold this for long,' Camron hissed; his forehead folded in lines of concentration. '*Hurry.*'

It took everything in me not to lose myself to the view beyond the portal. I tore myself away, moving back to the infirmary, bile slithering up my throat. Bathed in the light of fire, I entered the room beyond to find every set of eyes on me.

But it was the sight stood before them all, that settled my spirit.

Simion straightened in Leska's hold, taking a shaking step towards me. His shoulders were slumped, his posture weak, his skin ashen. But there was a strength settled into his golden eyes that dispelled any idea he was weak at all.

As suddenly as the siren call to the Gathrax manor started, it severed. That was never home. He was. Simion. *He* was my home.

I gritted my teeth, fighting the new urge to fall into his arms. My eyes cast over the room, to the fearful gazes of the novices, to the still bodies of the suffering led out on the beds.

'I have a way off the island,' I said, heart beating in my throat. 'But we must go—now.'

* * *

The novice's each woke one of the phoenix-possessed victims. We had not the time to begin removing Camron's feathers from them now, but it was their first command the moment they got them to safety. Those who could walk, walked. Those who couldn't were pushed on the wheeled cots. Leska fortified the infirmary doors with layers of roots, vine and stone, preventing anyone from coming in, or going out.

Simion helped others, but his eyes never left me. Or Camron. But he didn't act, he didn't attack Camron because that was not for him to do. No matter if his gaze alone could slay him if necessary. I knew Simion shared the desire I had, but that time would also come. Just not yet. Because if I went to him, I would have to tell him about Beatrice.

I recognised my weakness.

It was easier to allow Simion these moments of focus before I tore his heart apart with three words.

Beatrice is dead.

'You must protect them,' I said to Leska for a second time, ignoring her initial refusal. 'We don't know what is waiting for you in the Gathrax estate, but it is our only chance.'

'Maximus, the way you are speaking makes me think you are not coming.'

She had the uncanny ability to see through me. 'I'm not.'

Ahead of us, the line of novices passed through Camron's portal on quickened feet. They either didn't notice him, or it was his presence that made them rush into the portal.

Inyris lingered in the far reaches of my mind. Every second that passed the bond between us strengthened. Enough that I could sense the bars of stone she was kept within. If I focused enough, I felt the brush of cold earth against scaled limbs as though I was the one kept in a cage. Not only could I not leave Inyris, but my mother was here. I wouldn't leave without her, I couldn't.

Simion hobbled over towards the portal, a phoenix-possessed victim hanging from his side. I held my breath, knowing what was to come the moment he passed through into the safety beyond.

Camron had his orders, he knew the single caveat I had asked of him. When they were all through, he would close it.

'Does he know?' I whispered, knowing Leska could see where my attention was. She also knew what I referred to.

'No.' Leska swallowed hard, skin glistening with sweat. 'There hasn't been a moment to destroy his world.'

I looked to Simion's face, the determination in his snarl as he fought towards Camron's portal. The flames reflected off his skin, highlighting his beauty. His life had been focused on bringing his family back together. Even with Beatrice back in Wycombe, she had been kept just out of reach. Just when he believed he had her, Beatrice was ripped out of his grip.

It would break him.

'He needs to know,' I said, eyes stinging again. 'Just not yet.'

Fingers gripped my hand and squeezed. When I looked back to Leska, shocked at her touch, it was to find eyes overwhelmed with concern. 'I trained you. If you don't make it out, that is a reflection on my abilities as a teacher. Don't you *dare* let me down.'

I nodded, because if I spoke, she would have heard my pending betray in the shake of my voice. Leska enveloped me in a strong hug, arms wrapping around me like vines of iron. It was sure and fast, then I was free, and she was moving away.

'Wait,' I called out, but it was swallowed by the dwindling flames of Camron's portal.

Leska didn't stop, though I know she heard me from the way her body flinched—she forged ahead. In seconds, she took the patient from Simion's grasp, replaced it with a sword from her belt and then left us. Leska was the last person to pass through the portal, leaving Simion standing before it.

He looked down to the sword, then back to me. When his eyes settled on me, a smile born from relief crested across his face. Slowly, he lifted a hand in offering. 'Are we going, or staying?'

We. The use of the word was a weapon all unto itself.

It was that moment I would've told him. I should've just said it. But I was weak and pathetic. If I told him to leave without me, he wouldn't have. That was why Leska gave him her sword, because she knew what I would do.

'You can't stay,' I said. The portal spun at his back, casting Simion in wings of fire as though he, too, had melded with the phoenix. 'It isn't safe for you.'

'Nor can I leave you behind. So make the decision. We go, or *we* stay.'

There it was again. We.

'Quickly,' Camron hissed. The sparks of the spinning disc

spluttered, casting across the stone floor and singeing it black. 'I can't—hold it for much longer.'

In the end, it didn't matter if Camron could hold the portal open long enough. Before my arms could lift to push Simion through, the room crumbled. Light shone so bright it blinded me. A wall of stone shattered as the building broke apart. I dove over Simion just as a boulder careened towards his back. Then Camron was there, covering us both with tattered wings, bathing the world in the darkness of his shield.

We hit the ground as it all fell upon us.

CHAPTER 42

There was no slow recovery from the darkness that had taken me captive. One moment I was lost to it; the next I burst through the membrane, eyes flying open to find I had lost time. Cold metal bit my skin, pinching it raw.

Elder Cyder stood in the clearing of the island, burned tents nothing but ash and ruin around him. Thick dark clouds coated the sky, giving the world an orange haze as daylight broke through.

His rebels stood in formation, lines and lines of warriors; all their gazes settled on me. Dragons soared through the sky, crying out in warning or promise, I couldn't tell which.

There was so much to take in. But none of it mattered when I heard the groan beside me.

My neck screamed in pain as I turned to look at Simion. Seeing him caused both relief and panic. He was sat on a chair, the legs sinking into the ash-ridden ground. His arms, like mine, were tied to the back of the chair with metal chains. As were his legs and his waist. Blood seeped from a cut across his browbone, falling over his open, unblinking eyes. Eyes that were pinned ahead of him.

'Dryads, Simion,' I rasped, body aching, every bone brittle with pain. 'Don't look at him... look at me.'

When Simion turned to me, my universe almost stopped. Ash streaked his skin, making the bloodshot red of his eyes stand out. Clothes torn and coated in dust, Simion looked like a survivor. It was horrifying. And from the way he looked at me, I knew he saw the same.

'It is going to be okay,' he managed, heat licking behind his words. 'I am here with you.'

I am here with you. Those five words were the water to my scorched roots, the cool breeze on a warm day. Whereas I was entirely focused on him, my mind told me to search for someone else, but the agony in my skull made it hard to discover who it was.

'If you were not so important to me, I would kill you myself for what you have done.'

I snapped my attention back to Elder Cyder, my lips drawing back over teeth as I regarded him. Gone was his fatherly expression, his kind doughy face I had blindly trusted. Here was a man who longed to pull the strings of someone else, to control them. After years beneath Gathrax rule, I should've recognised someone of his kind.

A mistake I wouldn't make again.

'Oh dear,' I spat. Pain was everywhere, in every muscle and vein. My lungs were full of smoke, my skin coated with rubble. 'Have I ruined your plans, Cyder?'

He shook his head, smiling proudly to himself. 'Delayed them, but not ruined. Look around you, Maximus. These are the faces of those who will save this world from the mother of monsters. You may have taken away my means of creation, but nothing is stopping a journey to Voltar to reclaim another phoenix. It was their gravest mistake to reveal what their power could do, just as it was your mistake to try and stop me.'

He looked down at a heap at his feet. I hadn't noticed it until he gave it attention. My mind had just told me it was the ruins of some tent, but I couldn't have been more wrong.

Suddenly, I remembered the person my mind had searched for.

Camron lay before Elder Cyder, broken. Blood pooled beneath him, oozing from the wound at his back. One wing was a mass of twisted flesh and feather; where the other should have been was now a stump of rippled skin and jagged bone. He was bent in ways a body should not be. Vomit scratched up my throat as my eyes settled on the concaved skull, pale bones protruding through skin.

I choked, unable to catch my breath.

One glance behind me and I saw why. The stone building was no more than a heap of destruction. I could barely see Camron's cage from where the stones had fallen in on it, bent bars squashed beneath the weight of the broken wall.

I blinked and recalled him using his body to shield us.

He saved us. Simion and me. And Camron paid the price with his life.

Camron Calzmir was dead. And this time, there was no coming back. There were no ashes, only mangled flesh. But it was not his physical state that proved it. I glanced down, sobs quaking in the back of my throat, to my arm. Although my skin was covered with debris, I knew the silver marks were no longer there.

'Look at me,' Simion growled from beside me, desperately calling me to him. 'Maximus, it is going to be ok. Do you hear me? I swear it to you.'

I did as he asked, but it didn't offer reprieve. Camron's death was etched into my mind like carvings to stone.

'Lilyth is coming,' Elder Cyder snapped, demanding both our attention. I could tell from Simion's pinched expression that the name meant nothing to him. 'Whether you care to admit it or not. The great parasite, the mother of gods, will return for the source of power she stored in Aldian all those centuries ago. And when she does, we will be ready.'

Cyder was wide-eyed, hardly blinking. He barely glanced down at Camron, but when he did, I saw genuine sadness pass behind them. Not because of Camron's death, but what it meant to him.

'This doesn't have to be the way—'

'It is the *only* way,' Cyder interrupted with a shout, stepping over Camron's body until his blood-soaked cloak blocked him. 'I have seen into your mind, Maximus. The Heart Oak showed you what is to come, the doom Aldian will face if we continue to be powerless—'

Spit flew past his pale lips, a deranged look intensifying as his desperation grew hotter.

'—our people must be prepared. I hoped you would see the need for my hard work. I hoped you would understand my fight and join me without the need of force, but I see you have given me no choice.'

'We always have a choice,' I said. Those words, I had heard them before. Camron, he had said the very same thing to me after I murdered King Gathrax.

Heavy scales of a fanged serpent moved in the back of my skull. It panicked me, sensing Elder Cyder's power prying where it didn't belong. But there was nothing I had to hide from him now. Even if I sensed my magic slowly return, I kept my thoughts open to him.

'Another step,' Simion hissed, pulling forward in his chair until the leather bindings screamed beneath tension. 'Not—another —step.'

'Is that all you have to say, Master Hawthorn?' Elder Cyder called out, veering his gaze and settling it on the sentinel beside me. There was something different about Simion. A danger in his silence. 'I give you power, I give you a chance, and you threaten me?'

'Promise,' Simion replied with a smile, 'no threats. As you have said before, you know me. I *always* deliver.'

Cyder stopped, pausing for a moment as he veered his gaze between the both of us. 'Both of you will understand one day soon. When the stars fall from the sky, when Lilyth returns for her children and I stop her. When I save the world.' He began to laugh—slow, interrupted barks that felt completely misplaced. 'You will see.'

'Allow this Lilyth to come for us,' Simion said, fingers working at the knot of rope behind him.

'Not us. Them.' Cyder pointed back to the dragons flying circles above us. The formation was a thick wall, like vultures intimidating prey. 'Dragons. Dryads. Nymphs. Phoenixes. Lilyth is a parasite, a world eater. What matters is her children. The gods. What I am doing is simply finishing the task the dryads began. They gave us humans power, to use us as an army. I, too, am giving us access to more magic, more of a chance.'

Simion's laugh scratched at my skin. It was powerful enough to distract Cyder, who frowned like a displeased parent. 'All this talk of monsters, and here you stand the very father of them.'

'Mage Hawthorn is going to take some more persuading, I see.' Elder Cyder narrowed his blue eyes, scrutinising Simion. 'You have your mother's spirit. If only she was here to tell you that everything I have done, everything I will do, is because of her.'

'Don't listen to him,' I snapped, willing Simion to look at me. He didn't. Simion's golden gaze wouldn't look anywhere but Elder Cyder. If his stare had the power to kill, Cyder would've been a lump of ribboned flesh by now.

'Unfortunately,' Simion snapped, 'she is not here to debunk your ravings.'

'No,' Elder Cyder said, 'Celia isn't. But I have someone who can offer the same truth.'

He stepped aside, revealing the figure of a woman I never expected to see. Eyes as green as Galloway Forest. Skin marred by freckles. Wild, curly hair set into damp curls set around an expression brimming with concern and… disappointment.

'Mother?' I breathed, scanning her for signs she was forced to stand there. I found nothing to suggest she wasn't there by her own choice. Her hands were unbound and held before her.

'I wish I could tell you Cyder is lying.' I knew what was coming before Mother said it. 'But he is telling you the truth.'

'Thank you, Deborah. Please, offer them the answers they seek.' Cyder's eyes swept between Simion and me. 'Whether they believe you is up to them.'

I pulled at my arms, sensing Inyris fluster as my emotions echoed within the dragon. The Nytraith was fading, sharpening my senses. Without my amplifier, I couldn't utilise magic, but that didn't stop me from calling for my bonded. Our connection was muffled, so I couldn't discern where she was. But Inyris was fighting against her own bindings. Across the quiet, I could almost hear the dragon struggle to free herself from whatever prison Cyder had forced her into.

'It is true, everything Cyder has shared with you will come to pass.' Mother's green eyes settled on Camron. There was no hiding the wince of regret that passed over her face. 'Lilyth is real, and she will come. We must stop her, and finally we have a chance.'

I hated how viciously he smiled at her side. His round, flushed cheeks reddened to mounds of cherry, his eyes closed beneath the pressure of his grin. 'Please, Deborah, do go on. Tell them what we discovered all those years ago.'

Nobody made a sound. Everyone kept silent as they waited for my mother to speak her truth.

'The Queen had been hiding something from us. Simion, it was your mother who discovered it. Aldian has been built on mistruths, stories we are told as myth, they were as real as you and I. The dryads never worked for us, we worked for them. They used us, gave us access to magic, all for a purpose.'

Simion's jaw set firm, the muscles feathering as my mother

spoke. What made matters worse, is he likely reached into her mind and sensed the truth behind them.

'We all know our story. The dryads gave us magic to protect us from the South's greed,' Simion rebuked.

'No,' Mother said through an exhale, a soft yet sad smile on her face. 'That is not true. We are an army, created to face the mother of monsters. Lilyth. If Galloway and the dryad never fell in love, never were forced into the first Heart Oak, the dryads would never have known this was a possibility. Our history has been written for us, ever since that fateful day.'

'So, you see,' Cyder said, clapping as though my mother had just finished some grand performance. 'That is why I need you. Together, Maximus, we will ensure the world is prepared. You will refuel the Heart Oak with your essence.' Simion faced him, but I dared not look at him. 'And I will see that every being, young and old, is graced with the power of a phoenix. Then, when Lilyth comes, and she will, we'll have the power to resist her.'

Mother shot forward, gripped Cyder by his upper arm and span him around to face her. 'Maximus is left out of this. You promised.'

'And you have made promises to me that you have broken with ease.' He shrugged her off with ease. 'He was born for this. It is his only purpose.'

She gazed over at me, the air around her frame shimmering with heat. 'It will kill him, Cyder. Don't. I beg you.'

'Then Maximus should not have kept his little secret for so long. What matters is the Heart Oak is restored.'

My mother glowered up at him, green eyes darkening to a maelstrom of gold. Fire. It twisted in her gaze, the air around her skin sizzling. 'Do you wish for a repeat of what happened when you came for me?'

I sensed the danger before it struck. Jolting forward, I began to shout and scream.

Hands suddenly gripped my shoulders, a cold blade pressed to

my throat. I could only move quick enough to see the rebel who
accosted me. My head filled with the vision of the cottage, razed
by wytchfire. She had never lost control to the phoenix within
her. The fire was a reaction to Elder Cyder, it was her attempt to
fight him... because she knew what he had done... what he was
going to do.

'Look at your son, Deborah. Remind yourself what is on the
line.'

Her head snapped to me, the fire in her eyes dissipating as
they settled on the blade at my throat. 'You need him.'

'You are right. I do.' The blade released, the hands disappeared
and then I heard Simion grunt from beside me. 'How do you
think Maximus will fare if I take another love from him today?
Camron is dead. Beatrice is... well.'

Simion struggled at my side, thrashing like an animal in the
hands of those who held him down. Veins bulged in his neck, the
whites of his wide eyes staining red. 'What have you done to my
sister!'

More rebels flooded to him. I leaned into the blade, not caring
for the bit in my skin.

'Take your hands off him,' I cawed, rocking violently in my
chair. 'Simion, don't fight it. Please, calm down.'

Inyris sensed my fear and reacted to it. My own teeth ached as
my dragon used hers to bite into the stone bars and tear them
free, one by one.

'Now, everyone is going to need to stop this madness. We have
spilled enough blood today, isn't that right, Maximus?' Elder
Cyder said, stepping around Mother's side. His scales shifted over
my mind a moment before his mind-speak filled it. *How do you
think Simion will look at you when he discovers you have kept his
sister's death from him?*

Tears spilled down my cheeks, slicing lines through my ash-
coated skin. *If you utter a word, I will never help you.*

Yes. Maximus Oaken, you will.

'Cyder.' There was a tenderness to the way my mother said his name. It had the desired effect, because I was forgotten as he laid all his attention on her. To my surprise, she laid a tender hand on his cheek. Elder Cyder practically leaned into it, closing his eyes as though cherishing the moment. 'You lost your way, Cyder. What happened to the soft boy I knew? The boy who vowed to protect me.'

His eyes burned with held-back tears. 'He broke when you ran from him. When you left him.'

This connection, it spoke of a history I couldn't even begin to comprehend. A history that churned my stomach into a knot of sickness at the possibility.

'I left because I knew what you would do with him,' she said, almost whispering. 'You would use him to fuel the Hawthorn cause. The Queen would've used him to fuel the Heart Oak. That is no life for *our* child.'

Elder Cyder and my mother looked at me at the same time. Both with differing expressions. Mother with regret as hot as coals, Cyder with wonder he couldn't begin to fathom.

'Release him, Cyder. Do not do this. We can find another way, together.'

I could barely focus on his silent contemplation of her request. Not as my soul twisted in on itself, my skin wishing to flay itself from my body.

'He is... mine?'

Elder Cyder voiced my own question, likely pulling it from my mind. I looked to my mother, truly looked at her, searching for a sign she was lying. Something to tell me this was all some illusion crafted to give me a chance.

'Yes,' she said, as tears welled in her eyes. 'Once the Queen's gleamers inserted her egg within me, it was your seed that gave me the greatest gift.'

The air was knocked from my lungs. No matter how I tried to grasp a full breath, my body refused it. I watched Elder Cyder's face change as he passed through a string of thoughts. From his face alone, I could tell he struggled with the revelation, as did I.

Yet it was the certainty in my mother's eyes that proved to me she was speaking the truth. That was more painful than hearing her say it. This was not some grand trick to stop him, distract him. It was the most powerful thing in the world, it was raw truth.

'This changes... everything,' Elder Cyder said, shaking himself out of his trance. 'Everything.'

My mother kept close to his side, grasping his hand and squeezing. 'Yes, yes, it does. I'm sorry I left you, I am sorry I lied. Please, prove me wrong. Do right by me, do right by our child.'

'He is mine,' Elder Cyder repeated, his gaze lost to the world for a moment.

'Yes—'

'So, he belongs to me.'

The atmosphere changed too fast to act. Elder Cyder drew a blade from his robes in a blink. He spun until my mother was held before him, the sharp edge pinned above her stomach, a hand grasped around her throat. 'You took my child, allowed another man to raise him. How dare you.'

'Simion,' Mother gasped, calling for him instead of me. 'Now.'

There was no more room for thought or hesitation. Fire hissed from somewhere out of sight. I expected to feel the burn, but it was not my skin that sizzled.

Simion Hawthorn spat at the rebel who held the blade at his neck. Instead of phlegm, it was fire that came out. He expelled a hissing serpent of red light across their face. The rebel fell back, blade dropped, hands clasped to his melting skin. When he pulled his hands back with a scream, he pulled away the top layer of his flesh with them.

Inyris. I filled my mind with the dragon's true name. It was a siren call; it was a command. The connection was stronger. By the time Simion had freed himself, burning metal in pools of liquid, Inyris was almost free from the imposing cage of stone she was kept in.

Simion was beside me, fire curling from the tips of his fingers.

Fire he had conjured. Fire that should've been impossible, because the feather had been removed from his skin. Except there it was, curling over his russet skin without burning him.

'Go,' my mother screamed, eyes boiling as she looked at Simion. 'Take him far from here. Find your—'

'Enough,' Elder Cyder screamed, pressing the blade into Mother's stomach enough for her to stop her pleading. 'No one is going *anywhere.*'

It seemed even the world was against him, because it responded to him with a roar.

Elder Cyder stiffened, silencing himself, as a far-off sound reached the island. Countless bodies shifted as one, heads turning to look out across the ocean. Everything stilled. No one dared make a sound, as though patiently waiting a command from something unseen.

My mother was the only one who spoke. Even though she whispered, her words sounded as thunderous as a shout. 'You're destined to lose everything you cherish. It was the same then and it will be the same now. It is over, Cyder.'

I reached out to my dragon, thankful she was close. But it wasn't Inyris who responded. The noise came again. A violent roar, followed by another, and another. They built on top of each other, layering into a storm of sound that split the sky.

From the clouds surrounding the island flew a speck of black scales. Smoke dissipated around the dragon as it entered the island's boundaries. I held my breath, knowing exactly who it was that came through. As impossible as it was, I knew this was not an illusion.

Glamora expelled a cry that sang with ire and hunger. Inyris answered the call through me, her talons gouging at the stone cage with more enthusiasm, more will.

Before the first archer could level the scorpion bows atop the wall, they faltered. For Glamora was not the only dragon it had to take down. There was another. Then another. A riot of dragons passed through the curtain of the nymph's power. It was a mass of scales, sparks of silver-garbed mages catching the fading light of day at their backs.

These were not rebel dragons. These belonged to Elder Leia and her Council.

Wycombe flew towards the island, levelling the playing field.

I found my mother's eyes, losing myself to the Oaken gleam, hating myself for what I saw within them. She smiled at me, a silent knowing passing between us. It was as though I left my body and watched from somewhere else, some sunken place.

There wasn't a chance to shout out. To stop her.

Wytchfire, as black as death itself, coursed down Mother's arms like liquid night. It dripped across Elder Cyder's hand, melting the skin down to bone, and bone down to dust.

He screamed, but my mother's fire screamed louder.

She leaned into the blade he held over her gut, barely reacting as it entered her. It was almost relief that softened her face as she was skewered to Elder Cyder. Two bodies, one blade, together. He didn't react with the same peace. I knew it passed through him as his eyes widened and the scaly presence of his magic receded as though severed.

She brought her lips and whispered something in his ear. I couldn't hear it, but Cyder's reaction told me it was a powerful choice of words.

The fire was never meant to kill him, she knew that. I knew that. But the sword. This was her way of levelling her chances. This was her way of protecting me. Of giving me a chance.

Elder Cyder pushed my mother away with a pained cry, forcing her body to fall forward, tearing the sword out of him. I felt the thud of her body on the ground as though it was me who fell.

'Doomed.' Elder Cyder grasped at his gut, fingers catching the blood that seeped from the wound. 'You have doomed us all.'

CHAPTER 43

I gathered Mother into my arms, cradling her to my chest. Around us the island raged in battle, but none of it mattered. The world could've chosen that moment to shatter apart, and I wouldn't have cared.

Because my world crumbled before me, into a million pieces that could never find their way back together.

Mother reached for my face, cradling my cheek with blood-slicked hands. Her touch was as warm as summer sun. When she smiled up at me, it was with tired eyes she could barely keep open. Her teeth were stained with blood—it was everywhere. She bled from her stomach, she coughed it up from internal wounds.

I had experienced death enough to know it was coming, but that still did not prepare me. Nothing would.

'Everything...' Mother spluttered, blood falling over her mouth. 'Everything that you've learned... it *is* true.'

I brushed strands of hair from her forehead, hating just how boiling her skin was. There was something distant about her eyes, how they gazed up at me, as though she looked through me.

'You're going to be okay,' I hissed, failing to convince myself, let alone her. 'Do you hear me? Someone can heal you, we can fix this. I promise, we can.'

I had been screaming for Simion, but he never answered. Not as dragons clashed in the skies, mages called upon lightning and rebels called upon fire. It was as though I was physically present, but a phantom. A ghost watching a memory, just like the one that the dryad showed me during the Claim.

Her hand dropped from my face, falling to the ground as the energy quickly seeped out of her. 'I'm so sorry, my boy.'

I'd regret the moment I looked away from her. It would haunt me forever. As I threw my eyes over the island, the life left her, the final string tethering me to my humanity snapped.

To my left, Camron's broken lifeless body was crumpled. To my right, Cyder was led out across the ground, a puddle of blood seeping beneath his back, spreading like wings of death.

'Help!' I screamed, watching the fight around me. Hope kindled in my chest as I found Simion. He threw his flame-coated fist into the face of a rebel, breaking bone before sweeping to the next. The battle waged across the island and throughout the sky. Dragons tore into one another whilst the Council's battlemages met the rebels on the muddied battlefield.

I pulled my mother closer to me, my scream building to new heights. 'Help me, please!' *Simion.* I forced out the mental cry, hoping that would command him. *She is dying.*

But my voice was drowned out by the song of war.

Camron was the only one who looked at me. His arms bent and broken, his face laid out to the side as blood leaked from his glassy eyes. Fire licked up his leg, his waist, slowly eating away at his ruined body. And yet, despite the state of him, despite the torn flesh and concaved skull, he looked peaceful.

A new presence graced my mind, a feral and ferocious one. Then gold shot across the sky, scales glinting like rusted lightning. Before the rebels could reach me, Inyris was there. Her powerful body landed atop theirs, crushing them to pulp. Blood sprayed across the ground; flesh pierced between her talons.

She was fury embodied in scale, and there was not a rebel who did not discover it.

Seeing my dragon was a relief. Inyris had heard my call and aided me. Except, when she lowered her storm-grey eyes to the body in my arms, my heart panged. An emotion shared between our bond. She threw out her barbed tail, knocking down the rebels who made another attempt to reach me, horns slicing through them like butter.

Simion roared too, more fire curling from his hands, pouring over the face of an enemy he held clamped between his fingers. He was fixated on the rebel before him, he didn't notice the silver blade raised at his back.

Protect him. Inyris acted for me, swinging her neck around, jaw parted. My dragon snatched the rebel from the ground, serrated teeth separating him at his waist. I must have screamed because Simion finally turned around, eyes settling on me.

'Save—her.' I couldn't see him through the tears. 'Please.'

His mouth parted, his mask of fury softening. Even across the battlefield, through the screams of death and the shouts of war, I heard Simion clear as a bell in my mind.

I am sorry, my love.

I dropped my attention back to my mother and hoped for her to provide me with peace. Everything slowed. The world came to an abrupt stop. Her eyes were open, but they saw nothing. Empty and glazed, they stared mindlessly up at the sky. I pressed my muddied fingers into her neck, searching for a pulse.

'No... no. No.'

I found nothing but silence.

Heartbreak was as powerful as any god or any magic they could offer. It was all consuming. It was a tidal wave that broke over me and swept me far away.

I drew my mother's limp, lifeless body to me and screamed.

My power collided with the earth. It spilled out of me in waves of magic. Essence. In my desperation to keep her with me, I did the only thing my soul could conjure. I encased her in Heart Oak. From the depths of the earth, roots settled and anchored themselves into her very core.

The force of power stole her from my arms, lifting my mother skywards as her skin hardened to bark and her limbs pulled, extending into the gargantuan branches of her eternal encasing.

It was as though I was the leaf on the tallest branch, watching the world from new heights. Roots broke from the earth, spearing through the bodies of our enemies. They were like a sea of vipers, piercing bodies, stealing from their essence and feeding the Heart Oak's growth. Stabbing through time. I blinked and I was in many places, all at once.

I sensed my mother, deep in its centre, hidden behind a shield of bark, sap and earthen armour. My scream didn't stop. I continued unleashing my power as the tree grew and grew, thrusting high, as if it wished to pierce the veil of this world and enter the next. I was everywhere.

I was the furthest branch as it sliced through clouds. I was the deepest root, coiling around the earth's centre.

Then, I was gone.

I dreamt of another mother.

She moved on a thick tail, her back pierced with the leathered wings of dragons. Black hair fell from her head, twisting like the deepest waters of the ocean. On her head she wore a crown of flames, dripping like molten gold. In her taloned hand, she held a sharp point of wood. A spectre. In the other, a shield. Around her opalescent arm was the gleam of a silver cuff bejewelled by gems.

Leashes, that is what they were.

We called her Lilyth, chanting the name over and over, bellowing from an army of shadows. Her shadows. The damned. Those we had failed... those we could not save.

The world was not luscious with earth and beauty. It was void and dark. The skies were a boiling red, clouds bubbling as though filled with blood. The earth was scorched, the air was heavy with heat, hot enough to peel the skin from my body. Barren and flat, in its centre stood this woman. A monster, a mother. Lilyth.

She sensed the world's coming demise. I felt her panic as though it was mine. I could taste the desperation on her tongue. Her weakness. Her suffering. Mother had never been this close to death, and she knew it. This world, it had resisted her more so than any other. She had won, as all parasites. But at a great cost.

I couldn't move as I watched her. As though my body was made of stone. No, not stone. Bark. I was a tree; I was a Dryad. I was her child.

Lilyth. Her name rang out across the land of destruction. It was an unspoken thing, but I knew this was her doing. When she looked over the lands, it was with pride in her serpentine eyes. Relief. Then they widened as a beast of wings and air flew towards her, jaws parted, ready to devour her whole—

The view shifted, as though I turned. Spread across the land were bodies. Torn, ruined, fragmented bodies of the bravest of us. Her children, dead. Sorrow hung in my chest, aching in my heart. And there was guilt—a guilt born from feeling as though we were the cause.

We had failed.

This was home, until it was a tomb.

Mother gathered us up. The clouds parted at her command, showing a night sky I recognised. She lifted a finger and pointed to a star, one that burned the brightest, a beacon of golden light. She cried over us, saddened at our betrayal. Never had she been so weak, using the last scraps of power we gave her to make her final move.

The dream shifted again to another landscape I knew well. It was as though I flew on Inyris's armoured back, gliding at the tallest height of the world, looking down on the smudge of earth that was Aldian. But it was not from a dragon I sat but nestled in the hand of my maker.

Lilyth spat flames upon the land, casting her favoured into pits of fire. She cried tears from her eyes, conjuring oceans, rivers and lakes. She breathed into the mountains, locking her heirs in cages of stone. And she took us, those who had conspired to finally stop her, and carefully sowed our seeds deep into the earth itself.

All with the promise she would return. Because Mother needed us. We were her children; we were her power. And we had betrayed her.

It was a feeling, a deep-rooted knowing, that she would return. She always did.

As the darkness smothered me, blocking out the world in a blanket of soil and earth, I made a promise. A vow. One that would not be broken.

When Mother came, we would be ready.

Not to join her, but to end her.

CHAPTER 44

I sat up, gasping as I tore myself out of the grip of the nightmare. It was as though I drowned in soil, choking on the earth that filled my lungs and roots that strangled around my throat.

Something strong held my shoulders, forcing me down. I reached up, ready to claw myself out of the earth's grip, when my fingers found the soft press of flesh. Then I heard a voice, willing me to calm down.

'Maximus, I have you.'

It was not root and vine that held me down, but hands. Familiar, kind hands. It was as if seeing the person before me was enough to shed the grasp of the nightmare. I could finally breathe, could blink away the darkness to find Beatrice Hawthorn, haloed in light.

She leaned over me. Brown skin glowed in the faint light, smudged with ash along her striking cheekbones. Her single braid rested over her shoulder and a single scar ran down the curve of her jaw—a scar I had not noticed before.

There was no thinking, no contemplating if she was real of not. I threw my arms around her, tugging her in close, feeling the physical press of her body on mine. She was... real.

'You're alive,' I exhaled, burying myself into her neck, inhaling the familiar scent.

'It will take more than that to kill me off, Max.'

My grip tightened. I couldn't wrap my head around how this was possible. 'But I saw you... you fell...'

'If you don't ease off me, you'll suffocate me to death,' Beatrice said, as another figure moved at her back. She encouraged me from her, drawing me back. 'Take it slowly, Maximus. Your body has been through a lot.'

A gleamer with the heart-shaped face and soft eyes was fussing, trying to make me lay back. These were Elder Leia's gleamers, dressed in the ivory-silver robes of Wycombe's city infirmary. Panic clawed up my throat, overcoming my body. I tugged at my ankles, expecting to find them bound. They weren't. Nor were my wrists, which lifted as I wrapped my fingers around Beatrice's arm and squeezed.

Wide-eyed, I couldn't shake what I had seen.

'How?' I exhaled, shaking violently, knuckles paling as I held onto Beatrice as though she was an illusion seconds from fading.

'As it turns out, the nymphs that Cyder kept beneath the island were no better than the abducted novices he stole from Saylam Academy. Cyder was able to... control them. But we are yet to understand how,' Beatrice said with a smile, although it didn't reach her eyes.

'That still doesn't explain that an arrow cut into Glamora's wing and you both fell beyond the mist...'

Beatrice flashed me a smug smile, eyes narrowing as she waited for me to work it out.

'You saw what the nymphs wished for you to see. An illusion. Cyder may have been able to control them, forcing them to stay in their pools beneath the island to do his bidding, but that didn't stop them from rebelling all on their own.'

What I had seen was real. Glamora had fallen into the ocean, brought down by the monstrous arrow that ruined her wing. It had been real. All of it...

'An illusion,' I repeated, grasping her face until her warm skin tickled beneath my palm. 'So it was all not real?'

Her smile faltered, her eyes dropping away from mine. 'No, Maximus. I'm sorry.'

I shook my head as a sharp pain speared through it. No, it wasn't pain, it was grief. There was no hiding from it anymore. As the dream subsided to cinders, the knowledge of what I had lost returned.

A scream tore out of my chest, from the deep hollow part of me.

'What's wrong with him?' Beatrice asked the question, but it was not for me.

The gleamer answered. 'It will take time for Mage Oaken to recover. His heart is a fragile thing. We can heal wounds of the body and mind, but not of the heart, Mage Hawthorn. We must allow him to come back around slowly. In the meantime, I can take away the—'

'No,' I growled, 'no more burying it. I... I can face it.'

The gleamer stepped back, nodding with eyes as wide as plates. I knew he offered to take away my grief just as Simion had done before. But this time—this time I would face it head on.

Beatrice took my hand and squeezed. 'Listen. Glamora got me out. We flew straight to my aunt and told her everything. Max, we came back as quickly as we could... I'm so sorry we didn't get here in time to...'

I didn't need to ask her what she apologised for.

'She's dead,' I whispered, breathless as the realisation sank in. 'My mother... she is gone.'

I already knew the answer—but hearing it from another was what I thirsted for.

Beatrice simply looked at me with her wide golden eyes, drinking me in as her brows furrowed. She screwed her mouth up, unable to find the words. 'Yes, Max. Deborah sacrificed herself to kill Cyder. It's over.'

Ire coursed through me. So sudden I almost didn't notice the high-pitched scream the gleamer released. When I looked to them, it was to find Inyris's golden snout poking through the tent's flap—forked tongue crackling with ice, searching for the cause of my anger.

Inyris fed off my emotion. Our bond was bright and clear—no longer smothered by the Nytraith.

'Calm down, Max, or more mistakes will be made,' Beatrice warned, one hand raised to me and the other towards Inyris.

It was close to impossible to reign in my anger. No matter how I tried, it was out of my control. Twisting into a cyclone until I could speak only a single word.

'Simion.' The name alone had the power to calm me. 'I need Simion.'

As sudden as my anger arrived, it dissipated, leaving only disappointment in its wake. Not disappointment for Cyder's death, but because I was not the cause of it.

It was all coming back to me slowly, in fragmented and out-of-order memories. I saw Camron, flames spewing from his back. Then I saw him on the ground, wing smashed, fallen stone, the silver fast-marks fading...

There was no need to roll up the sleeve of my shirt to see my unspoiled skin. But I did it anyway. It was the distraction I required for Inyris to settle herself, returning back to the curled mound of scale and muscle that waited outside the tent's entrance.

I turned my arm around, searching for a sign that it had ever been inked by a bond before. There was nothing but the memory to prove it was ever real.

A resounding hollow ache filled my chest.

Only in death shall you part.

The bond between Camron and me had not been smothered by Nytraith. It was broken. Because he was dead.

I was free.

Then why did I feel so pained at the thought?

I swallowed down my reaction, not wishing to show her.

Although, from the look that passed over her eyes, I knew I couldn't hide it. Beatrice would always be able to see through me.

'When you are feeling up to it,' Beatrice squeezed my hand with encouragement, 'we can deal with everything that has happened. Until then, you must be kind to yourself.'

'Bea,' I said, distracting her. 'I asked for Simion, and you ignored me.'

This time she didn't look away. 'Simion is not here. He was taken with the other phoenix-possessed. My aunt thought it best they were cared for in the city.'

I kicked my legs over the side of the bed, urgency boiling through me. Fuck all the agony in my body; hearing Simion was far over the ocean panicked me. 'But they removed the feather. He is *not* possessed.'

'Yet he can still conjure flame with a thought. Elder Cyder was leading on those who were plagued. Only he had the knowledge as to what happens to those who were infected with Camron's feathers.'

In the dark of my mind, I saw Simion with hands curling with fire.

'Will she...'

'My aunt will not harm anyone. Things have changed. Simion is proof of that. Proof those who had been plagued can be... freed of the possession.'

'But he isn't free, is he?'

'His mind is, but his body may not be. It is going to take time for us to understand everything. But first you must focus on *you*.'

How could I possibly do that, knowing what I had seen?

What I had witnessed.

What I had learned.

'Leska.' Saying her name was a challenge. It was like forcing the word out through a stone-filled throat. Beatrice's face seemed to open at the sound of Leska's name. Her eyes brightened; her cheeks flushed with warmth.

'You saved her. Once everything is prepared, we will send a

convoy to the South to retrieve Leska and those she has with her. If my aunt allows it, I will go since I am so familiar with the Gathrax manor. Until then we must first focus on this, what has happened here.'

I shook my head, eyes filling with tears. 'It was Camron. He saved them, not me.'

'He did what was needed of him. It's over now, Max. All of it.'

She spoke of Elder Cyder. She spoke of Camron and our broken bond. And Beatrice believed every word. There was peace in the way she said it, how her features relaxed and the tension in her shoulders faded. I didn't have it in me to ruin it for her. But in time, I would. Not because I wanted to, but because I had to.

There was a new burden on my shoulders, one given to me by the Heart Oak.

'I must speak to her,' I said, unable to finish the rest of what I wished to say. *She is my sister.*

'I know,' Beatrice said softly, as though she read my mind. Part of me longed to hear her tell me I was wrong, and it was my mother's attempt to stop Cyder from using me. Deep down, I couldn't deny it. Out of everything that happened, it made the most sense.

I buried my face in my hands, finding the darkness easier to bear. 'When you go for Leska, I am coming.'

'That will not be for me to decide,' Beatrice said. 'My aunt—'

'Is not in control of what I do. No one is.'

Beatrice narrowed her eyes at me, pride glittering in them. 'Then allow the gleamer to finish healing you up. We're going to need you at full strength with what we must face next.'

I swallowed hard, feeling my mind sink back into the haunting vision of Lilyth.

'You have no idea.'

CHAPTER 45

Dawn painted the sky in blush tones of pink and orange. It swaddled around my Heart Oak, kissing the rich brown bark, flickering through the full crown of foliage that cast a shadow over the island.

I sat on one of the roots, legs crossed beneath me, fingers brushing over its rough skin as my essence continued to feed it. I laid my hand upon the new Heart Oak, fingers caressing the armour encasing my mother. How could I grieve her when she was still here? The Heart Oak was a living, breathing thing with memories, an awareness and, more importantly, a heartbeat. It fluttered beneath my fingertips, offering me some sense of relief.

Inyris hadn't left my side since I had woken in the gleamers' tent. She had curled herself around my body, offering me her presence as comfort. I had no doubt she saw into my dreams—even if they were not dreams at all. Now she was perched in the far reaches of the Heart Oak's branches, grey eyes fixed on the horizon to the materialising view of ships.

The ocean's surface was glass-like, calm. No longer did the mist cling to the outer boundaries. Since the nymphs had been freed from their imprisonment in the caves beneath the island, they were no longer leashed to Elder Cyder.

It was a control I didn't understand. But I would.

Dragons flew to and from the city, bringing supplies or taking back those who were gravely injured to Saylam Academy for healing.

Memories. They lingered in the far reaches of my mind every time I laid a hand on my mother's tomb. Pretending what I had seen was simply an illusion—of an exhausted mind and broken heart—was not an option. It was real.

Lilyth was real.

It was the Heart Oak that told me of my visitor. It whispered in my ear as the approaching person brushed over one of the many roots that pierced the island.

'Leia,' I said, turning to face her.

'Mage Oaken,' she greeted me with a bow. 'It is good to see you up and about, but I would have preferred for you to stay with the healers.'

Nails tickled over my open mind, but never pried further.

'There is no need for them to waste their magic on me,' I replied, peeling my fingers from the Heart Oak, severing the drawing sap as it drank from my essence. 'Not with all the work they have on their hands.'

Inyris raised her neck, teeth bared as a slow hiss erupted from her chest. I lifted a hand and she stopped, lowering herself back to the branch. I finally turned my back on the great tree and levelled my stare with my visitor.

Elder Leia stood amongst a group of her battlemages. Silver armour wrapped around her frame, emphasising just how powerful her bloodline was. Like Beatrice, Leia was built for greatness. Her ivory hair had been gathered into a single braid. A blade hung at her hip, her amplifier gripped tight in her hand, her eyes fixated on the Heart Oak.

'Are they for my benefit, or yours?' I asked, cocking my head in her guards' direction.

Elder Leia looked to the guards fanned at her back, each with a hand not straying far from their amplifiers. 'Mine.'

Inyris emitted a low gurgle that was more akin to a laugh.

'I don't wish you any harm, Leia.'

'Nor I you.' Her smile was short-lived. It seemed Leia couldn't spend long looking at anything but the Heart Oak. Awe glittered in her eyes, as did the reflection of the Heart Oak's glow. A glow only I could see. 'Of all the secrets I thought you were keeping from me, this was certainly not what I expected.'

You have no idea. I couldn't help but feel a spike of discomfort in my gut at the final piece of knowledge I had yet to share.

'I am sorry for your loss, Maximus.' Leia lifted her fingers and placed them over her heart.

'But I haven't lost anything,' I said. 'My mother is still here. She will be forever.'

Leia lowered her eyes, bowing her head. 'Of course.'

'She is finally home,' I added, looking back out across the oceans. 'A place she can rest, a place she can look out across the ocean and feel at peace. And I will not leave her, Leia. You understand, don't you?'

'I am not here to arrest you, Max.' Leia plucked the thought from my head and answered it.

'Even though I led the rebels into breaking out of Saylam Academy?'

'That penance will be paid in assisting with rebuilding of the Academy,' she said, voice firm. 'Just as you will help rebuild a united Wycombe.'

She knew. Of course, she did. The Heart Oak I had conjured around my mother's corpse was proof of the blood in my veins. I stiffened, unable to stop myself from speaking out. 'A united Aldian, Leia.'

We wouldn't survive what is to come without it.

'Lilyth,' Leia said the name as though it soured in her mouth. 'I hadn't heard that name since my sister was… cast out of Wycombe. I did not believe her then, but I get the impression that was a mistake.'

'A grave mistake,' I said.

Leia swallowed hard. 'I feared as much.'

There is something I must show you. I forced my voice into my mind, knowing Leia could sink her nails in and hear me. And she did. Her eyes widened, mouth tightening into a taut line.

'Then do so,' Elder Leia replied aloud.

Alone.

I watched as my emotion slammed into her. Leia didn't refuse me again. She turned to her guards and dismissed them. There was no hesitation when they left us, filtering back towards the makeshift tents that had been erected over the sodden, charred ground.

Only when we were alone, with the Heart Oak and Inyris as our witnesses, did I dare speak.

'Something troubles you,' she said, stepping towards me cautiously. 'I sense it.'

The vision prowled my mind. Since waking, it hadn't left my thoughts, replaying over and over. It was a burden I didn't care to harbour—I hadn't the strength to deal with this alone. It was the same dream that the Queen's Heart Oak had shown me all those weeks ago, except mine was clearer—real. It was not a vision, but a memory. A point in time.

'Elder Cyder didn't lie,' I said. 'Nor did Celia. Something *is* coming.'

Leia shook her head, refusing to look at me. 'I remember, many years ago, when Cyder used to follow Deborah and my sister around like a puppy. He idolised them. Treated them like queens. I never understood it because they were all so different. But something bonded them together. This idea that there is something else out there, something powerful enough to threaten everything we know. Stories, Maximus. That is all it is—'

'No,' I said, filling my mind with the vision the Heart Oak had showed me. 'It is real. Lilyth is real.'

'You sound like my sister.' A frown creased over her face, eyes lingering back towards the gleamers' tent I had left. 'Maximus, you have been through a lot. I think it is best you are seen by the gleamers until we can get you back to Wycombe. You will find it easier, in time, to deal with what has happened.'

'It would be easier to lie to you, Leia. But I won't. I can't, in good faith, hide this from you.'

She extended a hand for me. 'Come, I really think you need to get some rest.'

I snatched her hand before she could withdraw. With my spare, I laid it down upon the Heart Oak's bark. In exchange for my essence, it offered me the same story it had showed me. As it filled my mind, I shared it with her.

I stood, hidden from view, as we watched it happen. The ground was cool beneath our feet, the breeze dusting our skin, the sun blistering our scalps. It was real, all of it. Every detail, every feeling and sense and colour and image. Leia saw it all.

The Queen had been the keeper of this secret. She had allowed the dryads to use humans to create an army, one that would be ready to resist Lilyth when she finally returned for her children.

That was the lie the mages were built upon.

Leia pulled free, stumbling back, hand shaking as she pressed it over her mouth to stifle her gasp. Although she looked at me, it was as though her mind was elsewhere. Like me, Leia could not deny what I had just shown her. It was more than a vision or memory kept by the earth.

Aldian, both the North and the South, had been brought up on the tales of the four elemental gods. But what that tale didn't account for was who put them here. Lilyth did. Whatever happened to the world the vision had first showed had led Lilyth to place her children here, in Aldian.

The Heart Oak showed me. And I had felt it. The soil in my lungs, the roots binding me in the pits of the earth. That had been the dryad, forced beneath the ground just as the dragons had been locked in their cages of stone—the Avarian Crest.

'United,' I said, holding her eyes as Leia slowly withdrew from her trance. 'It is the only chance we have of stopping Lilyth. Together. North and South.'

'If...' Elder Leia took a hulking breath. 'If what has been shown is true, there is no saying when this being will come. Where has this *mother* been all this time?'

I didn't have the answers, but I would. I would claw them from the earth, draw them out of this world until I knew them all.

'We still must prepare. Whether Lilyth comes for her children tomorrow, the day after or in a hundred years from now. We must be ready. The world it showed... the one in ruin. That will be Aldian. Those bodies, the shadows... will be *our* people.'

'Our people? It sounds to me as though you are ready to face your fate, Maximus Oaken.'

Since the Queen's death, I had fought against the weight that rested on my shoulders. That wasn't a luxury I had any longer.

'I am,' I replied finally, sensing the Heart Oak swell at my answer. Mother was there, her presence in it as much as mine was. Pride thrummed at my back, offering me comfort. As though she stood there, resting a hand on my shoulder.

Elder Leia withdrew something from the pocket of her trousers. I didn't see what it was until her fingers uncurled, revealing my amplifier resting on her palm. 'I believe this is yours.'

I regarded it, gaze caressing the smooth wood of my amplifier. It called to me, power to power. When I took it, slipping it onto my finger, the world sang to life with cords of silver.

'Lilyth can wait a few extra days,' Elder Leia said, bowing her head. 'Take some time. Grief must be experienced, not put in a box and locked away for a convenient time. When you are ready, there is a seat for you at the head of our Council. Then we can discuss how we are to unite the North and South.'

She withdrew from my mind, leaving it entirely. Unlike before, it was not the gouging of nails, but a soft tickle that set the hairs on my arms to standing. If she had stayed, she would have seen the vision again. Not all of it, but a single part I couldn't quite ignore.

The four elemental gods, each held in the hands of Lilyth.

They were power, they were her greatest asset. So great she travelled through the stars and found a world to hide them on.

Uniting the North and South of Aldian was the beginning.

'It will take more than a combined Aldian,' I answered, curling my fingers into a fist. 'Like the dryads and dragons have joined forces, we will need more. We will need the nymphs, the phoenixes. Only then will we have a chance. We fight fire with fire, water with water. That is the challenge we have to face.'

The world seemed to still. It was as though the very elements listened in, weighing up if they were to agree with me or not.

'Then I know someone who will be able to help us,' Elder Leia said, gaze flittering across the oceans as though in search for someone. 'But first, we must find her.'

'Who?' I asked, the single word loud across the island.

'My sister.'

Celia Hawthorn. The thought of her alone sparked something deep in my chest. I recognised it for what it was. Hope. Not for me, but for Beatrice and Simion. A chance I would never get again, but they... they could see her.

'Where is she?' I asked.

A haunting shadow passed behind Leia's eyes. It hung heavy as a storm cloud riddled with danger. She stepped in, as though what she had to say was for me, and me alone.

'My sister was not simply exiled. What happened to her was far more... permanent. All I know is the Queen took my sister to see the dryads. Only one of them returned... I do not know where she was sent, but, with you, we can find out.'

'Do you think she was... killed?'

Leia shook her head. 'No, Max. I think my sister is... *lost*.'

CHAPTER 46

The Mad Queen tavern bustled with life. It was the sound of survival, of victory. There wasn't a table empty, a space free of flesh and song.

I pushed open the door, my senses flooded with the warmth of bodies, the tang of ale that had stewed in barrels for far longer than it should have. The bell over the door chimed, but no one paid mind to me as I entered.

A small band played music in the corner, all the tables and chairs pushed back to allow for the swell of the crowd to dance. Drinks spilled from tankards, splashing over the sticky floor, turning the worn wood to a bog that clung to the bottom of shoes.

This was joy. It sang to my blood and coddled my spirit.

Nicho was behind the bar, attempting to settle all the patrons who wanted a top up of whatever it was they drunk tonight. His wife, Iria, was no help. She was in the middle of the room, bouncing to the beat of the music whilst she swung her dirtied rag over her head. It was as though she sensed me because our eyes locked.

I didn't need to say why I was here, or who I looked for.

Over the sea of patrons, her eyes lingered towards the narrow staircase hidden in the tavern's corner. She cocked her head in that direction, Simion's name whispered on her lips. Then the music changed, and she forgot me, throwing herself back into her dance.

My heart was in my throat as I passed through the crowd. There was a draw, one that longed to pull me back into the room. It reminded me of the Dance of the Dryads. The string in my heart pranged at the memory as though the musicians reached into my chest and plucked it.

The last time I had visited the Mad Queen, I had only ventured into the bathing chamber in the cellar room. Although I had often wondered what Simion's bedroom was like, I had not yet seen it. Until now. I stood before a door at the top of the stairs. The ceiling bowed on either side of me, creating a triangular shape to the roof.

Before I could lift my knuckles to knock, the door was opened. Simion stood waiting.

'Hello.' His deep voice resonated with the low bass of drums from far beneath us. Just like the music, Simion's voice had the power to make me move. And I did, straight into him, forcing his arms around my shoulders.

I buried my face into the crook of his arm, delighting in the heat that lingered on him.

The door closed behind me. It did well to quiet the sound of the tavern beneath us, but the floor and walls seemed to vibrate.

If I was not so focused on the relief of seeing him, I may have wondered why he seemed to hesitate. Although his arms were around me, his hold was subtle. As though his arms didn't have the strength to grasp me. His hands hardly touched me, fingers hovering just over my shoulders.

It wasn't until I pulled free that I noticed it. Simion quickly stepped away, placing his hands behind his back. His gaze trailed to the floor.

'What is it?' I asked.

He shook his head, offering me a smile. But I knew him, I knew his face and the way his body moved. And I knew he lied when he spoke without locking eyes with me. 'Nothing.'

I stepped towards him. He stepped back.

'Talk to me,' I said, wanting nothing more than to touch him. For him to touch me. 'Don't you dare shut me out.'

I reached out for him again, but he jerked away.

'Please…' His voice broke.

This had been a mistake. Coming here was wrong. I had thought we had not seen each other because he was still under surveillance by the Council, but clearly, I had been wrong; I had gone to the holding and found Simion had been discharged yesterday.

He never was kept from me by anyone else but himself.

'I'm sorry,' I said, choking as tears stung in my eyes. 'Whatever I have done to cause this… There is no one else, Simion. I need you. I am—'

Simion's eyes snapped to me. This time when he spoke, he held my gaze. 'You haven't done anything. It is me.'

'Say it,' I urged, although the words came out as a muted whisper.

He looked down at his hands with hate dripping from his amber eyes.

'I don't want to hurt you,' he forced through clenched teeth.

'That would be impossible,' I said, carefully closing the space between us. I was cautious as I lifted my hands to his chest. Simion was like a deer, spooked in the deep forest. One wrong move and he would bolt. I had to take my time with him.

'I gave you the Nytraith. I allowed Cyder to poison you. Trusting him will haunt me forever.'

He didn't flinch as I lifted a finger and pressed it to his mouth.

'Simion, we all trusted him. And you weren't to know what the Nytraith would do. Believe me when I tell you that I don't want for you to punish yourself. Not now. Not when I can finally be yours.'

His gaze fell to my arm. Where his eyes brushed, the hairs prickled. I knew he searched for a sign of the fast-mark, but there wasn't a single mark left.

'It has gone,' I said, barely audible over our shared breathing. 'You cannot hurt me.'

If I expected to find relief rush over his expression, I was wrong. Simion's frown only deepened, his tired eyes hollowing with shadowed skin.

'That isn't what I'm referring to,' Simion said, exhaling a heavy breath. 'When I say I can hurt you, it isn't a metaphor. I'm changed, Max. I'm not the same as I was before—'

Smoke curled from his fingers, his skin reaching a fever until the air around him seemed to boil.

'—I have become the thing you feared.'

Camron's feather had changed him. Altered him. There was no knowing if these abilities would falter in time, the more the body was allowed to heal after the feather was removed. Or, if this was the body's way of adjusting to the trauma it was put through. Either way, I did not shy away from him.

As a spark of fire curled around Simion's fingertip, I regarded it without blinking. I refused to look away.

'I'm not scared of you,' I said, speaking to the fire, to Simion.

'There is no controlling it, not around you. I don't trust it.'

'Didn't you hear me?' I said, locking eyes with Simion. 'I'm not scared of you. This is not a curse. It is a gift.'

One that we may require, soon enough.

I snatched his hand in mine. As we touched, his fire dwindled to a thin stream of dark smoke.

'And I trust you, Simion.'

There was a slight resistance as I laid his hand upon my cheek. It was a delight in its warmth. How smooth his palm was against my skin, how his fingertips drummed over my jawline before settling.

'We have navigated worse than this,' I said. 'One step at a time. We've done it before, we can do it again.'

'Some risks aren't worth taking, Max.'

'And some are, Simion.'

The corner of his lips lifted into that familiar smile—one I would've traversed the earth to see again.

He took a breath, preparing himself to feed me another excuse when I silenced him. Not with my finger, but with my mouth.

Our lips met, gently at first. I leaned into him, allowing the pressure of his hand to flatten against the side of my face. He used it for leverage, just as I reached for the leather cord around his neck, wrapped it around my hand and anchored him to me.

There was nothing in this world with the power to ruin this moment.

My body prepared for pain, tensing as though I would be overcome at any moment. Nothing happened. No agonising stab of agony as the fast-mark punished me for going against the sacred bond.

Camron had freed me from it.

No, not now.

I deepened my kiss, parting Simion's mouth with my tongue, distracting my mind with his taste, his touch. Now was not the time to think of Camron. In this moment, there was only Simion.

Simion withdrew, breathless and lips bruised. When he looked down at me, it was as though I was the only thing in the world.

'Don't stop,' I urged, leaning my chest into him, knees weak with my desire. If it was not for his arm around my waist, I may have fallen.

'Not until I say this,' Simion added, thumb brushing my cheekbone.

His eyes trailed every inch of my face, memorising my freckles, my lines and scars. Then I remembered, there was no need for him to do that. He already had me memorised—enough that he could have an entire outfit made for my body without the need for measurements.

He saw me, just as I saw him. Completely. Entirely.

'I'm your family,' Simion said, finally breaking the silence that brewed between us. 'Beatrice. Me. You will never be alone. Not ever.'

He forgot to mention Leska, and I was almost glad for it.

Grief uncurled in my chest like a rose. Beautiful and thorned. With a single look, Simion reminded me that such an emotion didn't need to be destructive. With the sharp thorns came the beauty of the flower. If pruned, if treated with care and love, it didn't need to shred one from the inside. It could grow as a reminder to what came before.

I was never good with my words. Where I hoped for something meaningful to come out, it was always laced with sarcasm. But that was my way of coping, my way of showing love.

'Does that mean,' I said, gazing around as I chewed my lower lip, 'this is where I'll be staying? Because I admit, it beats the apartment your aunt has offered me.'

Simion huffed out a laugh. 'The key is yours, if you want it.'

I leaned into him, gazing up through lashes at his face. 'I think a tour is in order first. Before I make such a decision.'

'Of course,' he pressed a kiss to the end of my nose. 'Where would you like to start?'

It was the easiest answer to give. 'The bedroom.'

'Is that so?'

I narrowed my eyes, feeling a swell of excitement bubble in my chest. 'Lead the way.'

Simion scooped me into his arms, the suddenness of his movement snatching another laugh from me. I wrapped my arms around his neck, holding on, as he padded from the foyer of his apartment towards our destination.

The bedroom was modest in size, leaning walls and a narrow ceiling, which meant Simion had to bend his head to the side as he carried me to the bed. A single window was in the wall behind the bed, giving view to a star-filled sky. There was something entirely peaceful about the night. I wasn't certain how long it would last, but dryads knew I would make the most of what I could take.

Simion discarded me onto the large mattress, the fall softened by a mound of pillows and blankets discarded over it.

'What do you think?' Simion asked, looking down at me where I lay. I was trapped beneath his stare, pinned to the sheets like a butterfly to a cork board.

'It will do, I suppose.'

'You suppose,' Simion repeated, one brow raising into a peak. 'It sounds as though you will need some persuading.'

'I think you are right,' I said, taking my fingers to the buttons of my shirt. I popped the first away, delighting in how Simion's eyes widened in knowing. He quickly copied, standing at the end of the bed, undressing himself.

We didn't stop until there was nothing but air between us.

Simion crawled onto his bed—our bed—across the sheets, until he leaned over me. His amplifier dangled from the leather cord, tickling the skin of my chest.

My back arched off the sheets until every inch of me pressed into every inch of him.

Fingers trailed up the inside of my thigh, littering my skin in prickled flesh. Simion didn't stop until his warmth brushed over my hip, across my navel and up the centre of my torso.

'Convinced now?' he asked.

Far below, the music of the tavern reached a crescendo. It mirrored the thunderous beat in my heart.

'I am—'

As suddenly as I was in the bedroom, I was taken from it. My mind snatched by another's until I looked through the grey eyes of my dragon.

Inyris sensed something. She filled my mind, taking my consciousness from Simion, from the room, to the outcrop of rocks she rested on. It was as though I saw through her eyes, looking at the Nests—the collection of rocks just shy of

Wycombe's shoreline—as Dragons stirred awake and each looked out across the dark oceans.

The boom came first.

Inyris's scales prickled, as did my skin. I gazed through her eyes as a circular cloud rushed over the world. The hot air bubbled the waters of the ocean. It was suffocating as it passed over my dragon.

Then there was light. Far off in the distance, a pillar of molten flame shot skywards, splitting the night sky.

I was vaguely aware of Simion shaking me, but I couldn't break free from this connection to tell him what was wrong. I couldn't do anything but watch through her eyes.

Voltar erupted. It was so great it could be seen at a distance, as the mountain spat its fire into the sky. My dragon rose into the sky in a cloud of her kin, each one screeching ice and wind in reaction to what they sensed.

My mind translated their panicked caws, forming words in my mind, a chant that I had heard before. A chant that would haunt me until this was truly over.

And I knew exactly what this was.

There was nothing natural about this disaster. Not as the Thassalic Ocean reacted, lifting in a wave to stifle the boiling dark clouds that began rolling out from Voltar.

None of this was happening by chance.

I snapped back to the attic room in the Mad Queen. Simion was there, face pinched in worry as he called my name. He was shouting it, but it sounded more like a whisper. My ears were clogged with the boom as Voltar shattered apart in flame.

'It is a signal,' I said, shaking violently. I knew Inyris was flying from the Nests to find me. Even back in the room, I felt the winds sliced apart by her wings as though it was me who flew through the sky.

'A signal to what?' Simion asked, his bare chest rising and falling in rapid succession. Mine did to. Without clothes, tangled in the sheets of his bed, I felt frozen to the bone.

I gazed beyond the window; Simion's attention followed. My eyes fell upon the glittering night sky. Falling from the darkness beyond the heavens, a boiling red shape slithered through the stars. It was large and fast, the edges burning with flame. And it was coming directly for Aldian.

'Lilyth,' I replied, repeating the panicked caw Inyris and the other dragons expelled into the dark. 'She is coming. Now.'

A LETTER FROM BEN

Dear reader,

I want to say a huge thank you for choosing to read *Heir to Frost and Storm*. If you did enjoy it, and want to keep up to date with all my latest releases, just sign up at the following link. Your email address will never be shared and you can unsubscribe at any time.

www.secondskybooks.com/ben-alderson

I hope you loved this next instalment of Maximus's story. If you did, I would be very grateful if you could write a review. I'd love to hear what you think, and it makes such a difference helping new readers to discover one of my books for the first time.

This book has been so much fun to write. Taking the characters, putting them through more trials and tribulations. Poor Max, will he ever catch a break? At least he has a dragon now, am I right? I am writing this letter whilst I am halfway through writing Book 3, and let me tell you… there is SO much drama left to come. World-ending monsters, magical objects and countless battles that will have you at the edge of your seat. I am so excited for you to see where we go after this book.

I love hearing from my readers—you can get in touch with me on social media or through my website.

Thanks,
Ben Alderson

KEEP IN TOUCH WITH BEN

www.benalderson.com

 facebook.com/BenAldersonAuthor
twitter.com/BenAldersonBook
instagram.com/benaldersonauthor

ACKNOWLEDGEMENTS

Readers, thank you for taking the time of your day to read this book. Your ongoing support is what motivates me. The messages, the shares and comments and likes and messages, it makes my day. Your love for this series has been so heart-warming. Thank you.

Second Sky Books, thank you to the entire team for the continued support during this fabulous collaboration. This book, this world, characters and story, would not be what it is now without you.

Beth, thank you for being my muse. Your endless hard work, the art you have made for this series, it truly makes the entire process so much easier. Thank you for also becoming such a wonderful friend during this process. I look forward to working on more art pieces for this series with you.

Maria. I am in awe of the covers you are making for this series. Thank you for bringing the characters to life. Working with you is always a pleasure. I am honoured you chose to work with Second Sky to help bring this book to life.

Printed in Great Britain
by Amazon

44191066R00249